TAKE ME TO BED

S0-ARM-852

Books by Joan Elizabeth Lloyd

THE PRICE OF PLEASURE

NEVER ENOUGH

CLUB FANTASY

NIGHT AFTER NIGHT

THE SECRET LIVES OF HOUSEWIVES

NAUGHTIER BEDTIME STORIES

HOT SUMMER NIGHTS

MADE FOR SEX

THE MADAM OF MAPLE COURT

TAKE ME TO BED

Published by Kensington Publishing Corporation

TAKE ME TO BED

JOAN ELIZABETH LLOYD

KENSINGTON BOOKS
http://www.kensingtonbooks.com

KENSINGTON BOOKS are published by

Kensington Publishing Corp.
850 Third Avenue
New York, NY 10022

Copyright © 2008 by Kensington Publishing Corp.
The Pleasures of JessicaLynn copyright © 1996 by Joan Elizabeth Lloyd
Velvet Whispers copyright © 1999 by Joan Elizabeth Lloyd

All rights reserved. No part of this book may be reproduced in any form or by any means without the prior written consent of the Publisher, excepting brief quotes used in reviews.

All Kensington titles, imprints and distributed lines are available at special quantity discounts for bulk purchases for sales promotion, premiums, fund raising, educational or institutional use.

Special book excerpts or customized printings can also be created to fit specific needs. For details, write or phone the office of the Kensington Special Sales Manager: Kensington Publishing Corp., 850 Third Avenue, New York, NY, 10022. Attn. Special Sales Department. Phone: 1-800-221-2647.

Kensington and the K logo Reg. U.S. Pat. & TM Off.

ISBN-13: 978-0-7582-1278-8
ISBN-10: 0-7582-1278-X

First Kensington Trade Paperback Printing: November 2008
10 9 8 7 6 5 4 3 2 1

Printed in the United States of America

This book is dedicated to Ed,
my editor,
my conscience,
my partner,
my friend.

And my thanks to Angela Preston
for her short story entitled "Assimilation,"
which I use with her permission.
A talented writer,
Angela has a bright future.

CONTENTS

THE PLEASURES OF JESSICALYNN
1

VELVET WHISPERS
221

The Pleasures of JessicaLynn

Chapter

1

"Steph, it's Jessie." Thirty-six-year-old JessicaLynn Hanley kicked off her high heels and stretched out against the mountain of pillows on her king-sized bed. She crossed her stocking-clad ankles on the paisley bedspread and, holding the cordless phone between the pillows and her ear, unfastened the thin gold bracelet she had just bought.

"I thought about you a lot today," Jessie's best friend Stephanie Carlton said from a thousand miles away, "and I was hoping you'd call. Is it done?"

"Done," Jessie said, glancing at her watch. "According to my lawyer, for three hours and seventeen minutes I've been a legally separated woman. All the papers neatly signed by the judge. It's over." Through surprisingly misty eyes, she glanced around the tastefully decorated room in which she had slept for the last nine years of her marriage and the fourteen months since Rob moved out.

"You knew this day would come," Steph's soft voice said. "Weren't you prepared?"

"Oh, I guess I was," Jessie said, taking a large swallow from the can of diet Pepsi she had grabbed on her way upstairs, "but, I guess I wasn't quite as ready as I thought I was."

"How do you feel about everything now?" Steph's voice was filled with concern.

Jessie let out a long breath. "Mixed emotions. I thought about Rob a lot this afternoon and, hell, he's still the person I spent all those years with, thinking we were happy. Part of me is sad, like something died." She shook her head. "Of course, most of me still wants to shoot the bastard." She closed her eyes and the moment that changed her life played behind her lids like a movie.

It had been more than a year since she had arrived at her husband's dental office late one afternoon with swatches of fabric for new chairs for the waiting room. His receptionist had left for the day, so Jessie had wandered back toward his private office where he often worked late getting his paperwork in order. As she glanced into the main operatory, she had been greeted by the vision of her husband's bare ass, muscles clenching, back arching as he crouched over the contour dental chair and drove his cock into his recently hired twenty-two-year-old dental assistant. "Harder Robby baby, harder," the girl had been screaming. "Fuck me good. Fill me up."

Snapping back to the present, Jessie said, "You know, Steph, all I could think of when I walked in on the two of them fucking was the old joke about the voluptuous woman who goes into the dentist's office. After a brief exam, he tells her that she needs quite a bit of very expensive dental work. 'Oh fuck,' she says. 'Okay,' says the dentist, 'just tell me which cavity you want me to fill and I'll adjust the chair.' "

Jessie enjoyed her friend's deep husky laugh. During their senior year at Ottawa High in Ottawa, Illinois, Steph, her steady boyfriend and now husband Brian, Jessie and Rob had hung out together. They had gone to the drive-in in LaSalle in Rob's father's Pontiac and pretended to watch the latest movie, shared burgers and fries at Bianchi's or the Root Beer Stand, and planned their futures.

"Wall Street," Brian had said, over and over. "I'm going to make millions and then Steph and I will get married and have a dozen kids."

Immediately after graduation Brian, true to his dreams, had moved to New York and had made a great deal of money as a commodities trader. He had sent for Steph and they had married and moved to Westchester County. Unfortunately, their only child, Theresa, had been killed at the age of nine. She had been riding her bicycle near the elementary school when a drunken driver ran his car onto the sidewalk and struck the child.

"I'm going to be a doctor or dentist and make scads of money," Rob had said from the driver's seat of the Pontiac. "I'll join the country club and play tennis every Thursday afternoon." And Rob had done just that; gone to college and dental school while Jessie had worked to support both of them. Insisting that he wouldn't make a good father, Rob had also decided that the couple would have no children.

Through the years, though a thousand miles apart, Steph and Jessie had kept in touch and had remained close. Jessie had even visited the Carltons' home in Harrison occasionally.

"It's good to hear that you haven't lost your sense of humor," Steph said.

Jessie sat on the edge of the bed and began to pull the pins from her carefully arranged titian French knot. An attractive, green-eyed redhead, she had freckleless ivory skin and a slender figure with ample curves in all the right places. "My funny bone is still intact. Actually, I feel a little sorry for the jerk. I get weekly reports from some of our old supposedly well-meaning friends who think I need blow-by-blow accounts of their comings and goings, pardon the pun. I understand that he's going to marry the bimbo. She has the brains of a thumbtack and giggles all the time, but you know all the stories about the seven-year itch. Rob always was a bit slow. It took him thirteen years to feel it. I hope they'll be very happy, snarl. I'll retract my claws now." Jessie's voice dropped. "Anyway, maybe she's good in bed, better than I ever was." Jessie was amazed at the knot of bitterness that was lodged in the pit of her stomach. She and Rob hadn't had a volcanic sex life but she had been content. Content. What a horrible word to describe a sex life.

"Do I hear a note of self-pity?" Steph asked. When her comment was followed by a long pause, she continued, "Cut that out, Jessie."

"I know. It's just that I thought we were happy. I feel duped, somehow." She stood up and walked to the window, overlooking the backyard. She raised the sash and inhaled the fragrance of freshly cut grass. "And suddenly I feel very lonely, very foreign here."

Steph changed the subject quickly. "Are you changing your name back?"

"No. I thought about it, but so much of my business life is under the name Hanley that I'm going to keep the name. And, after all, it's so much easier to pronounce and spell than Florcyk."

"Lord knows you're right about that," Steph said. "Remember, in school, how we always waited for the teacher to get to your name the first day. No one could ever say it right."

Jessie smiled. "Remember Mr. Honeywell? He never did learn to pronounce it. He got as far as Fler-cuck and called me that all year." Jessie pictured their senior English teacher. He had held all the girls spellbound with his sensual reading of eighteenth-century English poetry.

"God, he was something," Steph said with a small sigh. "I still get the hots just thinking about him. He had the greatest buns in those tight jeans he wore."

"A tight, flat rear and that fantastic bulge in the front. We speculated for hours about whether he wore padding in his shorts." Jessie smiled. She hadn't thought sexy, outrageous things like that in years, and, she suddenly realized, she missed it.

"And what about men in your life?" Steph asked. "Are you dating yet?"

"Yes and no. There's a guy I've known for a few months. We've been to dinner a few times in the past few months and I think he's interested."

"And you? How do you feel?"

"I don't know. Maybe I'm not ready yet. Steve, that's his

name, Steve's sweet and kind and thoughtful. But I feel, I can't explain it, sort of closed in."

"So come back here and stay with Brian and me for a few weeks or longer." Steph had been trying to convince Jessie to visit for months. "You're selling the house so you have to move anyway. Let someone in your office handle the arrangements and get the hell out of town for a while."

"Oh, Steph, I wish I could."

"Why can't you?"

"I have responsibilities here."

"Like what?"

"Like the office." Jessie owned Ferncrest Realty, a small but successful real estate agency specializing in newly built town houses. "And selling the house. Packing, organizing, you know."

"You've told me over and over that the office runs like clock-work. I'm sure you hate to admit that it can get along without you, but it can and it will. And how will it feel showing strangers through your house, knowing that they're criticizing your land-scaping and your wallpaper? You don't need that right now."

Jessie looked down at the backyard. She remembered planting most of the red, white, and pink azaleas that blazed in full bloom along the foundation. "I know that, but I don't mind selling the house. It was always too ostentatious for my taste. Rob was the one who wanted a big, showy house in which to entertain. His lawyer told me that he wanted to keep it, buy me out but I told him no. I won't have Rob and bimbette living here." Her eyes misted as she stared into the master bath and took in the new fix-tures she and Rob had had installed just a month before 'the event.' "I just can't bear that."

"I understand, Jessie. If, God forbid, anything like that ever happened to Brian and me, I wouldn't want him to live here ei-ther."

"Everything has two sides, you know, and sometimes my feel-ings change from minute to minute. There's a big part of me that still feels the history in here. So much entertaining: the bridge games, the country club crowd that Rob wanted so much to be a part of, barbecues on the deck." Jessie tucked the phone between her ear and shoulder and, with all the pins now removed from her long, red hair, combed her slender fingers through the strands and rubbed her scalp. "That's all over now."

"So, why stay there? Come to Harrison and stay with us. You know this huge old place has plenty of room. You could have the entire end of the house you had when you were here two years ago. All the privacy you could want, and all of my company you can stand."

"Oh Steph, it sounds so tempting."

"I wish you'd come. Harrison has so much to offer you, especially at this point in your life. It will be like old times. Girl talk, movies. We can lounge by the pool and talk about life, love and good sex, not necessarily in that order."

"What about my life here? I've got to find a place to live."

"Do it later. You don't want to make any long-term decisions right now anyway and you can certainly afford to dump most of your stuff. Put things you really want to keep in storage and split." Jessie paused, so Steph continued, "It would be so great. You and me, on our own near the big city. Nobody gleefully keeping you up to date on Rob's escapades. Just Broadway plays, expensive restaurants, museums, Bergdorfs, Bloomingdales, Saks, Lord & Taylor's, the works."

"Not too many restaurants," Jessie said, running her palm down her flat stomach. "My figure couldn't stand the calories."

"Calories are overrated." Steph stopped suddenly. "Whoa. Wait a minute. Was that a yes I heard?"

Jessie flopped back onto a stack of pillows. "Why the hell not? For a couple of weeks anyway."

Steph squealed like the girls had when they were kids. "Wonderful. I never believed you'd actually agree."

"Are you sure you're not regretting your offer now that I've said yes?"

"Of course not. It will be great. I don't mean to push my luck but how soon can you get here?"

Jessie giggled and pulled her datebook from her bedside table. She flipped the pages. "Okay. It's May seventeenth." She planned out loud. "Give me a month to get a few arrangements made. Make it six weeks. I'm selling most of the furniture anyway, so all I have to do is sort out some personal stuff. God, the amount of crap one collects in nine years."

"Just pull out what you want and let Rob sort out the rest. Since you're there, you get first dibs."

"It's all in that long-discussed separation agreement anyway. Now let's see." She planned out loud, her pencil tapping the dates on the calendar in her book. "The house goes on the market July first. I'll put a few things in storage, pack a couple of bags. . . . How about I fly out June twenty-fifth. That's a Sunday. I'll plan to stay for. . . ."

"Leave your return open. Maybe I'll be able to convince you to stay for the whole summer."

"Okay. No return just yet." Jessie wrote 'Go to Harrison' across the space for June twenty-fifth, then slammed her datebook shut and dropped it onto the bed. "Oh Steph, thanks. Now that I've made the decision, I feel so relieved. I guess I didn't realize how much this divorce has taken out of me."

"Well I did, and I'm delighted that you've finally made the right decision."

The two women talked for another half an hour, and, after she hung up, Jessie pulled off her clothes and soaked in a hot bath. Then, after a dinner of pasta, salad, and a glass of Beck's Dark, she collapsed into bed and slept through the night for the first time in weeks.

Later that evening, in her bedroom in Harrison, Stephanie stretched out beside her husband Brian. "I can't believe I actually talked her into coming out here. It will be so good for her."

Steph was Jessie's physical opposite, tall and angular with long legs and a slender, tight figure. She had recently had her almost-black hair styled into a shoulder-length bob that framed her conventionally pretty face. She needed almost no makeup to highlight her doelike deep brown eyes, cute turned-up nose, and full, sensuous lips.

Brian rubbed his palm over his wife's naked hip. "What about us? You know. How much does Jessie know about the way we live?"

"Not much yet, love," Steph said, sliding her fingers through the heavy black hair on Brian's chest and gazing into his unusually pale, blue eyes. "But she will, soon enough. It will be an enlightening experience for her."

"I've always had the feeling that there was so much more to her than Rob ever saw. The jerk. While we were making out in the backseat, I used to listen to them in the front."

"You're kidding," Steph said, caressing her husband's flat stomach with the tips of her fingers. "I was always too busy trying to control your hands, or pretending to, to pay attention to anything else."

"Oh, I just heard bits and pieces, before and after. He always satisfied himself but I had the feeling that he didn't pay much attention to whether Jessie was satisfied or not."

"Tell me the truth," Steph said. "You always had the hots for her, didn't you?"

Brian's breathing quickened. "She was a sexy little number. I know there's animal sensuality hidden beneath the surface, fighting to get out through all that carefully orchestrated facade. I'd love to be the one to let it out."

"You and she never made it?"

"Unfortunately, no."

Steph wrapped her long fingers around Brian's hard cock. "There's still hope, you know."

"I know, babe," he said, sliding his index finger over her wet inner lips. "I know." Brian rolled his wife onto her back and slammed into her until they both came, screaming.

After a long and delightfully uneventful flight from Chicago, Jessie walked down the long corridor at Newark Airport and grinned as she saw Steph waving. Just outside the security gate,

Jessie dropped her carry-on bag and the two women hugged. Jostled from all sides, they moved out of the line of deplaning passengers. "You took tremendous," Steph said.

"You like?" Jessie said, turning so Steph could appreciate her new navy linen pantsuit and pale pink tailored blouse. "I went shopping yesterday. I'm new from the skin out." She lifted one foot and waggled it to show off her new navy low-heeled opera pumps. "And from the top down."

"You look fabulous," Steph said, "but I'm disappointed. I wanted to take you shopping myself. You need jeans, shorts, T-shirts, things like that. And, although I lead a denim kind of life most of the time, you'll need a dress or two."

"We will shop until we drop, to coin a phrase," Jessie said, settling the strap of her suitcase on her shoulder. "I only bought a few things and I brought my checkbook and my credit cards."

"You're doing okay, financially, I gather."

"I'm doing just fine. The business is thriving despite the economy and Rob, under mild duress, was very generous, bless his pointed little head."

"Are you getting alimony?"

"We hassled for a while. His practice nets him in the low six figures but I just wanted payment for the years I spent putting him through dental school so he could drill his bimbo."

"Bitter, darling?" Steph asked, raising one eyebrow.

Jessie sighed. "I have my moments. But on to better topics. What do we have planned for the next week or so?"

"I thought you might want to relax for a few days. Become a vegetable. So I arranged my schedule so that I'm at the gift shop at the hospital Monday and Thursday, but for the rest of the week, I'm yours." Steph had been working at the shop at the hospital for several years and, since her arrival, it had become a profitable business for the small local institution.

"You like working at the hospital. I wish I had something like that, something that made me feel good about myself."

"So do it. When you get back. . . . No, I won't talk about you going back to Illinois. It'll spoil my good mood."

"And how's Brian?"

"He's great, working hard and playing hard. He's got a tennis game this afternoon, but he said to give you a kiss and tell you he'd see you at dinner."

"God, I'm so glad to see you," Jessie said, hugging her friend again.

The two women walked toward the baggage claim area stopping occasionally to hug again. "How much luggage did you bring?" Steph asked, matching her stride to her friend's.

"Only one large suitcase with some essentials and enough clothes to hold me for a few days. I didn't want any leftovers." She heaved a great sigh. "The house is ready to go. And I do mean go. It's well priced and should sell quickly. And the office is better organized than I'd like to admit."

In the baggage claim area, they spotted the illuminated sign for the flight from Chicago and reached the edge of the carousel just as it started to move. "We're looking for a beige tapestry suitcase with brown trim," Jessie said.

As they watched, the first bag over the top of the chute and onto the turning plates was Jessie's. "That's never happened to me before," Jessie said, her mouth hanging open. "My suitcase is usually so far down the line that almost everyone has already left."

"Well," Steph said, "it's an omen." She hefted the bag from the moving platform. "Good luck and good things are coming."

"Oh, I hope so." Jessie fumbled in her purse for her baggage stub. "Sometimes I'm so up, excited about starting a new phase in my life." She looked her best friend in the eyes. "Then, at other times, I'm so down. Rob and I were comfortable and good together. I knew what he was thinking and he knew. . . ." Her eyes began to fill. "It's so final."

"None of that," Steph said, linking her free arm with her friend's. "Only good thoughts will be permitted."

Jessie shook her head and a wisp of hair fell from her French knot. Impatiently she stuffed it into one of the bobby pins that pulled her hair tight against her head. "Right. Only good thoughts."

They arrived in Harrison and had just pulled Jessie's suitcase from the trunk of Steph's BMW when Brian drove up the long driveway, honking the horn of his Lexus and grinning through the windshield. He pulled to a stop, jumped out of the car, and enveloped Jessie in a giant bearhug. "Oh, JJ," he said, reverting to Jessie's nickname from their days in high school. "I'm so glad to see you."

"Me too," she said, hugging him back. "I'd almost forgotten the days of being called JJ. You're the only one who calls me that anymore. It takes me back."

"If you hadn't been so hooked on Rob, I would have jumped you back then and Steph would have had to find someone else."

"You are so full of it, Brian," Jessie said, laughing, swatting him on the ass. "You should have been born Irish."

"Okay, okay, so I exaggerate a bit. But I am glad to see you."

Jessie pushed Brian to arm's length and looked him over. Although he was not particularly tall, Brian was a big man, with large hands and feet and an open, ingenuous smile that lit up his ordinary-looking face. His tennis whites accentuated his oversized arms and legs, all covered with heavy black hair. His skin was heavily tanned, making his eyes look even paler than she remembered. She hugged him again, enjoying the feel of a virile man after so many months alone. "You look fantastic, sir," she said, a bit embarrassed by the erotic thoughts his tight shorts aroused. "And happy."

Brian reached out and draped his arm around his wife's shoulders. "Happy doesn't describe it." He pecked Steph on the cheek, then said, "When's dinner? I'm starved."

"Everything's in the fridge and ready to go. You get the fire started and I'll show Jessie to her room."

"Will do. I'll start the grill, then take a quick shower. Dinner should be ready in less than an hour."

Just over an hour later, the three friends were filling their plates with rare steak, a rice pilaf that Steph had just removed from the microwave, and a crisp green salad with tiny shrimp and bacon bits. "I hope you're not watching your calories," Steph said. "At least not for today. I decided that in honor of your arrival I would make all the things I don't ordinarily eat. To hell with cholesterol."

Brian uncorked a bottle of California Cabernet and poured some into each glass. Jessie looked at the label on the bottle. "Stag's Leap. 1984. Very nice wine."

Brian lifted his glass. "For a very nice lady and her new life. To JJ." His eyes locked with Jessie's and, after a moment, she looked away.

This is silly, Jessie told herself. It feels like he's flirting with me. It only goes to show that I've been celibate too long. He's my best friend's husband, for heaven's sake. She shook it off and spent the rest of the evening chatting amiably with Steph and Brian.

The following day Jessie unwound. Between Brian's job and Steph's stint at the hospital, Jessie saw nothing of either of them. Content to be alone she sat beside the pool until her skin turned a luscious shade of soft apricot, read a romance novel, soaked in a bubble bath for an hour in the oversized jacuzzi-tub in her bathroom, and generally exorcised Rob from her consciousness.

She saw Steph briefly late that afternoon. Jessie had grabbed a container of yogurt from the fridge and was sitting at the table in the kitchen, eating with one hand and holding her book open with the other.

"Hi, Steph," she said, looking up from her book. "What's up? How was your day?"

"The day was great, but I now have a delightful idea. Brian got two tickets for a concert tonight from some client and we can easily get a third. Very last minute. It's the Julliard String Quartet. Brian and I love them and we don't get to hear them very often. How about us both joining him in the city? Dinner, the concert? It would do you a world of good."

"I'm not a concert kind of person, Steph. All that music, particularly after a good dinner, just puts me to sleep. You go, and have a great time."

"But we haven't spent any time together. You've been alone all day."

"And I've enjoyed every minute of it. Go and enjoy your concert. I want to get to bed early anyway. All this relaxing is making me tired." To emphasize her drowsiness, she yawned. "I don't want you to feel you have to entertain me. I do just fine on my own."

"I feel so guilty. But we're best friends and I'll trust you to be honest. So if you're sure you don't mind I'd really like to see this. And the next two days, and Friday as well, are ours. Shopping. Bloomies maybe?"

"Done. See you in the morning."

The next morning, dressed in jeans and a white tank top, Jessie sat in a long white lounge chair in her favorite room in the Carltons' house. Jessie knew that, when Steph and Brian had bought the house a dozen years before, the room had been an open flagstone patio overlooking the pool, shaded at each end by a huge red maple. The couple had immediately seen its potential and had enclosed it with louvered windows and white wood. They had furnished it in white wicker and cluttered it with dozens of pillows in primary colors.

Once the room was constructed, Steph had worked with a florist, learning everything she could about houseplants. She decorated the room with carefully selected specimens, and then tended them with loving care. One end contained cactuses, many blooming with either flowers or colored globes. The other end was all greenery, with ivys, ferns, and a six-foot-high fig tree. In the center, where there was sun most of the day, Steph had put florals with several plants in bloom at all times—African violets in exotic shades, orchids and lilies, anything that caught her fancy. One section was her hospital. The owner of the florist shop frequently gave Steph plants that weren't doing well, for her to nurse back to health. She spent time almost every day misting, watering, pruning, and removing dead blooms.

Jessie had gotten up early that morning and, although it was only eight-thirty, she was sitting and reading, a cup of fresh coffee at her elbow. As she read, she suddenly became aware of sounds from the pool. She shifted her position and peered through the leaves of a deep orange hibiscus. She couldn't believe what she saw.

Not twenty feet away, beside the pool, Steph lay, stretched out on a lounge chair, dressed in only the top of a tiny black bikini. The bottom of the suit lay on the concrete beside her chair. Her legs straddled the cushions and a man lay between her thighs, his head buried in her pussy. "Ummm," Jessie heard Steph mumble. "That's wonderful." As Jessie watched she became aware of a smooth, tanned back and a tight, tiny ass. She realized that the head that bobbed in Steph's lap was blond. It was not Brian.

Jessie could hear slurping sounds and moans. Wanting to turn away yet fascinated, Jessie watched through the leaves and blossoms.

"Oh Tony," Steph moaned. "Do that more." Her legs trembled and her fists clenched and unclenched. "Yes, just like that." She reached behind her back and untied the top of her bathing suit to free her breasts. As the young man lapped, she pinched her nipples and squirmed. Jessie saw Tony hold Steph's hips still as his mouth worked its magic. Jessie's body throbbed and she could almost feel Tony's tongue as it brought Steph closer and closer to orgasm.

"Oh baby," Steph yelled, "don't stop!"

Jessie wiggled her hips to scratch the itch that grew between her legs. She clenched her vaginal muscles as Steph yelled, "Now, baby. Stick me now!"

Tony plunged two fingers into Steph's body. His arm worked like a piston as Steph's hips thrashed. "Yes," she screamed. "Yes!" As she clutched the arms of the lounge chair and arched her back, the man could barely keep his face against her cunt and his fingers pistoning.

Jessie could almost feel her friend's orgasm and, as she heard

Steph's heavy breathing slow, Jessie snuck back into the house and up to her room.

What the hell was that all about? she wondered as she closed the door to her room and dropped onto the bed. She took a few deep breaths to calm her excited body, then propped her head on the pillows. Steph had been a bit wild as a kid, she remembered. She had dated several boys before she met Brian and had told Jessie in great detail about one particular gymnast who finally convinced her to go 'all the way' in the backseat of his father's Oldsmobile. "Boy," Steph had told her, "his gymnastics aren't limited to the gymnasium.

Jessie shook her head. I never thought she'd cheat on Brian like this, she thought, her eyes filling. What is it about sex that makes good people like Steph and Rob do such impossible things, lie and cheat? What is it about sex?

It was after ten when Jessie heard a light knock on her bedroom door. "You up?" a voice whispered.

Jessie wiped her eyes, composed her face and, trying not to look as upset as she felt, said, "Sure. Come on in."

"Well, good morning sleepyhead," Steph said. She had changed into a pair of tight-fitting jeans and a short-sleeved, navy-blue shirt.

"Good morning yourself," Jessie answered, not totally successful at keeping the edge from her voice.

"What's wrong, Jessie?" Steph said. "You sound upset."

"Nothing's wrong," Jessie said. "Just a bit cranky this morning."

"Don't kid me, babe," Steph said, plopping onto the edge of the bed. "Something's up." When Jessie was silent, Steph dropped the novel Jessie had been reading onto the bed beside her. "I found this in the plant room. Does this have anything to do with your mood this morning?"

Jessie picked up the book and put it on the bedside table. "I must have left it there last evening."

"Don't, babe. You never were a very good liar. You saw Tony and me earlier, didn't you."

Jessie blushed, but remained silent.

"You're embarrassed. I can understand that, but what Tony and I did was just clean, honest fun. He comes to tend to the pool and, occasionally, he tends to me as well. It's really nothing."

"Nothing?" Jessie spat. "What about Brian? I'm sure he wouldn't think it was nothing if he knew."

"Of course he knows," Steph said softly. "Come on downstairs. Let's get some coffee and I'll explain everything. I was going to tell you about things before this, but I haven't gotten a chance."

"What things?"

"Coffee first. I need some right about now. I promise I'll tell you everything."

Fifteen minutes later, the two women sat in the plant room, each with a fresh cup of coffee and a toasted english muffin. The coffeepot sat on a warmer near Steph. As she munched on her muffin Jessie's lay untouched on the plate beside her. They had not spoken a word.

"Okay, Jessie," Steph said with a long sigh, "let me try to explain." She sipped her coffee. "About three years ago, Brian was infatuated with a single woman in his office. He told me about it and, for a while, telling about what it might be like if they ever got together made for wild times in bed. Finally, I asked him if he'd like to actually be with her. You know, make love. He said yes."

"He told you that he wanted to go to bed with another woman?" Jessie was horrified.

"There isn't a man on this earth who hasn't thought about doing that at one time or another. Brian was just honest enough to admit it. He would never lie to me and I knew that he wouldn't do anything without telling me."

"And you allowed him to be with someone else?"

"Allowed is an interesting word. I hate to think that I'm in charge of his sex life. I gave it a lot of thought and I decided that I wanted him to be happy. I guess I'm very strong because I didn't feel threatened. It wasn't that kind of thing. He wasn't in love with her, just in lust."

Jessie laughed and started to relax. "In lust. That's an interesting way to put it."

"Well, that's really what it was. Haven't you ever felt that pull, that almost irresistible urge to jump into some man's pants?" When her friend was silent, Steph continued, "You, my love, haven't lived. It's a great feeling, even if you never get to do anything about it."

"I guess I've got no sex drive," Jessie said softly. "And no sex appeal either."

"Bullshit," Steph said. "You just haven't discovered them yet. Anyway, getting back to Valerie. That was her name, Valerie. I never saw her, but Brian described her to me. Tall and shapely, with big, soft tits and great, long legs. But it wasn't her body that turned Brian on. It was her obvious attraction to him. Her eye contact, smiles, movements."

"He told you all that?"

"He described everything in detail afterward, in bed. And the telling got him so hot that we fucked like bunnies."

Jessie shook her head. "I don't believe it. You lay in bed discussing another woman fucking your husband."

Steph nodded, silently letting Jessie absorb what she had heard.

Jessie picked up her muffin and took a bite. "Amazing. How long did it last?"

"He was only with her for about two months, then it all wore off for both of them. So much of being in lust is the expectation, not the actuality. Reality is frequently a letdown."

Despite her amazement, Jessie was fascinated. "You still haven't told me about this morning."

"Give me time," Steph said. "It's a long story. It was several months after that and Brian and I had spent an evening playing Boggle with Lara and Hank Cortez, friends of ours from Scarsdale. Have you ever played Boggle? It's a word game and it's lots of fun. Your score is based on the number of words you can make that no one else wrote down. Well, everyone had had quite a bit to drink and, toward the end of the evening, we had gotten very silly."

Chapter

2

"I have only one word left," Hank said. "Pussy." He grinned at Lara and licked his lips. "Anyone else have pussy?"

"Not me," Brian said. "I haven't had any good pussy in quite a while. Except Steph's, of course, but a wife's pussy doesn't count."

Hank refilled the wine glasses and then threw the letter-dice again. "Cunt," Hank said, triumphantly pointing out the word among the letters before anyone had had time to write anything. "And look. You can make *suck* and *fuck*."

Lara giggled and squeezed Brian's arm. "Such nice words, don't you think?" She looked up at Brian and blinked.

Brian looked at Steph, then stroked Lara's face. "Very nice words."

"I've got an idea," Hank said. "Let's play strip-Boggle. The winner is the one with the most dirty words and everyone else has to take off one article of clothing." He looked at Brian and Steph. "Game?"

Hank was not a particularly good-looking man but the twinkle in his eye and his delightful sense of humor made him attractive. Steph had always been interested in him, but had never before thought about doing anything about it. "Want to?" Brian whispered into Steph's ear.

Steph thought a minute. Yes, she really did. She gave a tiny nod. "Okay, let's do it," Brian said.

After six rounds of the game, the men were down to their socks and shorts, and Lara, who had won three of the rounds, was still wearing her blouse and underwear. Steph had a particular love of delicate undies, and was glad she had worn a black, demi-cup bra with matching lace panties, which, by now, was all she was wearing. "You are one gorgeous woman," Hank said, admiring the way Steph's small, yet soft breasts filled the tiny cups. "I knew you'd be sensational without clothes."

"Not without clothes yet," Steph said. "I'm not wearing any less than I'd be in a bikini."

"I know, but it's knowing that it's not a bikini that's such a turn-on," Hank said.

Brian was gazing silently at Lara's legs and the dark shadow he could make out through the crotch of her white nylon panties. She also still wore her short-sleeved, flowered blouse. "I feel I've been gypped," he said to Lara. "You're still decent."

Lara lowered her head and looked up at him through her lashes. "I'm afraid you won't have the same thrill. I haven't nearly the body that your wife has. As a matter of fact, I'm so flat-chested I don't usually wear a bra. And I've certainly got my share of stretch marks from the babies."

Brian reached over and brushed his hand down the front of Lara's blouse, feeling her erect nipple rub his palm. "I bet you're beautiful under there," Brian said. "Will you take the blouse off, just for me?"

Lara looked at her husband and raised one eyebrow.

"Does everyone understand where this is going?" Hank asked. When everyone nodded, he said, "Then why don't we separate this party. Lara, you and Brian can have the bedroom and Steph and I will take the guest room." He rubbed his knuckles down Steph's cheek. "I want this lady all alone."

As Brian stood up and took Lara's hand, Steph swallowed hard. She was suddenly terrified.

"Baby," Brian said softly, looking at his wife and immediately sensing her discomfort, "this isn't a command performance. It's supposed to be fun. You look like a deer caught in the headlights. Talk to me."

"Did you and Hank set this up? I don't think it's as spur of the moment as it might appear."

"We talked about it," Brian admitted. "Hank has had the hots for you for a long time, and I know he turns you on. It's kind of like me and Valerie. I think we will all get pleasure from this evening, but if you don't want to we can leave right now."

Steph looked at Lara. "What about you? Did you know about this?" Although the question sounded accusatory, her voice was soft and gentle.

"Hank and I have done this sort of thing a few times. It's a game, fun and harmless. We have our rules, of course. Things only happen if everyone's willing and anyone can call things off at any time. And, of course, condoms at all times."

Steph giggled nervously. Where have I been while all this has been going on?" she asked. "I always thought you two were so conservative."

"Shows how much you know," Lara said. She smiled and squeezed Hank's hand. "We have a few friends who like to play the same games we enjoy."

Steph took a swallow of her wine and looked at Brian. "You want to do this, don't you?"

"Only if you do."

Hank took Steph's hand and placed it gently on the crotch of his shorts. "I want you very much, and I'd love to show you how good it can be with someone new."

Steph sighed, torn between the indignation she ought to feel and the excitement that was making her pulse pound. Deciding that she did indeed want this, she relaxed her arm and let Hank use her hand to stroke his cock. She smiled and looked from Lara to Brian. "Why don't you two go upstairs. I need a few minutes to get comfortable with this and I think Hank is just the one to help me do that."

Arm in arm, Lara and Brian went upstairs and Hank, clad only in his shorts and socks, sat on the tweed sofa. "Why don't you come and sit beside me?" Steph moved to the couch and sat with a few inches of space between her and Hank. "Baby, I've wanted you for a very long time, but I can wait until you're ready. I want to touch you and hold you. I want to make you wet and hot."

Steph sighed and leaned her head on the back of the sofa. Without touching her, Hank rested his head beside hers and spoke softly. "You know what I'd like to do? I'd like to take off that bra and watch your nipples get hard. I'd like to lick them and then blow on the wet skin. Your nipples will get as hard as tiny pebbles."

Hank watched Steph's body relax, then warm to the sound of his voice. "Then I'll take one nipple between my thumb and index finger and pinch it, hard. You'll think it should hurt, but it won't. It will make your pussy twitch and you'll have a hard time keeping your legs together. While I'm pinching one, I'll take the other in my mouth and bite it gently."

Steph's eyes closed as Hank continued. "I'll alternate, pinching one nipple and sucking and biting the other. Can you feel it, Steph? Can you feel my fingers and my teeth on your breasts? Tell me. Can you?"

"Yes," Steph said, squirming, unsuccessfully trying to keep her body still.

Hank moved his mouth closer to Steph's ear, his hot breath adding fuel to her fire. "Oh yes, I know how you feel." He grasped the snap between the cups of Steph's bra and unclipped the fastener. As he separated the sides, freeing her breasts, her hard, erect nipples reached for Hank's mouth. "Like this," he purred, pinching Steph's left nipple. "And this." He pinched the right. "And this." He leaned over and nipped at her pebbled breast. "So delicious."

When Steph reached out to touch Hank's arm, he gently pressed her hand back onto the back of the sofa. "This is entirely for you. I want you to lie there and just enjoy. I've wanted to do this for so long."

Her voice hoarse and breathless, Steph asked, "What exactly did you imagine?"

He leaned close to her face, his breath hot on the side of her neck. "I imagined breathing into your ear and watching you shiver with pleasure." He caressed the skin on her cheeks and forehead with the pad of his index finger. "I imagined stroking your face and touching your lips with the tip of my tongue." He licked the sensitive skin around the edges of her lips until it was almost torture for Steph not to rub the ticklish spot. He brushed his tongue along the joining of her lips until her mouth opened. "And I dreamed of tasting you." He pressed his mouth against Steph's until their tongues found each other and played deep inside the sensual depths.

"Oh, baby," Hank purred when they separated. "I knew it would be this good."

Steph opened her eyes and gazed at Hank. She should be ashamed of what was happening, but she wasn't. She was revelling in the sensations and in the knowledge that this wasn't her husband. This was a sensual man who wanted to make love with her. In the small part of her brain that was still capable of coherent thought, she realized that it was okay. No, she corrected herself. It was wonderful. She smiled.

"Oh yes, baby," Hank said, almost able to read her mind. "Let me make love to you. Shall we go upstairs to where we can be more comfortable?"

Steph stood and, barefoot, wearing only her tiny, lace panties, she followed Hank upstairs to the guest room. While he ripped the spread off the bed and heaped the covers on the floor, she stood in the center of the room now eager to let Hank make love to her.

Hank turned and allowed his gaze to roam over Steph's almost-naked body. "I can't believe this is really happening," he whispered.

"It is happening," she purred, feeling sexual power and strength flow through her.

When she started to pull the tiny wisp of lace down over her hips, Hank knelt and took her hands. "Let me do this the way I've fantasized." Then he pressed his mouth against her flat belly, flicking his tongue into her navel. He slowly lowered her undies and inhaled her fragrance. He helped Steph step out of her undies, then nudged her legs apart to make it easier for him to touch and taste and smell her.

He reached his tongue between her legs and pressed it against her swollen clit. He felt her legs tremble. "So excited," he whispered, standing and scooping her into his arms and gently laying her on the cool sheets. He crawled between her spread legs and lowered his face to her cunt. He blew hot air through her pussy hair, further inflaming her, then brushed his chin lightly against her fur, just barely touching it, watching her hips buck and reach for him. "Tell me now, baby. Tell me how hot you are."

"Oh God, Hank, I need you so much. I want you."

"And I want you. My cock is so hard that most of me wants to climb onto you and fuck you until we both come. But I'm going to wait. I'm going to give you more pleasure than you think you can stand." He brushed her pussy with his finger, then slid the length of her slit, parting her lips but not entering.

"That's torture," Steph moaned. She raised her hips but Hank kept his fingers just touching her.

Hank's laugh was deep and sexy. "Yes. It certainly is." He pressed just a tiny bit harder so his finger penetrated only a small way.

"Oh God," she moaned. "Oh God."

Hank tightened his tongue and flicked the tip over Steph's hard, swollen clit.

With his breath on her skin, his tongue stroking her nub, and his finger rubbing her pussy lips, Steph could hold out no longer. "I'm going to come," she cried.

As he felt her body begin to spasm, Hank forced three fingers deep into her body and sucked her swollen clit into his mouth.

Waves of liquid heat pulsed through Steph's body, filling her belly and cunt. He seemed to know just how to rub and lick, when to make it hard and when to stroke. Her orgasm continued for what seemed like hours.

"Hold on to it and don't let it down," Hank said as he climbed over her quivering body.

Steph wasn't sure what he meant, but she concentrated on not relaxing, on reaching for more of the glorious sensations and not letting them ebb. When Hank plunged his fully erect cock into her soaking passage, it triggered more spasms of erotic pleasure. He thrust into her over and over until he climaxed and she came again.

"Lord," Hank said as his breathing returned to normal. "It was even better than I dreamed."

"It was fantastic," Steph said.

Back in the kitchen in Harrison, Jessie listened to her friend's story with increasing amazement. When Steph sat back on the kitchen chair, Jessie was silent for a long while. "I'm flabbergasted," she said finally. "I'm . . . I'm . . . I don't know what I am."

Steph stared into her empty coffee cup. "Horrified? Disgusted?"

"No, of course not." She got up and poured a fresh cup of coffee for herself and her friend. On the way back to her chair, she gave Steph a quick hug. "Not horrified or disgusted. Surprised and, I guess, a bit curious. Can I ask you a few questions?"

"Of course. This wasn't intended as a monologue. I wanted you to know. For lots of reasons."

Jessie remembered the picture of Steph, draped over the lawn chair. "This obviously wasn't the only time."

"Actually, Brian and I are now what you would probably call swingers. We have a wonderful life together, but we also have other relationships." When she saw Jessie's eyebrow go up, she said quickly, "None serious. Just playtimes."

"You have people you go to bed with and Brian does too? Like a lover? It's not just the occasional couples swapping partners?"

"That's exactly what I mean." Steph wasn't sure how much Jessie was ready for so she decided just to react to questions for a while. "Right now I have two men with whom I get together from time to time, and Brian is currently seeing a wonderful woman, a systems designer in the computer department at his office."

"The mind boggles," Jessie said, then giggled. "That's how it all started. Boggle, I mean."

Steph let out a deep breath. She hadn't been sure of Jessie's reaction but she had wanted very badly for her best friend to understand. "You're okay with this?"

Jessie reached across the table and took Steph's hand. "I'm fine with this, as long as it works for you and Brian. It was the lying that upset me so much before. But you don't lie to each other. This is all very new to me, but I love you both and you seem very happy." She pulled back and grew thoughtful. "I guess I never thought about women who make love to other people's husbands."

"Hold it," Steph said. "I never make love to anyone who is married, unless the wife knows what's going on. No lying. That's my first and most important rule. No lying. To Brian, to the man involved, or to wives. Period."

"No lying," Jessie said softly.

"In my mind, that's the cardinal sin, the commandment, if you will, that Rob broke with his bimbo, as you call her. He lied to you and he probably lied to himself. It's the dishonesty that makes me want to wring his scrawny neck."

"I guess I never looked at it that way, exactly. For me it was two things. The dishonesty, of course, but it was also the fact that I obviously wasn't good enough for him in bed." Jessie's eyes filled and she looked down.

"Bullshit!" Steph put a finger under Jessie's chin and gently raised her head so the women were looking into each other's eyes. "Listen to me good, JessicaLynn Hanley, you're not good or bad in bed alone. If you and scrawny-neck didn't make it together, it was a mutual failing. Individuals aren't good or bad at making love. Only couples are."

"Yeah, but . . ."

"No 'yeah but.' You're a warm, caring person and you're as good in bed, or as bad, as the chemistry and communication between you and the man you're with." As she looked into her friend's face, she continued, "Don't look at me like I just told you that the earth was flat. It's true."

"But Rob told me . . ."

"Rob isn't the sexpert of all times, you know. Besides, was he ever with anyone else beside you?"

"He says that bimbette was the first," Jessie said, snuffing.

"What about before you two got married. Was there ever anyone else?"

"No. The first time for both of us was in the front seat of his father's Pontiac." Her face softened. "He almost came on my jeans trying to get them open."

"So what makes him the ultimate judge of sexuality? Certainly not experience."

"I don't know. If I were being brutally honest, I'd have to admit that it wasn't very good. He used to give me a shot of alcohol to 'loosen me up.' He said I was uptight and needed to relax." Her voice dropped and she wiped a tear from her cheek with the back of her hand. "He said I was frigid."

"He can say anything he wants, Jessie, but he can't make you believe it. And I don't believe it."

"But I don't think I've ever had an orgasm."

"And whose fault is that?"

Jessie's head jerked up and she was silent for a minute. "I never thought about it that way. You mean there might not be anything wrong with me?"

"Probably not. You're healthy. No physical problems. No drug abuse. You probably weren't excited enough to come. I read something a while ago that has stuck in my mind. Someone wrote that a man flames like a match and a woman heats like an iron. That timing requires some coordination. It takes a woman twenty or thirty minutes from a cold start."

"A cold start." She laughed. "That's an unusual way to put it. It makes me sound like an auto engine on a winter morning."

"Is that such a bad analogy?"

"Maybe not. I was always a cold start. I came to dread sex."

"Make that forty-five minutes to warm up," Steph said. "Jessie, relax. You're fine. It's scrawny-neck I want to kill."

"Thanks for that, Steph. You always were a good friend."

"And I still am. Let's table this topic for the moment, get dressed up and do some outrageous damage to your credit card at Bloomingdales."

Jessie took a deep, shuddering breath. "Good idea. You've given me lots to think about, and I'd like to continue this discussion another time."

"Any time, babe. I love to talk about sex."

Steph and Jessie spent the afternoon shopping. At first, Jessie selected outfits that were conservative and concealing. At one point, however, Steph convinced Jessie to try on a low-cut, Indian-silk sundress with a very full, soft skirt. When her friend came out of the dressing room, Steph grinned. "You look wonderful." The dress, in shades of soft peach and rose, complemented Jessie's red hair and sun-warmed complexion.

"I do? Isn't it a bit much?" She yanked upward on the neckline, trying to minimize her deep cleavage. "I mean isn't it a bit young for me?"

"Young? Come on. You're thirty-six years old. That's young enough for almost anything, except maybe being proofed at a bar. I think you look terrific, and with a little makeup. . . ."

"Don't get carried away." She swung back and forth in front of the mirror watching the skirt move with her body. As she watched herself, her smile broadened. "But although it's not my usual, I do like this dress."

"Now you need shoes to go with it," Steph said to Jessie's back as she disappeared back into the fitting room. "And a new bathing suit and a few other things I can think of."

When they arrived home, the two women dumped their purchases on the sofa and adjourned to the plant room with two glasses and a bottle of California chardonnay. When they had settled into long chairs side by side, and sipped some wine, Jessie reopened the earlier topic. "I guess I've digested some of our conversation of before. Now I'm curious. How did Brian react to your first encounter with Hank?"

"He was pretty quiet for a day or so, then, in bed a few nights later, he asked me all about it."

"He wanted the gory details?"

"Not specifically, but he wanted to know whether I enjoyed it and whether I came."

"Did you tell him? I mean, weren't you worried that he'd be jealous or something."

"Jessie," Steph said, turning to fully face her friend. "I will never lie to Brian. That's the bottom line. If he doesn't like something that happens we can change the rules but I will never lie. I told him it was wonderful. To me, lovemaking isn't a contest. It's not who's better than whom at this or that. It's pleasure for the sake of pleasure and that's all it is. And, of course, there's never a substitute for first times in bed together. It's the greatest kick in the world."

"Wow. That's quite an attitude."

"I guess, but it's one that Brian and I share completely. We have a deal that if something makes one of us uncomfortable, either about what we are doing ourself or what the other is doing, we talk about it and decide how to rearrange things, if necessary."

"Has he ever been jealous? Have you?"

"Once in a while one of us becomes obsessed with someone for a short time. But it's always hottest at the beginning and eventually it all cools."

Jessie hesitated. "Am I cramping your style?"

"Of course not. There are a few couples in the neighborhood who get together for fun from time to time and we will, either with you or without, in the near future."

"Me?"

"Yes, you. We've found quite a few honest, open kindred spirits." She smiled. "You know, some people who claim to be open-minded have said to me, 'Just don't tell my wife the details. I don't want her to know about. . . .' Honest my foot. They have more secrets than the FBI. We don't find that type of person very congenial."

"Hey, girls, your lord and master is home," a voice yelled from the front hall.

"Hi lord and master," Steph yelled back. "Bring a wineglass. We're killing a bottle of chardonnay and need an accomplice."

"Let me change and I'll be right in."

"You really found the best one," Jessie said wistfully.

"I know I did. But he didn't make out badly in the deal."

Jessie's head snapped up. "I didn't mean. . . ."

Steph laughed. "Of course you didn't. You know you could talk to Brian about all this too."

"Talk to Brian? I'd be too embarrassed."

"Nonsense. He can tell you better than I can how he feels about it all."

"I don't think I'm up to discussing this with him just yet."

"Do you mind if I tell him that we talked?"

"I guess not. It's just so, I don't know, so intimate."

"That it is. And try not to treat him differently because you know what's going on."

"That will be a tall order. I never dreamed there was a tiger under that teddy bear."

At that moment, Brian walked in, wearing a pair of form-fitting swim trunks and carrying a wineglass. The two women burst out laughing. "Okay," Brian said, filling his glass, "what's the joke?"

"We were just talking about what could be hiding under your teddy bear exterior." Steph took a minute to control her laughter. "Then you walk in in those tight little nothings you're wearing and we know you can't hide a thing."

Brian looked down at his body with its heavy black hair. "Okay, ladies, now I'm insulted. Teddy bear indeed. I've always wanted to be a centerfold." He posed with his arms flexed. "A sex symbol. Like Burt Reynolds."

"You're my sex symbol darling," Steph giggled.

Brian walked over and gave his wife a kiss on the top of her head then started toward the pool. "Thanks," he said over his shoulder. "I'll just take this teddy bear body and go for a swim. Join me?"

"Sure." The two women followed Brian to the pool and while he swam laps, Jessie and Steph talked about gardening.

As he swam, Jessie watched Brian's shoulders. He always did have great shoulders, she thought. He fools around. With other women. She watched his huge hands cut through the water. Now stop that, she told herself as a warm flush spread through her body. That's Stephanie's husband you're leering at. But, she said to herself, he fools around with Steph's permission. Interesting.

The following day was Wednesday, matinee day in Manhattan. Steph knocked on Jessie's door and Jessie called, "Come on in." She stood in her bra and panties, rummaging in the dresser drawers for a clean polo shirt.

"Good," Steph said, one hand buried in the pocket of her flowered terrycloth robe. "I caught you before you got dressed. Put on your best city duds, I've got a treasure." She raised her hand and waved a small white envelope. "*Phantom of the Opera.* This very afternoon. Two tickets, row eight."

"Oh Steph. I've wanted to see that show for ages." She slammed the dresser drawer and opened the closet door. "City duds. How's the outfit I arrived in?"

"Just fine," Steph said, looking at her watch. "I'd like to make the ten o'clock train. We can lunch someplace nice, then go to the theater. I'll give Brian a call and he can meet us for an outrageous dinner."

"Sounds terrific."

The day was perfect. The weather was unusually temperate for New York in late June, temperatures in the high seventies and low humidity. The two women window-shopped, ate a quick lunch at Twenty-One, and enjoyed the theater. Brian met them at Le Cirque and the three spent hours gorging themselves on fine food and memorable wine. After dinner, Jessie snuck out to the maitre d' and secretly gave him her credit card. When Brian asked for the check, the waiter nodded toward Jessie. "The madam has already taken care of it."

"Jessie, you shouldn't have."

"That's to say thank you for everything. You're the best friends anyone could ever have and I'm grateful."

Brian stood up, walked around to Jessie's chair and gave her a soft kiss on the cheek. "You're our best friend and we love you." He slid the tip of his finger up the nape of Jessie's neck, ending just below her tight French knot. A shiver slithered down Jessie's spine.

Thursday, Steph spent the day at the hospital and, since Brian had a business dinner, the two women ate in the kitchen, dressed in shorts and T-shirts. "Oh lord, Steph," Jessie said as her friend pulled a casserole dish out of the oven. "Franks and beans. I haven't had franks and beans in . . . gosh, since we were in high school. Rob always said that beans gave him gas and he always watched his fat intake so franks were out."

"So? You never made some just for you?"

Ruefully, Jessie shook her head. "You don't have any of that brown spiced bread we used to have, do you?"

Steph pulled the cylinder of deep brown, spicy bread from the microwave. "Only ze best for ze madam," she said in a bad, mock French accent.

Over coffee, Steph said, "Jessie, I'd like to invite some friends over to meet you on Tuesday night. That's the Fourth of July. Just a few couples we know and particularly like. I think you'll like them too."

"Couples you and Brian fool around with?" As soon as the words were out of her mouth, Jessie regretted them. "I'm sorry."

"That's okay. And the answer is yes and no. I'd like to invite three couples, nice normal everyday folks, one of whom we've swapped with, two we haven't. I challenge you to figure out which couple we've swapped with. I had intended to invite two single men so you wouldn't find the evening so couples-oriented but one of them, a wonderful man named Gary, is out of town. You will get to meet him too, eventually. He's a very long story, but suffice it to say that he gives the best parties. You'll have to attend one with us some evening. I know you'll like the other man I've invited. Eric Langden's a doll, divorced and gorgeous. And no, I've never been with either Gary or Eric. Exactly."

Jessie let that final remark pass, for the moment. "Are you trying to fix me up?"

"Frankly, yes. But not fix you up with someone specific. It's just that you should have some fun now. It's been over a year and Rob's past history. It's time for the next phase of Jessie's life."

"I don't think I'm ready for that yet, Steph."

"For what? All I'm planning is a nice evening with nice people. Period. No sex, nothing kinky. No future plans unless you want some. No awkward foursomes. Just people. And no Jessie and Rob. Just Jessie."

"Just Jessie." She nodded. "Okay. Sounds wonderful."

The long holiday weekend sped by. Tuesday afternoon, Steph and Jessie sat chatting in the plant room. "By the way, Jessie," Steph asked, "what are you wearing this evening?"

"I thought I'd wear that same navy linen suit. Why? Is it too dressy?"

"Well. . . ." Steph hesitated. "May I make a suggestion? I'd love to see you wear that print dress we bought last week."

"Oh no, Steph. Not for tonight. It's so, I don't know, so flamboyant."

"But it's a party and that light, pretty party dress will make you feel like a party. And anyway, what's wrong with a little flamboyance? Let's look at this as a coming-out party for a new Jessie, a JessicaLynn party."

"That's silly."

"It is not silly. Let's look at it this way. If you decide to leave sometime soon—and I'm not for one moment suggesting that you should—you'll never see any of these people again. If you stay, they'll have met the new you and I'm sure they'll love you as much as I do. Let's create a new look for you to match your new life."

"Oh Steph, I don't know."

"I know you very well, JessicaLynn Hanley, and somewhere inside you a little JessicaLynn-voice is saying, 'Do it. Have some fun for a change.' Another, louder Jessie-voice is saying, 'That's ridiculous. Be yourself, conservative and proper.' Tell that Jessie-voice to stuff it and let JessicaLynn out."

Jessie laughed. "You do know me well, don't you. That's exactly what's going through my brain. I would really like to be JessicaLynn, fun-loving party-girl, but on the inside I'm still Jessie, proper and restrained." When Steph didn't respond, Jessie raised an eyebrow. "The flowered dress?"

"The flowered dress."

"The strappy sandals we bought to go with it?"

Steph nodded, then added, "And no tightly organized French twist. Wear your hair softer, maybe even loose."

"But that's not me," Jessie protested softly.

"It's JessicaLynn."

"It's JessicaLynn," she whispered. "Okay. I'll wear the dress and the shoes, but I don't know about the hair."

"Yippee. JessicaLynn gets to come out and play."

The party was scheduled for eight o'clock so the three friends had a bite to eat around six. Then Jessie went to her room, took a long shower, and scrubbed her long red hair until it squeaked. She wrapped herself in a towel, then wandered into the bedroom, opened the closet door and stood before the full-length mirror. Her fine, soft hair was already drying and flowing softly around her shoulders. The summer sun had turned the ivory skin on her face, arms, and legs a soft peachy color.

She hadn't really looked at herself in years, so Jessie took a deep breath and dropped the towel. Her figure was softer and more rounded than it had been in high school. Her breasts were high and full, her nipples deep smoky-pink. Her hips were wide enough to accentuate her small waist. Her legs were long and shapely. She smiled. I should be thinking about my thick thighs and my not-too-flat stomach, she thought. But JessicaLynn wouldn't do that.

She put on a white lace bra and panties, added a short half-slip, and then she was ready for the dress. Jessie took the hanger from the closet and, without looking in the mirror, pulled it over her head and zipped it up. She looked down and all she could see was the deep shadowed valley between her breasts. She wiggled her hips and pulled up at the neckline. "I can't do this," she said. Then she glanced up and looked at her reflection. "Wow," she said.

The dress was perfect. It hugged her upper body and cascaded in soft flowing lines over her hips and thighs. The skirt fell to just below her knees and below her short slip it was slightly translucent. She looked five years younger than she had looked a half an hour before and, she admitted to herself, she felt ten years younger.

She struggled with the tiny straps on her sandals and finally got them adjusted to her satisfaction. Again she looked at herself and grinned. "Okay, JessicaLynn, what about this hair?" Part of her wanted to put it into her traditional French twist but she stopped herself. She brushed it until it was soft and dry and pulled it back from her face. She tried a ponytail at the back of her head, then one at the nape of her neck, and finally one on top of her head. None of them were right. She pulled it one way, then another. Nothing looked the way she wanted.

She almost surrendered and put her hair up in her usual style when she remembered a long silver-colored comb she had once pushed into the fold of her twist. She found the comb in the bottom of her cosmetic bag and used it to pull one side of her hair back behind her ear. "Oh my God," she muttered as she saw the sexy woman in the mirror. "Is that me?"

It is if you want it to be, JessicaLynn said in her mind.

But is this the conservative midwesterner you've always been? Jessie asked.

No. And so what? JessicaLynn answered.

But what would Rob think?

Out loud, JessicaLynn said, "Who gives a fuck!" She dusted her cheeks with blush, pencilled on a line of eyeliner, and colored her lips with a coral lipstick. "Well, JessicaLynn, here goes."

Chapter
3

Jessica walked into the kitchen where Steph and Brian were doing a few last-minute things for the party. They had bought several party platters at the local gourmet food store and, while Steph filled a bowl with mixed nuts, Brian was dropping fresh fruit into the blender. Steph was wearing a white cotton halter-top dress with a navy belt and sandals. Brian wore identical colors, a white short-sleeved shirt, white duck slacks with a navy belt, and navy deck shoes.

"Did you two dress to match on purpose?" Jessica asked.

At the sound of her voice, Brian and Steph turned. "Holy cow," Steph said while Brian just whistled long and low. "You look fabulous."

"Now I see what I've always known," Brian said, staring. "You are not only a lovely looking woman, you're sexy as hell."

"JessicaLynn," Steph said, "you're amazing."

"JessicaLynn?" Brian said.

"We decided that the person you've seen for the past week is Jessie, but it's time to let her sensual alter ego out." Steph waved her arm at the gorgeous woman standing in the doorway. "This is JessicaLynn."

"Actually, I'd prefer to be Jessica for the moment. I'm not yet ready to become JessicaLynn but this," she swirled her skirt, "isn't Jessie either."

"Okay, what's this name thing you two have got going?" Brian asked.

Jessica motioned for Steph to explain. "Jessie lives in the midwest. She's a bit conservative and sexually repressed."

"Steph!"

"Well, she is," Steph said.

As Brian laughed, he asked, "And JessicaLynn?"

"She's a swinger. She loves sex and games and fun." Steph gave her husband a peck on the cheek. "Like us, darling."

Brian looked at Jessica and, after a moment, said, "You're telling me that you're halfway there."

"Not yet. I am telling you that I'm trying to open my mind to everything. But it's a slow process."

"Okay, Jessica it is," Steph said.

"Well, lovely lady," Brian said, crossing the kitchen and wrapping one bearlike arm around Jessica's waist, "I like your new name and your new attitude. Will you dance with me?" He swept her into his arms and they twirled around the kitchen.

"You know, Brian," Jessica said, laughing, "I never knew you were such a good dancer."

Brian pivoted, raised his arm, and let Jessica twirl underneath it. "You never gave me a chance." They danced into the living room and, gazing into her eyes, he bent her over his arm in a deep dip.

"You're flirting with me," she said, moving from his embrace.

"And why not?"

"Your wife, my best friend, is in the kitchen. Remember her?"

"Of course. But I know she told you about our unusual relationship and I've wanted to hold you for a very long time." As he watched the confusion flash over Jessica's face, Brian said, "Haven't you ever thought about how it might feel to be in my arms?"

At that moment, the doorbell rang, signalling the arrival of the first guests. "Saved by the bell," Jessica said.

"One last thing. I would never make you uncomfortable, JJ, I mean Jessica. You know that. I'll back off any time you say. But you're sexy and attractive and I enjoy playing with you, wherever it leads."

Jessica smiled as she heard Steph's footsteps in the hallway. "I understand, but it does make me a little uncomfortable." When Brian looked crestfallen, Jessica added, "But it's a nice discomfort."

As they separated, Brian ran his fingertip up Jessica's spine, then walked toward the hallway to greet their guests.

As the first couple walked into the living room, followed almost immediately by two more, Jessica remembered Steph's words. *I challenge you to figure out which couple we've swapped with.* As she was introduced to each, Jessica had to admit that she had no idea who Brian and Steph had slept with. All six people were delightful, bright, interesting, and interested.

Chuck O'Malley worked at the same brokerage firm as Brian and his wife Marcy was the vice president of an international bank. They had a married daughter who was expecting their first grandchild in two months. "Of course," Marcy said as she settled in the living room, "I'm only going to be a grandmother because I had Betsy when I was six years old."

"I know," Chuck said, "and Betsy's only nine now."

"Right!" Marcy said, giggling. "That makes me. . . ."

Chuck snatched the drink Brian offered before Marcy could take it. "That makes you only fifteen and too young to drink."

Pete Cross worked at General Foods as a research chemist and his wife Gloria was deeply involved in local politics. They had five children, ranging in age from seven to eighteen, and regaled the group with tales of their adventures in parenthood.

Steve Albright was the biggest, blackest man Jessica had ever seen. At six foot six, with skin that was almost blue, he was an imposing figure. In contrast his wife Nan was five foot one with cafe au lait skin that was stretched to its limit by her eight and a half months of pregnancy. Steve was a junior partner in a prestigious Wall Street law firm and would be a full partner before he was thirty-five. "Our first," Steve said, lovingly rubbing his wife's belly.

"And, if this pregnancy is any indication," Nan said, easing her body into a soft chair, "my last. I waddle like a duck, I sleep sitting up and I haven't seen my feet in six weeks. I've finally had to stop working, too." Jessica's ears had perked up when she learned that Nan had worked for a local real estate agency and would go back to work part-time after the birth of the baby.

"I've been wondering," Steve added, "why they call it morning sickness. Nan's been nauseated since day one, all day."

"I think they call it morning sickness because it starts in the morning," Nan said, sipping the glass of club soda Steve handed her and nibbling on the saltine crackers she always kept at hand. "But only a couple of weeks to go. The doctor says that little Stevie's right on schedule."

"You know it's a boy?" Jessica said, her envy obvious to Steph.

When Jessie and Rob had married, she had wanted several children. Over the months and years, Rob had talked her out of it. 'We want so many things. Travel, freedom. Kids would just get in the way,' Rob had said. Jessica gazed wistfully at Nan's enlarged belly.

"It's a boy. Steven James Albright Junior." She beamed at her husband. "But the doctor also said that he's already over seven pounds. Another two weeks and he'll never be able to get out the old-fashioned way."

Steve winked. "He got in there the old-fashioned way."

Over the laughter, Nan cocked her head to one side, paused, then said, "Oooohhh, yes. I remember. That sex thing. It used to be very nice, back when such a thing was possible."

"Don't give us that," Steve said. "We've found ways. Oral sex has never been as pleasant."

"Oral sex is always pleasant," Gloria said.

"And we found the most delicious goo in a sex catalog," Pete added. "I hate the ones that taste like fruit juice. This one's cinnamon. Very spicy."

Gloria winked. "Just like me."

Jessica was amazed with the openness of the talk about sex. Rob had always found the subject distasteful, so it never came up in conversation with their friends.

As the group chatted in the large living room, the doorbell rang again. That must be Eric, Jessica thought, her palms damp. Not a date, Jessica told herself. Just a man coming to a party.

Eric Langden was about six feet tall with iron-gray hair and a well-trimmed, iron-gray moustache and beard. An architect, he had been divorced for five years. The group was obviously comfortable together and they all made an effort to draw Jessica into the conversation.

Over rum and fruit drinks that Brian whipped up in a constantly whirring blender, they talked for several hours about everything from world tensions to real-estate prices, from television shows and movies to crabgrass. When she stopped to think about it, Jessica realized that she hadn't had such a light, tensionless evening in a long time.

"By the way, did anyone see Sally Jessie this afternoon?" Nan asked, sipping her club soda.

"Most of us have to work," Marcy said. "And anyway, since when have you been interested in the adventures of dysfunctional families airing their dirty little secrets in public?"

"I'm practicing to stay home for a few months at least. You have to watch at least two hours of talk shows and an hour of soaps each afternoon to keep your daytime TV certification. Actually, there's not much else on."

"So which dirty little secret did Sally Jessie reveal today?" Steph asked. "Transvestite lesbian cannibals?"

"People who've had plastic surgery on their penises," Chuck said.

"Women who've been fucked by Elvis's ghost."

"Couples who've been abducted by alien polar bears."

"A family of seven who've lived at the bottom of a well for three years."

"All right," Nan said, holding up her hands. "Take pity on the pregnant lady, will you? The show was about sexual fantasies and it got me thinking. They had couples dressed up as their favorite fantasy. One was a pirate and his captive, one was an Arabian guy with his harem girl, you know. The nice thing was no one had a Barbie and Ken shape or anything. They were just regular people and very free with their conversation."

"Sounds kinky," Chuck said with a leer. "Like Gary's party. Remember?"

"Who could forget that night?" Marcy said. "But that was before you guys moved here," she said to the Albrights.

"We've heard about Gary's parties," Steve said, patting his wife's belly. "We're not up to that yet."

When Jessica looked particularly puzzled, Steph winked at her and said, "It's a long story. I'll tell you at length sometime."

"Actually, Sally Jessie was interesting. God I hate to hear me saying that. Talk shows and interesting in the same sentence. Ugh. But anyway, some of the people discussed how difficult it had been in the beginning to tell their wife or husband about their fantasy."

"It must be for some people," Steph said seriously.

"These days I fantasize a lot," Nan continued. "I think it's lack of good sex that does it. And I know it would be hard for me to share the details with Steve. I was just wondering whether any of you have fantasies and whether you tell each other."

"You know," Marcy said, "now that you've admitted to having fantasies that you haven't shared, Steve will force all that sexy information out of you." She twirled a nonexistent moustache. "Force you to tell all the yummy details, all those sexy four-letter words."

Steve and Nan looked at each other, their look saying, 'We'll talk later.' "I guess he will," Nan said. "But now I'm curious. Do you have fantasies and have you shared them?"

As Brian poured another round of fruity drinks, he said, "I've shared most of mine with Steph, but I've kept one or two secret."

Steph jumped in, "You have?"

"Yes. Telling a fantasy and acting it out, as we have, is delicious. And yes, we've acted a few out so you guys can all eat your hearts out. But it also takes the erotic edge off of it somehow."

"What's your favorite fantasy?" Nan asked Steph and Brian.

Steph answered, "He likes to pretend that he's kidnapped me and taken me to a cabin deep in the woods. That way he can have his way with me in private."

"Oooo, yummy," Gloria said, winking at her husband.

"Would you like me to abduct you?" Pete asked. "I could have my way with you and you couldn't object."

"Why do you suppose so many fantasies revolve around being made love to forcibly?" Nan asked. "I've always thought it was evil somehow."

"Rape fantasies aren't about rape," Brian said. "They're about power. I love to have Steph under my control. That way I feel free to do some of the things I might not otherwise. I can demand. But I also know that Steph will let me know if I've gone too far."

"And I enjoy being under Brian's control," Steph said, sipping her drink and enjoying the buzz she had developed. "I don't have to worry about my reactions, what I'm supposed to be doing. I can lay back and enjoy things."

Jessica sat there enthralled. She had never heard people admit to having sexual fantasies before, much less discuss the plot. "You sure do speak your minds," she said softly.

"I'm so sorry, Jessica. Are we embarrassing you?" Nan said quickly. "You fit in so well with us that I forgot that you're new to this little group. We're pretty open-minded."

"And openmouthed," Steve added.

"I'm not really embarrassed." Jessica paused then added, "Yes I am, but it's a fun embarrassment. And I'm fascinated by the way you all talk about this stuff so freely."

"Didn't you and your ex talk about sex?"

"Rob? Not a chance. I think his only fantasy was to have a larger dental office. Sex for him was a routine. Releasing his precious bodily fluids. He wasn't the creative type."

"That's sad," Eric said. "How can you understand what you like and don't like unless you try different things?"

His look lingered on Jessica's face a bit longer than was necessary. She could feel the tingle deep in her body. "I never really thought about it. I guess we were pretty 'missionary position' and totally noncreative."

"My ex and I had a dynamite life in bed," Eric said. "It was out of bed that we fought like cats and dogs."

"How about you guys," Nan asked, turning to Chuck and Marcy. "Any sexual fun and games you'd like to share?"

"Actually," Marcy said, "Chuck has the greatest hands. He gives the most interesting massages." Chuck blushed and silently munched on a cracker and brie. "I guess," Marcy continued, "that we'd show up on Sally with me dressed in a towel and Chuck in a white uniform."

"Pete and I have a fantasy too," Gloria admitted. "We haven't acted it out, but we like to turn out all the lights and. . . ."

"Hey, babe," Pete said. "Aren't we going to have any secrets left?"

"Not a one. We're among friends. We tell a story in the dark. He's a doctor and I'm his unsuspecting patient."

"Babe . . ." Pete warned.

"Okay, okay. I'll say no more."

"Have you ever actually acted it out?" Nan asked.

"So far, no," Gloria said. "But now that you mention it. . . ."

"This conversation is making me very hot," Pete said. "Anyone for a swim?"

"Not me," Nan said, rubbing her belly, "but I'll sit by the pool."

"I turned the heater on just before you folks got here," Brian said. He turned to Jessica. "Suits are optional. Some wear them, some don't. Dealer's choice."

"I think I'll put a suit on," Jessica said, "if that's okay. I'm not that liberated yet."

"You won't be upset if I don't, will you?" Brian asked.

"I don't think so. If I am, I'll look the other way."

In her room, Jessica pulled her three bathing suits from the drawer. The one she had brought from Ottawa, a one-piece floral print, held her in in all the right places. Too conservative and definitely Jessie. She held up the bikini that she and Steph had bought on their recent shopping trip. It barely covered any of her. She dropped it back into the drawer and compromised on a one-piece black suit that mock-laced up the front and left a panel of barely concealed flesh from waist to cleavage. As she wiggled into the suit, she realized that she was slightly drunk, totally relaxed, and very aroused. Her nipples were hard and showed prominently through the tight black fabric.

This sexual tension was a revelation. Poor old Rob, she thought. He would never do anything like this. He missed a lot, and so have I. Well, she told herself, maybe he experiments with bimbette. You know, I really hope he can. She shook her head. I must be mellowing, but I do hope he's getting some good sex. I know I will get mine, eventually. Maybe sooner, rather than later. She fluffed her hair and, barefoot, she ran down the stairs.

When she arrived at the pool, all the patio lights were out with just the underwater lights to illuminate the soft mist rising from the water. Nan was stretched out in a lounge chair with Gloria and Pete sitting in chairs on either side of her. Everyone else was in the water and through the choppy surface it was impossible to tell who had clothes on and who didn't. Steph and Steve were involved in a splash fight at the shallow end, with Chuck egging them on. Brian, Eric, and Marcy were hanging onto the ladder at the deep end, talking. Jessica found herself looking at Brian's muscular shoulders and wondering what he looked like without a bathing suit.

Jessica walked to the deep end and dove cleanly into the eight-foot-deep water. She came up beside Brian, facing the side of the pool, holding on to the edge. "The water's perfect," she said, pushing her sopping red hair out of her face.

"So are you in that bathing suit. I could rape you right here," he whispered, pressing his obviously naked body with its ridge of hard male flesh against her side. "You look so sexy." He released the pressure of his body. "But I won't rush you. I just want you to know that our time will come, eventually, if I have my way." He let go, pushed Marcy under the water and together they swam to the other side, leaving Jessica with Eric.

"That suit looks terrific," Eric said, moving nearer. "It's actually more sensual than being nude." When she was silent, Eric continued, "I'm sorry if I come on too heavy. You're new to this crazy life we have here. But we're just free spirits and we do what feels good and doesn't hurt anyone else. I won't embarrass you, but I would be less than honest if I denied that you turn me on."

Remembering that Eric had been divorced for several years, she asked, "Were you and your wife swingers?"

"We had occasional flings, with each other's knowledge, of course. We were very creative in the bedroom."

"If you'll pardon me for asking, what caused your breakup?"

"Money, mostly." He pulled himself from the water and sat on the edge of the pool while Jessica remained in the water next to his ankles. As water sluiced from his torso she admired his body, substantial in his brief red trunks. "I made some, she spent more. She always wanted me to do things that made more money, I wanted to do things that made me happy. When I was offered a new job with a large architectural firm in the city at an unseemly increase in salary, she begged me to take it."

"You didn't want to?"

"Not really. Commuting was not my idea of how to spend three hours a day. And that job would have also meant weeks, even months travelling. I had commuted and travelled before and it took too much out of me. That's why I took the job in Scarsdale in the first place. It was a small firm but we created some wonderful buildings.

"So we argued about the job. She whined about all the things she wanted out of life. I tried to explain that all I wanted was to stay in Scarsdale, enjoy my ten-minute drive to work, and have enough money to do the things that were important to me. And that wasn't a big house, a maid five days a week, and trips to Europe several times a year."

"What is important to you?"

"I love my kids. They're boys, twins, and they were fourteen then. I liked being able to get to their soccer games and parent conferences. She wanted them in a private school. I like tennis and golf. And I like my friends." He looked around the group. "I wanted to have something left at the end of the day, not get up at the crack of dawn, work, come home, eat, fall into bed so I can get up with the roosters and do it all again."

"And your wife wanted you to take the city job?"

"She demanded. She gave me the 'If you loved me' bit and I thought about it and discovered that I didn't love her. At least not enough to do everything the way she wanted. So we split. We still see each other occasionally, though not as much now that the boys are in college. I miss them, especially since they're spending their summer together in Colorado. Anyway, Marilyn lives in Hartsdale, in a large condo I bought her, and I think she's happy. But her happiness isn't my responsibility anymore. It took me a long time to realize that nothing I did was going to make her happy anyway."

"That's a very grown-up attitude," Jessica said.

"How about your divorce. Was it very difficult?"

Jessica told him about Rob and bimbette. "I find I'm becoming less bitter day by day. Being here has opened my eyes a lot."

"And, if you'll pardon my asking, was your sex life really as boring as you alluded to before?"

Jessica sighed and sipped the drink Brian had set on the edge of the pool for her. "I guess so. I'm not sure how much was his fault and how much was mine."

"Why does it have to be anyone's fault?"

"Not fault, exactly, but I'm just not responsive enough." Why in the world had she admitted that? Now he won't be interested. She looked at the glass in her hand and put it down. And she realized that she wanted Eric to be interested.

"Did he tell you that?" When she nodded, he said, "A sensual woman like you? He has to be a jerk."

Jessica laughed and, bobbing in the warm water, moved slightly

away from the side of the pool and kicked her legs. "Thanks for
that. But why do you say I'm sensual? What do you know about
me?"

"I know that your nipples are hard and it's getting difficult for
you to hold still." When her cheeks pinked, he said, "And you're
blushing. I love that." He grinned. "I know this is sudden, but
could we get together one evening soon?"

"Is this a proposition, sir?" Jessica said, flirtatiousness coming
easily from somewhere deep inside her.

"Maybe. I have to admit that I'd love to teach you how sexy
you really are, but let's start with dinner. It can progress as quickly
or as slowly as we like from there. Or not at all, if that's what we
decide."

Jessica smiled. This man was making a pass at her and she was
revelling in it. "I'd love to have dinner with you."

"Friday? I can pick you up here at about six?"

"Friday it is."

"Did you have a nice evening?" Steph asked as she and Jessica
tidied up the kitchen. They could see Brian, a towel around his
waist, wandering around the pool area, stuffing plastic plates and
glasses into a large black garbage bag.

"I had an amazing evening," Jessica said. "Your friends are terrific people. I like them all so much."

"I knew you would. They're the greatest."

"Okay. I think I'm ready for the big revelation. Which of them
have you slept with?"

Steph laughed. "Couldn't tell, could you."

"Not a clue. Everyone's so open and sexy. I'd sleep with any
one of the guys."

"So, my dear, would I. However. . . ." She stuffed a large platter into the dishwasher. "Okay, okay," she said, catching Jessica's
look. "Steve and Nan only moved here about a year ago and they
were trying desperately to get pregnant. We discussed our lifestyle with them, and they were tempted. Isn't he the most gorgeous thing? Makes me sweat just to think about those arms

around me. Anyway, they didn't want to confuse things. I hope, after the baby's born. . . ."

"You're right about him. He's got the greatest body."

"That's my Jessica talking. I think Jessie's long buried."

Jessica sighed. "You may be right. What about the others? Who did and who didn't?"

"Pete and Gloria discussed it and decided that they didn't want to risk the jealousy that they were both afraid would surface. They tried swapping once, many years ago, and Pete particularly found it very hard to deal with the thought of someone else making love to his wife. They go to most of the parties but they stay together."

"So you've been with Chuck and Marcy."

Steph just grinned as Brian walked up behind her and wrapped his arms around her waist. "The four of us," Brian said, "spent a weekend in the Adirondacks together last January. Get Steph to tell you about it sometime. It was incredible." He nibbled his wife's neck. "Just incredible."

"Certainly was," Steph agreed. "And, by the way, I also spent a creative evening with Gary about six months ago. I was sorry he couldn't come tonight. He's the sexiest man I know, with the exception of Brian, of course."

"Is he very handsome?"

Steph thought about it. "Actually, not at all. He sort of reminds me of Ichabod Crane. He's about six foot two or three and probably doesn't weigh one fifty. Long legs, long arms, sort of like a stork. He wears mismatched clothes that hang on him. He always looks like he's just lost fifty pounds and his wardrobe hasn't caught up."

"But you said. . . .

"I said sexy and attractive, not handsome. There's a big difference."

"Like . . . ?"

"He listens when you talk and concentrates like you're the only one in the world who matters at that moment. He touches you, accidentally on purpose, if you know what I mean. A hand on your shoulder as you sit down, or a palm in the small of your back to guide you through a doorway. And he looks at you like he wants to make long slow love to you all the time."

"Where was Brian all this time, while you were out with Gary?"

"I was here," Brian said, walking through the large sliding glass door. "It doesn't have to be a couples thing with us. I've had my . . . adventures too. Solo. It's really okay with us."

"And what did you think of Eric?" When Jessica blushed, Steph continued, "Did he ask you out?"

"We're having dinner on Friday," Jessica said softly.

"That's great," Brian said. "He's one of the nicest people I know and you two should get along well."

"I liked him a lot. He's bright and so open about things."

"Well," Steph said, "I'm beat." She closed the dishwasher and turned it on.

Jessica glanced at the clock on the microwave. "Holy cow. Is it really after one?"

"Yup," Steph said. "Time sure rushes by when you're having fun."

Brian grabbed Steph by the arm and dragged her toward the sliding glass door. "Let's go out by the pool so I can ravish you before bed."

Steph giggled. "Weallll suh," she laid on a thick southern accent. "What kahnd of a girl do you tahke me foah?"

"I know what kind of girl you are," Brian said, still tugging. "That's why I want to take you out to the pool."

"Nighty night, Jessica," Steph said as Brian dragged her out the door.

"Good night, folks," Jessica said. "I love you both."

Brian blew her a kiss and he and Steph disappeared into the darkness.

Upstairs, Jessica pulled off her bathing suit, took a quick shower, and collapsed onto her bed. Despite the late hour, she couldn't sleep. Images of the people she'd met that evening and an image of herself so different from anything she could have imagined a few weeks before crowded her brain. Finally, she dropped into an exhausted slumber.

In her dream she rode on a merry-go-round. The calliope played random notes that didn't combine into anything she recognized, but surrounded her and filled her head with erotic music. Multicolored lights winked and flashed in a primitive rhythm.

She was gloriously naked. The snow-white horse rose and fell between her thighs, cool against her heated flesh. She leaned forward and pressed the cool metal bar against the valley between her breasts, against her flaming forehead.

As the merry-go-round turned, Jessica closed her eyes and let the wind blow her hair until it flew behind her like the tail of the horse she rode. Up and down the horse moved, carrying her with it.

Suddenly, there was a man seated on the horse with her, the fronts of his thighs against the backs of hers. She felt the prickle of the coarse hairs on his legs against her delicate skin. Just ignore him, she told herself. But she couldn't. When she started to turn to look at him, he placed his hands gently on the sides of her head, effectively preventing her from seeing who he was. When he lowered his hands to her waist, she didn't try to turn again. Around and around they rode, his hands on her waist and his thighs against her legs.

Gradually, he leaned forward until the length of his chest pressed against her back. Hands splayed on her belly, he used the tip of his tongue to tickle the hollow just behind her right ear. Holding her against him, he bit the tip of her earlobe, then sucked it into his mouth.

As the erotic power of his mouth held her against him, he slid his hands up to cup her aching breasts. He filled his hands with them, weighed and massaged them. Jessica looked down and admired the contrast between his dark fingers and her white skin. She watched in fascination as the hands kneaded her soft fullness and moved ever closer to her fully erect nipples. Squeeze me, she whispered to herself. Pinch me. Make me feel you.

"I will," the man's voice breathed into her ear. "I will give you everything you want. But at my pace." He caressed her breasts lightly. "Just ride the horse. Feel the wind in your face. Close your eyes. Feel." His fingers reached her nipples and he held the left between his finger and thumb. "Feel." He pinched and pulled, causing a sensation that was almost pain.

Erotic heat knifed through her body, stabbing deep into her secret spaces. Don't stop, she thought. Oh God, don't stop. She wanted to tell him, say it out loud, but she couldn't. The words echoed in her head.

"You don't have to say it," he whispered. "I won't stop." One hand pressed her belly and forced her buttocks to cradle his mammoth erection. The other hand shifted to her right breast, grasping it tightly and twisting.

"You're hurting me," Jessica said, not sure whether it was true.

"No, it doesn't really hurt although you think it should. It gives you pleasure; hot demanding pleasure. It makes you hungry. So hungry that you are being devoured by it. Aren't you?" When she remained silent, he moved his hips so his cock slid more deeply into the crack between her cheeks while his fingers worked on her nipple. "Aren't you?"

"Yes," she sighed. "Oh yes."

He shifted his hips and lifted her body. Suddenly his cock was touching her hot, moist entrance. "You want this," the voice whispered, the heated breath tickling her ear. "But you'll have to take it."

Between Jessica's thighs, the merry-go-round horse continued its unrelenting up and down movement. She supported her weight on the stirrups and held herself above his cock. Her thigh muscles quivered from the effort of holding herself up.

"Take it," he whispered. "Let your body go. Take what you and I both know you want."

Yes, she admitted to herself, she did want this. Slowly, she lowered her body so she filled herself with his cock. The merry-go-round went faster and faster and with each note of the calliope the horse rose, carrying him deeper inside. She rode him, synchronizing her movements with the rhythm of the horse. Her mind splintered, sensations darting from the fingers on her nipples to his mouth on her neck to his cock, filling, caressing. Faster and faster she rode until she was a bubble about to burst. And burst she did, a million colors surrounding her. The lights of the carousel flashed, penetrating her lowered eyelids. She screamed, but then couldn't get her breath. She flew, then plunged with the horse and the man beneath her, the wind unable to cool her body. On and on they rode, climax after rending climax, until she collapsed.

Jessica awoke in a pool of sweat, the sheets tangled around her naked body. Her breathing was rapid and her heart pounded. She could almost hear the music and see the lights. She lay in the darkness until her body calmed, then took another shower. Afterward, she climbed back into bed and slept dreamlessly until morning.

Thursday evening Eric called and he and Jessica talked for almost an hour. "About tomorrow evening," Eric said. "If you agree, there's a concert at a place I think you'd enjoy called Caramoor. There'll be a small jazz group playing in a part of the estate called the Venetian Gardens. I thought we'd have a little picnic on the lawn before the music."

"That sounds lovely."

"Great. Wear jeans and something long-sleeved. It's supposed to be cool and it does get a bit buggy. I'll bring the dinner and the bug spray and pick you up around six."

"I'll see you then."

Jessica flopped back onto her bed. She was both jittery and excited, looking forward to the following evening with a combination of terror and delight. Okay, she thought, jeans. She mentally flipped through her small collection of clothes and selected a soft buttercup-yellow silk shirt. Should I take a jacket? It's only a picnic. But it might get cool later in the evening. But I might look pretentious. Sneakers? Maybe loafers? Or what about sandals?

That night and most of the next day while Steph was at the hospital, Jessica selected, discarded, and reselected. She sat in the garden room and tried to read, only to get up and pace around the pool. "This is ridiculous," she said aloud. "I'm acting like a kid on her first date." Then she grinned. "I am a kid on her first date."

At about four o'clock, she soaked in a tub and managed to relax for a short while. Then she put on the clothes she had selected, changed her shirt, then changed back. At six o'clock, Jessica was dressed in the outfit she had first selected, yellow shirt, soft, well-washed jeans she had had for many years, tennis shoes, and socks. Then, at the last minute, she added a fitted denim vest.

She put her hair up, then held a pair of earrings near her ears. She discarded them and picked another pair, which she also dropped back into the drawer. Something bigger, she thought. But it's only a picnic. Maybe no earrings. She settled on a pair of medium-sized wooden hoops. She gazed into the mirror, smiled, added blush and lipstick and hurried downstairs, glad the house was empty.

As she heard Eric's car in the driveway, Jessica stood inside the front door debating whether to open it and walk outside or wait for him to ring the bell. You're jumpy as a cat, she said to herself, turning the knob in her right hand and pulling the door open. Eric stood with his hand poised above the doorbell.

God, he's sexy, she thought as he stood, openly appraising her. He was dressed in tight jeans and a white tennis sweater with the sleeves pushed up to the elbows, showing off well-muscled forearms. He wasn't gorgeous and she doubted that anyone would stop in their tracks and stare at him. But there was a gleam in his eyes as he looked her over that created a small flutter deep in her belly. His eyes lingered on her breasts as they pressed against the silky fabric of her shirt, then wandered lower to her narrow waist and full hips.

"Very nice," he said. "Although I've seen you in a bathing suit, I still enjoyed speculating about the way you'd fill out your jeans." As she colored, he continued, "You're blushing again." He used the knuckle of his index finger to raise her face, then he dropped a light kiss on her lips. "It's sort of virginal. I love it." Then he took her elbow and guided her out the door.

Together they walked toward the driveway where Eric's vintage BMW 2002 was parked. Bright red with slick black leather upholstery, it was in mint condition. "That's some car," Jessica commented.

"I love old BMWs. I found this one about a year ago and I had it restored. It cost more than buying a new one and it's silly of me, but I get a kick out of it. Drivers of these old cars flick their lights at each other in recognition and I like that kind of camaraderie."

Jessica stroked the supple leather seat beneath her, silently wondering how he could afford to 'restore' a classic car like this one. Did architects make that kind of money?

Eric and Jessica passed the next twenty minutes in comfortable conversation, driving along the tree-lined roadways of Westchester County. They arrived at Caramoor, passed through the big iron gates and drove to a grassy parking area. He helped her out of the car and, arm in arm, they walked along the dirt pathways toward a small picnic area. Before they arrived at the tables, however, Eric turned into a small area of lawn surrounded by a low hedge. In the middle was an old fountain, now filled with flowering plants.

"By the way," Jessica said, her stomach reminding her that she hadn't eaten since breakfast, "you're not carrying any basket. I thought you mentioned dinner."

"I did."

They approached a large plaid wool blanket spread on the lawn under a large maple tree, set with fine china plates, full settings of silverware, and crystal champagne flutes. Each place setting was accompanied by a white linen napkin and a red leather seat cushion.

But it was the man who stood beside the blanket who caught Jessica's attention. He was immense, probably over two hundred and fifty pounds, but well muscled with a long golden ponytail and a heavy gold hoop in one ear. He looked like he might have been a football player or a prize fighter, with gigantic hands and a face that looked like it had taken a punch or two in its time. Beautifully groomed, the man wore tan slacks and a forest-green polo shirt. He was obviously waiting for the lady he would share his feast with.

"Isn't that lovely," she said to Eric. "What an elegant presentation."

"Why thank you," he said, approaching the blanket. "I'll tell Timmy you're impressed."

As Jessica turned to Eric, puzzled, the man near the blanket said, "There you are, sir. I was afraid the food would get warm."

"Not to worry, Timmy," Eric said. "I know better than to keep one of your sumptuous meals waiting." He turned to Jessica. "Jessica, this is Timmy Whitmore. He's my right-hand man and my chauffeur when I want one. He's in charge of my house and he's the best damn cook in the county."

Timmy inclined his head slightly. "It's nice to meet you Ms. . . ."

Totally nonplussed, Jessica answered automatically. "Hanley. It's Jessica Hanley." She turned to Eric who looked sheepish. "Didn't you say you were a modestly well-off suburban architect who used to argue with your wife about money?"

"I did, didn't I. I know that I owe you an explanation but can it wait until after dinner? Timmy's meals are always works of art and he gets very huffy if his food isn't presented just so."

"Of course it can wait," Jessica said. "But you'll have to give me a moment to adjust." Eric held her arm as she settled onto one of the leather cushions.

With a flourish Timmy pulled two plates from a hamper a few feet away and set one in front of each of them. Artfully arranged on fresh lettuce and watercress were half a dozen of the largest shrimp Jessica had ever seen, with a dollop of dill sauce and a few small toast-rounds on the side. "Good grief, Timmy," Eric said. "These shrimp look like they should have saddles."

"I know," Timmy said, looking downcast and a bit irritated. "I tried to get U12s but all they had were U5s. They're really too large to be as tender as I'd like, but the man in the fish store swore that they were superb. If they're not. . . ."

Eric tasted one. "Well, Timmy, your man was right. They are delicate and crisp, cooked exactly right. Not chewy at all."

Timmy beamed, the smile giving his singularly unattractive face an appealing glow. "Thank you sir."

Feeling like she was in the middle of a James Bond movie, Jessica speared a shrimp with a slender shrimp fork and tasted, then dipped the shrimp into the sauce and took another bite. "These are delicious," she said and watched Timmy's smile grow still wider. "I make cold shrimp often, but with cocktail sauce with extra horseradish, or a cold mayonnaise. I've never made anything like this sauce. It's wonderful."

"Thank you. I've met only a few people who appreciate shrimp with mayonnaise," Timmy said.

While they ate in silence, she watched Timmy deftly open a bottle of Dom Perignon and fill two flutes, each half full. "This meal is delightful," Jessica said as she lifted her glass.

"And the company is a perfect complement," Eric whispered, holding her gaze until her hand shook. He lifted his glass and touched the rim to hers, enjoying the single clear note it produced. "To an enjoyable evening, the first of many I hope."

"To an enjoyable evening." She sipped the wine, knowing she was already intoxicated.

When they had finished their shrimp, Timmy whisked the plates away and replaced them with larger, prearranged dinner plates. "I made cold smoked breast of duck with a chilled pasta primavera." Moving with surprising grace for such a large man he placed a sauceboat on the blanket. "There's a light vinaigrette for the duck." He placed small bread plates, each with two tiny hot rolls, beside Eric and Jessica. Jessica was amazed that the surface of each butter pat was covered with a tiny staff and notes of music. "These are beautiful, Timmy," she said.

"I enjoy doing that. You might call it a hobby of mine."

"That's along with cake decorating and baking the most delicious breads you've ever tasted."

"Actually, I once worked as a food stylist on photos for a cookbook," Timmy boasted, removing the champagne glasses and replacing them with white wine glasses. "I have a sauvignon blanc from Chili, 1992. It will go perfectly with the duck and was very reasonable."

"Timmy haunts the local wine stores."

"I found this one at Zachy's actually. It was so well priced that I bought us a case," Timmy said.

"Jessica?" Eric asked.

"If Timmy recommends it, how can I argue?"

Timmy beamed as he uncorked the wine and poured a small amount into Eric's glass.

"Anyone can find a good fifty-dollar bottle of wine," Timmy said. "I can find a good bottle of wine at under ten dollars. What do you think?"

Eric tasted and nodded. "Right as usual."

Beaming, Timmy handed Eric the cork and half-filled each glass. "Keep the cork," Eric said, handing it back to Timmy, "and you can recork the bottle before you leave. If we finish even half of this wine, I'll never be able to drive home."

As they ate, they made small talk. "Do you know why the host breaks the wine cork?" he asked.

Jessica took a sip of wine to moisten her dry mouth and tucked her legs underneath her. "I always wondered why the waiter hands it over, but I didn't want to sound as unsophisticated as I felt so I never asked."

"Most of these rituals are left over from the dim past when there was a real need for precautions. Now it's mostly just snobbery and uptight people who like to make a simple glass of wine into a Japanese tea ceremony." He reached out and Timmy handed Eric the cork which he in turn handed to Jessica, his fingers lingering on hers. "You'll notice that the imprint of the winery is on the cork, with the year." He laid the cork in Jessica's palm, rubbing the rough surface along her skin. "In the olden days unscrupulous people used to fill an empty bottle with jug wine, then recork it and sell it as the expensive stuff. So, rather than break the expensive bottle so that wouldn't happen, they broke the inexpensive cork."

"Oh. That makes sense." She held the cork under her nose. "Why do they smell the cork?"

"Before wine was sterilized, pasteurized, and otherwise purified, occasionally bad yeasts would get into the vats and, instead of fine wine, you'd get fine vinegar. Actually the word vinegar is from the French, *vin* meaning wine and *agre* meaning sour. And if the wine was sour, you could smell it in the cork." Eric smiled. "These days, wine is never sour and there's no need to smell the cork. The only ones who sniff it are those who want everyone to think they know something." He reached over and wrapped his long fingers around Jessica's then slowly drew the cork from her hand.

As his fingers slid from her hand, Jessica's breath caught. She gazed at the attractive man who sat across from her, then looked at her plate. She lifted a small forkful of the duck to her mouth and tasted it, unsure of whether she'd be able to swallow. To break the tension she was feeling, she said, "This is very unusual, Timmy. I really like it."

"I'm so glad. I didn't know anything about you or your taste in food, so it was difficult to plan the meal."

"Well, Timmy, I'm easy. I enjoy tasting new things and I can't imagine anything that you created that I wouldn't like."

Eric gazed into her eyes. "I'm glad you enjoy trying new things, Jessica."

The food turned to cardboard in her mouth and she sipped her wine to moisten her lips. Although it was difficult for her to eat with Eric's hot gaze on her, she couldn't insult Timmy so she finished every bite along with two glasses of wine.

"I'm so glad the meal pleased you, Ms. Hanley," Timmy said as he removed the plates and the wine glasses. "I have a triple-crème blue cheese and fruit for dessert. There's coffee and I've taken the liberty of opening a 1971 Chateau D'Yquem. It will go superbly with the cheese and fruit. The pears are especially good." Leaving the platter with the fruit and cheese, china mugs for coffee beside the filled carafe, the decanter, and new glasses for the sauterne, Timmy efficiently packed everything else in a hamper. "I'll be leaving, now. I've left a small basket over there," he pointed, then lifted the heavy hamper as though it weighed nothing. "Everything should fit quite nicely."

"Timmy," Eric said, stretching out on the blanket as people wandered through the gardens around them, "you've done a wonderful job, as usual."

"Thank you, sir," he said, "and it was so nice meeting you Ms. Hanley."

"Thank you for the wonderful meal, Timmy," Jessica said. "I don't think I've ever had better."

"Good night," Timmy said and walked toward the exit with a surprisingly light step for such a big man.

Chapter

4

"Try the cheese with the sauterne," Eric said. He cut off a bit of pear, spread a small amount of cheese on the morsel and held it in front of Jessica's mouth. She ate from his fingers and he quickly handed her the wine. "Close your eyes and drink this so the tastes are in your mouth at the same time."

When she had sipped the thick, deep yellow liquid, he asked, "What do you taste?"

"Cream and pear and . . . pineapples." She opened her eyes, amazed.

He took a bite of pear and cheese, then sipped his own wine. "Pineapples. Wonderful. A few years ago, someone introduced me to the combination of sauterne and blue-veined cheese. There's a strange synergy. The whole taste is so much more than the sum of its parts." He spread another bit of cheese on another piece of fruit and offered it to Jessica.

She took it from him, placed it on her tongue, and sipped the sauterne. "It is wonderful, but if I have much more to drink, I'll be incoherent." She dropped onto her back on the soft blanket.

Eric took the glass from her hand. "I certainly don't want you incoherent. I want you to be fully aware of everything that happens."

"And what is going to happen?" Jessica asked, the words out of her mouth before she could stop them.

Eric grinned and licked a tiny crumb of cheese from her lower lip. "Everything and nothing."

"What does that mean?"

"Everything means that I'm going to spend the rest of the evening seducing you with wine and food, music and evening breezes and me."

"And nothing?"

"Nothing means that as much as I want to, and, I hope, as much as you will want me to, I'm not going to make love to you tonight."

"Why not?"

"Because I want you to anticipate how wonderful it will be with us when I undress you and touch you and lick every inch of your skin. I want you to wonder how it will feel when I slide, ever so slowly, into your body and feel your hips reaching for me, unable to wait any longer.

"Then I want you to think about it in the cold, sober light of day. Sex for the sake of sex. Not love, just desire. Then you can decide whether that is truly what you want."

Jessica sighed and closed her eyes. Her thighs were trembling and her heart was pounding. She did want him. Badly. She felt a tickling on her neck and reached up to brush it away. As her hand dropped she felt the tickling again. She slowly opened her eyes and saw Eric, his face close to hers, a blade of grass in his hand. "I know what I want right now," she whispered, unable to stop the words.

"Maybe you do. But I know what we're not going to do. It's important to me that we don't make love because of too much wine or too long since the last time." He saw the disappointment on Jessica's face. "Oh lord," he said, smiling. "This is going to be a long and singularly frustrating evening." He tossed the grass aside and sat up. "I owe you an explanation. About Timmy and all."

Jessica sighed and partially shook off the cloud of desire that surrounded her. She sat up and poured herself a cup of steaming coffee. She looked at him and lifted a cup. When he shook his head, she put the decanter down and added milk to her coffee. "Okay. Tell me."

"Marilyn, my ex-wife, must be, in some ways, the unluckiest woman in the world. When we split, I was, as you put it, a humble architect. I made eighty thousand a year, a nice salary but not enough for her, so she went looking for greener pastures. Maybe there was a deeper reason. But money seemed to be all she thought about."

"Don't tell me you won the lottery or something."

"Let me give you a little background." He sipped his sauterne and watched the people wandering past them. In the far distance he could hear the sensual sound of a clarinet tuning up. "My father took off when I was seven. I think my mother was glad to see him go although it meant that she had to work. He was a heavy drinker, a gambler, a womanizer, and a general pain in the ass. He was never abusive, or anything like that. It was just that he was totally unpredictable. Rich and expansive one minute, poor and depressive the next. He wouldn't come home for days, even weeks at a time. Then he'd arrive home like the prodigal son, frequently reeking of perfume. Of course, at the time, I idolized him, thought he was the greatest, especially when he arrived with his arms full of presents."

"It must have been a tough life for you."

"My mom was a very sane, down-to-earth woman and I was a very happy child in spite of my on-again, off-again father."

Jessica smiled. "You were lucky."

"I guess I was. One evening, my dad arrived home after almost two weeks, and told my mom that he was leaving for good. He packed his things in an old black-and-white suitcase and disappeared. My mom cried for about a week, then pulled herself together and made a good life for herself. She had worked in a local nursing home as an aide and discovered that she enjoyed helping older people. So she put herself through nursing school, then made enough to put me through college. She died the year after I graduated."

"She sounds like a nice woman."

Eric's face softened. "She was the best. Anyway, about a year after Marilyn and I split, I received a visit from a lawyer. My father, it turns out, had done okay for himself. He'd ended up in Vegas and amassed a small fortune. Before he died, he had a will drawn up leaving everything to me. There was a letter from him for me, too. He tried to explain that although he didn't consider himself a bad man, he had been a terrible husband and a worse father and that we had been better off without him. He said that he had spent a lot of years broke and then started a run of luck and had gotten some money together. He hired an investigator who learned that my mom had died and that I was doing very well on my own." Eric ran his long slender fingers through his iron-gray hair.

"Personally, I think he didn't contact me then because we had almost nothing in common except some genetic material. I don't remember him as a bad father, but that's the way he thought about things. I'm just sorry that my mother didn't live to know that he still thought about us. Anyway, I inherited everything. Including Timmy."

"Including Timmy?"

"He was my father's bodyguard, and, I gather, he needed one. He was in some pretty ugly businesses with some pretty nasty people. My father won Timmy, who had spent a few years as a professional wrestler, in a poker game almost ten years before he died. His old manager put up his contract in lieu of five thousand dollars. Fortunately for both my father and Timmy, the manager's full boat, aces over sixes, wasn't as good as my father's four deuces.

"Timmy's a gem and a thoroughly nice man. He was unquestionably loyal and able to take care of himself and my father, particularly in my dad's final months which, I gather, were lousy. Timmy won't talk about those years and the things my father was

into. He says it's a closed book now that he's dead. And I guess it
is."

"How could he leave Timmy to you?" Jessica asked. "It
sounds like some kind of indentured servitude."

"Not at all. My father got to know Timmy very well. Although
he left him a generous amount of cash in his will, my father left
Timmy something more important. One section of the will guar-
antees him a job with me for as long as he wants. And that's all he
wants. I guess he's like my mom. He wants to take care of someone the way he took care of my father, and he stays because he
wants to. He keeps the money my dad left him in the bank. 'For
his old age,' he says."

"Your dad sound like a very perceptive man."

"He was."

"And Timmy's cooking?"

"That had been a hobby of his for many years. He used to
cook for my father, who taught Timmy to enjoy fine food and
good wine. After my father's death, Timmy told me that he had
always wanted to study seriously so I encouraged him to take a
year to study at the Culinary Institute. Now, as you've gathered,
it's more than just a hobby—it's a passion."

"That's quite a story."

Distant strains of jazz filtered through the evening air. "The
music's starting," Eric said, stretching out on the blanket. "They
discourage listening from here rather than going to the terrace,
but I bought six tickets and made a special plea to the staff so
they'll leave us alone."

Jessica stretched out beside Eric, her head buzzing with the
wine and the music and the feel of Eric's fingers entwined with
hers. Together they watched the sky darken and the stars appear
while they listened to an erotic baritone saxophone. From time
to time, Eric would lift Jessica's hand to his lips and kiss her
knuckles, or nip one fingertip. As the first half of the concert
ended, he sucked her index finger into his hot mouth and swirled
his tongue around the tip.

To calm her fluttering stomach, she said, "With this inheritance of yours, do you still design buildings?"

He chuckled. "Getting too hot for you?" He sucked her finger again, then answered, "Sure. I like to be productive and I don't know what else I'd do. I do one or two projects each year, overall design, not the bathroom fixtures or landscaping. I keep my job within strict limits. I never take on a project that will occupy more time than I want to give, leaving the rest of my time for the parts of my life that give me joy." He bit the tip of Jessica's finger, then swirled his tongue around the palm. "How about you? What was your family life like as a kid?"

Jessica struggled to concentrate enough to answer his question. "Dull. I was born and brought up in Ottawa, Illinois, a small town near Chicago. Steph and I went to high school together and that's where she met Brian and I met Rob, my ex-husband."

Jessica tried to gently withdraw her hand from Eric's but he held her fast. "Tell me about him. He must be some kind of idiot to let something as gorgeous and sexy as you get away."

"I don't mean to make him sound like a total jerk," Jessica said, finally pulling her hand away from Eric. "We met in high school and he knew precisely what he wanted out of life, so it happened. Dental school and a very busy practice in Ottawa."

When Eric took her hand again she sighed and didn't try to pull away. "I gathered from your conversation Tuesday night that you and he weren't setting the world on fire in the bedroom."

Jessica laughed softly. "No, we weren't. Most of our problems in bed were probably due to inexperience. We were both virgins or close enough for government work when we met and there never was anyone else for either of us. Not until bimbo."

"He found a sweet young thing?"

Jessica told him about finding Rob in his office that afternoon so many months before. When he laughed at her version of the story, he apologized. "Don't apologize," she said. "Now, looking back on it, it was pretty funny. At the time, however, it seemed my life had ended."

Eric propped himself up on one elbow and slid the tip of his tongue across Jessica's lips. "And how does it seem now?"

Jessica reached up, cupped the back of Eric's head and smiled as she touched her lips to his. "It seems like it might have been the best thing that ever happened to me." When she felt his mouth on hers, it was soft and warm and incredibly exciting. They kissed for a long time, savoring the taste and feel of each other's lips and tongue. Eric stroked Jessica's side until she longed for the feel of his hands on her breasts.

As the second half of the concert began, Jessica lay on her back on the blanket with Eric, who propped himself on his elbow, gazing down at her, "Even though you can barely see me in the dark, you make me self-conscious when you look at me like that," she said.

"Uncomfortable?"

"A little."

"Good. You make me uncomfortable too. All I can think of is how much I want you."

Jessica closed her eyes as Eric continued, "Do you know how it will be with us? It will begin with a glow, soft and warm and gentle. Slowly it will build until it will blaze with fire too hot to touch but too sweet to resist." His hand lay on her flat belly, fingers widely spread, "I can feel your muscles tighten when you're excited. Like now." He placed his mouth beside her ear, his breath tickling her. "I can tell you some of the things we're going to do. Would you like that?"

She groaned. "Tell me."

"First, I'll unbutton your blouse. Wear a blouse next time so I can open each button and lick your skin as I expose what's beneath the material." He ran his finger down her breastbone to the first button of her blouse, then up to the hollow of her neck, feeling her shiver.

"Then I'll open your bra so I can admire your beautiful breasts. I've seen them in my dreams, full and white with hard, dusky brown nipples. They'll be so hard and hungry that I won't be able to resist taking one in my mouth. They will taste of your skin, spicy, tight little nubs. I'll use my teeth and you'll try to pull away from the slight pain, until it turns to hot pleasure flowing through your body." He slid his hand lower, until his fingers rested between Jessica's thighs.

"Then I'll slide your bra and your slacks off until you're wearing only your panties. Have you ever been stroked through the silk of your panties? It slightly muffles the sensation, making it softer, and more delicate." He felt the heat of her body through the crotch of her jeans and slowly rubbed. "I'll rub you there, slowly, back and forth, back and forth until you're filled with such heat that it's hard for you to breathe." He rested his head on his upper arm and used his now-free hand to draw her hair from the comb that held it. "I'll run my fingers through your deep red hair, both here on your head and between your legs."

Jessica tried to draw air into her lungs, but she could only tremble and respond to Eric's touch. The rhythmic pressure of his hand between her legs was becoming almost torture. She wanted him inside of her, to fill her and satisfy the unending hunger he was creating. "Oh Eric," she whispered.

"You'll be so wet and slippery that I'll want to slide my fingers into your body. Maybe one finger, deep inside, maybe two or even three, filling you completely. And you'll be moving your hips, trying to capture my fingers, pull them in deeper."

As he rubbed her body through her jeans, Jessica felt the pressure build somewhere deep inside and flow through her groin and thighs. It grew hotter and hotter, like a fire consuming, yet not satisfying. "So good," she moaned.

Eric placed Jessica's hand over his between her legs. "Feel me rubbing you."

She rested her hand against his and felt the movement of his fingers. "Oh God."

"I'll keep stroking you until you want me more than you've ever wanted anything in your life. My cock will be so hard that it will hurt, but I'll wait until I feel your muscles tense and your back arch like it is now. Yes, baby, let it go. Come for me, baby. Do it."

The fire inside of Jessica's belly smoldered into life. She ignited hot and white, flames roaring in her ears. As she started to moan, Eric covered her mouth with his own, filling himself with her climax. Despite her writhing, Eric managed to keep his fingers between her legs, draining her of the remnants of her orgasm, drawing the final notes from her now-quieting body.

"Oh my God," Jessica breathed, shaking her head in amazement. "Never. . . ."

Eric grinned. "Never what?"

"Never before like that." She tried to catch her breath.

His eyes widened. "You mean no one's ever touched you like that. Your husband never. . . ."

Jessica reached up and pressed her fingers over Eric's lips. "I've never climaxed like that before." As he started to ask more questions, she kept his lips still with her finger. "Give me a sip of coffee and I'll try to explain. Let me catch my breath."

Eric poured Jessica another cup of coffee, then cooled and diluted it with lots of milk. She took the cup in a still-trembling hand and drank the contents. Then she dropped back onto the blanket. "Rob and I were into very simple sex. He loved my breasts. He said they got him hot just thinking about them. When he wanted to make love, which was two or three times a week, although much less frequently toward the end, he'd take off my pajama tops, suckle until he was excited and hard, then we'd do it. You know, missionary position."

"Nothing creative?"

Jessica chuckled. "Being creative wasn't Rob's strong suit. And I didn't know any better. Until now."

A grin split Eric's face. He'd done it for her. "Oh, Jessica. Making love to you is so good."

"It will be."

"It was. What do you think we just did? That was making love just as surely as fucking is. Making love is sharing all the sexual pleasures we can. And there are so many."

Eric became aware that the air was silent. No music. He sat up and looked around. Clusters of people were ambling toward the parking lot. He glanced at his watch. "Good grief, it's almost midnight. Time to get Cinderella back to her castle."

Together they packed the remains of the fruit, wine, and coffee in the hamper, folded the blanket, and placed it on top of the lid. Eric and Jessica each took a handle and they walked back to the car in silence, through the soft summer evening.

When Eric dropped her off at Steph's house, Jessica said, "I don't know what to say, Eric."

"I'd like to invite you to my house, but you need to make a decision before then. In the light of day and with a clear understanding of what it means."

"And what does it mean?"

"It means that I want to share some wonderful pleasures with you. I want to make love to you for several hours, then relax and make love again. It doesn't necessarily mean that I want to spend the rest of my life with you or that I want to be with you and you alone. That's very important. I like you and I want to fuck you until we're both exhausted."

"It's hard for me to grasp. Sex for the fun of it. Like tonight."

"Sex for the fun of it." He thought about it. "That's exactly right. Sex for the fun of it. Think about it, Jessica. I'll call you in a few days."

"I won't be able to think of much else."

Eric leaned across the gearshift lever and placed a soft kiss on Jessica's mouth. "Good night, sexy lady."

"Good night, Eric."

In her room, Jessica stripped off her clothes and climbed into bed. Sleep, however, was impossible. She lectured herself all night.

Sport fucking, she told herself. That's all it is. Fucking because it feels good seems so . . . sinful. But yet so wonderful. For once, my sexual world is filled with light and pleasure.

Am I in love with Eric? No, she argued, I'm not. Would it make it easier if I believed that I were? Yes. And no. I'm infatuated. That's what it is, and it feels good. And I want more of his lovemaking. It's like I have a new toy and I want to play with it.

And what's wrong with that.

By morning, she had debated, argued, vacillated, and finally arrived at the conclusion that she wanted to make love with Eric just because it would feel good. And, for once in her life she was going to do something for herself, just because she wanted to.

Steph and Brian were out for the day and Jessica needed an outlet for her new feelings of freedom. She called a rental car company that specialized in sports cars and asked them to deliver a tiny red Alfa Romeo convertible. When the rental agent asked how long she'd be keeping the car, she told them that she had no idea. "Just give me the weekly rate for two weeks and I'll call a few days before the end of the second week and let you know." She gave them her credit card number and hung up.

Two hours later, when the man arrived with her car, she drove him back to the agency, then put the convertible top down, pulled the rubber band from her hair and spent the rest of the morning driving around Westchester County. With the radio turned up loud and the wind in her hair, she felt fifteen years younger than her thirty-six years.

She drove to the Bronx Botanical Gardens and wandered the grounds, stopping to smell the flowers. She ate a hot dog at the Old Snuff Mill, then, realizing she was starving, ordered and ate another, this one smothered in sauerkraut and pickle relish. She drove up to the Bear Mountain Bridge, found a place to park at the Westchester end and walked across and back.

On her way home late that afternoon, she stopped at a delicatessen and picked up a pastrami sandwich with cole slaw and Russian dressing and a sour pickle. Back at Steph's she sat in the kitchen and devoured every bite, washing it all down with three Samuel Adams Dark Beers.

Then she dialed Eric's number. When she heard his voice, she said, "It's Jessica."

"Well, hello," Eric said, his voice tentative. "I didn't expect to hear from you."

"I didn't expect to call, but I wanted to thank you for last evening." She told him about the car she'd rented and the day she had spent. "I feel so good, I just had to thank you. It's like my life is just beginning."

"I'm so glad to be part of that."

"I feel a bit awkward, but I wanted to ask when we can get together again."

"You're sure you understand everything?" Eric said.

When Eric spoke, Jessica could hear the smile in his voice. "I know that what we did last evening felt wonderful and I want to explore," she said. "I'll probably chicken out several times before I see you again, but in my heart of hearts, I know that this is what I want. And, of course, I've had three beers and I'm smashed."

Eric laughed. "I don't want to take advantage. Are you really drunk?"

"No," Jessica admitted. "But it's a good excuse to let go and do what I want."

"Can I pick you up in half an hour?"

She glanced at the clock. It was 7:30. "I'd like that," Jessica said, smiling.

"I'll see you at eight o'clock."

Jessica hung up the phone and giggled. "I've got a date and I know what I'm going to be doing." Her body sang and her mound throbbed. "Jessica," she told herself aloud, "you're a piece of work."

She took a two-minute shower, then put on a short-sleeved red blouse, a pair of white slacks and white flats. She brushed on a bit of blush, lipstick and left her hair loose. She had just left a note on the kitchen table, telling Steph and Brian that she was out and she didn't know when she'd be back when she heard Eric ring the doorbell.

Jessica opened the door and Eric filled the opening. He was wearing the same soft jeans he had worn the evening before, this time with a tailored, navy-blue polo shirt.

"Oh Lord," he said, staring at her, "I feel like a starving man gazing at a gourmet feast."

"You're looking at me like I'm the blue-plate special," she said, squirming.

"Am I embarrassing you?"

"A bit. But I like the way you look at me." She grabbed her purse and closed the door behind her.

"Can we take your car?" Eric asked. "It's warm and I'd love to drive with the top down."

Jessica fumbled in her purse and found the keys. She tossed them to Eric who opened the passenger door for her. Then he climbed into the driver's seat and started the engine. "Do something for me," he said. "Take off your bra."

Jessica paused for a moment, then turned away from him. She unbuttoned her blouse, unhooked her bra, and wriggled it off. She rebuttoned the blouse, feeling the fabric brush across her erect nipples. She stuffed the bra in her purse, snapped her seat belt, and lay her head back against the headrest.

"Nice," Eric said. "That belt falls just in the right spot, right between your luscious breasts." He reached over and traced the belt with his fingers. "Unbutton the blouse so you can feel the wind on your skin."

Jessica gave him a questioning look. Then she opened the buttons and spread the sides so the red fabric just covered her areolas. The canvas of the seat belt was cold against her bare chest.

"Oh yes," Eric said. "We're going to have everything." He tuned the radio and, as they drove out of the driveway, Frank Sinatra's voice filled the warm night.

During the five-minute drive to Eric's house, Jessica closed her eyes and let the sensuality carry her. The wind was cool on her naked skin, the radio mellow. The air smelled sweet, of summer flowers. She was almost disappointed when they drove up the driveway of Eric's house. As the car stopped, Jessica couldn't believe the building in front of her. "You designed this?"

"Yes." The building seemed to be made of rock and glass, lean and low to the ground, almost growing out of the earth. Although the rooms appeared square, each one was at an angle to its neighbor, gently slanting roofs complementing each other. It was a strange harmony of unusual shapes, softened by lots of hundred-year-old maples. "It was an idea of mine that I adapted to this piece of land. You can't see much from here but there's a rocky pool with a little waterfall on this side," he pointed, "and woods in the back. Real woods. We cut down only one tree."

"I want to see it during the daytime. It must be magnificent."

His laughter was deep in his throat. "Some say yes and some think it's ugly. I like it and I'm all that counts." He ushered Jessica inside, through the darkened living room, up the stairs, through the master bedroom, and into the master bath. He lit a small oil lamp in the corner and began to light candles.

"Oh my," she said. The room was dominated by a huge two-person tub that nestled in an alcove surrounded by a redwood-and-tile ledge covered with pots of ferns, interspersed with dozens of glass containers of clear oil with wicks floating inside. Eric poured bath oil into the tub and turned on the tap. Then he lit each candle and they both watched as shadows danced and flickered on the walls and ceiling. The scent of greenery with a hint of flowers filled the room. "Lavender," Jessica whispered.

"Just a wisp, one candle. And, from now on, every time I smell it, I'll think of you." He lit the last candle, turned to a wine bucket he had placed beside the tub and picked out the bottle. He lifted Jessica's right hand, turned it palm up and cupped it in his large hand. Then he poured a tablespoon of cold wine into her palm, leaned down and licked it up with his rough tongue.

Then he filled his palm and held it out to Jessica. She held his hand in hers and slowly licked the wine from his skin. She slid the tip of her tongue down his index finger, then nipped at the tip. She was wanton. She was brazen. She was free.

"Oh, baby," he groaned as she nibbled on the end of his finger. "I thought you were new at this."

"I am," she whispered. "I'm just learning."

"You learn too well," Eric said, pulling his hand away. "I want to take it slowly. Very slowly. I want us to savor every step, every pleasure."

Jessica wanted to take it all slowly, but her body ached for what she knew would happen. She was excited, her body and soul reaching for something she knew she could have at last. She took a deep breath and stepped back. She looked behind Eric and saw the mountain of bubbles threatening to overflow the huge tub. "Eric," she whispered, "we're about to have a minor flood."

Eric turned around and grabbed for the taps, turning them off just before the water sloshed over the edge. "A long time ago I covered the overflow drain with tape so I could fill this beast as high as I liked. I've never lost track of time before." He released the drain to allow a little water to empty from the tub.

"Thank you. I take that as a compliment."

"Oh, believe me, it is." He filled two wine glasses and handed one to Jessica. "Sorry about the plastic, but I won't have glass in here."

"I like the cups we used a moment ago better," she said, raising the glass to her lips and looking up at Eric through lowered lids. She was flirting. She was playing. She tried to control her grin, but didn't succeed. "Oh God," she said, "I'm so happy."

"And a bit drunk?"

"Just enough."

Once a few inches of water had drained from the tub Eric replaced the stopper. "Our bath awaits." He pulled off his shirt, pants and shorts, kicked off his shoes and stepped into the bubbles.

Jessica saw only his back, smooth and firm with tight buttocks and well-muscled legs. He had just a little extra weight, enough to make him look soft and inviting. He kept his back to her, fussing with a few more candles.

Now she had to undress. Can I do this? Can I take off my clothes in front of a man I've known for less than a week? Quickly, while his back was turned, she pulled off her clothes, stepped into the water and sat down, covering herself with bubbles. This makes no sense, she thought. I've made a decision, I've licked wine from his palm and nibbled on his fingers. Why now am I afraid of his seeing me naked?

"Can I turn around now?" Eric asked.

"You knew?"

"Jessica, my sweet, your mixed emotions are written all over your lovely face." He turned, settled into the warm water, took her hand and held it. "I want this to be your decision all the way. I want you to want me and want my lovemaking. And I want you to explore all the things that give you pleasure. I will never knowingly embarrass you, although it might happen without my realizing it, I'm afraid."

"Thank you for understanding my confusion."

"I want you to promise me something. Some things we do will make you want to laugh. Silly stuff. And if you want to laugh, do it. I want this to be fun. Some things we might try will make you a bit uncomfortable and some discomfort is very exciting. But if we ever do anything that makes you want to stop, you must say so. Immediately. Just say 'Eric, stop' and I will. Promise me."

"I promise."

Eric placed a palm on each side of Jessica's face and gazed into her eyes. "If I can be sure that you will tell me to stop, I can do so many things we might enjoy."

"I do promise, Eric."

They were facing each other in the giant tub of warm, bubbly water. Holding her face in his palms, he caressed her with his gaze, softly sweeping from her sea-green eyes to her lips to the sensual line of her throat. "So lovely," he whispered, stroking her cheeks with his thumbs. "Half of me wants to grab you by that gorgeous red hair of yours, throw you down on the floor, and fuck you until we're both exhausted, the other half wants to savor this and make our loving last all night."

She remained silent, enjoying the warm, sensual web he was spinning around her. Slowly all worries about how briefly she'd known Eric ebbed. She wanted him to make love to her. It was that simple. She picked up a cake of soap and lathered her hands. She placed her palms on his shoulders and made lathery circles on his biceps. She felt him lower his hands into the water as she spread lather onto his upper chest. Smooth, tight skin covered his well-developed muscles.

As she slid her slippery hands up the sides of Eric's neck, she watched his head fall slowly backward, exposing his throat to her caress. There was something so intimate about the motion that she smiled and rubbed her thumbs along the line of his jaw. She closed her eyes and her hands returned to his chest, swirling through the soapy lather. "Mmmm. You feel so hard and smooth." Rob has curly chest hair, she thought, then pushed the thought aside.

She opened her eyes and found Eric looking at her. "I told you before that your face tells all. Were you thinking about your ex-husband?"

Without stilling her hands, she said, "Yes. But he's gone now."

"No he's not," Eric said, "and that's okay. He's the only man you've ever been with and it's natural that you should think of him right now. I don't mind."

"He's a fool."

"That may be true, but he's your only measuring device." Eric reached under the bubbles and cupped her breasts in his hands. "I, on the other hand, have had enough experience to know that you will be a sensual delight." He rubbed his thumbs over her nipples and felt them contract until they were tight under his fingers. "We will learn to share so many pleasures." He leaned forward and placed a soft kiss on Jessica's lips. Then he soaped his hands and rubbed the lightly scented lavender soap over her shoulders and upper arms. "Your skin is so soft." He increased the size of the soapy circles until his hands slipped under the water and caressed her breasts.

Jessica let her head fall back, soaking in Eric's touches as she soaked in the water. Her ribs, her underarms, her neck and arms, she felt Eric stroke them all. Then he lifted one of her hands out of the water and carefully soaped each finger, sliding his fingers between hers. Then he dipped the hand into the water and sucked the tip. "You taste soapy," he said. He picked up his wine glass and poured a bit of the cold, clear liquid over her fingers, then drew each, in turn, into his mouth. "Delicious," he whispered. He repeated the ablutions with her other hand.

"I'd like to make love to you right here," he said, "but we need to shower off first."

Puzzled, Jessica looked at him. "They always do it in hot tubs in movies."

"In movies, the actors aren't really covered with soap, that might irritate your tender body. In addition, let me show you something about hot water." He stood up, water and bubbles pouring from his slight belly.

Jessica couldn't help gazing at his penis, small and flaccid. I am a failure, she told herself. Rob was right. I am frigid.

Laughing, Eric said, "Hot water and too much wine. Not you, my love." He lifted her into a standing position and sluiced water and soap from her body with the flats of his hands. "Definitely not you." He caught the drop of soapy water at the tip of one breast with the tip of his tongue.

Jessica shuddered, not sure whether Eric was lying to save her from embarrassment. She watched Eric pull a shower curtain across the open side of the alcove, release the tub's drain, and reach for the shower controls. Suddenly the alcove was filled with soft, warm spray, coming from shower heads in each corner at once. "It's like a soft summer rain," she said.

"There are several settings, but this one is designed for moments like this." As water drained from the tub, warm water poured over their bodies and Jessica turned her face to the spray, rinsing off all traces of soap. "Done?" Eric asked.

"Ummm," she purred.

Eric turned off the water, opened the curtain and wrapped Jessica in a thick, thirsty bath sheet. As she rubbed her hair, Eric, a towel around his waist, walked out through the connecting door. Slowly, as she watched, candlelight began to dance on the walls of the bedroom.

Without giving Jessica time to think, Eric returned, swept her into his arms, and carried her to the bed. He spread a dry towel on the satin spread, laid her on it and stepped back, feasting on her naked body. "God, you're lovely." He nipped her toes and kissed his way up her shin.

Jessica looked at the wavy gray hair on the man who was quite purposefully making love to her. It wasn't Rob. It was Eric. Then she felt Eric's hot breath on the hair between her legs and she couldn't think anymore. Reflexively, she pulled her knees together.

"Oh, baby," Eric whispered. "You're so sweet." He pulled her legs open and blew a cool stream of air on the hot flesh between her thighs.

"But. . . ." She willed her muscles to relax, but they wouldn't.

"Rob never kissed you here?" he asked.

"No." Her voice was barely audible.

"Does it feel bad?"

"I don't think so. Just odd."

He lightly rubbed his index finger over her clitoris. "And this?"

Her mind was filled with colors, swirling reds and purples, oranges and bright sulfurous yellows. "God no. It feels . . . indescribable."

"How about this?" He surrounded her clit with his lips, swirled his tongue across it, then sucked it into his mouth. As he felt her body tighten, he slid two fingers into her drenched pussy.

The sensations were too much for Jessica. The colors exploded, pinwheels and kaleidoscopes, angles and shards of color and light. "Eric," she screamed, arching her back and clenching her fists. "Eric."

"There's so much more I want with you," Eric said, "but I can't wait right now." He unwrapped a condom, unrolled the latex over his engorged penis, crouched between Jessica's legs and pressed his cock against her opening. "Feel that?" he said. "Feel how hard for you?" He slid it into her passage, a bit at a time. "Feel how it fills you, stretches you? Feel how I want you." When he had filled her completely, he held still above her, balanced on the heels of his hands. "Open your eyes, Jessica. Look at the man who wants you beyond everything right now."

Jessica opened her eyes and looked at Eric, his face tight as he held his body in check for one last moment. She watched the control in his passion-clouded eyes. That passion and control is for me, she thought. A small smile curled the corners of her mouth. He was holding back. He was controlling his excitement. She clenched her vaginal muscles and squeezed the cock that filled her.

"Oh baby," he groaned, pulling back, then plunging deeper inside, giving in to the needs of his body.

Jessica's last coherent thought was that she had caused him to lose control. She, Jessica. One-time frigid wife of Rob the asshole. Oh lord, I've missed so much. But not anymore. Then waves of an incredibly intense orgasm overtook her.

Chapter
5

They lay together on the bed, and dozed for almost an hour. When she opened her eyes Jessica found Eric gazing at her. "You're staring," she said, a grin spreading across her face.

"I guess I am. I knew you'd be wonderful, but I didn't expect to be overwhelmed."

Jessica giggled. "I'm overwhelming, am I?"

"Jessica, you're priceless and wonderful. Not only do I get the joy of making love with you, but I get the delight of watching you discover yourself. What more is there?"

Jessica turned and propped herself on her elbow. "This takes a bit of getting used to," she admitted. "I guess I've been told that there was something lacking in me for so long that it's hard to grok that it wasn't true."

"Grok?"

"My word, actually Heinlein's, for something that's even deeper than just understanding. It's like someone telling you that the world really is flat and that round was just propaganda."

"You've got an unusually honest way of looking at things."

"Maybe I do. It's just that here and now, I find it necessary to put some things into words for which there aren't really words."

"Ummm." Eric took her hand. "Can I tell you something very personal, Jessica?"

Was he going to reject her? Tell her she really was frigid? Fearing the worst, Jessica tightened her abdominal muscles, closed her eyes, and nodded.

Eric barked a single laugh. "Oh baby, don't look so stricken." He kissed her fingers. "I just want to say that I'm starved. I was so excited when you called that I never ate dinner."

Jessica let out a long breath, then cocked her head to one side. "Me too." She rolled over on her back and grinned, sliding her arms and legs over the sheets like she used to as a child when she and her friends made snow angels. Life was fun.

Eric got them each a fluffy, terrycloth bathrobe and, laughing like schoolchildren, they ran down to the kitchen. Jessica walked into the white Formica room and gasped. It was larger than her living room in Ottawa.

"I know," Eric said. "It's ridiculous. But it's Timmy's playground and I let him design it when I built the house."

"I can see that," Jessica said, gazing at the wide counters, hanging baker's racks, and masses of cabinets and closets. There was a six-burner stove, a microwave, a conventional oven, and a convection one. Eric crossed to the industrial-size refrigerator that dominated one end of the room and opened the double doors. "You know," he said, reaching for a slice of strawberry cheesecake, "one should really eat healthy stuff, especially after good sex."

"One certainly should," Jessica said, looking over his shoulder at the second shelf, which held a plastic container of something that appeared to be chocolate pudding.

Eric put the cheesecake on the counter, then grabbed a jar of peanut butter and a loaf of bread from the refrigerator. "Good choice," Jessica said, grabbing the pudding, then shutting the door with her hip. "Got a toaster?"

"You're kidding. Toast and peanut butter was always my favorite. I haven't had it since Timmy arrived."

"And where is he tonight?" Jessica asked, inserting two slices of white bread into the toaster.

"I gave him a quarter and sent him to the movies." When Jessica laughed, he admitted, "Actually, Timmy lives in the guest house on the far side of the garage and I saw him earlier, just getting back from a day with friends in Jersey. When you called I asked him to stay away from the house for the evening." He winked. "Timmy said to say hello to you."

Blushing slightly, Jessica said, "He knows? About us? About this?"

"He knows that I find you exciting and that I intended to do something to scratch the itch, yes."

The toast popped up and Jessica put the two slices on a plate and put two more into the toaster. She handed the plate to Eric who slathered chunky peanut butter on each piece. "You know what goes with toast and peanut butter?" he asked.

"What?"

"V8."

"We must be long-lost twins," Jessica said, smiling. "When I was in high school on my way home I would stop at the store and get a loaf of bread, a jar of Skippy, and the oversized can of V8."

"Actually," Eric said, getting glasses from an upper cabinet, "you were much healthier than I was. I'd usually get a bag of potato chips, a container of sour cream, and a box of onion soup mix. That and a bottle of Pepsi and I was set for the afternoon. Peanut butter and V8 were for bedtime."

"Were you into sports or after-school activities?"

"I went to elementary and junior high school in Manhattan." Eric pulled out a large can of juice and filled two glasses with thick, red liquid. "There wasn't much of that sort of stuff to do. Then I went to Bronx Science High School, mostly eggheads with a calculator in their pocket. I guess I was a bit of a nerd."

"I was the artsy type back then," Jessica said. "Before I met Rob, I was into writing, both short stories and, of all things, poetry."

"Why do you say 'of all things' like that? What's wrong with writing poetry?"

"Nothing, really. I just wasn't the type."

"And why not? What type writes poetry?"

"People with things worth saying. Important things about life and love."

"Nonsense. People write poetry because they want to write poetry. Even I wrote some at one time. Did you write good poetry?"

"Oh lord. It was very free-form, sophomoric stuff filled with suppressed desire. You know, now that I think back, it was probably sexual frustration, pure and simple. In most of my images, two lovers raced toward each other across a flower-filled meadow. That sort of thing." The toaster popped and Jessica put a piece of toast on top of each peanut-buttered one.

"Ummm, suppressed sexual desire. I like that. But now that it's not suppressed anymore, you'll just have to write some erotic poetry and attend one of our evening readings."

"Readings?"

"You know there are several people, including a few whom you met at Steph's party, who make up a very enlightened group. We sometimes get together and read erotic literature out loud, and sometimes Gary tells a story."

"I've heard about Gary. Steph told me he gives great parties. She didn't elaborate."

"He does, and he has the money to indulge in all his hitherto suppressed sexual desires. He has the most wonderful imagination and has no reticence about using it to plan outrageous gatherings."

"Erotic readings?" Jessica smiled.

"Don't laugh. At one of his parties, Gary turned out the lights and we all lay around on the floor while he told erotic fantasy tales. There was a lot of suppressed desire when he was done, I'll tell you, although it didn't remain suppressed for long."

Jessica took a bite of her sandwich and chewed for a minute. This was still all so new to her. "Ummm," she said. "Good peanut butter." Her words came out muffled through the mouthful.

"You make a hell of a sandwich," said Eric. Sensing her need to digest more than the peanut butter, Eric let the conversation veer off in a different direction. They shared their companionable meal, then pigged out on chocolate pudding and Timmy's best strawberry cheesecake. When they had put the dishes in the dishwasher, Eric said abruptly, "I think it's time for me to drive you home."

Nodding, Jessica said, "I think I understand." Eric had made the rules and they both were keeping their new-found intimacy within tight boundaries.

When Eric grinned, Jessica continued, "But we'll see each other soon, I hope."

"That's the difficult part. I'm sorry to say that I have an assignment that requires my presence in San Francisco. My job only demands that I be on site occasionally, but this is one of those occasions. I found out today that I have to leave first thing tomorrow so I can be ready for Monday morning. Then I'll work all week and red-eye back Friday night. The timing stinks."

"Yeah. It does," Jessica said, disappointed that they weren't going to see each other for a week. Sexual freedom felt like her new toy and she wanted to play with it. "We can talk on the phone, though."

"Of course." He told her the name of his hotel and they arranged for her to call. Then he hugged her and they went back upstairs, located their clothes and dressed in silence. As they climbed into Jessica's car, Eric said, "We need to be totally honest from the outset. Sex can be good with anyone who has an open mind and a desire to please."

"I know. But I have just come to terms with extracurricular activities with you."

"Extracurricular activities. That's one way to put it. Just remember, however, that you have no curriculum anymore. Play. Have fun. Rob is history and good riddance."

"To bad rubbish."

It was almost one in the morning when they drove into the driveway and parked next to the Carltons' two cars. Eric kissed her hard, then quickly climbed into his own car and drove away.

Jessica gazed after him, then turned. She walked over to Brian's car and stopped, resting her hand on the cold hood. "Extracurricular activities." She slid her hand along the highly waxed surface, then walked into the house.

Stephanie found Jessica the following morning, sitting in the plant room staring into space. "Morning, Jessica," Steph said.

Jessica looked up. "Morning," she said, a strange look on her face.

"We saw Eric's car when we got in last evening," Steph said, "and I got your note. Wanna tell me about it?"

"Eric and I went back to his place."

"And. . . ."

Jessica burst into delighted laughter. "And wow and double wow. It was sensational. Lights, colors, bells, whistles, candlelight, and peanut butter."

"Peanut butter?" Steph settled into the chair next to her best friend.

"Oh, Steph, I'm so glad I came to Harrison."

"So am I. Are you and Eric an item? He's a really nice man and Brian and I are very fond of him."

"Not exactly an item. Not that way. We understand each other. We make love like rockets and supernovas, but it doesn't mean anything more than that."

"Sounds like you're a different person than you were when you left Illinois."

"Well," Jessica giggled, "I know I'm not in Kansas anymore. God, who's been hiding orgasms all these years. I think mine registered on the Richter scale at one point."

Steph leaned over and hugged Jessica. "I'm so happy for you. Maybe we should send scrawny-neck and bimbette a blow by blow. Pardon the expression."

"I don't even want to think about Rob. You know, though, I feel kinda sorry for him. He has no idea what he's missing."

"Are you seeing Eric tonight?"

"That's the sad part. Even as we speak, he's winging his way to the west coast. Some big job he's got to work on."

"Oh, Jessica, that's too bad. How long will he be gone?"

"Til the end of the week, he thinks. We have a date for next Saturday."

"That's great. Eric's a wonderful guy." Steph looked at her watch. "Okay. It's almost nine and Brian's still in bed. What shall we do today?"

"Let's drive around, have a high-calorie lunch, and pick up guys."

"JessicaLynn Hanley, I love you." Her voice dropped. "There's a party a week from Saturday at Gary's. Not just couples but it is a swinger's get-together. Fun and games, and I do mean games. Interested?"

"Being with Eric has opened up a whole new world for me. I want to explore. But I'm not ready for an orgy, I'm afraid."

"Not an orgy at all. These swingers' parties are very tightly controlled because not everyone is interested in the same thing."

"Controlled how?"

"Well, for example, the living room and kitchen are off-limits for any hankypanky. They're safe zones where people who don't want to play or haven't decided yet can gather. That way no one will ever be embarrassed by something they don't want to see or do. There are pieces of colored yarn on or beside every door. A black ribbon on the door means off-limits. Like, if we had a party at my house, your room would be off-limits. A red ribbon on a door means the room is occupied, stay out. Like that."

"Sounds like you've thought this through."

"We have. And we've made mistakes and learned. We want to have a good time and not hurt anyone."

Jessica thought a moment, then smiled. "I don't know whether I'm ready for something like that yet. Maybe. I assume that, if you guys go, they're all nice people. No weirdos."

"The only new faces will be people personally endorsed but mostly it's the same people. Like the ones you met here last weekend. And then there are very specific rules about safe words."

"Safe words?"

"We use 'cease and desist' for an absolute stop. If anyone says 'cease and desist,' whatever is going on that involves them must stop. Immediately. And you must use that phrase if things get uncomfortable. No martyrs or endurance contests. We use 'time out' for things like, my foot itches or my arm is cramped."

"I don't get it. Why don't you just say stop?"

"If you say stop, no one knows whether you really want to stop or not. It can be fun to say, 'Please no' or 'Don't do that' without worrying that someone will actually stop. Control games can be very exciting."

"Control games?"

"You're just beginning your sexual education. Let's leave control games for a graduate-level course. Suffice it to say that dominant and submissive fantasies have been around for centuries and can be a lot of fun to play out."

"I always thought you were so suburban yuppy, so conservative."

"Shows how much you know."

"You know what I'd like to do today, really? Let's drag Brian to the Bronx Zoo."

"I haven't been to the zoo in years. Great idea. Then seafood for dinner. I know a great spot on City Island." Steph stuck her head out into the hallway and yelled at the top of her voice. "Hey Brian, get dressed, you bum. We've got the day all planned."

The following Tuesday morning, Jessica stretched out on the bedspread in her room at Steph's. The room was cool, with off-white, grass-cloth wallpaper, green and off-white sheets and a dark green flowered comforter. The carpeting was thick and a deep forest green, giving the room the look of a forest glade.

Since she wanted to be free to say anything to Eric she picked up her cellular phone and dialed The Stanford Court, Eric's hotel in San Francisco. The switchboard connected her immediately. After only one ring, a sleepy voice answered. "Hello?"

"Good morning, Eric. You did say I should call you at this ungodly hour." Jessica could hear the rustling of Eric's body as he moved around in bed three thousand miles away.

"Good morning. And yes, this time is fine. I have to get up anyway and what better way is there to be awakened?"

Eric told Jessica that his job was going well. "I should have no problem getting back by the end of the week. How about you? What have you been doing?"

Jessica told Eric about her time with Steph and Brian, trying to put her feelings into words. "It's like someone just lit a lamp in a part of my life that I didn't know existed."

"Well, I'll be sure to have my flashlight with me at all times so I can illuminate more dark corners."

"It's so much more than sex. It's me. I'm free to do and say things I haven't done or said since I was in high school. I didn't realize how much of my life I've lived with the feeling that Rob was looking over my shoulder, judging me."

"It must be wonderful to feel so liberated."

"And, of course, it's all that good lovemaking we did. The only problem now is that my mind seems consumed with thoughts of you and your gorgeous body." As the picture of Eric's naked body flashed across her mind, she realized that he wasn't really well built at all. He was soft and a bit overweight. But he was sexy and attractive and a total turn-on.

"I'm glad you think I'm gorgeous, although it does make one wonder about your eyesight. By the way, what are you wearing?" Eric asked.

"That's a question out of left field. I'm wearing shorts and a polo shirt. Why?"

"Well, I'm not wearing anything, and I want you the same way. Put the phone down and take your clothes off." When there was silence, Eric added, "Please."

"This is silly."

"Come on. Pull the shirt off over your head, take your bra off and get out of those shorts and underpants."

Jessica giggled, then complied. She cradled the phone against her ear and lay back down on the bed. "Okay. I've taken my clothes off. Why?"

"Because we're going to make love."

"Three thousand miles apart?"

"Yes, three thousand miles apart. Stretch out on the bed and close your eyes. I'll close mine. What are you lying on? A bedspread? A quilt?"

"A comforter."

"Okay. Feel the cool, smooth cloth on your back. Feel it on your buttocks and calfs, on your heels. Stroke the comforter with one foot and feel the smoothness against your sole. Can you feel it?"

"Yes."

"Is the window open or do you use the air conditioner? It was pretty cool when I left."

"It is cool and I have the window open."

"Good. Feel the air that is coming in the window. Feel it against your skin, all over. Listen to the birds and the leaves rustling. Smell the green smell of the grass and the trees. Part your lips and breathe in through your mouth. Now run your tongue around your lips and taste the cool air. Feel the coldness as you breathe in again."

Jessica did as Eric asked. She had never been as aware of all the sensations around her.

"Lick your thumb. Taste your own skin."

She did, feeling only a tiny bit silly. "It's tangy, spicy kind of."

"Good. Now put your fingertips on your breast bone, right between your beautiful breasts. Stroke up and down, from your throat to your belly. With my eyes closed I can imagine that I'm watching and touching you."

Still feeling awkward, Jessica placed her fingertips against her chest and stroked her skin the way Eric wanted her to.

"Are you doing it?"

"Yes," she said softly.

"Does it feel good?"

"Yes." It did feel good. Soft and gentle.

"Jessica, have you ever touched yourself, explored your body?"

"I shower every day," she said, laughing nervously.

"That's not what I mean and you know it. When I was a kid, I touched my body, rubbed my cock, discovered the things that felt good. It was hard not to because all the feel-good parts were right out there, aching to be touched. I think every boy knows those places, if not before puberty, then about twenty minutes after. But, somehow, I don't think girls do. Did you ever touch yourself like that?"

"No," she admitted. Jessica could hear more rustling through the phone. Eric was obviously moving around in bed.

"How can you know what will feel good when a man touches you," he said softly, "if you don't know yourself? How can you help him to find the feel-good places if you don't know where they are?"

"I never thought about it."

"Well, you will now. Let's find out together. Swirl your fingers over your right breast. Your fingers feel the soft skin of your tit, and your breast feels the rougher texture of your fingers. Don't touch the areola, just the soft white skin. Are you doing that?"

"Yes," she whispered, torn between the erotic sensations and the feeling that she shouldn't be doing this.

"And it feels good. Don't answer that. Just indulge me for a few minutes. Just do as I ask without thinking. Now, slide your fingers up your side, to your underarm. Are you ticklish?"

"Not really."

"Good. I know that feels good, but we're looking now for places that make you hot. Slide your fingers over your neck and behind your ears, then across your face. Touch yourself."

Jessica was doing exactly what Eric was asking of her and it did feel good. Her skin tingled and she felt more alive, somehow.

"Now slide your fingers back to your breast. I know how sensitive your nipples are. If I close my eyes I can see them getting hard and tight. Fondle them and make them hard. Squeeze and pull. Make it feel good."

Jessica sighed, and touched her right nipple. She felt it contract and become more erect under her fingers. She dropped her hand and took a breath, about to tell Eric that this was ridiculous. Then she stopped herself and put her fingers back on her nipple. "It does feel good. It does."

"I know it does. And it makes other parts of your body feel good too. You are becoming aware of the heat between your legs. You don't really want to think about it, but you can't help it. Your mind keeps travelling to the tightness low in your abdomen and you can feel the area between your legs swell and get hot and wet. Slide your fingers down your belly and make large, swirling circles. Use your palm."

Jessica could hear him chuckle and she smiled. "What are you laughing at?"

"I know what's going on in your brain right now. Part of you wants to explore, wants to find out what mysteries are hiding between your legs, waiting to have the light shone on them like the lights we turned on a few nights ago. But part of you is still, wondering whether nice people do things like this. Your brain is yelling words like 'masturbation' and remembering all the things your mother told you would happen if you touched yourself."

Jessica nodded, "She said I'd spoil it for lovemaking with my husband. She told me that if I touched myself, then I would always need that kind of stimulation in order to become excited. It would become a habit. Therefore I would never get any pleasure from relations with my husband. It sounds so uptight when I say it out loud now."

"Lots of people believe it. But, if you never know your own body and what gives you pleasure, then how can you ever help a man to know how to please you?"

Jessica was still sliding her palm over her belly. "Men were just supposed to know."

"Yeah. Right. That's been the bane of men's existence since we lived in caves. Don't help us, just expect us to know. No wonder sex becomes tedious."

"I guess that's not really fair."

"No, it's not. But it's a very common attitude. I enjoy making love and I've made love to lots of women. It's a unique experience when I find someone like you and I can introduce you to all kinds of exciting new activities, but I also like it when a woman knows her body and what she enjoys." His voice dropped and softened. "What do you enjoy, Jessica?" Without giving her time to answer, he continued, "Do you like it when the ends of your fingers brush the springy hair between your legs? Do that. Just brush your bright red bush very lightly."

Jessica did as Eric asked. She had washed herself every day in the shower, but this was different. She never thought about her body in the shower. Now she could think of little else.

"Part your knees. Let your legs open wide. Feel the cool air on the hot, wet skin that's probably never felt cool air on it before."

"That feels strange," Jessica said, "forbidden somehow."

"I can hear your mother now. Keep your knees together. It's not ladylike to allow anyone to even think about what's between your legs." As if sensing her feelings, Eric said, "No, no. Don't slide them closed. Keep them spread wide apart. Reach between your legs and touch the hair there."

"How do you know what I'm thinking,"

"You're a sensuous woman who's never had any opportunity to revel in her sexuality, in her body. This is all new, exciting, and a little scary. Am I on the right track?"

"Actually, it's very exciting and very scary."

"Good. Scary is exciting, too. Are you touching yourself?"

Jessica's fingers just grazed the hair between her legs. She knew she got wet, but she'd never actually felt it before. God, it felt good, both on her fingers and on her swollen lips. "Yes," she whispered.

"Touch yourself more. Let yourself explore. Feel. Your body is slick, and rubbing it makes you want things you've never allowed yourself to want before. Are you touching all the crevices and folds? Tell me, Jessica, are you?"

Jessica was sliding her fingers into places she'd never touched for pleasure before. And it felt so good. Her outer lips were open, giving her access to the areas within. Her inner lips were covered with slippery wetness. She found that some places felt better than others. "Yes," she answered.

"This will be more difficult for you, Jessica, but I want you to touch your clit. You've been avoiding touching that part, but your clitoris can give you intense pleasure. Slide two fingers into the fold between your outer lips and find that hard, swollen little nub of nerve endings. Slip one finger on either side and stroke back and forth. And shut off your mind, except for the parts that feel and hear. Just rub. And if you find a spot that feels particularly good, rub more. Find the places that make your toes curl and your back arch. Find the places that seem darkest and most erotic. Stroke yourself, baby. Do it for me."

Jessica touched her swollen clit. Torn between the intense pleasure and the feelings left over from her past life, she did as Eric's voice told her to. She rubbed. And she rose higher and higher. It became easier and easier to touch the places that gave her the most pleasure. She closed her eyes.

Eric's voice was husky as he continued. "Let me tell you what I'm doing while you're touching yourself. I've got my hand on my hard cock and I'm squeezing and stroking it. I'm caressing my balls, then holding my cock."

Knowing that Eric was touching himself made what she was doing seem less dirty somehow. This was part of a mutual experience.

"Remember how it felt when I touched you? Reach for those feelings. Do things that bring you closer to those swirling colors you told me about. Touch just the right places. Pretend that those are my fingers, if you need to, but feel the erotic intensity growing."

"Oh yes, Eric. It feels so good."

"Don't stop. Prop the phone against your ear and take the other hand and use your index finger to rub your slick inner lips. Rub the opening of your slit. If you want to, slide one finger into your body. If that doesn't feel good, don't do it."

"It all feels good."

Jessica heard Eric chuckle. "You're magic, baby," he said. "Feel the orgasm coiled inside you, waiting for you to release it. Find the places that tighten that coiled spring. Find them. Use them. Wind it tighter and tighter."

Jessica was burning. She rubbed her body with both hands, and squirmed on top of the comforter. She rubbed her feet on the material and arched her back. She found a tiny ball of light and touched the places that made the light grow. Higher and hotter, she didn't want to stop. Her slippery fingers offered her ecstasy and she reached for more. The light changed from soft yellow to white and grew brighter. Suddenly it exploded, enveloping her in heat and brightness. "Oh," she said, her breathing hard and fast. "Eric."

For long moments she was filled with lava, reaching every nerve in her body. She was lost in it, yet aware of every sensation. Never before had anything like this ever happened while she was alone. And somewhere a tiny part of her was sad for all the lost opportunities.

"I came with you," Eric whispered. "God, that was great."

Jessica laughed. "It certainly was." She looked at the clock on her bedside table. They had been on the phone almost forty-five minutes. "Look at the time," she said.

"Time flies when you're having fun. But I do have to get to work. And a shower is most definitely necessary now."

Jessica lay on the bed, limp and smiling. "This is all so incredible," she whispered.

"Unfortunately, I have to get up," Eric said. "But you lay there until you want to move. And don't think. Feel. And when those thoughts about what's right to do and what isn't surface, and they will, tell them to get stuffed."

"Yeah. Get stuffed. I'll do that."

"I'll call you when I know my schedule."

She needed to tell him one last thing. "There's a party at Gary's a week from Saturday. Steph invited me to go."

"Great. Gary called me and I'll be there too. But even if I weren't going to be there, you'd have a wonderful time and get to explore the new you."

"But, you'll be there?"

"Yes. And I want to make love to you in every way possible, in every place possible. I want you to explore your new-found sexual understanding with others, too. Meet new men and make love if they turn you on. Women too, if that gives you pleasure. You're a new person, Jessica."

"I don't think I'm ready to do this alone."

"I'll be back on Friday and, if you're free, we can see each other Saturday night. By then, I'm sure you'll be more comfortable with the new you. Okay?"

"Great." Jessica took a deep breath.

"I'll call you later in the week if I can."

"Okay," she said, disappointed that he didn't say that he'd definitely call tomorrow. "Don't work too hard."

"Jessica, have a terrific week, and don't play too hard." They both hung up.

It was almost eleven when Jessica wandered into the kitchen. Brian was standing at the counter, pouring Cheerios into a bowl. "Good morning, JJ."

"What are you doing here?"

Grinning, Brian said, "I live here."

"That's not what I meant and you know it. Why aren't you at work?"

"Day off. I'm allowed, you know. Even us Wall Street types get time off for good behavior." He leered at her long legs, exposed beneath her brief denim shorts. "Or bad behavior."

Jessica blushed and sat down at the table.

"JJ, I'm sorry," Brian said, sitting across from her. "I don't ever mean to make you uncomfortable. Steph told me about you and Eric and I understand how you're feeling right now. I know Eric well enough to be sure that he's told you that he's a free-spirited guy with a girl in every port."

"He has, of course."

"This is all new and strange. You've suddenly realized that men are attracted to you and, if you wanted, you could enjoy more than dinner and a movie together." He reached across the table and took Jessica's hand. "And, you've never thought of me as anyone but Steph's husband. However, I am attracted to you. I won't deny that. Just understand that I will never knowingly do anything to hurt you. If I tease you a bit, or make a remark, it's because I care about you as a friend and as an attractive woman. Okay?"

Jessica smiled warmly. "Yes, Brian, I do understand."

"And I want to make love to you in seven different positions."

Jessica's laughter filled the sunlit kitchen. She looked at Brian for a moment, then added, "And maybe you'll get your wish, eventually."

Brian stood up and retrieved his bowl of cereal. "You give an old man hope," he said.

"Old, my foot," Jessica said. "You're exactly three months older than I am, if I remember correctly."

"But I'm several decades more experienced."

Jessica shook her head ruefully. "I certainly do have a lot of catching up to do."

Brian raised his hand high in the air. "I'll help," he said, waving the hand around. "Ooooh, oooh, pick me."

"Good morning, everyone," Steph said, interrupting the conversation. "What are you volunteering for so enthusiastically?"

"Never you mind, snoopy," Brian said. "That's between JJ and me.

"Sorry I asked." She grinned and kissed Brian on the cheek, then hugged Jessica good morning. "What should we do today?"

"I'd just like to lounge around the pool," Brian said. "And I've got a few errands to run. And how about some tennis later?"

The threesome spent the remainder of the morning beside the Carltons' pool then made chef salads for lunch. Late that afternoon, Jessica watched as Steph beat Brian in two sets of tennis at their country club. The two opponents were laughing together as they walked back to where Jessica sat beside the court with a diet Coke in her hand. Sweat dripped from their bodies, soaking their tennis whites. "I'd say six-four, six-two is a thorough trouncing," Steph said. "And that doesn't happen often."

"I was distracted looking at JJ's legs in those tiny shorts," Brian said. "She kept crossing and uncrossing them at just the wrong moments." He groaned. "And when you decided you needed more sunblock on your thighs I double-faulted three times in a row."

Jessica stretched her long legs in front of her and ran a finger up the inside of one thigh. "If you can't take the distractions," she said, then winked at Steph, "tough."

Brian whacked his wife on the arm. "Did you plan this?"

"Well . . ." the two women said in unison.

"JessicaLynn Hanley," Brian said, grinning, "you're becoming entirely too frisky."

Jessica grinned. "Thanks," she said. "And I'm not too frisky, but I am just right."

"You sure are. Okay, I'll meet you ladies in the bar in fifteen minutes," he said. "Gotta shower and shave." He walked toward the men's locker room.

"I'll meet you there," Steph said, handing Jessica her racket.

While Steph and Brian took showers, Jessica settled at a tiny table in the bar and ordered a Bloody Mary. As she nibbled on a piece of celery, a man of about forty leaned over the table. He was wearing crisp white tennis shorts and a light blue soft-collared shirt with a tiny Donald Duck stitched above the left breast. "You're Steph and Brian Carlton's friend JJ, aren't you? From the midwest."

"Yes," she said, warily.

"I thought it might be you. Brian described you several times. My name's Cameron Hampstead, but everyone calls me Cam. I work in the city and I ride Metro North with Brian. When I saw him yesterday, he mentioned that he and Steph had a tennis date this afternoon." He held out his right hand and Jessica placed hers in it. His palm was warm and soft, his grip strong.

"Hmmm," Jessica muttered. "And I thought this tennis game

was spur of the moment." Aloud Jessica said, "And how did you recognize me?"

"Brian's described you as a gorgeous redhead with green eyes."

"Oh," Jessica said, a bit nonplussed.

He looked at the other chair at the small table. "May I?"

"Sure," Jessica said, not totally comfortable with being picked up in a bar, despite the club's exorbitant annual dues.

He sat down and placed his racquet and tote on the floor beside him. "I guess this is where I'm supposed to ask you what your sign is, or something inane."

Totally puzzled, Jessica's head snapped up. "Excuse me?"

"I'm sorry, but this isn't my usual thing."

"Okay, you've lost me. What isn't?"

"Picking up women in bars. Brian told me yesterday that he and Steph would be here with you today and he suggested that I might meet you. He thought you and I would get along splendidly."

"He set this up?"

Cam smiled ruefully. "He did. He's a big fan of yours and, I suppose, of mine too. I guess he thought we'd hit it off."

"I'm very embarrassed," Jessica snapped. "I really don't need Brian fixing me up."

"I'm so sorry. I know he meant well. I'm the one who botched this." There was a slight trace of an English accent in Cam's voice, which had gotten more pronounced as the conversation progressed. "This was a really bad idea."

As Cam rose to leave, Jessica placed her hand on his, where it rested on the table. "This is dumb and awkward," she said, somehow warming to Cam's openness, "but not an entirely bad idea. Brian's intentions were good and your only fault is one that I suffer from as well. Honesty. Let's start again."

His grin lit Cam's ordinary-looking face. "Thanks." He sat back down.

"Hi." Jessica extended her right hand. "My name's Jessica. Jessica Hanley. Nice to meet you."

Cam's grin widened still further and he took her hand. "Mine's Cameron."

"Cameron. That's an unusual name."

"It's a family name." He deliberately broadened his accent. "Very British and all that. Actually, I hate it. Cam's much better."

"Well, Cam, until recently, people called me Jessie, and only Brian calls me JJ. Right now I prefer Jessica."

"Jessica it is." Cam ordered a glass of cabernet. "What takes you into the city on the train with Brian?"

"I'm in advertising. TV commercials. Lots of pressure, lots of late nights and coffee. Lots of famous people being temperamental and thinking that they know my business better than I do. And lots of sponsors who think they know my business better than I do."

"Sounds awful."

Cam smiled ruefully. "It does, doesn't it. To be truthful, I love it."

Jessica liked Cam's grin and she matched it with one of her own. "Someone has to," she said.

Over the next five minutes, Jessica told Cam briefly about her divorce and her extended visit to Harrison.

"I was married briefly," Cam said, "but my wife was killed in an auto accident." When Jessica looked distressed, he added, "That was almost fifteen years ago. I guess that I've idealized her over the years, and I just haven't found anyone since that I wanted to spend my life with."

Brian arrived at the table dressed in navy shorts and a plaid sport shirt, pulled up a chair and dropped into it. "Well, Cam, fancy meeting you here."

"I told her, Brian," Cam said. "Everything."

"Uh-oh." He looked a bit sheepish. "I got caught. I'm really sorry, JJ."

"You should be," Jessica said, wanting to make him suffer for a few minutes. "You made both Cam and me very uncomfortable."

Brian picked Jessica's hand up from where it lay on the table.

He kissed her fingertips, one by one. "Am I forgiven?" He gave her an I'm-too-cute-to-be-mad-at look. "Please?"

Jessica burst out laughing. "Okay. I'll forgive you. But just this once. From now on I'll select my own friends."

"I agree," Steph's voice said from behind Jessica. "When Brian told me about this. . . ."

"She didn't know in advance," Brian said, jumping in to keep his wife in Jessica's good graces. "I told her between our two sets. Honest."

"Hi, Cam," Steph said. "I'm glad to see you, even under these circumstances." She cuffed Brian on the arm. "You're impossible."

Brian grabbed Steph's arm and pulled until she plopped into his lap. "I'm entirely possible," he said. "And you love it. Am I forgiven?"

Steph wriggled into her own chair. "Buy me a club soda and I'll think about it."

"Jessica? Forgive me?"

"Well. . . ."

The four talked for about half an hour, then Brian glanced at his watch and said, "It's almost six-thirty. If I haven't entirely turned you two off about each other, I'd like to suggest that the four of us have dinner together. Cam?"

"I'd love to join you all for dinner. But only if Jessica has forgiven both of us for our subterfuge." He looked at her. "Have you?"

There was a boyish, attractive quality about Cam, Jessica thought. He's charming and good company. She thought briefly about Eric, then said, "I'd like that." She looked down at her bare legs. "I'm obviously not dressed for anything fancy."

"I know a great place for Texas-style barbecued ribs and chicken," Cam suggested. "It's up-county in Yorktown. A place called Rattlesnake's. And they have an appetizer platter with things called rattlers that will cook the fillings in your teeth."

When Steph looked dubious, Cam added, "Not everything is hot, but I happen to like chili peppers."

"Sounds good to me," Jessica said. "And I don't mind having my teeth rattled occasionally."

"Really?" Brian leered, waggling an imaginary cigar, Groucho-style.

"Sounds good to me too," Cam added, holding Jessica's gaze a fraction too long.

"Okay, you two," Steph said, wanting to bail her friend out of a potentially uncomfortable situation. "Enough of the double entendres. You're embarrassing the two refined ladies at this table."

"Where?" Jessica said. "I only see two grown women and two attractive guys, one of whom you're married to."

Both Cam and Brian beamed. "Thank you, Jessica," Cam said.

"Rattlesnake's, it is," Brian said.

After getting directions to the restaurant, they separated. Steph and Brian drove away in Brian's Lexus and Jessica and Cam in Cam's Toyota. After half an hour of good conversation, Jessica and Cam met Steph and Brian in front of the restaurant and they were shown to a table in front of a wide window. They ordered beers and, while the other three looked at the menu, Cam ordered the Rattlesnake PuPu appetizer platter.

When the platter arrived, they ordered a barbecued chicken and a rack of baby back ribs, deciding to share. Cam gave the other three a guided tour of the enormous plate of appetizers. He pointed to a shapeless lump, breaded and fried. "This is a popper, a hot pepper filled with cheese and deep fried, and this is a rattler, a shrimp stuffed with a hot pepper. Warning!"

Jessica picked up a rattler and bit off a small piece. Her mouth flamed almost immediately. "Holy cow," she said, grabbing a taco chip from the pile of nachos and stuffing it into her mouth. "These do smart a bit."

"How about the wings?" Steph asked.

Brian bit one and answered, "Just at the borderline of your heat tolerance. I think you'll like it."

Stephanie did, and the rest of the meal as well. When the check arrived, Cam laid his credit card on the tray. Jessica reached for her purse. "Brian, Steph, and I have agreed," she said. "We split checks." She wondered how Cam would react, and in her mind, it was a test of sorts. Would he be gracious?

"Okay, if that's what makes you comfortable," Cam said. "About twenty each ought to do it."

Jessica pulled a twenty-dollar bill from her wallet and handed it to Cam. Without fanfare, he tucked it into his pocket.

As they left the restaurant, Jessica walked with Cam toward Brian's car. "I'd like to take you to dinner," Cam said. "Would you like that?"

Jessica linked her arm in Cam's. He was charming, and refined, and, she admitted to herself, without any overt effort, very attractive. "I would, very much."

"Would tomorrow night be too soon? I could pick you up about six. I know an Indian place that makes the best shrimp vindaloo. It will sizzle your tail feathers."

"I haven't had my tail feathers sizzled in a while. I love vindaloo."

Again, Cam's smile lit up his face. "Six it is." Jessica nodded as she climbed into the backseat of Brian's car. "See you tomorrow," she said.

Cam leaned in through the open door and kissed Jessica lightly on the mouth, then ran his tongue across her upper lip. "Till then."

As they drove south, Brian said, "Hey, JJ. I hope I'm forgiven. I guess it was a bit sneaky."

Jessica pictured Cam's face. "You're forgiven, but no more. Okay?"

"Okay."

Chapter
6

The following day, Steph joined Jessica at breakfast. After some small talk, Steph asked, "Have you ever considered having your hair done? Maybe getting a body wave?"

"That's out of left field," Jessica responded. She ran her fingers through her long hair and tucked a strand behind her ear. "Actually, I wanted to cut and soften it a few years ago, but Rob thought it was pretentious so I dropped it." She made a face.

"I'd love to see you shorten it, and give it some soft waves."

"What brought this on?" Jessica asked.

"I've got a hairdresser appointment this morning and I was wondering whether you'd like to come along and maybe do something a bit experimental. Something more Jessica and less Jessie."

Jessica thought about her long, straight hair, which she now wore either in a ponytail or just hanging loose down her back. She fluffed out the sides, which fell back against her face. "I don't know. How about if I join you, and consider my options later?"

John's of Harrison was an incredibly opulent salon. Ten full-time operators cut, styled, blow-dried, and colored the hair of Harrison's rich and pampered. When anything new was considered for any of its slightly spoiled patrons, five-foot five-inch

John Matucci bustled over and discussed the changes at length. No one, absolutely no one, would make a move without John's specific approval. Several women put off stylings if John wasn't at the salon.

When Stephanie and Jessica arrived, the salon was only half full. A woman in a pink and gray jumpsuit hurried over. "Good morning, Ms. Carlton. We were expecting you. As you can see we're not very crowded so we can do as much as you'd like today."

"As much as you'd like?" Jessica muttered.

"You'll see," Steph said, turning to the perfectly groomed receptionist. "Gina, I'd like to introduce my friend Jessica Hanley. She's from my old hometown, here visiting for the summer."

"Ms. Hanley. How nice to meet you. Will you have time for anything today? You have magnificent skin," Gina said. "Maybe a facial?"

"Jessica, John's does massages, body wraps, waxing, just about anything you could want."

"Sounds delightfully decadent," Jessica said.

"Have you thought about your hair? Maybe a soft wave?" Steph asked.

Gina reached out and took a strand of Jessica's hair and rubbed it between her fingers. "Such wonderful hair. With a light rinse and loose wave, you'd be spectacular." She lifted one of Jessica's hands. "And wonderful long fingers. How about a manicure and an herbal hand-wrap?"

"Gina, down girl," Steph said. "She's just visiting. Don't go overboard."

Gina leaned over so her face was close to the two women. "John's here today and he's even got some time." She leaned even closer to Jessica's ear. "I could fit you in."

Jessica sighed and smiled. "Okay. What the hell. Tell John to do his worst."

"But, he will do his best," the woman said, unused to Jessica's bantering.

"Of course. It will be his best." Jessica and Steph laughed, then got ready to be pampered. While Jessica's hair was rinsed with a gentle highlighter then waved, she had an herbal wrap on her hands, a manicure, a facial, and an hour-long massage. When Steph replaced her on the massage table, she said, "Isn't that the most hedonistic thing you've ever done?"

"God, Steph," Jessica admitted. "I've never had a massage before. That's heaven."

"Imagine how it would feel if a man did it on his bed, with his hands awakening all those feelings in your body, then satisfying all those hungers. God."

Jessica felt the prickling between her legs. "I'll bet it would be unbelievably erotic."

While the manicurist massaged Jessica's feet, filed off the calluses, and applied bright red polish to her toenails, Jessica nibbled on a light tuna salad with melba toast.

When John combed out her hair and blew it dry Jessica was delighted with the subtle difference in her appearance. He had shortened her hair until it fell just at her shoulders, longer in back and waving loosely around her face. He had enhanced her existing style without making any dramatic changes. "What do you think?" the talented, officious salon owner asked.

"It's just lovely," Jessica answered, truly impressed by the improvement. "I look years younger."

"Lovely? Of course not. John does not do lovely." He seemed to refer to himself in the third person frequently. "John does magnificent. John does terrific. But lovely?"

Steph walked over. "John, it's sensational."

Jessica quickly agreed. "Yes, of course John," she said, trying not to laugh. "It's magnificent."

John smiled, and tried to look humble without success. "Thank you Ms. Hanley, Ms. Carlton." He took Jessica's hand and guided her from the chair. "And such soft hands." He kissed her knuckles.

Steph and Jessica settled their exorbitant bills with their credit cards and left the shop, giggling like schoolgirls.

* * *

Cam picked her up that evening and commented on how nice she looked in tight beige slacks and a soft off-white silk blouse. She wore her hair loose and it now flowed softly around her face.

"You look different," Cam said. "Softer."

The curry was terrific, hot enough to awaken every nerve in her mouth, but not so hot as to deaden her taste buds. They shared tales of past curries, compared life in England and Ottawa, Illinois, favorite movies, TV shows, and books. As they sat over rasamalai and spiced tea, Cam said, "I'm sorry to say that I've got to end our evening early. I've got an impossible job to finish that will take the rest of the week and all weekend."

"I'm sorry too," Jessica said. "When is it due?"

"Tuesday morning, at eight a.m., come hell or high water."

"Oh Cam, I'm sorry. You should have called and cancelled tonight. I feel so guilty."

Cam covered her hand with his. "Don't. I wanted to see you again and it was worth whatever time it took. I'm just sorry that we can't continue this evening. With final revisions and everything, I should be off the hook by the middle of next week. Could I interest you in a drive out to Connecticut for dinner? The traffic might be awful, but I know a place that has the best steamers and makes flounder that's so fresh. . . ."

"I'd love to, Cam." She was seeing Eric on Saturday, now Cam next week and the party the following Saturday. God, she felt good.

"Great. I'll call you at the beginning of the week and we'll set a definite date."

Cam drove her back to Steph's and helped her out of the car. As she stood up, he took her in his arms and softly pressed his lips against hers. They kissed for a long time, exploring each other, pressing their bodies tightly together, feeling the soft, yet building arousal. When he pulled away, Cam said, "If I keep doing that, I'll throw you into the car, take you back to my place, and ravish you in the driveway."

Jessica kept her arms around Cam's neck. "You would, would you?" she said, savoring her slightly aggressive feelings. She wanted him and they were both adult, single and capable of making their own decisions. Then she pressed her mouth against Cam's and kissed him for another long minute. "A bit more of that and I might let you."

Cam flashed her his most charming smile. "You're quite a woman, Jessica."

"And you're quite a guy, Cam. Thanks for dinner."

"Till next week?"

"Till next week. Call me when your job's finished."

Jessica turned and walked into the house, happier than she had been in a long time.

The following morning she called Eric. After a few pleasantries, she said, "I had a date last evening."

"Great. Have fun?"

"Yes. I did. It's a whole new thing, this dating."

"I'm happy for you, Jessica."

When she told him about her day at John's he asked, "Are you gorgeous? More so than when I left?"

"You know, I feel gorgeous and I've never felt like that before. I feel like men might want to look at me, might find me attractive. That's a new thing for me." She laughed. "I also had a massage. What an experience."

"If we're still on for Saturday, I'll give you one of Eric's patented massages, no holds barred."

Jessica felt heat flow through her body. "I'd like that," she said huskily. "Then could I give you one?" She had never explored Rob's body and now she found that she wanted to touch all of Eric's.

"That sounds like an offer I can't refuse." He picked up his watch from the table beside his bed. "It's after nine-thirty there. Are you still in bed?"

"Yes," Jessica said. She stretched, liking the feeling of cool sheets against her naked skin.

"Well, I need to know something. When I give you that massage where would you like me to touch you?"

"Where?"

"Where. Exactly."

"Oh, just everywhere," Jessica said, suddenly shy.

"Your breasts? Touch them and see whether they would like that."

Jessica pressed the palm of her hand against her breast and felt her swollen nipple fill her hand. "Oh yes."

"And you'll want me to rub your thighs and your beautiful ass. Then I'll rib your clit until you come. It won't take long, will it?"

Without thinking, Jessica slipped her hand between her legs and found her swollen, wet clit. She rubbed long and slow, then harder and faster. "No," she whispered. "It won't take long at all." She felt the familiar tight knot in her belly.

"Are you rubbing where it feels so good, baby?"

"Yes," she moaned.

"Don't stop. Stroke and touch. Do exactly what feels best. Reach out for the orgasm and pull it closer. Use your mind to see your fingers as they rub and give you pleasure."

Jessica reached for the climax and drew it closer and closer. As it flowed up her thighs, she tensed her legs and arched her back slightly. "Yes," she groaned and it overtook her. "Yes." It filled her, swirling in hot shards of orange and gold. It came so hard it almost hurt. She gritted her teeth and felt it curl her toes.

After a short silence, Eric said, "You did it, didn't you. You gave yourself pleasure. You were responsible for your own orgasm."

Jessica caught her breath. "I guess I was."

"I hope you've recovered from those feelings that Rob stuffed you full of."

She smiled. "Not entirely, but it's hard to feel frigid when a man can make you come over the phone."

She heard Eric's rich laugh. "True enough. Saturday? My place? Timmy's wonderful dinner, then whatever?"

"Yes. What time?"

"I'll come get you at about six-thirty, if that's okay."

"Great," she said, feeling her languid body sink into the mattress. "See you then."

The rest of the week sped by. As had become a habit, Thursday afternoon she called her office in Ottawa and talked at length to Vivian Whitman, her second-in-command and, next to Steph, her best friend. She made a few necessary business decisions and was gratified to learn that everything was running as smoothly without her as it did when she was there. "Viv," she said, "you make me feel unnecessary."

"Jessie, we all love you and we want you to take this time off. We're deliberately not bothering you with anything but the most important stuff." Viv's voice lowered. "Are you having any fun?"

Jessica could picture the slightly overweight black woman who, right now, had her head bowed with the phone tucked between her shoulder and her ear. One hand would be cupped over her mouth, as she always did when she was being conspiratorial.

"Oh lord, Viv," Jessica said, "I'm having more fun than I could have imagined." Leaving out the more lurid details, she told her friend about Eric and about Cam. "I feel attractive and sexy and free."

"That's great. I'm so happy for you."

Jessica could hear a note of sadness. "What's wrong, Viv?"

"I guess I'm scared you won't come back. I miss you." Viv and Jessie had become friends several years before although Rob had always declined offers to have dinner with Viv and her husband.

"I miss you too, Viv," Jessica said.

"Dates are not coming out of the woodwork here. Nice men are in short supply, as you may remember. I'm just afraid you'll decide to stay in New York."

Jessica felt uncomfortable with Viv's correct assessment of Ottawa, Illinois. It was a bit dull. "Any nibbles on my house?"

"We've gotten several repeat visits, but no offers yet. I'll call you if anything appears promising. Oh, and by the way, your ex seems to have dropped out of sight. Do you know anything?"

Jessica found that she wasn't hurt by the mention of Rob's name. Now, she was angry. "Not a thing, and I really don't want to either."

"Sorry."

"Don't be. And I didn't mean to sound waspish. I hope he's happy. Remember the line from *Fiddler on the Roof*? 'May God bless and keep the tsar . . . far away from us.' That's how I feel right now. They should be happy, and invisible." Jessica could hear Viv's giggle over the phone lines.

"Lord, I do miss you, girl."

"Me too, Viv. Talk to you next week."

"Till then."

Eric picked Jessica up that Saturday evening and they sped to his house. As they drove up the driveway, Jessica was struck by the way the low-slung, strong, rugged, rough-hewn house matched Eric's looks and personality. She glanced at his angular chin and close-cut, granite-gray beard and said, "The house fits you."

"Thank you." He stopped the car and pulled up the emergency brake.

"I didn't really see it the last time I was here. I was a bit distracted, if you remember. I'm awed by how perfectly your house suits you. It's beautiful."

"Thank you. And don't be awed. That's what I do for a living, you know."

"I didn't know you were so good."

"I'll bow modestly and admit that I'm damn good. Actually what I'm good at is finding out what people are and what they want." He rested his head on the headrest. "I get people to paint me a picture of the way they see themselves, then I design a frame to put that picture into."

"I've been selling real estate for a long time and I'm hard to impress." She waved her arm to take in the house and the subtle landscaping. "This impresses me."

"Thanks." He got out, rounded the car and opened the door for Jessica. "Very non-politically-correct."

Jessica extended her hand and Eric grasped it. "Very," she said as she unfolded herself from the tiny car, "and I like it." Without releasing his hand, she stood very close to Eric's body, looking into his smoky-gray eyes. The day was hot and humid, but it couldn't match the heat radiating from her body and Eric's.

He raised her hand to his lips and, without releasing her gaze, he swirled his tongue around her palm. Then he pulled a length of thick dark-gray yarn from his pocket and tied it around Jessica's wrist. "You may not remember from your last trip here, but my bedroom is decorated in shades of gray, from the palest hue, which looks almost white, to the deepest shade, the color of the ocean in a storm. This," he finished the knot, "is the color of the sheets on my bed. Tonight, you will be there, with your red hair spread on my pillow, your green eyes clouded with passion, your body needing me."

Jessica swallowed hard, around the lump in her throat.

"And you know what you'll be doing?"

"What?" she croaked.

"You'll be begging me to fill you up. And I won't. I'll tease you and drive you crazy."

"Oh."

He grinned. "But we have to have dinner first. Timmy's been expecting you." He aimed her at the front door.

They walked down a short hallway and through a formal dining room dominated by an oak table that could seat twenty. The chairs were upholstered in a soft rose damask and the deep plush carpeting was a richer shade of the same color.

"Ms. Hanley," Timmy said as they entered the kitchen. "I'm so glad to see you again."

"I'm glad to see you, too, Timmy, but could you call me Jessica?"

"Okay, Jessica," Timmy said, opening the refrigerator door. "You spoke about liking cocktail sauce with horseradish so I gambled that you'd also like Bloody Marys. Was I right?"

"Timmy, you're a mind reader. I love Bloody Marys, extra spicy."

Timmy withdrew a pitcher from the refrigerator and filled two glasses. He garnished the drinks with stalks of celery and thin slices of tomato and onion. "Actually," Jessica said, lifting the celery from the drink, "I like Bloody Marys but I love celery." She bit off a chunk and chewed loudly. "Aren't you having one, Timmy?"

"If I drink before I cook, I don't cook."

Eric patted Timmy on the shoulder. "Occasionally Timmy and I share a bottle of wine or something before dinner. First, the rolls don't get made, then the salad bites the dust. By the time dinner arrives, it's meat and pasta."

"Yes," Timmy said, "but I thought you were usually too sloshed to notice."

"Too true," Eric said. "What's for dinner tonight?"

"I've made a cold cucumber and yogurt soup, chilled chicken breasts with white grapes and watercress, and tabbouleh."

"What's tabbouleh, Timmy?" Jessica asked.

"It's a middle eastern salad made from bulgar, tomatoes, parsley, lemon, and olive oil."

"Bulgar's wheat, isn't it?" Jessica felt Eric ease around behind her. While she talked, he pulled the back of her blue-and-white-striped shirt out of the waistband of her white linen slacks.

"It is wheat, but I have no idea exactly what's been done to it."

Jessica felt Eric insinuate his index finger into the back of her pants and stroke the top of the crack between her buttocks. She swallowed then she said, "That sounds delicious."

"Oh," Timmy said, "it's so nice to have an appreciative audience."

As Eric's fingers lightly brushed the skin in the small of her back she sipped her drink, wanting him to stop, yet not moving away. As Timmy turned back to the refrigerator, Eric licked a wide swathe from her collar up to her hairline. She smiled as she remembered her debate about whether to sweep her hair up to the crown of her head with a silver comb and a narrow blue silk scarf.

"I like your hair up," he said, his breath hot on her ear, "but I want to see how it looks with its new styling."

"Would you like to have your soup now?" Timmy asked, oblivious to what was going on.

Eric tucked Jessica's shirt back in loosely and said, "I want to show Jessica the back. Let's say fifteen minutes?"

"Everything's served cold this evening, so take your time. I'll have soup ready whenever you like."

With Eric's warm palm in the small of her now-covered back, Jessica walked through a gigantic living area, cleverly divided into several seating groups. "Oh Eric, this is fantastic," she said, clearly awed. Although each area had a different pattern to the furniture—florals in one area, stripes in another, solids in a third—the areas were held together by the consistent use of southwestern shades of soft rose, sand, and slate blue. "I would have thought you more the chrome and glass type."

"I went to Tucson about five years ago and fell in love with the country, the people, and the ambiance. I had already built the house, so it's very steel, rock, and glass outside and soft and plushy inside."

"I know a lot of people like that," Jessica commented.

Eric smiled. "Now that I have it the way I want it," Eric said, "I don't use the house much, except for an occasional party."

"But you wouldn't sell this," Jessica said. "It's a part of you."

"I don't feel that way about things, I guess," Eric said, "but it would be a shame to leave this. I would, though, as long as I felt that I was leaving it in good hands." He led her through a sliding glass door and into the backyard.

A flagstone patio about fifteen feet wide ran the length of the back of the house. The area was edged with a three-foot-high wall of natural rock with water gurgling out at intervals into small pools and a six-foot-high waterfall at one end. Shrubs and low ground covers grew in crevices in the rocks and half a dozen large trees closed the area in. To Jessica it looked like an oasis out of an Arabian Nights fantasy or a secret cove on a tropical island. It should be tacky, she thought, but it isn't. It's glorious. Jessica looked around, taking in the beauty of the secluded spot. The air was heavy and humid, filled with the sweet aroma of distant flowering plants. "It's beautiful." A soft breeze brushed her face as Eric stood behind her.

"I pictured you here," he whispered, his fingers deftly unbuttoning her top. "I saw you naked, like some kind of jungle creature, wild and wanton." He unfastened the last button and pulled her shirt loose from her slacks. He took the drink from her hand and put it on a small wicker table. Then he removed her shirt, unhooked her bra, and slid it off her arms.

Jessica stood still, letting the warm breeze pucker her nipples and whisper over her skin. She closed her eyes and let her head fall back as Eric pulled the scarf, then the combs from her hair. She felt the soft mass cascade to her shoulders as Eric buried his fingers in the soft red strands. "You smell wonderful."

His hands were all over her body, touching, moving, dancing. He moved around until he was facing her, then he cupped her breasts and buried his face in the curve of her neck. "Just as I dreamed it would be," he purred. He stepped back and let his fingertips trail toward her nipples. "But not yet," he said.

When she felt him pull back, she opened her eyes, a silent question on her face.

"I want this evening to be filled with sensual pleasures. And I want it to last." He handed her her top, keeping her blue lace bra in his hand.

"I understand," she said. She slipped her arms through the openings and buttoned a few buttons. When he handed her her scarf, she tied it in her hair at the nape of her neck.

"Now feel your nipples against the soft fabric of your blouse." He lifted the end of the scarf and brushed it over her cheek. "Feel everything. Smell everything. Taste everything. We are going to make love all night." He kissed her softly, then led her back into the house.

They ate dinner in a small dining area adjacent to the kitchen. The table was oyster-colored Formica and the place mats and napkins followed the southwestern feel of the living room. The soup was cold but it cooled only a bit of her internal heat. The chicken was delicious, and the salad was the perfect complement. Eric poured each of them a glass of cold, crisp chablis, but she drank only a little. She was gently buzzed and didn't want to get any more so.

Throughout the meal, they talked about unimportant things. He amused her with stories of his travels and some of the unusual people he had designed for. She countered with tales of the weird couples for whom she had tried to find houses.

Although they laughed and shared and nothing overtly sexual was mentioned, a soft, sensual haze pervaded everything they did. Occasionally Eric would reach across the table and tug gently on the yarn around her wrist but she needed no reminders. The picture of her on Eric's bed was never out of her mind.

When they were finished with the main course, Timmy removed the plates and brought simple bowls of fruit sherbet for dessert. He placed a plate of chocolate truffles and tiny butter cookies in the center of the table. He poured coffee into their cups and put the pitcher on the table. "Unless there's anything else you want," Timmy said, "I'm going to go watch the Mets game."

"Nothing else," Eric said. "Who are they playing?"

"Los Angeles. Actually, I'm dying to see that Japanese phenom who's pitching for the Dodgers. Nomo."

"I've heard of him," Jessica said. "He's being considered for rookie of the year, but he's hardly a rookie. He's played for a dozen years in Japan."

"I'm impressed," Eric said. "I didn't know you were a baseball fan."

"When you live within spitting distance of Chicago, it's either the Cubs or the White Sox. I'm a Cub fan, myself, although I only watch games on TV."

"Maybe we can watch together some time," Timmy said.

"That would be fine," Jessica said. "Are you a Mets fan? We can watch a Cubs/Mets game and we can scream during alternate innings."

"I'm not a real rooter in that sense. I watch any sport and any team," Timmy said. "I just enjoy good competition."

"Timmy will watch anything from arm wrestling and surfing championships to chess and gymnastics. We watch a lot together on the weekends."

"Good night, Ms. Hanley." He caught himself, and said, "Good night Jessica. It was nice to see you again. And I'd love to watch the Cubs with you sometime."

"Good night, Timmy. Enjoy your game."

As Timmy left, Eric said, "We'll enjoy our games too." He took the spoon from her sherbet. "First game, no spoon."

"No spoon?"

Eric dipped his finger into the sherbet and extended it to her. She smiled, then licked the cold sweetness from his fingers. Then she scooped a dollop of sherbet and put it into the hollow of her hand.

Eric grinned as she held out her hand and he licked it from her skin with long, slow laps. "You taste heavenly."

Licking sticky sherbet from each other's hands, they ate their dessert. Eric poured them each a cognac, then they walked back onto the patio. As Jessica stood in the middle of the patio, Eric removed the scarf from her hair and held it in front of her at eye level. "May I?"

When Jessica looked puzzled, he lay the scarf across her eyes. "I want you to feel, not see. May I?"

Jessica thought only a moment before nodding. Eric tied the scarf across her eyes, then removed all her clothes, leaving only the yarn around her wrist. Jessica felt him lift first one foot and then the other to remove her sandals.

"Feel how cold the stone is on your feet," he said, stroking her insteps. "You're so beautiful," he said, sliding his hands up her legs. "Your legs are long and shapely, your thighs white and soft." He brushed his knuckles over her red pubic hair. "Red, like fire. Do you burn for me, Jessica?"

"Oh yes," she moaned. She felt him take her hand to lead her across the stones. Jessica hesitated. She couldn't see. What if she spoiled the mood by stubbing her toe or doing something equally awkward. She didn't want to ruin this.

"Trust me," he said softly.

"But. . . ."

He placed a finger against her lips. "Just trust me. Nothing will spoil this." He picked her up in his arms and carried her to the edge of the patio and sat her on the cold stones. Then she felt him take one of her hands and dip it into the cold water of one of the pools. "You're all sticky," he said, carefully rubbing the sherbet from each finger. He did the same with her other hand.

Then, when both her hands were cool and wet, he took her palms and placed them on her breasts. Cool water ran down her ribs in tiny rivulets, tickling her sides. She struggled to hold on to the mood but, as Eric dribbled water onto her belly, she started to laugh.

"Ticklish?" Eric said, laughing with her.

"Not usually, but right now, yes," she said, worried that she had ruined the mood.

"Good. Laughter is necessary." He licked the droplets of water from just below her belly button and she giggled again. Then he suckled at her right breast and heat stabbed through her, making her as hot as she had been. He took her nipple in his teeth and bit gently, just hard enough to make her squirm. "Like that," he said. He took one finger and slid it into her, rubbing the sides of her slick, hot channel. "And that." He withdrew, stood and lifted her into his arms. "Oh yes." He moved her body so her hip rubbed against the bulge in his slacks. "Come upstairs with me. I want you in my bed."

Still blindfolded and naked, Jessica felt herself carried through the house and up the stairs. "I've been dreaming of you in my bedroom all week." Eric set her down on the floor and said, "Sit down, love."

He placed her hand on the edge of his bed and she sat on the smooth slithery sheets. She felt the bed sway just a bit as she settled onto it.

"If you were as excited as I was last weekend, you were too excited to notice that this is a water bed and particularly delightful to make love on. And the sheets are satin, cold and slippery. Lie back."

She stretched out on the cool fabric and spread her arms and legs, moving to intensify the feel of the satin. "Ummm," she purred.

"Now I want to play."

Jessica felt something soft and velvety rub lightly up and down her arm. "That's a rose," Eric said. He brushed the flower across her face and she could smell its light fragrance. She felt the flower caress her breasts then her shins. "Don't move," Eric said when her hips began to move. "Just hold completely still." The flower was gone. "This is a piece of fur from the collar of an old coat." He rubbed the fur over her skin, touching her underarms, the insides of her thighs and the backs of her knees. When her hips moved, he said, "No, no. Don't move."

"But I want to move. it's very hard to keep still."

"That's part of this lesson," Eric said. "You must keep your body completely still. You can't see, you can't move, just feel. Nothing more. Concentrate."

Jessica held still despite the increasing difficulty of controlling her body. Now that she knew what she craved, the heat and orgasmic excitement, she wanted it. She needed it. She reached for it, but Eric skillfully kept it just out of reach.

"You're getting so aroused," he purred. "Your pussy is an open and hungry mouth. But I'm not ready to fill it just yet."

"Yeeooow," Jessica yelled as she felt something icy pressed on the hot, swollen flesh between her legs.

"That's an ice cube." Eric laughed deep and warm. "Hold still."

"I can't," she said as she squirmed to get away from the freezing cube. When she felt the ice being removed from her clit, she took a deep breath and willed her body to relax.

"You know that this is a game we're playing. I'm going to tease and play and you're going to hold perfectly still while I do."

"If it's a game, then what do I get if I win?" Jessica asked, giggling at the sheer joy of it all.

"If you win, you get the best fucking you've ever had."

"And if I lose?"

"Then I get to fuck your brains out."

Jessica laughed. "Then I guess it's important that I win."

She felt Eric press the ice against her right breast and take her left nipple in his mouth. The contrast between the cold and the heat drove her crazy. After about a minute, he switched, placing the ice against her warm breast and his hot mouth on her cold one. It's strange, she thought with the small, coherent part of her brain. The pleasure is the now, the feelings, the eroticism, not the anticipation of the fucking that will come later. It was a revelation for her. It's the journey, not the destination.

Eric took a deep breath and removed Jessica's blindfold, as though he sensed the change in her attitude. She looked at him and grinned.

"You understand what I'm trying to teach you now, don't you?"

"Yes. I always thought foreplay was just to get ready for fucking. But foreplay is fun just for itself."

"You get an 'A' plus. Okay, next lesson. What gives your body pleasure?" When Jessica hesitated, Eric continued, "I've touched you, caressed you, kissed you, made love to you. And I've taught you to do the same. What exactly, gives you pleasure?"

"That's really hard to talk about."

"I know, but I want you to tell me."

"I like it all."

He made a rude noise. "Cop-out."

"I like it when you kiss me."

Eric leaned over and licked Jessica's lower lip. He slowly inserted his tongue into her mouth and played with the tip of her tongue. He nipped at her lips and sucked her tongue into his mouth.

Heat flowed through her body. A moment before she had been relaxed but now she was tense and wanting. She reached up and held his head against her mouth.

He pulled back, took her wrist, and pressed it back against the sheets. "No hands. You're still under my orders not to move."

"Orders?" she said, the word causing heat to knife through her belly.

"Yes, orders. Now, that last answer was also a cop-out, but I enjoy kissing you too so I'll let it pass. Tell me where you like to be touched, where you want me to kiss you." She remained silent, so Eric said, "Is it difficult to say the words? Do you like it when I suck your tits?"

The crude word again sent waves of heat through her. "Yes," she whispered.

He licked her erect nipple, then said, "Tell me." A smile spread across Eric's face. "Makes you hot, doesn't it. Those words. Okay, first show me with your hands. Hold your tit for my mouth." He placed her hand on the underside of her breast and lifted, holding it upward for his mouth. He drew the hard tip into his mouth and sucked. "Say *tit*," he said as he blew cool air on her hot dusty-rose areola. "Say it."

"Oh baby," she moaned. "Please."

He couldn't resist her and he took her flesh in his mouth, laving and sucking it. "Where now?" he said.

Jessica took his hand and pulled it down, pressing his fingers against her swollen vulva, rubbing, kneading. "Please," she cried. "Oh God, please."

"You want my fingers in your pussy?"

Pussy. The word increased her excitement. The power of the words. She wanted to say them. She wanted to be forced to say them. She wanted. "Yes," she said, her breathing ragged and harsh. "I want your fingers inside me." Saying them felt so forbidden, so dirty, so good. She took a breath. "I want your fingers in my pussy."

Eric moaned, then plunged two fingers deep into her cunt, sawing in and out, fucking her with his hand. "Yes, baby, take it," he cried.

"Eric," she said, looking at his face, "fuck me." She saw it all, including the effect her voice was having on him.

He unrolled a condom onto his stiff erection and climbed over her. She grabbed his cock and rubbed it over her clit. The power to give pleasure, to excite, to drive him as crazy as he was driving her. It was intoxicating. She wanted to touch him, to drive him a little crazy too.

She placed her palms against his lightly furred chest and stroked his skin. As he moved, she caressed the skin over his contracting muscles. She wanted to touch his soft belly, and she did, sliding her hand lower and lower until she heard his harsh intake of breath.

"You'll kill me doing that," he groaned.

"But it will be worth dying for," she said, his passion making her bolder. She found his hard cock and did what she imagined would feel good. She laid his shaft in her palm and stroked the length of him.

"Oh, Jessica," he moaned and she revelled in the giving, exploring his excitement. She grew bolder, finding his sac and cupping his heavy testicles. She squeezed his cock and watched his face contort with pleasure. She wanted and needed and took. She placed the tip of his cock against the opening of her cunt, slid her hands to his buttocks, and pulled him into her.

The power of it was as enlightening as it was exciting. She moved with, then against him. They varied their rhythm, first fast, then slow and languid. He pulled out, then drove into her. He slid to the opening of her sheath, then slid in, inch by teasing inch. He was quiet inside of her, then pounded hard and fast.

Finally, she felt him tense and he reached between their bodies and rubbed her clit. "Yes," she screamed, "now, do that, yes. Do that." They came almost simultaneously, but the orgasm was only the culmination of the pleasure, not the pleasure alone. It wouldn't have mattered if she hadn't come, she realized with amazement. There were so many climaxes before her orgasm.

"It's so wonderful," she said later, running her hand up his side. "I never realized until now."

"Well," Eric said, panting, "I'm afraid I've created a monster."

Jessica propped herself on her elbow. "You have, you know. You certainly have."

Chapter

7

"Tell me about Gary," Jessica asked Steph the following Tuesday morning over breakfast.

"Gary Powell is quite a story," Steph said. "When he was in his early twenties he invented some kind of computer chip. I have no clue what it did, but it did it faster than anything else. So he started a manufacturing company and made a bundle. I mean a real bundle." She sipped her coffee. "About three years ago, someone offered him a couple of gazillion dollars for the firm, lock, stock, and patents."

"Obviously he took it."

"It was more than that somehow. He took the money and dropped out. Of everything. He was, and still is, mind you, single and very interesting. Although he's not especially good looking, he's always been sexy as hell. Now he's that and rich as Croesis as well. For a while mothers would invite him over to meet their eligible daughters, run into him accidentally at parties, whatever they could do to lure him into the family. Him and all that money."

"And . . . ?" Jessica said.

"Nothing. He owns a huge estate in Scarsdale. It's on about fifty acres with tennis courts, three pools, a ten-car garage. The landscaping is gorgeous, and you know how I feel about flowers.

"The house has to be seen to be believed. He gutted an old

inn, and had the entire thing rebuilt. Actually, now that I think about it, Eric designed the inside. It has a dozen guest bedroom suites, three entertainment rooms, a main kitchen and two auxiliary ones for people who stay over and want to make breakfast or what-have-you."

Jessica let out a long, low whistle.

"And the house has twenty-two bathrooms."

"Does he still work at the company?"

"That's the amazing thing. When they bought him out, they offered him a seven-figure salary to stay on as CEO, but he turned them down flat. He took his money and he decided to enjoy it. He travels, spends time in the city, dines at the best restaurants, sees shows and goes to concerts, sometimes with a woman on his arm, sometimes by himself." Steph laid her hand on Jessica's arm. "Get this. He even learned to ride and keeps a stable of thoroughbreds. He flies his own plane and goes to Boston for lunch. But he gets his jollies throwing parties."

"How do you mean?"

"He throws lavish parties and spends money like it's water. One party was a masked costume ball. He prepaid for everyone to rent costumes from one of the biggest Broadway distributors. We all went down and took our pick. Lord, that was some party."

"I'm impressed. Does anyone else give parties like that?"

"We all agreed early on not to play can-you-top-this. We all have the type of party we want to and leave the conspicuous consumption to Gary.

"Once he rented a yacht for an evening and we went out into the lower harbor and partied. Another time he flew us all to a private Caribbean Island for a weekend. He'd had the whole place set up with tents, food, wine, even a dance floor. Warm breezes, good champagne, and free love. For another weekend, he took over one of those hedonism resorts, the ones with the champagne-glass-shaped hot tubs in every room."

"You're kidding."

"He's a hedonist, with the money to indulge himself. The costume party was the one during which Brian and I first discovered one of our favorite pastimes."

"Don't tell me you discovered sex. I remember you and Brian in the backseat of a certain Pontiac."

"Not sex but a new and particularly exciting way to enjoy it."

"So tell me everything."

Steph raised an eyebrow. "I think you're ready to hear the next installment in my sexual education. I remember it so clearly, even though it was two years and many parties ago."

"We have to dress as our favorite sexual fantasy," Steph said.

"For what?" Brian said absently.

"For Gary's party a week from Saturday. It's a costume thing and we have to dress as our favorite fantasy." She turned the invitation over and there were the names and addresses of one costume shop in Manhattan and one in White Plains.

Brian looked up from the current issue of *Time* magazine. "My favorite sexual fantasy? In costume? I don't think so." They sat at the dinner table over dishes of fresh fruit and cups of coffee.

Brian's tone seemed harder than usual. Steph looked up at him. "Why not?" she asked, curious.

"I don't have many sexual fantasies but the ones I have are mine and I don't share. And certainly not in dumb costumes." He looked back down at his magazine.

"We've never talked much about sexual fantasies. I assume you have a few."

"Enough," he growled.

Ignoring his harumphing, Steph pushed a bit harder. "Come on, tell me. Chasing Heather Locklear around Melrose Place maybe? Or making love in the bathroom of a 747? Tell me. Please?"

"No."

Stephanie sensed that he was protesting too hard and might enjoy talking about his desires. She poured two glasses of brandy, walked to Brian's chair, pulled the magazine from his hands, and plunked herself in his lap. She handed a glass to Brian and said, "Come on."

"This is dumb," he said, sipping the drink Steph had handed him. "If you want me to tell you a fantasy, you have to tell me one of yours. And not one of those lightweight backrub or bubble-bath fantasies either. I assume you have a few, don't you?" he said, mimicking her question. When she was silent for a moment, he continued, "See. It's not easy to just tell someone that secret."

"I thought we didn't have secrets," Steph said, standing up.

"We don't," Brian said seriously. "Not real secrets. It's just that fantasies are personal. It's risky to tell someone that you want to, oh let's say make love in the pool."

"We've done that," Steph said.

"Don't pick nits with me. You know what I mean."

"Actually, I do." Steph was thoughtful. She did have some fantasies that she'd never shared with another soul. She was sure that if she said them out loud, everyone would know she was really perverted. Several vivid pictures flashed through her mind and her eyes glazed.

Several moments went by, then Steph snapped back to the present. She looked at Brian and found him staring at her. "You were a million miles away," he said. "Fantasies?" Steph's cheeks turned pink. "Holy cow," Brian said. "You're blushing."

Steph giggled and covered her face with her hands.

Brian picked up the two brandy glasses and said, "Follow me."

Steph followed him up to the bedroom. He placed the glasses on his bedside table, then placed one hand on each of his wife's shoulders and pushed her over backward onto their bed. He turned out all the lights, then stretched out beside her. "You know, I must admit that I'm so excited by this fantasy idea that my cock is almost painfully hard."

Steph propped herself up on one elbow, reached over and started to unzip Brian's jeans. He placed his hand on hers and removed it from his crotch. "Not yet." He hesitated. "This is really tricky," he said with a sigh, "but part of me wants to share a fantasy I've had for a long time. If I tell you one of mine, will you tell me one of yours?"

"Phew. This got serious in a hurry." She dropped onto her back.

"It's not serious, just intense."

"Why now, after all these years?"

"You started this, you know. And now we're playing with other people and, without realizing it, I've played out some fantasies with them. But part of me wants to play out a fantasy with you." Steph could hear his voice brighten. "Of course," he continued, "part of me is scared as hell."

"Scared I'll think you're weird?"

"Exactly."

"Scared to say it out loud? Because I'll think you're perverted?" When he remained silent, she added in a small voice, "Me too."

Brian rolled onto his side and kissed his wife softly on the lips. "Nothing you could tell me could make me think you were weird, at least any weirder than I already know you are."

"And nothing you could tell me would ever, ever make me think less of you. I promise," Steph said.

Brian took her hand and rolled onto his back in the dark. There was a long silence while each considered the new ground they were treading on. "Why don't I tell you a story," Brian said finally. "Let's see how far I get."

"Okay," Steph said.

"Once there was a young man. He was in his late twenties and he was the janitor at an all-girls high school. It was one of those schools where the girls all wear uniforms. You know the ones." Brian dropped her hand and lay not touching his wife.

"Sure," Steph said softly, trying to encourage what she knew was a difficult revelation. "Maybe the uniforms were blue-and-green plaid skirts and crisply starched white blouses."

"Yeah," Brian said. "Just like that. And this janitor, maybe his name's John, he likes to listen to the girls giggle. Most of the time they forget he's even around and they talk about their dates and boys and things like that."

Steph thought about taking Brian's hand, but didn't. She didn't want to do anything that might interrupt.

"John's particular favorite was a girl named Missy. She was all blond and blue-eyed, with a great body, only partly concealed by the dumpy clothes she was forced to wear. He would slowly sweep the floor and watch her as she talked about her dates. He'd watch her mouth and her hands and her hips and her large breasts. More and more, he became fixated on her breasts. He had to see them."

When Brian lapsed into silence, Steph encouraged, "Go on."

"Anyway, although he never wanted to really hurt anyone, over the months he decided that he had to see her, have her all to himself. So one afternoon he drove along the route he knew she took home every afternoon. He saw her up ahead, her cute tush swaying as she walked. He pulled his car to a stop beside her."

Brian took a deep breath. " 'Hi, Missy,' he said to her. 'Need a lift?' 'Oh hi, John,' she said back. 'Sure, if you don't mind. I just live a few blocks from here.' So she comes around to the passenger side of the car and opens the door."

Brian was silent for a long time. Steph took his hand in the dark. "This is really difficult for you. You don't have to tell me any more."

"I know I don't," Brian said. "And a lot of me wants to stop, but part of me wants to tell the story. God, telling it makes me horny."

"Want to get naked?" Steph asked.

"You know, it's funny but it's easier to do this with clothes on and in the dark."

Steph rolled against Brian's side and pillowed her head on his shoulder. "Okay. Missy's climbing into John's car so he can drive her home. Except I don't think he's going to drive her home. Is he?"

"No. He lives in a remote part of town, in a house where they won't be disturbed. That's where he's going to go."

"When does she catch on that they're not going to her house? What does she do?"

"Well," Brian said, slipping back into the story, "he's planned this all very well. He's got the car's seat belt rigged so it's really tight and doesn't release. Missy throws her books and stuff into the back and sits down in the passenger seat. John reaches over and pulls the seat belt over her, trapping her hands at her sides. He snaps it into the holder and speeds away.

"It takes a minute before Missy realizes that she's in trouble."

Steph slipped into the fantasy. " 'Let me go,' Missy says, squirming, unable to get loose. 'What are you doing? Where are we going?' What does John answer?"

"John is silent. He's enjoying her struggles. He likes to watch the way her breasts are separated by the seat belt and how they move as she wriggles. 'I'll scream,' Missy says. 'Don't bother,' John says. 'With the windows closed and the heater on, no one will hear you.'

"So eventually they arrive at John's house. Missy is thinking that she'll get loose when he tries to take her into his house, but he's thought all that through very well. He gets out, comes around to her side and, before she can yell, he's tied her hands behind her and put a scarf into her mouth so she can't scream."

Steph wanted to give Brian the option of a cooperative scenario. "Maybe she's only pretending to struggle. Maybe she has enjoyed watching him watch her all along."

Steph could feel Brian thinking about her option. "Oh yes," he said, "maybe that's right. She's a little tease and enjoys making the boys sweat before she lets them have her."

"Maybe," Steph said, "but she'll never let John know that."

"He wants her to fight, but it's comforting to know it's all an act."

"You know, I always wanted someone to kidnap me," Steph whispered. "And ravish me while I fought as hard as I could, knowing that I couldn't win." It had become so much easier to share her fantasy, too. It was the sharing that made it all right.

"Really?" Brian said.

Steph took Brian's hand and pressed it against her crotch. Even through the denim of her jeans, he could feel the wet heat.

"I never suspected," Brian said.

"Will you continue the story?"

"Sure," Brian said, his voice stronger. "John carried Missy into the house, placed her on the bed, spread her legs, and tied her ankles to the bedframe. He tied her arms to the headboard, wide apart."

Steph spread her legs and arms on the bedspread. "Turn on the light," she whispered.

Brian flipped the switch and looked at his wife, spread-eagled on the soft rose bedspread.

"Like this?" she whispered.

Brian drew a ragged breath. "Just like that, except she was tied."

"Was she?" Steph said softly. "How?"

"Shit, baby," Brian said, trembling. "Are you serious?"

"Tie me down, then tell me more of the story." God, she wanted this. It had been a fantasy of hers for as long as she could remember.

Brian pulled several stockings from Steph's dresser and awkwardly tied her wrists and ankles to the head- and footboards of the bed. Then, for a long time, Brian stared down at his wife. What had started as a small, risky story had turned into something far more intoxicating. Although she was still fully dressed, Steph looked so vulnerable. "Are you okay? Is this all right with you?" he asked hoarsely.

Steph wanted even more. "Am I allowed to speak?"

Brian looked as if she had ignited him. She had asked his permission to speak. "Tell me," he said.

"I am much more than okay. I'm so turned on I could come just listening to your story. Tell me more. Show me what John did in that remote house."

Brian swallowed hard. His voice was trembling. "John had Missy tied to the bed, but she still had her uniform on. He was prepared for that, though. He had a big pair of scissors and he slowly cut off all her clothes."

"Did he do it very slowly? Did he watch her face as she slowly revealed her body? Did she tremble as his fingers touched her bare skin?"

"Oh yes," Brian said. "He mostly liked looking at the white cotton underwear she had to wear under her uniform."

"I'm not wearing anything like that," Steph said, "but there's a pair of scissors in the hall closet." When Brian continued to stare at her she nodded. "Do it," she whispered.

He hurried to the closet and returned with the scissors.

"What did he cut off first?" Steph asked.

"He started with her socks." Brian worked around the stocking-ties and cut Steph's socks off.

"What do you see?" Steph asked as Brian gazed at her ankles.

"Those ties around your legs are the most erotic things I've ever seen." He looked into her eyes. "Next he cut her pants."

"I've got other jeans," Steph said. "And these are old anyway."

Brian smiled and started at the cuff of her right pant leg. He cut up to her belly, then repeated the process with the other pant leg. Then he connected the openings by cutting across just above her pubis. He looked at her tiny blacklace panties, then touched the crotch. "You're soaked," he said, incredulous.

"What did John do next?" Steph asked.

Brian unbuckled Steph's belt, cut up the front of her pants and pulled them open. With less hesitation, he cut up the front of her black sweatshirt, then down the arms until she lay in the tatters of her clothing, wearing only her bra and panties.

"Does he like what he sees?"

"John likes what he sees. Missy struggles, knowing what John has in mind. As she moves against the ropes that are holding her body wide open for him, he watches her breasts and her pussy, knowing they are his for the taking."

Steph pulled against the stocking holding her limbs. She writhed, her breathing uneven, her nipples pressing against the lace of her bra. When Brian reached underneath to unhook her bra, she said, "Cut it. Cut it off of me."

Brian cut the thin strip of fabric that connected the two cups, then the straps above them. He feasted his eyes on his wife's luscious body.

"God, baby," she said, "you're making me crazy. What next?"

A slow smile lit up Brian's face. "John did things very slowly. He liked to stretch out every part." Brian reached down and rubbed the nylon-covered flesh between Steph's legs. He found her swollen clit and rubbed and stroked until her hips were bucking beneath his hand. "He also had a few surprises for Missy. He had prepared for a long time for this moment."

Brian went into the bathroom, rummaged in the closet for a moment, then found an old plastic toothbrush holder. He washed it, then brought the phallus-shaped instrument back into the bedroom. He and Steph had never played with toys, but this was his fantasy and he would know it if he went too far. From the look on Steph's face, he suspected that she was hot enough for almost anything.

He stood next to the bed, brandishing the bright red phallus. " 'I'm going to fuck you with this, Missy,' John said. 'And you can't prevent it.' John pulled her panties aside and rubbed his toy all over Missy's pussy." Brian took the scissors and cut the sides of Steph's panties and pulled the fabric free. Then he rubbed the red plastic through the soaked folds of her cunt. "Then John slipped the toy inside."

Steph felt the cold plastic invade her body. She was beyond any coherent thought. "God, Brian, make me come."

Brian rubbed her clit with one hand and fucked her pussy with the plastic cock with the other. "Missy fought the orgasm," he said, "but John kept fucking her. Missy didn't want to come but John had complete control of her body." Brian bent low over Steph's bush. He knew just what his wife liked. "When he ate her, she couldn't hold it back." He slid the plastic in and out of Steph's pussy while his mouth sucked her clit.

Steph screamed, unable to control what was happening to her. She climaxed in a blaze of heat and clenching muscles. Usually her orgasms were sharp and short, but this one went on and on and Brian wasn't letting her body calm. She felt him rub and suck until finally she shrieked, tightened all her muscles, came again, then became limp.

Brian quickly untied Steph's wrists and ankles, then stripped off his clothes and stretched out beside her.

Steph's hand found his hard cock and her fingers wrapped around it. "You're so hard," she purred, "and so big. I'll bet Missy would be impressed." She squeezed. "But she couldn't use her hands if she was still tied up, could she?" She got onto her knees and, still trembling from her violent climax, clasped her hands behind her back and lowered her mouth toward Brian's cock. "All he could do would be to hold her hair, bend her head back, and force his cock into her mouth." Steph pursed her lips around Brian's cock and sucked it deep into her wet mouth. Up and down she bobbed, sliding her tongue and cheeks over his slick erection.

"Shit, baby, I'm going to come."

"Do it," Steph said.

"But. . . ."

He had never come in her mouth before but now she wanted it all. "Do it," she said, fucking his cock with her mouth. In only moments, he spurted deep into her throat. She had always been afraid it would make her gag, but, although it tasted strange, it didn't bother her at all. She swallowed some and let the rest of the thick fluid flow down her husband's penis. Then she lay her head on his stomach and wrapped her arms around his waist.

They gazed at each other silently, then burst out laughing. "That was not to be believed," Brian said.

"I'll bet people in the next county heard me scream."

"Was that really a fantasy of yours?" he asked quietly. "Yes," Steph admitted. "I've always wanted to be ravished."

"Why?"

"I don't know. I guess I like someone else to be in control. You can put layers of psychological gobbledygook on it, but I just like it. Wow, did I like it."

"Me, too, baby. Me too."

Steph finished telling Jessica the story. "I guess that's quite an admission, friend to friend. But I do love to be play-raped. Brian and I do that often now."

Jessica was silent for a long time.

"Are you shocked?" Steph asked, suddenly afraid she'd said too much.

Jessica grinned and patted Steph's hand. "Not at all. I'm sorry for my silence. I'm just thinking about my own fantasies." She chuckled. "Rob would be mortified to hear me say this, but I would lie in bed after we'd made love, frustrated and angry. I'd wish that he would do things to me, things that at the time I thought were dirty and weird. Let me tell you that I never even masturbated while we were married, but it would have helped at those moments. But I'd fall asleep remembering a scene in a movie I saw once. I was snapping past the Playboy channel late one night. I didn't even have the courage to watch the damn thing, although I was curious. But as I snapped past, a woman had a man on a leash and was ordering him to do things to her."

"Like what?" Steph asked.

"You know, the funny thing is that I was never sure what. Now, however, I've got a few ideas." She shook her head to clear her thoughts. "Did you go to that party?"

"Believe it or not we found a schoolgirl uniform in my size, just like the one in Brian's story. And we got a pair of coveralls for him, and a mop and bucket." She smiled dreamily at the memory. "We came home from the costume shop and, although he couldn't cut the clothes, we did the next best thing. He tied and untied me until he stripped me naked, then we fucked and fucked. . . ." Steph squirmed in her seat.

Both women took deep breaths. "I wasn't sure about going to

this party before but now I'm really looking forward to it," Jessica said. "Does it have a theme?"

"That's right. I got the invitation last evening, but I forgot to open it." Steph fetched the small square envelope and ripped it open. "Storytellers," she read, "have existed for thousands of years. In days of old they told tales of bravery, sacrifice, beauty, and devotion. More recently they tell of submarines and crime. The kind of story I like best tells of love and desire. So, for Saturday night, if you like, write an erotic story for us to share. Make it as hot as you like, as hot as I'd like. Submit it anonymously or sign it. Read it yourself, or I'll read it. I've already written one about an alien couple making love to an earth person, but of course you can pick your own subject. Have fun writing and I'll see you Saturday."

"What an interesting idea for a party," Jessica said.

"I love the idea of a story about making love with an alien. Are you going to write one?"

"I might just," Jessica said. Ideas were whirling in her head. "But I've never written anything like that. I've never even read anything like that, except for Hollywood novels."

"Come upstairs with me a minute." Steph and Jessica went to the master bedroom where Steph opened her closet and pointed to several large stacks of books and magazines. "My collection."

Jessica stared. There were copies of x-rated magazines, books of erotica, books of sexual advice, even books devoted to sexual games and fantasies. Steph pulled several out of the pile and handed them to Jessica. Then she added a few magazines to the stack. "Read."

"Wow.

"But I'm warning you that this stuff," she patted the magazines, "gets you very excited. Do you have a date with Cam tomorrow night?"

"He called last evening. He's picking me up about three tomorrow and we're driving to Connecticut."

Steph smirked. "You'll be eager to see him, I'm sure. And,

when you're ready to try writing a story, Brian's laptop computer's in the den."

"Can I take it upstairs?"

"Sure. Plug it in in your room. I'll use the one downstairs."

Jessica giggled. "I'm going to do a lot of reading, then we both can write something deliciously outrageous?"

"I think we must."

It was late that night and Jessica lay in the dark on her bed. A wide shaft of moonlight colored the room in a soft blue. Steph's story had fascinated her, opening new realms for her fertile imagination, as had the books she'd read all afternoon.

So much was possible. She could do anything, be anyone. It was as if someone had opened an entire area of her mind and thousands of pictures poured out. Pandora's box was open.

She looked at her body, glowing in the moonlight. She played Steph's story through in her mind for the dozenth time. It had become as familiar as if she had lived it. She was tied to the bed, helpless, not responsible for anything but taking pleasure. In the fantasy, however, she was also Brian, having someone under her control. She closed her eyes and thought about several stories she had read. Pieces moved, separated and reformed. Pictures, images, positions. I am JessicaLynn, she thought, in control of myself and my sexual destiny. She thought about her ideal partner in this new world.

He was tall, in his mid twenties, with sandy hair and deep blue eyes. He had a gorgeous body, honed by hours of daily heavy manual labor. His muscles were well developed and, because he worked without a shirt, his skin was heavily tanned, smooth, and hairless. When he lifted heavy two-by-fours his muscles rippled and sweat trickled down his chest and disappeared in the waistband of his jeans.

He worked for her, constructing an addition to a house she was selling. His crew had left for the day, but he remained to finish a small piece of work. His name was Walt.

As Jessica lay on the bed a soft breeze wafted across her naked skin and she smiled. Yes, she thought, his name is Walt.

"Ms. Hanley," Walt called from just outside the kitchen door, "I'm done for today."

JessicaLynn was dressed in a pair of short-shorts and a tank top that left little to the imagination. She had been aware of Walt's stares but she had been waiting for just the right moment to take advantage of the situation.

"How about a cold drink?" JessicaLynn asked.

"That would be great," he said. "Thanks." He walked into the kitchen and sat down at the table as JessicaLynn put a glass of iced tea in front of him. "It's really shaping up," he said, his gaze moving from her nipples to his hands.

"Yes," JessicaLynn said. "It's coming along nicely. You do excellent work."

"Thanks," he said, finding his eyes more and more drawn to her breasts.

"You look very warm. I'm sorry the air conditioning isn't working properly yet." She walked around behind him, leaned over his shoulder and took his frosty glass from his hand. "This might help." She wiped her finger through the beads of condensation on his glass, then down Walt's spine. "Better?"

His only answer was a quick intake of air.

JessicaLynn placed the cold glass against his overheated back and, when he jumped, placed the flat of her tongue against the cold spot. "Sorry," she whispered, "I didn't realize it would be so cold."

He turned in his chair and looked up at her, the obvious question in his eyes.

"Yes," she said, "but my way." She paused, watching passion darken his eyes. "You can leave at any time. But, for as long as you stay, you will belong to me. And it will be the most fantastic time of your life."

"That's all right with me," Walt said softly.

"In which case, you will obey the following rules. You will call me Mistress and speak only when you are spoken to. Do you agree?"

"Yes."

"Yes?"

"Yes, Mistress."

"You will do as you are told without hesitation. If anything is distasteful you may say, 'Only if you wish it' and I will reconsider. Do you understand?"

"Yes, Mistress."

"And you will not be restrained in any way. At any time you may leave. If you do, however, you may not return to me for this, just to work on the house. You will do what you do willingly. Do you understand?"

"Yes, Mistress."

JessicaLynn cupped her right breast through her tank top, extending it to Walt. "Suck," she said. When he reached out to wrap his arms around her waist, she added, "No hands."

Walt leaned forward and took the fabric-covered nipple in his mouth. He sucked and licked until the material was slick with his saliva. JessicaLynn backed away. "Enough. I'm going to change now, and you will sit here." She watched his fists clench and unclench. She reached down and pressed her palm against the fly of his jeans. "And that is mine. You may not touch it without my permission and I do not give my permission. Do you understand?"

"Yes, Mistress," he said.

JessicaLynn pulled the tank top off over her head, exposing her naked body to Walt's eager gaze. "You will be able to do wonderful things that will excite both of us, but only if you behave."

"I will, Mistress."

"You know," JessicaLynn said as she headed toward the kitchen door, "I like that eager look in your eyes. I like knowing how much you want me. You'll do anything to have me, won't you?"

Walt sighed. "Oh yes, Mistress. I'll do whatever you want."

JessicaLynn smiled. "Of course you will." She walked out and upstairs. While she changed clothes, she thought about Walt, sitting in the kitchen, waiting for her hungrily.

As Jessica lay on the bed in her moonlit room, creating the scene in her mind, she slid her hands over her ribs and up to her full breasts. He's so hungry, she thought.

When JessicaLynn arrived back in the kitchen she was wearing a tight black-leather teddy with metal studs and openings and covered with chains and hooks in various places. Her breasts were uncovered, as was her pussy. Her matching high-heeled leather boots came to just below her knees and she wore narrow, butter-soft black leather straps around her wrists and a wider one around her neck. She had several matching straps in her hand. She walked to within a foot of Wait and watched his eyes.

He stared, his gaze moving slowly from her out-thrust nipples to the tangle of red hair that peeked out through the open crotch. He looked at her face, now made up with heavy eye shadow and liner and deep crimson lipstick, then lowered his gaze to the floor.

"Do you want this?" JessicaLynn asked.

"Oh yes, Mistress," he said.

She reached out and ran her hand over his smooth, rock-hard chest. "Nice," she purred. She fastened a leather collar around Walt's neck and one around each wrist. "You're not restrained in the usual sense," she said. "But these straps mark you as my possession. Strip."

Clumsily, his hands shaking, he pulled off his work boots, socks, jeans, and shorts. His cock was fully erect, rising from a thatch of sandy hair.

JessicaLynn handed him a leather jockstrap. "Put this on."

Walt stared at the tiny garment, then down at his enormous cock. "But. . . ."

JessicaLynn raised one eyebrow.

"Yes, Mistress," Walt said, pulling the garment on and stuffing his cock into it as best he could.

"Now," she said, "you like sucking my tits, don't you?"

"Oh yes, Mistress."

JessicaLynn placed two kitchen chairs about two feet apart. "I want you to kneel, one knee on each chair."

Walt scrambled to obey. With his knees widely separated, the awkward position left his jockstrap-covered cock and balls exposed.

"Clasp your hands behind your back." Walt did.

JessicaLynn moved so her erect nipple touched Walt's cheek. When he turned to take it into his mouth, she backed up. "No," she said. "Move only when you are told to." He turned back and she rubbed her nipple over his cheek, his chin. She watched as he licked his lips, but made no other movement. She heard his thick, heavy breathing, saw his thighs begin to shake with the exertion of his strained position. Finally, she brushed her nipple against his lips and he opened his mouth slightly. "That's fine," she said. "Open your mouth but don't move unless I tell you to."

He did and JessicaLynn rubbed her erect nipple over his teeth and tongue. "Such a good boy," she said. "You may lick it."

She felt his tongue lave her flesh, gently caressing. "Suck," she said, needing him, wanting him.

He was like a man first starved, then given a feast. He sucked and licked, pleasuring first one breast, then the other. The erotic sensations were so intense, JessicaLynn felt as if she could come just from the feeling of his mouth. But that wouldn't do at all.

Jessica opened her eyes and looked down at her moon-bathed body, naked and so hot. Her hands played with her nipples, pinching them and making them hard and tight. She felt the heat in her belly and slid her hand down, tangling her fingers in her red bush. She found her flesh warm and moist as she had several times in the past few days. She knew now where to touch to give herself the most pleasure. She touched those magic places.

"Enough," JessicaLynn snapped. She grabbed Walt's crotch and squeezed his cock. "You're very good at that. It pleases me."

"I'm so glad, Mistress. I like giving you pleasure."

JessicaLynn smiled. "Are your legs tired?" She ran her hand down one steel-hard thigh, straining from the difficulty of holding himself up for so long with his knees separated.

Walt hesitated, then said, "Not if it does not please you, Mistress."

JessicaLynn patted his pouch, then said, "Come inside."

Walt took a moment to stretch his aching thigh muscles, then followed JessicaLynn into the living room. His feet sank into the thick carpeting and he watched her stretch out full length on the black leather couch, one foot on the back and one foot on the floor. She snapped her fingers and pointed so he knelt at her side at the level of her knees.

She handed Walt a comb. "I like my bush looking nice," she said. "Comb it nicely."

He used the comb so the teeth just touched her skin, caressing her with the plastic.

"And I like my thighs to be very soft." She handed him a bottle of baby lotion. As she watched intently, he filled a hollow in his palm. When he took some on his fingers, she added, "It must be warmed first."

He held the lotion in his cupped hand until it was body temperature, then rubbed it into her thighs with long, powerful strokes. He rubbed the lotion into every inch of her skin, raising her legs so he could stroke the backs as well.

"Is it all to your pleasure, Mistress?" Walt asked.

JessicaLynn reached down, ran a finger through her dripping cunt, then extended it for Walt to lick. "Do I taste good?" she asked.

He sucked her finger. "Oh yes, Mistress."

"Would you like to lick my pussy now?"

"May I please?"

JessicaLynn nodded and Walt lay the flat of his tongue against her clit, pressing gently. She placed her hands on his muscular shoulders and felt the play of his muscles beneath his skin as he caressed her with his mouth. "Yes," she said, "right there. Lick it and suck it good."

Eyes glazed in the moonlight, Jessica's hand slid through her folds, rubbing her clit. She inserted one finger of her other hand into her waiting cunt, filling herself, driving herself higher. In her fantasy, she came, yet in her bedroom she wanted more, and she now knew what it was.

As spasms rippled through JessicaLynn's cunt, Walt filled it with his fingers, pumping, rubbing, spreading. He licked, sucked, rubbed, and caressed until her body was drained of every ounce of her climax. She lay, panting, while Walt watched her. "That was very good," she purred. "But there's more. You watched me come, now I get to watch your pleasure too."

Walt looked a bit startled.

"Haven't you ever touched yourself with someone watching you?"

Walt paused a moment, then said, "No, Mistress."

JessicaLynn stared at his swollen crotch. "But you're so excited, you want to come very badly, don't you."

Walt groaned. "Oh yes, Mistress."

"Well then, you'll have to do it yourself." She pointed to the leather jockstrap he wore. "Take that thing off."

She smiled as she watched his hesitancy. She loved his embarrassment. "There are no shackles on you. You know where the door is. But, if you want to stay, take that off."

While his eyes remained staring at the floor, he wriggled out of the leather garment. He stood, trembling, his engorged cock jutting from his body.

"Pull that glass table over here," JessicaLynn said, indicating a chrome and glass coffee table in the corner of the room. Walt pulled the table near the sofa. "Now kneel," JessicaLynn said. When he knelt on the soft carpeting, his cock was just above the level of the table.

JessicaLynn reached out, placed her hand on top of his cock and pressed it down against the cold glass. "Feel good?"

"Yes, and no, Mistress. I like your hand on me, but the glass is very cold."

"You take the good with the bad," JessicaLynn said. She stroked his cock, keeping it pressed against the table. She could feel him twitch, almost ready to come. She pulled her hand back. "But I said I wanted to watch you. Touch it yourself."

Hesitantly, Walt touched his cock with one hand. "Wrap your fingers around it, rub it with long strokes." She grabbed the lotion. "No wait, hold out your hand." She filled his palm with lotion. "Now do it."

JessicaLynn watched his face as he drifted deeper into his own sensation. She could see as his pleasure took precedence over his embarrassment. "Use both hands," she said.

His other hand joined and they rubbed and squeezed. "Oh," he moaned. He was lost. Spurts of thick come erupted from his cock, splashing onto the table.

"That's a good boy," JessicaLynn purred. "A very good boy."

In her room, Jessica couldn't hold back anymore. The vision of a man masturbating while she watched drove her over the edge. She gave in to the spasms that filled her body, feeling the rhythms that filled her. She sighed audibly, long and low as her body continued to climax. She touched the spot that extended the climax and trembled, panting, the picture of Walt coming filling her mind.

When she was calm again, she thought about her fantasy. She wondered whether it was best to keep this idea in her mind. No, she decided. if she had the opportunity, she would act this one out. But with whom?

Chapter

8

"I guess I've always found sex to be a bit of a letdown for me," Cam said as he and Jessica walked, hand in hand, along the water. They had driven to a small strip of beach in Fairfield, Connecticut, after a sumptuous dinner at a local seafood restaurant. They had removed their shoes and walked across sand still warm from the heat of the day, to the water's edge. Cam had rolled up his pantlegs and now walked calf-deep in salty foam, with Jessica on his left, only ankle-deep.

"A letdown?" Jessica said. Jessica had been puzzled by the fact that, although this was their third date and Cam talked about how sexy she was and how much he wanted her, he hadn't made a serious pass at her.

"I've dated lots of women, don't get me wrong, and I've been to bed with many of them. But it hasn't been, well, you know, skyrockets, the earth moving, that sort of thing. From what you've told me, you seem to have found that in the past few weeks, and I'm envious."

"I guess I thought that you men had it easy. You're always ready, willing, and able and you can do what you want in bed."

"Not so. I spend most of my time worrying about whether I'm making my partner happy."

"Haven't you ever had anyone ask for what they want? Wouldn't that make it easier for you?"

"Sure it would," Cam said, standing still and gazing out over the ocean, watching the sky darken. "But not many women are willing to do that. Or at least I haven't found any."

"Take a big risk with me," Jessica said, holding Cam's hand tightly. "Describe to me your perfect sexual evening."

"Phew," Cam said. "That's really difficult."

"I know it is, but it may just get you what you want. Is the risk of telling me worth that reward?"

Cam took a deep breath and let it out very slowly. "I don't think I can."

"Okay," Jessica said, holding Cam's hand tightly. "Let me try to help. . . ."

Interrupting, Cam started walking. "This is going too far," he said. "Let's just walk and enjoy the evening."

"Stop," Jessica said. "Stand right there." Jessica felt the tightening of Cam's hand as he stopped in his tracks. "That's better," she continued. "Now, I really want to know what you're thinking because I think there's something very wonderful here. Do you trust me?" Cam nodded. Jessica leaned over and kissed Cam on the cheek. "I'm going to say a few things and, if what I say excites you, squeeze my hand. Okay?"

"This is really silly," he said.

"Scary is more like it," Jessica said, noticing that Cam's erection was now clearly visible under the fly of his navy trousers. "Will you trust me?" Cam remained silent, so Jessica continued. "You said you would enjoy making love to someone who told you exactly what to do to give them pleasure. What if a woman was very clear and forceful about what she wanted? What if she told you how to give her pleasure?" She felt Cam's hand tremble. "What if she went further? What if she ordered you to do things?"

Releasing her hand, Cam turned his back to Jessica and stared out to sea.

Jessica stood behind him and reached around his waist. Since he wasn't much taller than she was, she moved her mouth close to his ear. She deliberately switched from 'she' to 'I.' "What if I told you to take both of my hands in yours?"

Slowly, Cam's hand covered hers, his fingers interlocking with hers. Jessica's breathing quickened. This was her fantasy, and, it seemed, his too. She was going to make the decisions. She had read so much about it but had never actually experienced anything like this. Should she go slowly? Should she jump right in? In for a penny . . . she thought.

"Cam, unzip your pants." When he hesitated, she whispered, "Do it."

"But. . . ."

"No talking," she snapped. "Do as you're told."

Jessica could feel Cam's body tremble and he moved his hands slowly to his fly. Ever so slowly, Cam pulled his zipper down. Jessica reached for his cock, which peeked through the opening in his clothes. "Touch it," she said, moving to his side so she could see his hands. "You know you want to, Cam." With a groan, he moved one hand toward his erection, then dropped his hand and again turned his back.

"It would give me great pleasure to see your fingers wrapped around your cock," Jessica said, placing her hands on his shoulders and turning him to face her. "Do it to please me."

Cam looked into her eyes and Jessica watched the battle raging within him. Then Cam's shoulders dropped and his facial muscles relaxed as he gave in to what was happening. He took his cock in his hand and held it. "Oh yes," Jessica said. "You're so beautiful and so excited. Nothing has ever felt like this before, has it?"

"No," he whispered.

Jessica took his free hand in hers. She had to ask him for confirmation one last time. "You don't have to tell me anything with words, but tell me with a squeeze of your hand. Is this what you wanted?"

Jessica felt Cam's hand squeeze hers.

"This is a fantasy of mine, Cam," Jessica said, clearly able to see how excited Cam was. "You're going to be mine for tonight.

But I don't want you so hot that you're in pain. Do you know what would please me? I want to see you come. Right here, right now."

Cam looked stricken. "I can't."

"Oh yes, you can," Jessica said. "You know you're so close now that if you slid your cock into my pussy you would come immediately. Close your eyes if you need to and think about pleasing my demanding pussy." She touched Cam's hand, and the hard cock within. "Tightly," Jessica said. "Hold it and think about my pussy. Later tonight, you'll know how wet it gets, how it feels, how it tastes." She felt his free hand twitch. "Tasting me. Is that what you want? Then I'll order you to lick and suck me until my juices are flowing into your mouth."

She watched Cam's eyes close and his hand begin to stroke his cock. "Maybe I'll sit in a chair and order you to your knees in front of me. . . ." Cam's cock erupted, spraying thick fluid into the ocean water. "It's so beautiful to watch you come."

The two were silent for a few minutes as Jessica pulled a tissue from her pocket and handed it to Cam. When he had cleaned himself off, he mumbled, "I don't know what to say."

"Don't say anything. But watching you has made me so horny that I want you right now," Jessica said. "Is there a nice motel nearby?"

They drove to a small motel in town and Cam registered for them. He drove around back and used the key to open the door to room 203. It was a standard room, with a double bed, several chairs, a table and a long dresser. Jessica walked inside. "Close the door," she demanded, "then I want to see all of you. Take off your clothes."

Clumsily, Cam stripped off his slacks, shirt, and shorts.

"Now stand there while I look at you." Jessica walked around Cam's naked body, slapping his hands when he started to cover his limp penis. "Keep your hands at your sides," she said. She ran her hands over his shoulders and back, soft, with an extra layer of fat under the skin. She took a handful of his buttocks in each of her hands and dug her fingers into the soft flesh, pulling the cheeks slightly apart. She smiled as she felt him quiver. There were so many things she wanted to try, but one step at a time. She walked around and stood, facing him. Because he had climaxed only a half hour before, his cock was still soft.

"There are so many things I want you to do to pleasure me," she said. "But I need to be sure of one thing. If I do anything, or ask you to do anything that doesn't make you feel good, tell me. Say 'Please no,' and we'll stop. Promise me."

"I promise," Cam whispered.

"Unbutton my blouse." Slowly and awkwardly, Cam pushed each silver button on Jessica's gray silk blouse through its buttonhole. "Now unhook my bra." He worked at the center-front clasp until the fastening parted. "Do you want to see them? Touch them? Lick them?" God, she wanted him, but she was enjoying extending her pleasure by making both of them wait.

"Oh yes," Cam said, his eyes glazed.

"I like gentle fingers and soft lips," Jessica said as Cam parted the sides of her bra, exposing her breasts. Softly, reverently, he swirled the pads of his fingers over her skin. He traced the line between tanned skin and creamy white flesh.

Jessica cupped her right breast and held it up. "Suck."

His lips touched the tip of her nipple and shots of electricity stabbed through her body. She pulled back and dropped into a chair. She pointed to the floor and Cam knelt beside her chair. "Yes," she purred, "suck my tits."

Hungrily, Cam's mouth pleasured her breast, kissing, sucking, tasting. She wanted more, and suddenly realized she didn't have to wait until he decided what to do. She could ask for anything she wanted. "Pinch this one," she said, guiding his hand to her other breast. "Harder. Make me feel it."

"But I'll hurt you," Cam said.

"That's not your decision. You do as I ask."

"Oh yes," he sighed.

He pinched her nipple, driving heat through her. "Enough," she said, standing. "Undress me."

She stood, stepped out of her shoes and Cam quickly removed

her blouse, slacks, and underwear. When she stood in the middle of the motel room, gloriously naked, she watched Cam's hungry eyes as he looked at her. "Do you like what you see?"

"Yes," he groaned. "And I like what you're doing."

"That's good," she said. "Very good." They were both learning, she realized, each trying to find the ideal place for this fantasy to go. "Is there anything particular you want to add to this?"

"Yes," he said.

"Tell me."

"I want to be able to see it all," he said. The closet doors in the vanity area were mirrored and, slipping out of his submissive role for a moment, he opened first one then another. Soon he had a three-sided, floor-to-ceiling, mirrored area in which his naked body was reflected over and over. He pulled a chair over, repositioned it a few times, then nodded. "If it pleases you," he said softly.

"Oh it does," Jessica said, as she seated herself in the chair. She could see her cunt for the first time between her widely spread legs. Watching in the three mirrors, she slid her fingers through her springy hair, then pointed to the floor between her feet. Cam sat. "Very nice," she said. "We can both watch everything." As Cam stared at Jessica's wet, swollen pussy lips, she asked, "What do you see?"

"I see that your body likes what's happening."

"It does," Jessica purred. "It wants you to touch and watch as you do it."

Cam's fingers slid up the insides of her thighs, and Jessica saw them reflected over and over in the mirrors. She slid her hips forward and pushed Cam's head against one leg to improve her view. She guided Cam's fingers to just the right spots. "Rub here, very slowly. Yes. Faster now. Oh yes." She revelled in being able to tell Cam exactly what she liked.

"I want your mouth," she said, suddenly. "Lick just where your fingers have been. Lick with the flat of your tongue. Yes. Like that. Now suck my clit into your mouth and flick your tongue over it." She was soaring. She closed her eyes, then opened them so she could see Cam's moving head reflected in the three mirrors. Would she let him bring her off this way, with his mouth? Was that what he wanted? But this wasn't for him. It was for Jessica-Lynn. "Put two fingers inside me," she said. "Fuck me with your hand. Hard. Now."

He did and, only a moment later, Jessica came, her fists tangled in Cam's hair. "Don't stop," she yelled. "More." As her orgasm continued she felt Cam's fingers continue their rhythmic fucking while his mouth worked its magic. She spasmed for what felt like hours, then, as her orgasm ebbed, she told Cam to stop.

He laid his head against her belly and said, "I've never felt a woman climax like that," he said. "I could feel the sensation on my hand." He looked up at her and grinned. "It was truly remarkable."

"It certainly was," Jessica said. She looked down at Cam's cock, surprised that he wasn't erect.

Cam's laughter warmed her. "I got a great deal of joy from your orgasm," he said, looking at his limp penis, "but I'm not as quick to recover as I once was and I came less than an hour ago. I'm not ready to make love so soon again."

"I've learned a lot recently and the most important thing is that we *have* been making love. For hours."

"Yes," Cam said. "We have, haven't we."

They stretched out on the bed, pulled the quilt over themselves, talked and napped. Later, they touched and stroked each other, free now to share what gave each of them pleasure. When Cam's hard cock finally slid into Jessica's waiting body, it was a completion to an evening of loving.

Hours later, as Cam's car pulled into the Carltons' driveway, Cam said, "I hope we can see each other soon again."

"Me too. How's your schedule?"

They made plans for the following week and Cam promised to consider new ways that he would like to make love. "Think about something totally outrageous," Jessica suggested. "Then, if it turns me on, we can do it. If not, we'll think of something else."

Cam smiled and kissed her. "With you, this all seems so possible."

"It's all possible," Jessica said, climbing out of the car. "Everything's possible and most things are probable between us."

All day Friday, Jessica worked on an erotic story for Gary's party. She wrote, edited, printed, but wouldn't let anyone read it. When it was as good as she thought it could get, she printed it, without her name on it. "Did you write a story?" she asked Steph Saturday morning over coffee in the plant room.

"Brian and I coauthored one about an alien and a human. We only wrote a few paragraphs at a time. I think we fucked more yesterday than we have in ages."

"At least you had someone to work out your frustrations on."

"You can borrow Brian any time, you know."

"You say that, but it feels weird."

"Eventually, you and Brian will find the right time and the right place. If and when it feels right, you'll know it's fine with me."

"I guess," Jessica said, patting her friend's hand.

"So we each have a story for tonight," Steph said. "Do I get to read yours?"

"Not a chance. I've mentally chickened out several times already, and almost threw it away twice. But I've now decided that Gary can read it at the party tonight. Probably."

Steph laughed. "Brian and I agreed that we'd allow Gary to read ours too. But, even though it's fiction, it's so personal, somehow."

"Yeah. I know what you mean. What are you wearing?" Jessica asked.

The two women discussed the party, then, when Brian returned from a tennis game, the three friends spent the day anticipating the evening to come.

"And you must be Jessica," the tall, almost emaciated-looking man said as he took her hand. "I've heard a lot about you." His eyes held Jessica's.

She inhaled deeply. "And I've heard a lot about you, too." Gary had deeply set eyes and hard, angular features. He's almost homely, Jessica thought, fleetingly, enjoying the heat that his gaze engendered.

"Hello, Gary," Steph said from behind Jessica. "We're here too. Remember us?"

Gary's laugh was rich and deep. "I do remember you," he said, dropping Jessica's hand, grabbing Steph by the waist, lifting her up, then sliding her down the length of his body. He placed a deep kiss on her open mouth, then set her down. He reached for Brian's hand and clasped it warmly.

"Jessica," a voice from the living room called, "it's so nice to see you again."

Jessica remembered Marcy from Steph's party. "It's good to see you too," she said, walking into the enormous living room, comfortably decorated in shades of soft blue, toast, and ecru and filled with comfortable chairs and sofas. Plants softened the otherwise masculine aura and a heavy tweed carpet, overlaid with small patterned area rugs, covered the floor.

"Great news, guys," Marcy said to the three newcomers. "Steven James Albright, Junior weighed in at eight pounds fourteen ounces."

"Fantastic," Steph said. "When did Nan have the baby?"

"Late this afternoon," Marcy announced. "Steve is already saying how considerate his wife was. She woke him about six this morning and the baby was born at five. Eleven hours of labor with no lost sleep and no midnight rides to the hospital."

The room filled and, when everyone had a drink in hand, Marcy said, "To Steven James Albright, Junior." The dozen or so people touched glasses and drank. It was an interesting group. Besides Marcy and Chuck and Pete and Gloria whom she knew from Steph's party, there were three other couples, all between thirty-five and fifty. Jessica considered her previous notion of what swingers would look like. This slightly conservative group wasn't it.

The doorbell rang yet again. "Sorry we're late," a female voice said. "The baby-sitter was late."

Steph leaned over and whispered to Jessica. "Hank and Lara. You remember I told you about them." When Jessica didn't immediately connect, Steph said, "The Boggle game? My first outside activity?"

"Ah yes," Jessica said, looking at the balding man who entered the room, followed by his laughing wife. "I do remember." Steph quickly introduced Jessica to the newest arrivals.

Finally Eric arrived, looking particularly attractive in a black sport shirt and white slacks. Heat flowed through Jessica's body at the sight of the familiar grin. God, he's sexy, she thought. Eric, as if reading her mind, winked.

"Steph," Jessica said softly, "doesn't Gary have a date?"

"Sometimes he does and sometimes not," Steph explained. "Sometimes he does a threesome with another couple. And, of course, couples form, dissolve, and reform during one of these evenings. I can guarantee that I won't spend the evening with Brian, and Gary won't end up alone. It's whatever anyone wants."

Jessica gazed at Eric, who was talking with another couple, then wondered where Gary would end up. "Are there any people here who don't play?" she asked.

"Not tonight," Steph answered, looking around, "although Pete and Gloria won't swap, at least not yet. But they get really excited nonetheless, and take a bedroom and make love all night."

"Anyone who wrote stories," Gary said, "put them on the mantel within the next half hour, with or without a name. Then we'll have my dramatic reading. I've written a fantastic piece of pornography, by the way. Maybe I can even get it published."

"Modesty was never your strong suit, Gary, my love," Marcy said.

"How can you be modest when you're as terrific as I am?" Gary answered.

For the next half hour, the party was not unlike many that Jessica had attended with Rob. People talked about everything from politics to the weather. They ate crab puffs, shrimp in pastry, miniature bacon and spinach quiche, and lamb riblets. Eric made her close her eyes and fed her a roasted green chili stuffed with goat cheese. Some drank champagne, others a soft, Chilean merlot, and still others fruit and rum. A few of the guests drank soft drinks. Jessica slipped away from Eric for a moment, took her story from her purse, and put it on the mantel, with several others.

At about nine o'clock, Gary got everyone's attention. "Okay, reading time. Everyone cuddle up with someone, or some ones, and I'll turn out most of the lights."

People pulled pillows into the middle of the floor, others stretched out on sofas, or sat one atop another in chairs. Gary turned out most of the lights, leaving only a small spotlight shining on the chair in which he sat. Eric had pulled several pillows together and he and Jessica lay side by side, holding hands.

Gary cleared his throat. "Okay, I thought I'd read mine first, just to loosen things up." In a low-pitched, mellifluous voice, he began to read.

THE ALIENS

Louise lay in bed, unable to sleep. She kept thinking about the strange incident at the pool today. The couple who had come over and sat beside her as she dangled her legs in the water were two of the most attractive people that she had ever seen. They had asked her questions about herself that were so personal that she would not have answered them if asked by anyone else. But somehow, after talking with them for only a few minutes, she had felt completely comfortable with the intimacy of their questions. Although she had never met them before, she had felt their warmth, their caring, and their seemingly genuine interest in her. When they got up to leave, Louise had felt an almost overwhelming urge to go with them. Now, lying in bed, she was creating the most wonderful fantasies about them as she stroked herself beneath her nightgown.

As she slid her fingers between her legs, Louise became aware of a glow outside her bedroom window. As it grew brighter and brighter, she became frightened and jumped out of bed to see what was happening. Suddenly she was engulfed in a glowing light that rendered her powerless, unable to move. She felt hands pull her nightgown over her head and lift her into strong, muscular arms. Although she was still afraid, she also realized that the hands and arms that held her were gentle. She somehow felt certain that they would not hurt her and she felt most of the fear flow from her.

Louise opened her eyes to find herself lying on her back on a table in a brightly lit room with bare walls. Her wrists and ankles were bound to the corners of the table by a material that was both the softest she had ever felt and totally unyielding. Strangely, although she should have been uncomfortable, the table was the most restful thing she had ever been on. It molded itself perfectly to her body, firm, yet softer than down.

Suddenly Louise became aware of the couple from the pool, standing, looking down at her. They were wearing long robes of a transparent, shimmering material that seemed to flow over their bodies like a glowing liquid. It was also obvious that they wore nothing underneath.

"Where am I?" Louise asked.

"You wouldn't understand," the man replied, in a voice so warm and soothing that Louise found herself relaxing despite her fear and the strangeness of her surroundings.

"We're not going to hurt you," the woman said in a low, throaty voice. "I am called T'Mar and this is P'Lan. We're from a place that's very far away, but we have learned from long contact with the people of your planet that we're a lot like you. We have been sent here to study the ways our two races are the same and explore the ways we differ. Our particular field of study is sexuality."

"We have been observing your people's mating rituals," P'Lan said. "In many ways, it's similar to our ways of lovemaking. But we prefer small groups rather than pairs. And we have certain sexual abilities that your people don't seem to have. The experiment that we are about to do is designed to find out whether our abilities have sufficient stimulative effects to permit mating between your people and ours."

Louise realized that she was going to be the subject of a sexual experiment and she was helpless to do anything about it. But, she realized that she felt more excited than frightened.

"I'm going to touch your breast," T'Mar said. "You will feel a sensation, but it will not hurt. Just relax."

The woman slowly brought her hand toward Louise's body. Instinctively, Louise tried to move away, but she could not. The woman kept her hand open so that the palm of her hand touched Louise's nipple. Louise's body jolted against her restraints as a sensation instantly made it contract and turn hard. The sensation in her nipple was echoed by an instant feeling of wetness between her legs. As T'Mar placed her other palm on Louise's other nipple, then cupped both of her hands over Louise's breasts, Louise felt an incredible pleasure and heat spread through her. An electric tingling combined with an irresistible need overwhelmed her, and her body bucked and strained against the restraints. She could feel wetness flow between her legs.

T'Mar removed her hands from Louise's body and, as Louise relaxed, smiled down at her. "Now you know what the restraints are for," she said. "They're not to keep you from escaping. Just to prevent you from hurting yourself when we stimulate you."

Louise's head was spinning. All fear was now gone. All she wanted now was to be touched again by this wonderful creature.

Suddenly Louise realized that P'Lan had been watching her while she was being touched by T'Mar. He had seen her naked body writhe and had heard her moan with pleasure. Through his flowing robe, she could see that his erection was not unlike those of the men she had made love with in the past, although thicker and longer. She felt her face turn hot as he gazed into her eyes and smiled knowingly. His face said that he knew she ached to experience his touch. Without realizing what she was doing, Louise spread her knees slightly.

P'Lan tried to explain the wondrous sensations Louise had

just experienced. "In your world, there are creatures that use electric currents for defense or for capturing prey. On our world, our bodies are able to generate electric currents also, but we use it only for sexual stimulation—as part of our mating ritual." His eyes conveyed a loving warmth as he continued. "We are going to stimulate you in various ways. If you look around, you will see that you are surrounded by machines that will record your body's reactions to our probing. The only difficult part for you is that you will not be allowed to climax until we have completed our experiment. Now, we want you to just relax."

Relax? Louise's body tensed in anticipation of what she was going to feel. She watched the woman move toward the head of the table and the man toward her legs. Suddenly she felt a warm glow and soothing vibration as the woman began to stroke her temples and forehead. Just as she began to calm, she was jolted against the restraints as the electricity from P'Lan's fingers touched her inner thighs. The calming warmth of the hands on her head only intensified the sexual intensity of the burning pleasure as the man's fingers stroked the bare backs of her knees and the entire length of her naked inner thighs, stopping only when he reached the crease. She gave herself up to the pleasure and whimpered as she felt his hand move over her mound and caress her.

T'Mar bent forward and Louise could see her breasts through the shimmering robe. She slid her hands over Louise's breasts until her robe touched Louise's face. Suddenly Louise realized that the robe was not a solid material. It was warm and flowed across and around T'Mar and over Louise's face like water. As the robe flowed over her nose and mouth, Louise could feel the woman's nipple touching her mouth. The electricity sent a burning pleasure over her lips. Instinctively, she opened her mouth and began to suck the woman's pillow-soft flesh. She felt a warm, electrically charged fluid enter her mouth and felt the hot pleasure spread down her throat just as the man's fingers began to stroke the insides of her labia and her clitoris. Desperately she sucked the woman's tit and felt the electricity of the woman's hands caressing her body. She cried out as the man inserted fingers deep into her cunt and she helplessly strained against the restraints, begging T'Mar to let her come. "Just a little longer," the woman crooned. "It will be over soon."

Finally P'Lan looked at the woman and said, "I think we have almost all the data we need. We'll just do the anal stimulation study and then we can give her relief. But you had better hold her. The restraints may not be sufficient."

As Louise began to tremble, T'Mar came alongside the table and stretched out across Louise, belly against belly, breast against breast, leg against leg, pinning her entire body to the table. Louise felt bathed by the warm liquid flow of the woman's robe over her skin, and T'Mar gently spoke into Louise's ear. "Because of the intensity of the erotic stimulation, this part will be difficult to bear but we will soon be finished."

Louise's entire body tingled where the woman pressed against her, and the woman's nipples burned as they pressed against Louise's breasts. Suddenly she felt P'Lan's finger slide between her legs and under her until it touched her anus. With no hesitation, he plunged into her ass and the burning need that filled the entire lower part of her body made her shriek and press upward frantically against the woman who was holding her down. With the man's finger still in her ass, Louise felt the woman slide her hand down between Louise's legs and plunge her fingers into Louise's cunt. For a few seconds there was no electricity, just the sensation of both her ass and her cunt being filled. Then T'Mar crooned in her ear. "Are you ready, Louise? Do you want to come?"

"Please, please," was all Louise could whimper.

The woman looked at the man and in a low, gentle voice said, "Now."

Suddenly Louise shrieked and strained as the electric current from the invading fingers melded into a flame of molten heat and she felt the sensation of her throbbing clitoris spread to every limb, every vein of her body. She felt her cunt contract against T'Mar's fingers and her sphincter contract around P'Lan's hand as wave after wave of orgasm wrenched her body. Moments later she was enveloped in a warm glowing light. And then there was darkness.

Since that day Louise searches the sky every night. She loves to masturbate under the stars, pretending that she is being made love to by aliens. Most people think she's crazy. . . .

Eric's hand had been teasing Jessica's nipple while Gary read the story and now she was squirming, anxious to wrap her legs around his waist and drive his cock into her hungry cunt.

"I do love that story," Gary said. "It makes me so hot to read it." He looked around at the assemblage of hungry bodies. "Don't leave yet. I have other stories and no one's allowed to satisfy hungers with anything except strawberries until I'm done."

Jessica had a flash of Eric rubbing a strawberry on her hot, swollen tissues, then pushing it inside and sucking it out.

Gary's laugh was a deep, rich, highly erotic sound, and, as if reading her mind, said, "And you can't do that either. At least not until I'm done."

"You, dear sir," someone said, "make the Marquis de Sade look like a wimp."

Gary laughed again and Jessica wondered how that laugh would feel rumbling against her nipples as she held him. "Good," he said. "That's exactly what I had in mind." He picked up a second set of pages. "This one was written by Steph and Brian and, at first glance, it looks like another alien story."

Jessica looked across the room and saw Steph sitting on the floor with Marcy and Chuck, then found Brian stretched out near a woman named Angela.

Gary cleared his throat. "This one is called 'Assimilation.' "

"What have you got?" I asked, looking through the observation glass at the humanoid who had been brought in from sector seven. His back was facing the glass as he sat on the bench in the middle of the sterile room. I could see that he didn't look like any of the inhabitants we'd encountered from the planets in this part of the galaxy. All I had been told was that the alien had walked into sector seven almost one solar day ago and had come to our facility willingly. The report said he seemed to be waiting ever since. Waiting for what? We had no idea. I knew that the research team had been monitoring him since his arrival here, trying to determine his level of intelligence.

"Hi Libby," said Dirk, our chief scientist. "We're not sure what he is. He appears to be a humanoid, but he hasn't responded to any language we've used. He's six feet tall, weighs about two-hundred pounds, and by his build, we're assuming most of that is muscle. His skin looks leathery and he seems to have no hair anywhere on his body." He continued reciting the notes off his clipboard as we walked around the corner to view him from another angle.

"We've been referring to him as male," Dirk continued, "but as you will notice, he has more than one phallus." From the angle at which I was observing, I couldn't make out what Dirk was referring to.

"Has anyone gone in?" I asked, looking at the alien's face from the side. It was smooth and round, giving him an almost human look, except that he had no eyebrows and his eyes were widely spaced, giving him a curious expression.

"No," said Dirk. "We were waiting for you." I was in charge of the research lab and authorized all first-contacts with aliens.

"I'm going in," I said, taking off my clothes.

"Are you crazy?" yelled Dirk. "He could snap you in half in a minute."

"You can use the force shield if I run into problems," I said, pulling off my jumpsuit.

"Do you really need to take off your clothes?" he asked as I handed him my jumpsuit. "It's a little disconcerting."

"Thanks, Dirk, but you know how this works. Tell them I'm going in." I was used to being naked in front of the research team. Throughout our space travels we had found that most civilizations did not wear any type of clothing and it had become a standard practice to take off ours when we interacted with any non-humans.

Dirk looked at me as he pressed a button on the neck of his jumpsuit and spoke into the tiny mike. "Libby is going in to observe. Be ready with the force shield in case she has problems."

I opened the door slowly and the alien turned to look at me. His eyes were peaceful and I saw no tension in his body. I let the door close behind me and entered the room. He was only a few feet away from me when I stopped.

"Hello," I said, smiling at him. "Can you understand me?"

He stood up slowly and turned to face me. My eyes immediately dropped to his groin and I stared at the unique combination of sexual organs. He did not appear to have any testicles, but instead had one penis in the front and a longer one hanging behind it.

He held his hands palm outward in front of him, extending them to me. Looking down at my hands, he nodded for me to raise them. He was only a foot away from me and I swallowed hard as I held my hands toward his.

"Be careful Libby," I heard Dirk say through the intercom.

Our fingers touched and I could suddenly hear his thoughts and feel his emotions. "I am many people, called by many names," he said with his mind. I looked in his eyes, and my thoughts told him my name was Libby.

"Where am I?" he asked telepathically. I told him our galactic location. He explained that he had found our outpost after his ship had been hit by a meteorite. He was a scientist, exploring the galaxy, studying and learning. Then, ever so slowly, his eyes lowered to my breasts and I could feel his sexual need increase.

"Are you okay Libby?" I heard Dirk ask.

"Yes," I said back. "He's communicating telepathically through his fingers."

I could hear his thoughts as he asked me if he could touch my body. I nodded yes and he dropped one of his hands and slid it down my chest until it stopped at my breast. The nipples I had noticed on his chest slowly inverted and started making a sucking sound as he moved his hand from one of my nipples to the other.

I looked down and saw the front penis had extended itself. His hand slid down my stomach and touched the hair around my pubis. When his finger slid between my legs and touched my clit, then rubbed my soaked vagina, I shuddered.

He brought his hand back up and touched his wet fingers against mine. The intensity of his sexual hunger flashed through my body as he stared into my eyes. I felt myself being pulled toward him and I took two steps nearer.

"Are you sure you're all right?" said Dirk over the speaker.

"Yes," I said, keeping my eyes on the alien.

We were standing face to face and he slowly lowered our hands to our sides, keeping our fingers touching at all times. He leaned toward me and, as my nipples touched his inverted breasts, like tiny mouths, they drew them in. I couldn't believe the sensation of the leatherlike suckers on my breasts.

Over the sound of my pounding heart I heard him tell me not to be afraid. He wanted to join with me. The magnetic pull was so strong that I was soon spreading my legs as he pushed his knobby penis inside. I let out a gasp as I felt it slide deeper, moving in and out even though he was standing completely still. Little knobs around the penis-shaft pulsated against my vaginal walls as it pushed in and out. Soon tiny lips appeared above his penis, locked onto my clitoris, and started sucking.

"Libby!" I heard Dirk yell. "What's happening?"

"Oh God!" I said, trying to keep my knees from buckling. "I'm getting fantastically fucked!"

"Do you want us to stop him?" yelled Dirk.

"No!" I yelled. The sensations were magnificent and I most certainly didn't want them to stop. I felt something touch my buttocks and I suddenly realized that his secondary penis had extended itself up to my anus. He heard the panic in my mind and somehow made me relax with his thoughts. His rear penis felt wet and oily as it touched my rear opening, then slowly inserted itself into the hole. It pulsed against the thin wall in unison with the one in my vagina. I wasn't sure how much longer I could stand there. My knees were buckling.

His eyes were intense as he stared at me, but no other visible signs indicated what was going on. His breathing was normal even though I was visibly panting. I tried to move my hands away, but he gripped them and held them tightly against my buttocks, holding me still against him.

His penises were moving in and out seemingly with a life of their own and the lips around my nipples and my clitoris were increasing the pressure of their sucking. I could feel an orgasm building inside of me but I heard him tell me to wait. Then, as he pressed his forehead against mine, a jolt of pure pleasure shot through me that set off a chain reaction. I came. I tried to scream but no noise escaped my lips. I suddenly understood that, despite his physical immobility, he was sharing my orgasm as we stood frozen against each other.

The climax pulsing through my body wouldn't stop and I wondered how long it could go on. "Much longer," I felt him say. Instead of deflating, his penises became harder and pumped in and out faster than before. The sucking became more intense against my clitoris and my nipples, and I felt my legs give out. His arms held me securely as he braced my body against his. Our foreheads still touching, wave after wave of orgasm continued until I thought I could take no more.

"It's time," I heard him say in my mind,

"I don't know what you mean."

"It's time to become one," he said.

"One?"

"Follow the orgasm." His pumping became harder, faster, increasing the sensations. I could hear Dirk yelling at me, but now I couldn't respond. I was drawn further and further back into his mind with each wave of the orgasm until I saw myself standing next to him. I was somehow inside his mind. It was warm, soft, and unbelievably peaceful as I flowed within him. I watched my body go limp in his arms.

Dirk and two others came running in and pulled the body that had been me out of the room. Then Dirk ran back in, his face filled with rage, and pointed a laser gun at me.

"Wait Dirk!" I said holding up my hand. "It's me." I could hear my voice coming out of the alien's body.

"What do you mean it's you, Libby? What happened?"

"We joined, Dirk," I said. "I'm now a part of him." I now understood everything, and it was wonderful. I watched Dirk drop to the bench and stare at the alien, at me, at the one that was us.

"This is why he travels the galaxy. Every time he mates," I explained, "he incorporates the mind and spirit of the person into him, me, us. I have become part of some complex entity. In addition, when he joins, he takes a body part he needs to grow. He chose my voice because he didn't have one." I/we reached over to pat Dirk's hand and he jumped up off of the bench and bolted toward the door.

"I'm sorry Libby," Dirk said. "I have to consider this for a while."

"I understand, Dirk," I said. "I need some time to adjust as well. But don't be angry or afraid. It's the most miraculous feeling I've ever had."

Chapter
9

A fter Gary had read several more stories, he said, "I have one more." Jessica knew it had to be hers. "It's called 'Educating Paul' and," Gary grinned, "it doesn't seem to have anything to do with aliens." Feeling the now-familiar tightness she placed her hand on Eric's thigh as Gary began to read.

It was a bright sunny day and, since Paul's parents were away for the weekend, he was all alone in the house. Although he was a reasonably attractive seventeen-year-old boy, he was painfully shy. Girls thought that he was snobby and aloof and generally avoided him. On his rare dates, he was clumsy in his sexual approaches, and usually did not get very far. He was still a virgin.

As he usually did when his parents were away, Paul had taken advantage of the rare period of privacy by pulling out his collection of erotic pictures and masturbating. It was a treat to be able to spread out his collection of magazines and pictures without having to hide or worry about being *caught*. As he gazed at the pictures of beautiful naked women, he tried to imagine what it must feel like to be touched by one, to feel a girl's tongue against his tongue, to suck a girl's nipple and to feel his hard cock slide deep into her cunt. His cock was rock-hard as he lost himself in his fantasies.

Suddenly he heard the doorbell. Shit, he muttered to himself. He remembered his mother telling him, "I've asked the Jacksons next door to check on you while we're gone." But he had seen the Jacksons drive away about an hour ago. When the bell chimed again he decided to ignore it. Whoever it was would think no one was home and leave him alone. Then he heard the front door open and a woman's voice call, "I know you're home Paul. I saw you through the window."

Paul immediately recognized the voice. It belonged to Terry, the Jacksons' twenty-one-year-old daughter. She had been away at college all year, but she must have come home for the summer. Terry had flaming red hair, long legs, and was gorgeous. Although she was the subject of many of Paul's fantasies, Paul had never had the nerve to talk to her.

"My folks asked me to check up on you," Terry called, as Paul heard her close the front door behind her.

Quickly, Paul shoved his magazines and pictures under his pillow and started to throw on his clothing. Paul wondered what she had seen through the window.

"I'll bet you're in your room," Terry called.

Paul met her at the doorway to his room. They faced each other, Paul's clothing in disarray, his face flushed and Terry dressed in a sundress that displayed the tops of her ample breasts. Her skirt came to mid-thigh and her legs were bare.

Terry smiled at him and looked at the rumpled bed. "Well, it's a good thing I came up to check on you," she said, teasingly. "What have you been doing?"

"Nothing," Paul mumbled, not knowing what to say.

Terry brushed past him, her breasts grazing his arm, and walked over to the bed. Paul's arm felt as though 1000 volts of electricity had gone through it at the point of contact. Sunlight streamed through the window onto Paul's pillow and the corner of the magazine that protruded from beneath it.

Terry slowly reached over and pulled out first one magazine, then the others, along with pictures that Paul had hidden under the pillow. She sat down on the bed and smiled as she slowly leafed through everything. Paul stood and watched, unable to move. "I guess now I *know* what you've been doing," she said with a grin. "But looking at pictures isn't nearly as exciting as looking at the real thing. Come over here," she ordered.

Now trembling as much from excitement as embarrassment, Paul walked over to Terry and looked down at her as she sat on the edge of the bed. Her skirt had ridden up almost to her hips and the sight of her bare thighs and her nipples poking against the thin material of her sundress was making Paul's cock so hard that it was forming an obvious lump in the front of his pants.

"Come closer, Paul," Terry said, her voice low and throaty as she looked directly at the crotch of Paul's pants. She spread her knees apart. "I want you standing right between my knees."

As Paul stood between her legs, Terry calmly and efficiently undid his belt and pulled down his pants and underpants. Then she carefully began to fondle his swollen cock and balls. "What a big cock," she said, stroking the length of its shaft with her right hand while cupping and gently squeezing his balls with her left. Looking up at him she said, "I saw you looking at my tits. I'll bet you're thinking about what it would be like to suck them. Aren't you?"

Paul felt his face get red and the trembling of his body increase.

"And, I saw you looking at my legs. I'll bet you want to touch them. Have you ever put your hand between a girl's legs, Paul?"

Paul's throat was so tight he could not reply.

"Well, I think it's time you learned a few things. Such a big, beautiful erection shouldn't be wasted." Her fingers danced over his skin from his anus, across his balls to the tip of his cock. Suddenly she removed her hand. "It will be all over too quickly if I keep doing this," she said. Terry reached out and took Paul's right hand and gently pressed it against the front of her dress.

The feel of her nipple and the softness of her breast burned the palm of Paul's hand. He found himself gently squeezing her breast.

"That's very good," Terry said. She removed his hand and

slipped the straps of the sundress over her shoulders, lowered the top, then put Paul's hand back on her naked breast. She guided his hands as they roamed across the softness of her bare tits.

"I want you to kneel between my legs now," Terry said. As Paul kneeled, Terry cupped her right hand under her right breast and sliding her left hand around the back of Paul's neck, pulled his face toward her tit. "It will taste so good, Paul," she crooned as Paul opened his mouth.

As Paul sucked, he felt Terry stroke the back of his neck. Her breathing quickened and he heard small sighs and felt her nipple harden in his mouth as he sucked and licked. After a little while, Terry pulled his head away and gave him the other tit. As he sucked and gently bit her nipples, Paul began to stroke Terry's legs and the inside of her thighs. He felt her spread her legs wider, inviting him to explore.

"Don't be afraid, Paul," she encouraged. "It feels wonderful there." As he sucked her tits, she gently took his right hand and slowly guided it deeper into the cleft between her legs. She wore nothing under the dress and soon Paul felt the hot, soft wetness of her mound. He heard Terry sigh as she guided his middle finger along the center of the heat and moisture. He felt the lips separate and then his finger was stroking the slippery insides of her labia.

Terry held Paul's head tightly against her breast, and demanded, "Suck it good, baby, suck it good." She was groaning and her hips were pressing against his hand. With her hand, she guided his finger to her swollen clitoris. "Can you feel that?" she asked him.

"Yes," Paul replied breathlessly, releasing her nipple from his mouth.

"Well, I want you to lick right there. Flick your tongue across it."

Paul hesitated.

"Now do it like a good boy," she ordered, pressing Paul's head down toward her lap, and spreading her legs even wider. "That's such a good boy."

Paul inhaled Terry's wonderful musky aroma as he buried his head between her legs. She tasted delicious when he ran his tongue along the length of her crack then began to suck on the knob of her clitoris. As he licked Terry's cunt and clitoris, she whimpered with pleasure. His balls and cock were aching for Terry to touch him again and he knew that now the slightest touch would make him come. He had never been so excited.

Suddenly Terry's naked thighs clamped hard against the sides of Paul's head and her hand pressed his face hard against her cunt. She cried out as her hips began to press rhythmically against his mouth. After a short while she relaxed, then placed her hands on the side of Paul's face and guided his face away from her.

"Did I do something wrong?" he asked, puzzled, looking at Terry sitting on the edge of the bed, bare-breasted with her dress bunched up around her hips.

"Definitely not," she smiled. "You gave me a wonderful orgasm. And now it's time for your reward. Take off the rest of your clothes."

Paul stepped out of his pants and underpants, still bunched around his ankles, then pulled off his shirt while Terry pulled off her dress and, completely naked, stretched out on the bed with her legs spread. She held out her arms. "Come here, baby. It's time to fuck me."

As Paul positioned himself between her legs, Terry gave his cock one long stroke, then guided it to her pussy. For the first time, Paul felt his cock slide deep into the ripeness of a woman's cunt. Looking down at her face, he saw her smile as he slowly withdrew then again pressed his cock into her until his naked hips were grinding against hers. Suddenly he was out of control. He pounded his cock as far into her as he could, over and over, until, with a shriek, clutching her naked body, he felt himself spurt deep inside her.

Terry and Paul spent a lot of time together that summer. Sometimes Terry would be the *teacher* but, since Paul learned quickly, sometimes, he would do the *teaching* and Terry would pretend to be a virgin. Paul was sad the day Terry returned to college, but, over the years, he found many other girls he could teach and be taught by.

"And that, ladies and gentlemen," Gary said, "is the last of our wonderful stories. There are drinks and food for any who want them, and you know your way around the house."

"Good stories."

"That last one was your story, wasn't it?" Eric asked softly, his mouth close to Jessica's ear.

"How did you know?"

"I could tell by the tenseness of your hand on my thigh and generally in your body." His hot breath on her neck made her quiver. "Which person were you when you wrote it," Eric continued, "the student or the teacher?"

"Sometimes I was one, sometimes the other. I was feeling what each of them felt at the time."

"And right now, which are you? Or are you something else entirely?"

Jessica propped her chin on her palm. She was excited and curious about all the things she had yet to experience. "Actually, I'm open for almost anything. The more I read and the more I experience, the more interested I become. There were a lot of things in the stories that Gary read that I've never done."

"That's what I had hoped you'd say." Eric walked over to Gary, whispered something in his ear, then returned. "Gary has a special room downstairs. I'd like to show it to you."

"Special?"

"He and I designed it when we redid the house. It's full of toys and equipment to play with." Eric took a deep breath. "I've got another question. How do you feel about Gary?"

"He's very nice, why?"

"Look at him," Eric said, directing her gaze to the tall, angular man still draped over his chair. "Think about his hands on you, my mouth sucking you while he does enticing things to your body. Does that sound exciting?"

Jessica looked at Gary, who was talking to another couple. She watched his long hands move as he talked and thought about them on her skin. She thought about two men making love to her at once and her knees shook and her hands trembled. She felt herself swell and moisten. "Yes," she said hoarsely.

"I'd like to invite Gary to join us. Would that be all right?"

"Yes," she sighed. "Is it all right with you?"

"Gary and I go way back and we, shall we say, understand each other. I'd like to share your pleasure with him."

Jessica nodded and watched as Eric approached Gary again. As they spoke, Gary turned to look at Jessica and his gaze travelled all over Jessica's body. A smile spread over his face, then he winked. Jessica couldn't help but return his grin. She trusted Eric completely and, without having exchanged more than a few sentences with him, she found she trusted Gary as well.

Gary mouthed 'Are you sure?' and Jessica nodded. Gary winked again, then said something to Eric, who returned to her.

"Gary will be along in a little while. He has a few host duties to attend to. Let me show you the downstairs."

Shaking with excitement, Jessica followed Eric down a flight of carpeted stairs into a large entertainment room. There were both a pool table and a ping pong table, several pinball machines, two television sets, and an octagonal card table with eight chairs. In addition, there were several comfortable seating areas and a fully stocked bar. Surprisingly, the room was empty.

Answering her question before she asked it, Eric said, "Most of the guests prefer the comfort of the bedrooms upstairs. The room I told you about is used only on special occasions, or with special people."

"Oh," was all Jessica could say.

They crossed the large open room and Eric used a key to unlock a door, almost totally hidden by cleverly designed panelling. "Remember that if anything makes you uncomfortable you have to say so." Eric opened the door and flipped on the lights.

Jessica stared. Two opposing walls were upholstered in white leather and the other two walls and the ceiling were mirrored.

Eric turned the dimmer switch so the recessed lights gave the room a soft glow. In the center of the room were several benches of differing heights and shapes and a few chairs. The floor was covered with a thick white carpet. Eric crossed the room and pulled a small handle in one of the leather walls. A closet door opened. "Would you like to pick something to wear?" he asked her.

Jessica looked into the closet. On one side hung stretch-lace cat suits, teddies, stockings, garterbelts, and bras in every color. On the other were leather outfits, collars, masks, hoods and, on the back of one door, whips and paddles of every description. Jessica was awed.

"You aren't into the whip stuff, are you?"

Jessica looked saddened. She momentarily thought about saying what she thought Eric wanted to hear, but then remembered her promise. "I don't think so. Are you?"

"When the moment is right I enjoy giving pain. But only when it's pleasure for my partner."

Jessica swallowed. "I don't know."

"Then the answer is no. It must be pleasure for you yourself, not pleasure because it excites me."

Jessica smiled weakly. "I know. But if something gives you. . . ."

"It won't please me unless you enjoy it. Enough said. Now, pick something fun to wear. And think about who you want to be for a few hours. Do you want to be the one in control?"

Eric turned his back and Jessica rifled through the clothes. She selected a navy-blue teddy with matching stockings. As she pulled off her clothes she thought about what she wanted for the evening. "Shouldn't this be a mutual decision?"

"It will be. I need only one thing from you and that's who do you want to be?"

As Jessica pulled the left stocking on, she said, "I don't know."

"Okay. Let's do this. Let's pretend it's one hour from now. Tell me about how you feel. Are you excited?"

Jessica pulled on the second stocking, sliding her fingers up her leg, feeling the springy nylon hugging her legs. Still having a difficult time sorting out her feelings, she said, "Oh yes."

"Are you watching me as I try to get free of my bonds, or are you tightly bound?"

Almost unable to pull on the teddy, she took a deep breath and said, "I'm bound." She adjusted her clothes, stepped into her shoes and walked up behind Eric's back. She rested her head against his shoulder and said what was in her mind. "I want to be crying for help, knowing no one will help me."

Eric turned and took her in his arms. He pressed his pelvis against her and Jessica could feel his excitement. "Can you feel what that idea does to me?"

Jessica giggled. "It's hard to miss."

"Okay. We need safe words. Rather than 'cease and desist' which I'm always afraid someone will forget, let's use 'red' and 'yellow.' Red if you want me to stop *for any reason*. I mean any reason. Yellow for 'I need a moment to catch my breath,' or 'My foot's asleep.' Is that okay?"

"'Red' and 'yellow'. I think I can remember that. Are we really going to do this?" Jessica was incredibly excited.

Eric kissed her deeply. "Oh yes. We certainly are." He stepped back. "Mmmm. I love you in that outfit." He ruffled her hair, which fell loosely at her shoulders. "Now," he said, "we have to talk about the rest of the evening. First, do you trust me?"

"Absolutely."

"Let me tell you about Gary. He's a dominant. That means that he enjoys being in complete control of his sexual experiences. He likes to give the orders and have them obeyed without question. Do you think you could enjoy letting someone else control everything?"

Jessica thought about the story that Steph had told her about being tied to the bed and having Brian 'have his way with her.' "I think I could really get into that. I've sorted a lot out."

"Good. Tell me."

"Well," Jessica said, trying to put her feelings into words, "I've fantasized about being in complete control and it makes me a bit uncomfortable. It bothers me that I might not be giving my partner complete pleasure. I don't much like that responsibility. When I tried it, it was satisfying, but. . . ."

"And giving up complete control? Does that excite you?"

"The idea does, but I don't know about in reality."

Eric wrapped his arms around Jessica's waist and pulled her toward him. He slid his fingers into her hair, cradled her head, and pressed his lips against hers. After a long, hot kiss, he said, "I love your honesty. I would have worried if you had said anything else. Do you remember what I told you about the words 'red' and 'yellow?' "

"Yes."

"And do I have your promise that you'll speak up if anything disturbs you. Anything at all?"

"Yes." Jessica shivered. She assumed that Gary was going to join them, somehow giving orders about what they were going to do, all three of them. God, she was excited at the prospect. "And Gary's going to join us?"

Eric's smile was warm and caring. "Yes. And thanks. I've been looking forward to this ever since we first got together. I'm going to tell him that we're waiting. Would you like something to eat? Some wine, maybe?"

Jessica took a deep breath. "A glass of wine would be nice."

"I'll only be a minute."

While Eric was gone, Jessica prowled the room. There seemed to be several doors of varying sizes concealed in the leather paneling. She touched one of the three benches, and found the white leather covering to be butter-soft and supple, with lots of foam padding beneath.

Every time she looked up, it was almost impossible not to look at herself, reflected on both walls, then rereflected again and again. She ran her fingers through her hair, fluffing it out, giving it a wild, almost animal appearance. When the door behind her opened, she jumped. Eric walked back into the room, a drink in each hand. Jessica took a glass from Eric and took several swallows. She heard the door open again and turned.

"Jessica," Gary said, looking at the teddy and stockings she wore, "you look enchanting."

Jessica stared. Gary's angular, slightly mussed appearance had been radically altered. He now wore a pair of skin-tight, black leather pants that disappeared into a pair of thigh-high, black leather boots. His slender upper body was covered by a matching black leather vest, and his hands were covered with leather gauntlets. All he needed, Jessica thought, was a sword and a scarf around his head and he would be the stereotypical pirate. Ichabod Crane had been replaced by Jean LaFitte.

"Eric says that he's told you about my sexual preferences."

"He has."

"And you're willing to be mine for the rest of the evening. With or without Eric?"

Jessica looked at Eric, whose smile reassured her. "Yes," she said.

"Wonderful. Eric has told you the safe words. Now the rest of the rules. First, you will do whatever I ask without question. If what I ask, or what I do, makes you uncomfortable you will use a safe word. If I can be sure of that, I can do anything I want."

"I understand," Jessica whispered.

"I like to be addressed as 'sir' at all times."

Jessica looked at Gary's boots and said, "Yes, sir,"

Gary grabbed a handful of Jessica's red hair and used it to pull her head backwards. He captured her mouth, driving his tongue into the dark, moist depth, tasting, probing, inflaming. He let her go and stood up while Jessica caught her breath.

"Eric," Gary said, "she's magnificent. We shall have a delightful evening. Now, fix her clothes."

"Yes, sir," Eric said. He went to the closet and got a pair of scissors from a drawer. He cut the cups from the teddy, just above the underwires, and then cut across the crotch both front and back, and removed the small panel of fabric. "Gloves, sir?" Eric asked.

"Yes," Gary said.

Jessica watched as Eric opened another drawer and pulled out a pair of long, fingerless gloves. He handed them to Jessica. As she pulled them on, she noticed one side of a zipper ran up the inside of each. When she had the gloves on, Eric pulled her arm behind her and somehow zipped the two gloves together. Now Jessica's arms were imprisoned, held behind her, forcing her breasts forward. She felt a moment of panic.

"Test them, Jessica," Gary said. "Try to pull your arms out. Get used to the fact that you belong to me now. Be afraid of the helpless feeling, then let it go. Release yourself to me and to all the new pleasures you will feel this evening." He walked up to her, cupped her chin and looked into her eyes. "If you can't let go of the fear, tell me and we'll stop now." He continued to gaze into her eyes. "You will feel no more fear, just intense, tightening pleasure."

Jessica felt the fear ebb. She wasn't afraid. As the panic faded, it was replaced with a flood of heat through her body. She looked into Gary's eyes and smiled. "No fear at all," she whispered.

"Oh God, Eric," Gary said, "she's perfect. Eric tells me you're not turned on by pain."

"I don't think so, but I've never thought about pain as pleasure before."

Gary took one of Jessica's nipples between his thumb and index finger and twisted, hard.

Jessica gasped.

"Good or bad?" Gary asked as he released the pressure.

Jessica looked down at the hard, deep brown point that extended from her breast. The pain had been erotic and had made her very wet.

Gary pulled off one of his gauntlets and slid one finger between her legs. He laughed when she trembled at his touch. "You're soaking, Jessica. I may try a little light pain and I think you'll enjoy it. If you don't, you know I'll stop any time."

Jessica smiled as her trust in the two men increased. She could completely let go. It was a level of freedom different from any she had experienced before.

"Eric, release her hands for a moment," Gary said, and Eric unzipped the glove-connection.

"Offer your tits to me, Jessica," Gary said.

Jessica slid her hands up the sides of the satiny fabric of the teddy until she cupped one breast in each hand. "It's Jessica-Lynn, sir," she said.

"JessicaLynn it is. And what a tasty morsel you are." He leaned over and drew her erect nipple into his mouth. He motioned to Eric who suckled at her other breast.

The intensity of the sensations was almost too much for Jessica-Lynn. "Oh my God," she whispered.

When the two men stood up, Gary said, "You spoke without my permission, JessicaLynn. I understand that this is all new to you, but independent actions are not allowed."

JessicaLynn looked at the floor. It was hard not to smile, but in her most serious voice, she said, "I'm sorry sir."

Gary took one nipple in each hand and twisted. "I'm sure you are.

The feeling that started in her nipples and stabbed through her belly wasn't pain. It was molten fire, irresistible and un-quenchable.

"Eric," Gary said, "refasten her arms." Eric did. "And let's begin with the chair."

Eric reattached the gloves behind her back, then opened a panel and pressed a button. A strange-looking chair attached to a sliding platform glided into the room. "Sit down, my dear," Gary said.

The chair had wide, leather-covered arms and legs and virtu-ally no seat. There was a ledge around the border of the seat-space and, when JessicaLynn sat on it, it supported her weight but left her cunt exposed. It was an excitingly vulnerable posi-tion. Quickly Eric attached her lower legs and her thighs just above the knee to the chair with wide elastic bands. Then, with her arms behind her still encased in the gloves she felt Eric pull a wide elastic band from behind the chair around her ribs and fasten it in the front with velcro. It encased most of her upper body, but left her breasts exposed and available.

"My god, you're a succulent piece," Gary said. "What size would you estimate, Eric?" Gary asked.

What size for what?

"The queen or the rook, I'd guess," Eric said, handing a large box to his friend.

Gary opened the case and showed the contents to JessicaLynn. "I bought this on a trip overseas a few years ago. These are hand-carved phalluses. Notice that there are eight smaller ones, then two of each of three larger sizes, one each of the large and the largest, here." He pointed and JessicaLynn suddenly smiled. "You've guessed," Gary continued. "It's a chess set made up of dildos."

"Amazing," JessicaLynn said, then added, "I'm sorry for speaking, sir."

"You do show the proper respect, and I like that so I'll excuse it one last time." He lifted one of the larger phalluses and showed JessicaLynn a notch around the base. From a drawer in the base of the box, he withdrew a holder with a large ring attached then fitted the phallus into the holder. The holder created a small flange around the base of the phallus, with a ring attached. "You see? Isn't this clever? This is the rook." He held it in front of her face. "Now I want your mouth to experience what your delicious little pussy will feel in a few minutes. Open."

JessicaLynn opened her mouth and sucked the cool smooth wooden cock into her mouth. Gary moved it in a fucking motion as she sucked. As she started to close her eyes, Gary said, "You will look at me at all times. You may look me in the eye or you may watch in the ceiling."

Jessica's gaze strayed to the ceiling. She saw herself, bound, half naked, as Gary fucked her mouth with the dark dildo. She saw Eric stroking Gary's shoulder with one hand and her breast with the other.

Gary looked up. "Oh yes. That's quite a sight, isn't it." He held Jessica's head and forced her eyes to lock with his. "But, when you're being fucked by me or by Eric, I want you to look into my eyes."

JessicaLynn looked deeply into Gary's eyes and saw his excitement. Out of the corner of her eye she could also see Eric, standing, fully clothed, at Gary's side, obviously enjoying the tableau as Gary pistoned the dildo into and out of her mouth.

"Yes, that's fine," Gary said, pulling the large phallus from Jessica-Lynn's mouth. He tipped the chair back slightly on its rear legs and, to her surprise, it remained at that rakish angle, her head resting against its raised back. "Yes, this chair does some wonderful things. I had it built to my specifications." He caressed Jessica-Lynn's wet pussy, then slipped the large dildo into her.

She was full. She arched her back, trying to pull the smooth, cool wooden dildo farther into her body. She squeezed her vaginal muscles, hugging the penis inside of her.

"Too small," Gary said, removing the dildo from her body.

She felt bereft and yearned to be filled again as Gary removed the queen from the phallic chess set. He connected the holder, then handed it to Eric. "You do the honors," he said.

Eric slowly inserted the larger dildo into JessicaLynn's body, stretching her almost to the point of pain, but not quite. She groaned and it took a tap under her chin from Eric to remind her to look Gary in the eyes.

Gary pulled a slender strap from the elastic cincher at the small of JessicaLynn's back, ran the end through the ring on the end of the dildo-holder, then fastened it to the elastic in the front. The large wooden phallus was now imprisoned deep in her body, filling her, stretching her, but unmoving.

JessicaLynn didn't want the dildo to remain quietly in her body. She wanted it moving, fucking her. She moved her hips, trying to move the dildo, trying to satisfy the growing craving.

"No, my dear," Gary said, "that won't help. That's part of the fun of this. Like that woman in my story, you will climb higher and higher and get no satisfaction until I decide it's time." He smiled and stroked her thigh. "Oh I love to see a woman's plea-sure pushed to its limits." He turned to Eric. "Strip," he said. "Then give yourself to me and don't move."

JessicaLynn watched as Eric quickly removed his clothes. His erection stuck straight out from his body like the branch of a great tree. Gary cradled Eric's cock in his hands, then ran his fin-gers up and down the length of it. Despite Gary's order for her to watch only his eyes, JessicaLynn stared at the soft look of plea-sure on Eric's face, then at his huge erection. She wanted that cock for herself, to hold and stroke it. She was envious of Gary's freedom to use his hands to give pleasure.

Gary looked at her. "You want this, don't you?"

"Yes, sir."

She watched Eric's head fall back, his arms hanging limply at his sides. "I can deny you your pleasure," Gary said to her. "I can give him satisfaction this way." He caressed and petted Eric's cock. "But you've been so good, I'll let you. Suck him."

Quickly, Gary tipped the chair farther back until JessicaLynn's mouth was level with Eric's cock. "Eric, don't move your hands." Eric moved so his cock brushed JessicaLynn's lips. Gary held it and stroked her mouth, cheeks, and chin with the wet tip. "Open." JessicaLynn opened her mouth and Gary pushed Eric's cock inside.

She felt so complete. With Gary's hand on the back of her head, JessicaLynn caressed Eric's cock with her tongue. She trapped it between her tongue and the roof of her mouth and moved her head slightly so it rubbed the rough surfaces. She couldn't get enough. When she again started to close her eyes to savor the sensations, Gary tapped her cheek and she gazed into his eyes as Eric, unable to hold back any longer, erupted, groan-ing and ejecting semen deep into her mouth.

As Eric continued to pump his hips against JessicaLynn's mouth, Gary tapped on the end of the dildo, causing heat to rip-ple through her body. When he reached under the slender strap and touched her puckered anus, JessicaLynn almost came. But she knew that Gary wouldn't let her. Not yet.

When Eric's cock was finally small and soft, he withdrew. Gary filled a bowl with warm water and used a soft cloth to wash his friend's body as JessicaLynn watched. When everyone was calmed, Gary said, "I think we need the pawn, too."

JessicaLynn had no doubt what he had in mind. She was frightened for a moment as she stared into Gary's eyes. She took a deep breath, then let it out slowly. It was all right.

"Good," Gary said, knowing what she had been thinking. He opened the chess box again and pulled out one of the smallest dildos and fit it into another holder. With deliberate slowness he took out a jar of lubricant and slathered it over the dark wood. "You know where this is going, don't you, JessicaLynn?"

JessicaLynn swallowed, then said, "Yes sir."

"Have you ever had your lovely ass fucked before?"

"No sir."

Gary grinned. "Wonderful. That's an added pleasure for me." Gary unfastened the crotch-strap and wiggled the end of the dildo, still buried deep in her cunt. He said, "Eric, hold this and move it just a bit. I want her right at the edge."

Eric held the ring on the end of the dildo and rotated it slowly in JessicaLynn's pussy. "Ohhh," she moaned.

"Let's let her come when I do this." Eric nodded. "That way she'll always associate having her ass fucked with a good, hard climax." Gary rubbed the slippery dildo against her anus, then slowly pushed the tip inside.

JessicaLynn felt her body tighten. "No," she said. "Don't."

"You know the words," Eric said.

"Red or yellow," Gary said.

"Oh please don't."

Both men laughed. "She knows how to increase our pleasure, doesn't she?"

Whether it was increasing their pleasure or not, it seemed important for her to protest, although she wanted to be filled more than she could have imagined. "No more, please."

Gary pushed gently and suddenly JessicaLynn's body opened to the new invasion. She felt the dildo slide into her ass while

Eric withdrew the one from her pussy, then pushed it in again. The pleasure was too much. "Yes," she screamed. "Do it, do it, do it."

Gary nodded. "Watch me as you come, JessicaLynn," he said as Eric fucked her cunt with the large wooden phallus. "Look up."

She climaxed violently, watching her body writhe in the mirror on the ceiling. Heat and light blazed through her. Eyes on the ceiling, she felt the two penises continue to fuck her. Over and over she came, her pleasure almost too much to take.

When she was finally calm, Gary put the dildos aside and kissed her deeply. "I like to come in someone's hand," he said. He unfastened the cincher and freed JessicaLynn's arms. "I want both of you to touch me."

He unfastened his leather pants and his cock sprang free. Gary moved close to the chair and JessicaLynn took his cock in one hand. Eric wrapped his hand around hers, fingers intertwined, all touching Gary's penis. "Watch our hands," Eric said to Gary.

Eric spread a gob of lubricant on their hands, then the ten fingers formed an elongated tube. Eric placed one hand in the small of Gary's back and pushed his cock into the slippery passage. As the two hands massaged Gary's cock, he grabbed each by a shoulder, bucked his hips and came, spurting thick fluid on the arm of the chair. "Yes," he growled.

Later, having showered and redressed, Gary guided Eric and JessicaLynn to the front door. "That was quite an experience," she said.

"I hope you enjoyed the evening, JessicaLynn," Gary said.

"I did," Jessica said. "Tremendously. And out here, I'm still Jessica."

Gary kissed her deeply. "I understand," he said. "And I'll tell Brian and Steph that Eric drove you home."

"They're still here?"

"I think so," Gary said, pointing to their Lexus in the driveway.

Jessica grinned. "I hope they are having as wonderful an evening as I did."

"I'm sure they are," Gary said.

Eric helped Jessica into the car and started toward the Carltons' house. "Are you sure that wasn't too bizarre for you?"

"If you had asked me yesterday, I would have said that it would be. But it was all terrific."

They drove up the driveway and Eric helped Jessica out of the car. "I'll call you," he said as she found her key in her purse.

"I'll look forward to that." Jessica unlocked the door and walked inside.

Chapter
10

Jessica slept until after eleven the following morning, then showered and dressed in a pair of white cotton slacks and an olive-green camp shirt. She wandered downstairs, both eager and a bit reluctant to share her experiences with Steph.

"Good morning," Steph said as Jessica carried a cup of coffee and a toasted English muffin into the plant room. "Did you enjoy the party? I lost track of you after the stories but Gary said that Eric had driven you home."

"I had an incredible evening," Jessica said, settling into a lounge chair. "And you?"

"Let's just say it was incredibly satisfying."

"Where's Brian?" Jessica asked.

"He had a tennis date at noon so he just left."

"Oh," Jessica said, nibbling at her muffin. "This is almost as awkward as going to the party in the first place. Part of me wants to tell you everything, and hear about your evening, and part of me is. . . ."

Steph's head snapped around. "Not ashamed?"

"Absolutely not. Not ashamed at all. Just a bit embarrassed. I did things last evening that I didn't know existed a month ago. Hedonistic and more damn fun than I've ever had. Are you ashamed of anything you did?"

"Not in the least," Steph said. "But, it was unusual."

"I'd love to hear about your evening," Jessica said, "but only if you want to tell."

"Tell me about yours first."

"Well, let me begin with the fact that JessicaLynn was in her glory." Jessica spent almost half an hour telling Steph about her adventures in Gary's special room. Except for an occasional 'You're kidding' Steph was silent.

When Jessica was done, Steph said, "Oh Lord, that sounds so terrific. I'm shaking just thinking about it."

"I'm excited just talking about it. It was the most intense orgasm I've ever had."

"What about you and Eric? Is this getting serious?"

"I hope not. I care about him a lot. I love the time we spend together, in and out of bed. I enjoy Cam too, and Gary is a wonderful lover and I'm hoping he'll call and we can continue some of the adventures we began last night. I'm not ready to even consider something exclusive and I don't think Eric is either."

"You amaze me, Jessica," Steph said. "I never would have expected this from you. You were so serious, so married."

"I always thought so too," Jessica said. "But that was the Jessie inside of me. Now that I've grown and become Jessica, I realize that there are so many wonderful things to try. Do you want to tell me about your evening? You don't have to, you know."

"I know that, silly. But I'd like to tell you. It's a bit offbeat. It seems that we both had a new experience."

"You mean that you did something last night that you've never done before? From all you've told me, I didn't think there was anything left."

"Oh, there are things I've never done and some I never want to do. But last night I got to try one of those secret things that tickles your mind but you never believe will actually happen."

"So tell all," Jessica said, refilling her coffee cup, then Steph's.

"Well," Steph began, "during the storytelling, I was sitting with Marcy and Chuck. You remember that I told you that Brian and I spent an adventurous weekend with them in the Adirondacks last winter. Well, halfway through that story about the teenaged boy, he whispered in my ear, "What are you doing after the show?' "

"What did you have in mind, Chuck?" Steph answered.

"Marcy and I have been talking about you."

"And . . . ?"

"Later," he said, turning back to Gary.

Later. The word echoed in Steph's mind. She and Chuck had been together a few times as part of a foursome with Brian and Marcy, and she had always found him to be a talented and intuitive lover. He always seemed to know what she wanted, sometimes before she knew herself. And he had no hesitation about doing the unusual.

After Gary finished the final story, Steph, Marcy, and Chuck talked. She noticed Eric and Jessica walk to the stairs toward the downstairs playroom. Steph felt Chuck's hand on the back of her neck, but decided to wait until he was ready to explain about the rest of the evening.

Finally, he said, "When we spent that weekend together last winter, I got some feelings about you." Steph remained silent. "My relationship with Marcy has changed since that weekend." Chuck reached over and lifted Marcy's hand from her lap. He held it so that Steph could see the heavy gold bracelet she wore. "Marcy belongs to me, now, body and soul." He fingered the tiny gold charm on the bracelet. Steph looked more closely at the tiny gold object and saw that it was a tiny pair of handcuffs. "She does what I want, when I want, and she loves it.

"May I?" Marcy asked.

"Of course," Chuck said.

"It's wonderful. At work I have two secretaries, three private phone lines, and a stack of incoming information that I have to digest each morning." Marcy was vice president of a medium-sized, international bank. "I make decisions that involve tens of millions of dollars every day. But when I get home Chuck tells me exactly what he wants me to do to please him."

Steph was surprised. Marcy had always been a no-nonsense type in her early fifties with salt-and-pepper hair cut in a short businesslike style. Ever organized and efficient, she had been the one to orchestrate their reservations and transportation for their weekend away.

Chuck picked up the story. "Remember that evening when the four of us made love on the floor in front of the fire?"

"How could I forget?" Steph said, memories of naked bodies flashing through her mind. She pictured a particularly exciting moment when she held Brian's cock in one hand and Chuck's in the other.

"At one point, I ordered Marcy to jerk me off, and she did. When we got home, we talked and discovered this mutual need, hers to serve, mine to give the orders." He ran his fingers through the wings of silver hair above his temples. "It changed everything."

"We've been together several times since," Steph said. "You never shared this before."

"I know," Chuck said, "but we had to get completely comfortable with it ourselves."

"Are you two happy?" Steph asked.

The smile that lit Marcy's face was dazzling. "I've never been happier. It's the perfect life for us right now. The kids are long gone and we can play to our hearts' content in the house."

"You're the first person we've told about this," Chuck said.

"I'm honored," Steph said, getting genuine pleasure out of the fact that these two people chose to share their discovery with her. "I have the feeling that there's more to this revelation than just information."

"We want you to join us this evening," Chuck said. "Just the three of us." He paused, then said, "I told you before that I had a feeling about you." Again he ran his fingers through his hair. "I think you might enjoy following my orders for an hour or so." He grasped Steph's wrist in one hand and his wife's in the other. He tightened his grip. "I brought a few toys for us to play with, if you're willing."

Steph's heart was pounding. She looked down at the hand encircling her wrist, then at Marcy.

"I would enjoy it too," Marcy said.

With a smile, Chuck said, "I can feel your pulse and your heart is racing. The idea excites you, just as it excites Marcy and me. Play with us. Say yes."

"Yes," Steph said.

Marcy got a small paisley tote bag from the hall closet and the three of them climbed the stairs. They found a bedroom with a red ribbon beside the door, tied it around the doorknob to indicate that the room was occupied, then went in and locked themselves inside. "This is a fantasy come true," Chuck said as he set the bag on the desk in the corner. The room was masculine, with navy, red, and white bedding, a red rug, and white wallpaper with a thin navy stripe. Chuck switched the radio to a music station and stretched out on the bed. He interlaced his fingers behind his head, sighed and said, "Okay, ladies, I would like to see a bit more of you both. Take off your clothes for me, slowly and sensually."

Steph realized that her decision to wear a sleeveless black sundress that zipped up the back hadn't been a wise one. In order to unfasten it, she would have to twist her arms into an awkward, very unsensual position. Chuck read her mind as he often seemed to do. "Marcy, help Steph undress."

Marcy's red silk blouse hung open, revealing a shiny red waist cincher. She walked around behind Steph, found the tab on the zipper and stroked Steph's back as she pulled the zipper down.

Steph had never been caressed by a woman before. She liked the smooth soft feeling of Marcy's fingers. She felt Marcy slide the dress from her shoulders and guide it down over her hips. She stepped out of it and Marcy draped it over a chair.

"Turn around, Steph," Chuck said.

Steph turned to face him, knowing that her choice of undergarments had been much better than her choice of dress. She wore a black-lace demi-bra through which her dark brown nipples showed prominently. Her black-lace bikini pants matched it, as did her thigh-high lace stockings.

"I had almost forgotten how beautiful your body is. Now you, Marcy," Chuck said, not moving from his regal position on the bed.

Marcy removed her blouse, then opened the full-length zipper on her black skirt. It parted and she put both garments aside.

"It's latex," Steph said, gazing at the tight red waist cincher that raised Marcy's full breasts and squeezed her body tightly. The garment went from halfway down her breasts to just above her black bush. Long garters down the front and sides held up her red stockings.

"Yes," Chuck said, "it is. And it's very tight. Sometimes, when we go out, I make Marcy wear it. She feels it all the time and it reminds her of me. Show her the chain," he added.

Marcy reached into her pussy-hair and showed Steph a thin gold chain that attached to the cincher front and back, stretching tightly between her pussy lips. "Every time she walks," Chuck said, "a special gold loop rubs her clit. It keeps her wet for me at all times. Move your hips for me, Marcy."

Marcy swiveled her hips hula style and Steph could see her knees tremble as the loop rubbed her clitoris. "Not too much," Chuck said and Marcy became still.

"Stand face to face," Chuck said and the two women did as he said. Because they were of similar height, they stood eye to eye, breast to breast. "Closer," he said and they moved so their nipples touched, Marcy's bare, Steph's barely covered by the lace of her bra. "Oh yes," Chuck said, "I've dreamt of this."

Steph looked into Marcy's eyes, soft and kind and almost loving. "I've dreamt of this too," she heard Marcy croon. She felt Marcy reach out and touch her hair, caress her cheek, run her fingertips over her eyebrows and lips. Marcy's hand slipped behind Steph's neck, drawing her close. She pressed her soft, warm lips against her friend's.

Her lips are so much softer than a man's, Steph thought, her breath sweet, her touch ever so gentle, like a butterfly caress. She sighed, then sank into the kiss, matching lip for lip, tongue for tongue. Steph's hands held Marcy's face as their lips changed position to draw forth every nuance of sensation. Steph felt Marcy's hands slowly make their way down her upper arms to rest on the sides of her breasts. Featherlight fingers teased the lace, then slipped inside to flick the erect nipples beneath.

"Have you ever been with a woman before?" Chuck asked softly, not wanting to break the spell of the moment.

"Not until now," Steph said.

"Nor has Marcy," Chuck said. "But we've talked about it and I know that Marcy has fantasized about being with you."

That remark gave Steph a strange, warm feeling deep in her belly. She smiled, and Marcy returned her grin. The women separated.

"Marcy," Chuck continued. "Pull off Steph's panties, then get the vibrator from the case." As Marcy complied, Chuck said, "I know each of you has masturbated with a vibrator before, and I've watched Marcy make herself come. Now I want to watch you pleasure each other. Steph," he said, taking her wrist, "lie here." He positioned her on the bed, arms over her head, legs widely spread, then lay beside her, his body in the opposite direction, his head close to her pussy, his fully dressed lower body level with her head.

Steph was liquid inside, filled with heat and longing. She made small purring sounds to assure both Chuck and Marcy that she was anxious to continue.

"I can smell your juices," Chuck said, sliding one finger through her bush. He brought the finger to his lips and licked. "And I always did like the way you tasted." Steph felt the bed move as Marcy joined them. "Marcy, think about what gets you hot, then do it to Steph."

Steph heard a click, then the hum of the vibrator. Suddenly a bolt of heat speared through her as the cool plastic tip of the vibrator touched her inner lips. Like an expert, Marcy slid the humming machine around Steph's cunt, touching all the sensitive places, driving Steph closer and closer to orgasm. When

Marcy rested the vibrator against Steph's clit Steph cried, "You're going to make me come!"

"Finish her with your mouth," Chuck said, taking the vibrator. Steph felt Marcy's warm lips draw her clit into her mouth. The sucking and a finger, she didn't know whose, penetrating her slit drove her over the edge. Sharp contractions of pleasure knifed through her, making her scream as she came.

Chuck pulled his clothes off and lay on his back, motioning to Marcy who mounted him, filling herself with his cock. Chuck took Steph's hand and placed her fingers on Marcy's clit. "Hold still," he told Marcy. Then to Steph he said, "She likes to be rubbed right here," he said, holding Steph's fingers against his wife's sopping pussy. Steph rubbed, feeling Marcy's clit swell under her touch.

"It's hard to hold still," Marcy groaned.

"Another moment," Chuck said, releasing Steph's hand. "Do it," he told her. "Make her come the way she made you come."

Steph probed, inserting her fingers between Chuck's pelvis and Marcy's. She could feel Chuck's cock as it filled Marcy's body. She rubbed, watching Marcy's face, sharing her increasing excitement. She explored, reaching every part of Marcy's cunt she could. Hearing Marcy's sharp intake of breath Steph knew she had found the spot. She rubbed and stroked until Marcy moaned and her body became rigid.

Steph was surprised that she could actually feel the tiny muscle movements of Marcy's climax.

"I love to feel you come when I'm inside you," Chuck said. "Now for me," he moaned. As Marcy rode Chuck's cock, Steph reached between Chuck's thighs and tickled his balls. As she sensed his approaching orgasm, she rubbed the band of flesh between his balls and his anus. He roared, arching his back and holding Marcy's bucking hips tightly against him.

"Jesus," Jessica said as Steph finished her story. "It must have been sensational. I'm a wreck just hearing about it."

"It was remarkable," Steph said. "I never suspected that making love with a woman would feel so different."

"I don't know how I'd feel. I don't have many hang-ups left, but that one. . . ."

"If you are exposed to the possibility sometime you'll decide then. I didn't think I could do it before last evening either."

"Will you do it again?"

"Same answer. If and when the time comes, I'll decide."

"It was quite an evening for both of us," Jessica said.

"It certainly was."

The weeks sped by. Jessica spent time with Eric and Cam, learning about them and about herself, growing and changing. One morning in August, Jessica joined Steph for one of their frequent mornings in the plant room.

"Steph," Jessica said, "I'm going back home for a few days."

"Just a few days, I hope," Steph said, her face showing her unhappiness.

"Just a few days for now, but I can't stay here forever, you know."

"Sure you can, if you want to. You can get your own place and I'm sure there are dozens of real estate agencies that would be glad to have someone with your talent."

Jessica hugged her friend. "I'm sure that's true. I could make a life here. That's part of the reason I'm going back, Steph. I don't know where I belong anymore or what I want to do or be for the rest of my life. I've seen and experienced so many things and it's all confusing the hell out of me right now."

Steph looked bemused. "I can imagine that," she said.

"Actually, I talked to my friend Viv, you know, the woman in my office. There are several people seriously interested in buying my house and she thinks that my presence might just push one to make an offer. She also thinks I might get close to my asking price."

"That would be great, babe," Steph said. "One less thing to think about."

"And Viv also said that Rob has been asking for me. He and bimbette split."

Steph looked incredulous. "You're not thinking of seeing the louse when you go back?"

"Actually, I am. I loved him for a lot of years, and I think seeing him might help me sort out my feelings for Eric and Cam and who and what I am."

"You're a big girl now, Jessica, but just be careful. You've changed a lot over the past month. You're not the same woman who loved Rob for all those years."

"I know that, but I have to do this, Steph."

Three days later, Jessica disembarked at O'Hare Airport from an early morning flight and rented a car to drive to Ottawa. The air was hot and steamy, but it smelled like home, the breeze filled with the odors of farm and fields. Despite the heat that dampened her underarms and caused a tiny trickle of sweat to run down between her breasts, Jessica rolled down the windows of her rented Ford and a grin spread across her face as she approached her home.

She wanted her house to stay perfect-looking so Jessica had made a reservation at a local motel. Since it was barely noon, however, she decided to stop at the office. Ferncrest Realty occupied a small house on a side street in Ottawa. Jessica pulled her rented car into the small lot in front of the building, got out and straightened her tailored white blouse and navy linen pants.

"Jessie," three women squealed as she walked through the front door into the cool, cozy sales area. "You look sensational," one said. "I love your hair," a second said. "Oh Jessie," Viv said, standing quietly behind her desk, "we missed you."

After the three women hugged Jessica they filled her in on the details of the past weeks. "Well," Jessica said when they finished, "things seem to have gone very well. You can't even tell I was gone."

"We knew," Kathy, a short, round, and bosomy agent said. Kathy had a knack for knowing exactly what a potential buyer was looking for. Once or twice a month she could be heard on the phone saying, "I have three houses to show you, but after the first, you won't want to see the others. I've found one that's perfect for you." Usually it was and Kathy made a good living for herself and her ailing husband.

"We missed you a lot," Marie, the second woman, said. She was tall and appeared slightly anorexic but she had a charm that made her beautiful. Viv would giggle as she relayed all calls for 'the lovely tall, skinny woman with the great smile' directly to Marie. "Are you back to stay?"

"I think I still need some time," Jessica said. "But you are doing so well without me that maybe I'll just stay gone."

"You're not serious," Viv said. Warm with her friends, but shy with strangers, Viv was Jessica's best friend in Ottawa. She had tried selling early on, but had found that her strength was in organization and paperwork. She kept everything running smoothly and each time she took a vacation, the office took weeks to recover.

Several phones rang simultaneously, and Marie and Kathy directed their attention to their customers. Jessica crossed the office and dropped into the comfortable chair beside Viv's desk. "I don't know what I'm going to do in the long run," Jessica said with a sigh. "The liberated life has been fantastic. Hot, heavy and very exciting, in all ways." Jessica spent the next half hour telling Viv some of the details of her weeks in Harrison. Viv's eyes widened at her descriptions of Cam and Eric, and widened still further as Jessica shared some of the details of her adventures.

"It must seem really boring here," Viv said, sadly. "We're so low-key we look forward to the next issue of *Cosmo*."

"How would you know anything about the sexual adventures of the average Ottawa citizen?" Jessica said. "You and that husband of yours have been monogamous forever."

"True. And I like it that way." She looked abashed. "I didn't mean that the way it sounded."

"Of course you didn't," Jessica said, sitting forward in her chair. "Anyway, let's order pizza and talk about my house."

Over slices of pizza the four women discussed the people interested in buying Jessica's house. "I hope you don't mind, but knowing you were coming in today, I arranged to meet the Mac-Donalds at the house at three. They're so nice that I really wanted you all to meet."

"Great," Jessica said. "Let me drive over and return this rental car, pick up my car, and I'll meet you there."

At quarter of three she drove up the driveway of the house that she and Rob had shared for nine years. It had been just this time of year when she and Rob had finally moved out of their tiny apartment, having saved enough for a down payment. As she crunched across the dry lawn she remembered how they had danced around the empty living room the day they closed, knowing that their few pieces of furniture wouldn't make a dent in the lavish space. They had made love right then, in the middle of the bare bedroom floor, she remembered. Marie pulled up with the MacDonalds's car right behind.

For the next hour, Jessica wandered through the rooms with their carefully chosen furnishings, showing the MacDonalds all the advantages of the house. "I love your furniture," Mrs. Mac-Donald said wistfully, "although it will be a long time before we can afford anything this nice." The couple was in their late twenties and Mrs. MacDonald was quite obviously pregnant. "The only thing I would change is that your husband's den would make a great nursery

"That's the perfect place for it," Jessica said, smiling at the young woman. Jessica liked the young couple more and more as they toured the outside. She and Carol MacDonald shared a love of azaleas and they spent five minutes discussing fertilizers and acidifiers before Mike MacDonald dragged them back to the driveway.

As they walked, behind the young people's backs, Marie winked at Jessica and gave her the thumbs-up sign.

"Darling," Mike said, "let's think about it and we can call tomorrow."

"That will be fine," Marie said.

"And listen," Jessica said on the spur of the moment, "I was planning to sell all the furniture but I think that, if you decide to make an offer, we can come to some understanding about the contents too." She suddenly liked the thought of the charming couple eating breakfast at her table or storing their clothes in the matching dressers in the bedroom. And a baby. . . .

Carol MacDonald wrapped her arms around Jessica's neck, bumping her pregnant belly against Jessica's flat one.

"You'll really like it here," Jessica said as Carol climbed into the couple's seven-year-old Nissan. "It's a good house."

The MacDonalds left, followed immediately by Marie, leaving Jessica to wander the grounds, glad she had hired a yard service to keep things tended. As she arrived back at her car, she saw a familiar black Honda Del Sol speed up the driveway. Her heart pounded as Rob got out, stood and stared. "Jessie, my god, you look wonderful. What have you done with yourself?"

Jessica fluffed her shorter hair and straightened her back. "Hello, Rob. How have you been?" He hadn't changed a bit, she realized. He looked exactly the same as he had when she had last seen him, his sandy brown hair carefully blown dry, his short beard and moustache neatly trimmed. He was wearing his uniform: gray slacks, a light gray shirt, tiny-print paisley tie, and a navy blazer with gold buttons.

"I've been the same, but you . . . You look stupendous." He enveloped her in his arms and hugged her close. Jessica stood stiffly, not yielding to the familiar embrace. Funny, she said to herself, the things you notice. He still smells of Old Spice.

"I know," Rob said, backing away. "I've been a louse. The whole thing with Suzanne."

Suzanne. Jessica had forgotten her name. She tuned back in to Rob.

"That's all over. I guess it was some kind of midlife thing. I don't know what could have made me do something so dumb."

"I don't know either," Jessica said dryly.

"I've missed you something fierce, Jessie," he said, "and I'd like to see you now that you're back."

"First of all, I'm not back. I'm just here showing two wonderful young people the house. They remind me of us years ago, except she's pregnant." When Rob remained silent, Jessica continued, "And by the way. How did you know I would be here?"

"I've been driving past here several times a day. Viv let it slip that you'd be coming back to show the house and I wanted to see you." He hugged her again.

He smelled so comfortable that this time Jessica hugged him back automatically.

"Oh Jessie," he said. "It's so good to have you back."

"I use the name Jessica sometimes, now," Jessica said.

"Jessica? Nah. You're not the Jessica type. You're my Jessie." He looked at his watch. "Look. I've got a patient at five, but he's the last for the day. Meet me at The Grotto for dinner." When Jessica hesitated, he smiled his most charming smile. "Please? We've got a lot of catching up to do."

The Grotto. Their place. She hadn't been there since about a week before the infamous bimbette-in-the-dental-chair incident. "Okay, just for dinner."

Rob leaned forward and pressed a quick kiss on Jessica's lips. Without thinking she kissed him back. "I'll see you about six," he said, sprinting toward his car.

Puzzled by her reaction to her ex-husband, Jessica drove to the motel, registered and found her room. As she hung up the few clothes she had brought she wondered. Have I been wrong about him all this time? Have I been wrong about myself? She pictured Eric and the erotic room, then Cam and his deliciously subservient attitude. Was this all her own mid-life crisis? Was it something she had had to prove to herself? Something that wasn't real?

She showered, dressed in a conservative white summer dress and paisley shawl and met Rob at the Grotto. Hector, the owner of the family-style Spanish/Italian restaurant, greeted them like long-lost relatives and indicated a quiet table in the back. "I'll get you a bottle of Rioja on the house. I'm so happy to see you

Dr. Hanley, Mrs. Hanley. It's so good to see you two together again." He hustled away.

"Together again?" Jessica whispered to Rob.

"I called when I got back to the office and reserved our special table. I guess he just assumed."

"A powerful assumption," Jessica muttered as Rob possessively took her elbow as they made their way between the tightly packed tables.

They sat and, when Hector returned, Rob ordered for both of them without looking at the menu. "We'll both have the gazpacho, we'll share an order of the roasted peppers with anchovies and, for the main course, we'll have linguini with your lemon and dill pesto."

"Hector," Jessica said, "didn't you used to make a garbanzo bean salad with an herb dressing?"

"Of course, Mrs. Hanley. Shall I bring you some?"

"Please," Jessica said. She hadn't had that salad for many years.

"Jessie, you know that gives me gas."

"Then don't have any," Jessica said, glaring. "I'd like some."

"Well, oh yes. Of course. Then you should have some," Rob said and Hector disappeared. "Now," he continued, leaning across the table and taking Jessica's hands in his. "Tell me about your little vacation in New York."

Jessica pulled her hands back, then told Rob a severely expurgated version of her last few weeks.

Looking surprised, Rob said, "You seem to have enjoyed yourself with Steph and Brian. It's good for you to get some of that, you know, carrying on, out of your system. One needs that sort of thing. It should help you to understand my Suzanne silliness."

"Silliness?" She swallowed the rest of her comments as Hector brought the wine and the gazpacho.

"Tell me about the shows you saw," Rob said as they ate their soup.

She told him about *Phantom* and he smiled enviously. "I wish I had been there," he said wistfully. "Maybe next time."

Jessica almost choked on her soup. Next time? "How's your practice going?" she asked, changing the subject yet again.

"Oh it's about the same." He brightened. "Actually I've gotten at least a dozen new patients. . . ."

Jessica sat back and looked more closely at Rob as he chattered on. He was wearing a different shirt. The one earlier had been pale gray while this one was pale blue, carefully ironed, with a different small-patterned tie that was so like all his others. She tuned out his conversation and just looked at him. It was as though there were two images, superimposed. One was the Rob of high school, young, charming, and a bit daring, with dreams of their life together. He was arrogant but enthusiastic. Then, as Jessica forced that image aside, there was an older Rob. Still sure of himself and arrogant, but with a hard edge that robbed his face of any of its previous boyish charm.

She brought herself back to the present when Hector arrived with their peppers. "These aren't totally skin-free," Rob said, covering his annoyance with a smile. "Your kitchen staff is slipping."

"I'm so sorry doctor," Hector said. "I'll replace them immediately for you."

"Don't bother, Hector," Jessica said. "They're just fine. If there's a bit of peel on one, I'll take it."

"Jessie," Rob said, "I'm paying good money for this and it should be perfect."

Jessica patted his hand, a placating gesture that was surprisingly familiar. "It's fine Rob."

Hector placed the plate of garbanzo salad beside Jessica's water glass. "I'm sure you'll enjoy this too, Mrs. Hanley."

Rob looked dubious, but said nothing.

During the rest of the meal, they talked about trivialities. Rob handed his credit card to Hector and signed the receipt. As they were leaving, Rob again took Jessica's arm. "I'm so glad you've missed me as much as I've missed you."

"Did I say that?" she asked.

"You don't have to say it. I know you've been lonely. I can see it in your eyes. And I understand why you went to New York. You thought it was all over between us."

"Is that why?" Jessica found she was gritting her teeth.

"Of course, Jessie. What we had was good and," he draped his arm across her shoulders, "we could have it again."

Jessica thought about how she had once longed to hear those words. She almost laughed. He was such an ass. How long had he been like this? Was this the Rob she had been married to?

"I know you've been as hungry for me as I've been for you." He hugged her to his side and smothered her breast with the hand that had been loosely on her shoulder until a moment ago. He kneaded her flesh, then grasped her hand and pressed it against the crotch of his slacks. "See what you do to me? Let's go back to the office and I'll remind you of how good it used to be."

What an idiot, she thought. I can't believe him. She was so astonished that she didn't move for a moment, during which he continued to knead her breast with one hand and use her hand to stroke his erection with the other. "Remember?" he whispered in her ear.

She remembered. She remembered all the evenings he had insisted she have a shot of bourbon to get her relaxed enough for his lovemaking. She remembered him sucking on her nipples, then spitting on his palm to make his cock wet enough to penetrate her not-yet-excited body. She remembered his lectures about how she should read a few books about how to be better in bed. She remembered it all.

Slowly, a smile crept across her face and she nodded imperceptibly. Then she squeezed his cock. "I remember," she said. "Let's go back to your office. That's a wonderful idea." She walked to her car. "I'll follow you there."

On the short ride to Rob's dental office Jessica turned the radio up loud and sang along to several old Beatles songs. As she pulled into the parking space next to Rob's car, she smothered the urge to laugh. She had all her plans made.

Holding hands, they went up to the second floor in the elevator and Rob used his key to open the glass door to the plush outer office. His face was flushed, his breathing rapid as he flicked on the lights. He quickly loosened his tie and unbuttoned his shirt.

"Let's go in the back," Jessica said, noticing that he never had changed the fabric on the chairs in the waiting room. They seemed even shabbier to her now. She glanced at the glass door to the hallway, then at Rob. "It's too public here."

"Of course, Jessie. Whatever you want. Oh babe, you turn me on."

They walked back toward the operatory where she had stumbled upon him humping bimbette all those months ago. "You know, Rob," she said, "I've changed a lot since we were together."

Rob was panting, pulling his shirttails out of his slacks. "I'm sure you have."

"I like to take charge of lovemaking now."

Rob flipped on the light in the operatory, threw his shirt on the counter, and turned to Jessica. "You do?"

She realized that she had accidentally alluded to her other lovers, but he didn't pick up on the slip. If he wanted, he could believe for another minute or two that she was pining for him. "I like to do all kinds of wonderful things." She reached underneath the waistband of his slacks and grabbed his cock. "I've learned all kinds of new ways to have fun." She squeezed and Rob groaned. "Let me show you." As Rob stood in the middle of the room, stupefied, Jessica unzipped his pants and pulled them off, along with his shorts, shoes, and socks. Kneeling, she took his cock in her mouth and sucked, looked up through her eyelashes at his wide eyes.

"Oh, Jessie. Oh God, Jessie." His fists clenched and unclenched at his sides.

"It's Jessica," she said. "How about playing with me?" She pushed him, now totally naked, into the dental chair. "You just watch." She turned her back and slowly unzipped the back of her dress. "It unzips just like this, all the way down." Her voice was low and throaty. She turned and lowered the front of the dress until it fell at her feet. Her gaze never left his eyes as he stared at her breasts, half exposed in her white lace and satin bra. She pinched her nipples, making them hard and pointed.

"Jessie," Rob moaned, "you're making me crazy."

She lowered first one shoulder strap, then the other, lifting her breasts out of their cups, then, finally, unfastening the clasp and dropping the tiny garment on the floor.

"Do you want to touch? You always did love my tits." She walked over to the side of the chair. When he reached out to grab her tits, she held his hands. "No, no. My way, Rob." She took his hands and pressed the palms against her erect nipples and watched his head fall back against the headrest of the chair.

"You've got the greatest tits. And you feel so good," he groaned.

"Do you want a taste?" She placed his hands in his lap and moved closer to the side of the chair.

"You know I do. I want to suck you as much as you want me to," Rob said.

"You have no idea," Jessica said, rubbing one erect nipple across his cheek. When he reached for her, she said, "I said my way. You're very grabby. Maybe we should do something about that." She opened a drawer in one of the rolling cabinets and pulled out a roll of adhesive tape. She placed Rob's right forearm on the arm of the dental chair and taped it down tightly.

"This isn't like you, Jessie."

"I know, but it's like Jessica. And it makes you excited, doesn't it?" His cock was enormous, bobbing in his lap as he moved.

"Oh yes," he said.

She taped his other wrist, then wrapped tape around the chair, then around his thighs and ankles. "That's much better." Jessica massaged her breasts while Rob watched, pulling at the nipples until they stood out from her white flesh, firm and tight. Then she slid her hands under the front of her lacy panties and buried her fingers in her wet pussy. She was hot, but not for the reasons Rob was thinking. She loved this. He was hers. He was all hers. And she could do what she now realized was what she had wanted ever since getting off the plane that morning.

She rubbed her pussy until she could hold back no longer. Watching Rob's eyes on her hands and seeing his cock twitch, she came, shuddering, standing in the middle of his operatory. "Good," she purred. "Very good."

"I don't believe this." He struggled, but couldn't move. His cock stood up in his lap, a tribute to Jessica's power.

"I've changed a lot in the past few months," Jessica said, slowly putting her clothes back on. "And this evening has been a revelation." She zipped her dress, slipped back into her shoes and picked up her handbag. "You, my darling ex-husband, are a jerk. You're worse than that, because you had me convinced that I was the one who was sexually incomplete. You had me convinced I was frigid. Remember all those 'discussions' we had? Remember how you threw that word at me? *Frigid.*" She stared at his lap. "Your cock doesn't think so." She went into the receptionist's area and returned with several sheets of paper from the copy machine. "I was hoping that your receptionist still smoked so she'd have these." She brandished a pack of matches.

Rob struggled to get his hands free of the tape that held them against the arms of the dental chair but neither his arms nor his legs would move.

"I was going to leave you here until morning, but you might get sick or something and I wouldn't want anything to happen to you, Robby baby." She twisted the paper tightly into a torch, then struck a match and lit it.

"What are you going to do, Jessie?" Rob asked.

"You never will understand that it's Jessica. JessicaLynn. And by the way, are you still doing the dental work for that fireman's organization?" When he didn't answer, she nodded. "I thought so. Try explaining this." She waved the smoking torch under the smoke detector. As the alarm started, she said, "It should be only a few seconds until the sprinklers go off and then about two minutes later the fire department will arrive." She grinned. "Bye-bye, Robby, baby."

As she crossed the reception area, water started to gush from the sprinklers. She shook her head like a wet puppy and laughed as she walked down the single flight of stairs. She sat in the car for a few minutes, and watched as two fire engines pulled up. Still laughing, she drove back to her motel and booked a flight back to New York for the following day.

At nine-thirty the next morning, on her way to the airport, Jessica stopped by her office. "The MacDonalds made an offer," Marie told her as she walked through the door. "Only five thousand below your asking price, but I don't know how much higher they can go. I think they're pushing their ability to get a mortgage now, with the new baby and all."

"You know," Jessica said, thinking about Eric's reaction to the house he had built, "I've made a nice profit on that house and I like that couple so much. Take their offer and offer them most of the contents for another five thousand."

"Five thousand? You're nuts. You spent twenty times that on the furniture."

"I know. But they liked it and I want them to have it. I just want the right of first refusal if they sell any of the contents."

Marie shook her head. "If you're sure, Jessie."

"I am."

"Jessie," Viv called. "Telephone."

"I didn't even hear it ring." When she went to pick up the extension on Marie's desk, Viv said, "Pick it up in your office, why don't you."

With a quizzical look at her friend, Jessica walked into her office and lifted the receiver. "Jessica Hanley."

"Jessie," a gravelly male voice said, "it's Steve. Steve Polk."

"Steve, how are you?" She pictured the tall, bespectacled man in his early forties with whom she'd had dinner several times the previous spring.

"I'm fine. I've missed our dinners together. How has New York been for you? Replenishing?"

"Very. A good way to put it. How did you know I'd be here this morning? I'm leaving at noon."

"I asked Viv to call me. I really have missed you. It's too bad you're leaving. I was going to invite you to lunch today."

He sounded so disappointed that Jessica smiled. "Listen. I was going to rent a car and drop it at O'Hare but, if you can get away, how about driving me to the airport. We can talk on the way." A successful local contractor, he might be able to take some time off.

"Great. I'll pick you up in fifteen minutes."

"Meet me in front of the municipal lot next to Hertz at . . ." She looked at her watch. "Make it ten o'clock."

She hung up and walked back to Viv's desk. She leaned over and placed both palms on her friend's blotter. "Have you and Steve been conspiring?"

Viv grinned. "Maybe just a little. I wanted you to remember that Ottawa does have a thing or two to recommend it."

Jessica leaned over and kissed Viv's cheek. "Thanks babe. You're right. I need to figure out a balance to all this."

"Oh, and by the way. Did you have anything to do with the craziness at Rob's office last evening? The fire department responded. Then they had the cops and lord knows who else."

Jessica winked. "Did he get into trouble?"

"Nah. The fire chief wasn't happy about the false alarm, but he went upstairs, and then, I understand, he came back down laughing."

Viv came around her desk and the two women hugged. Then Jessica bade farewell to Marie and told both women to say goodbye to Kathy, who was out showing houses to a young man who had just been hired by a large local computing firm.

Jessica drove to the municipal lot and put her car in a special section for long-term parking. When she exited the lot, Steve was waiting for her. They embraced, then he took the suitcase from her. "I missed you more than I thought I would."

They had been friends for about six months and things had never gone any further. Suddenly, her arms around Steve's muscular body, Jessica began to wonder what he would be like in bed. Down girl, she told herself.

On the way to the airport, they talked and Jessica remembered why she had liked him so much. He was comfortable, never pushing her, seemingly content to wait until she felt ready to move things to a more personal level.

"How long will you be gone this time?" Steve asked.

"I don't really know. I'm going to coast for the rest of the summer, then make some decisions around Labor Day."

He concentrated on the view out the front window of his car. "I'm worried that you won't come back."

"You're the second person who's said that to me."

"We're not New York here," he said, speeding East on I80, "but I just want to be sure you remember that there are things here for you, too." He placed a hand on her knee. "All kinds of things when you're ready for them."

Jessica felt her heat rise. There was certainly no doubt that he was propositioning her. How long had he been suggesting this? She had no idea, since she wouldn't have been aware of his offer two months previously. She patted his hand. "I understand, Steve. I really do."

An hour later, as she took her suitcase from Steve in the parking lot, she said, "I'll stay in touch. And keep the fires warm for me for a while, will you?"

Steve leaned over and kissed her gently. "For you, certainly."

She walked toward the terminal with a happy spring in her step.

"How was your trip back home?" Eric asked the following evening. He and Jessica were sitting on the flagstone deck sipping Timmy's extra-spicy Bloody Marys.

Jessica started to laugh. Over the next half hour, she told Eric the story of her encounter with Rob. "You're a pisser, woman," Eric said. "I admire your style."

"Thanks. You know what the last straw was? He kept calling me Jessie. He refused to understand that I'm a different person now, and that it went much further than a name. But the name was a symbol of everything, somehow."

"Well, Jessica, you're too much."

"Thanks, Eric," Jessica said. "But, despite Rob, I am seriously thinking about moving back to Illinois after Labor Day."

Eric was silent for a few moments, then he said, "I'd like you to stay here."

"Part of me would like that too. But this is an interlude, a piece of another world. I feel like I belong in Ottawa. Anyway, I can't sponge off of Steph and Brian forever."

"You could move in here." Surprised that the words had slipped out of his mouth, Eric suddenly realized that he meant it. The thought that this wonderful woman would disappear from his life made him miserable. "No commitment. No exclusivity, unless that's what you want." He moved on quickly. "You could have the same sort of setup here you had at the Carltons'."

Jessica grinned and squeezed Eric's hand. "Thanks for the offer, Eric, but the more I think about it, the more I realize that Ottawa feels like where I belong. This is an island, a refuge, but not a life, at least not for me."

"Don't go back to being Jessie."

Jessica leaned forward and kissed Eric warmly. "I'm not going back to being Jessie. I'm taking Jessica back with me."

"Shit, Jessica." Eric looked deeply unhappy. "What about us? I love you, Jessica. Very much."

"Whoa, Eric. I thought this was a non-exclusive, just-for-kicks thing between us. I love you in a very special way, but not the way I think you mean. The airplane is a terrific invention. I hope you'll visit me and I'll be here once or twice before the first of the year." Jessica winked. "Gary invited me to his party the first Saturday in October. I wouldn't miss that for anything."

Eric leaned forward and grasped Jessica's hand. "You're not getting my message. I love you."

Jessica pulled back, raised an eyebrow querulously, and smiled.

After a moment, Eric's shoulders relaxed and he smiled. "Okay, Jessica." He chuckled. "You're right. I guess I got a bit carried away but the thought of your leaving makes me sad."

"It makes me sad too, Eric. But I have a real life to lead and this just isn't it. Still, I also want you to be part of whatever comes after. Visit me. I'm just a quick plane flight away."

"And we have the rest of the summer."

Jessica's conversation with Cam was similar, and they also agreed to spend time together both in Harrison and in Ottawa.

"Jessica," Steph said one morning the following week. "I need to explain something to you and it's important that you under-stand."

"Okay. Shoot."

"I am going to be away next Friday night."

"And . . . ?"

"With a man you've never met."

"Oh."

"This is really weird, but I wanted you to understand some-thing."

"Hey, Steph, it's okay. If you want to spend a weekend with some guy who lights all your bulbs, go ahead. This is Jessica, not the Jessie who arrived here a few weeks ago." Sometimes the changes that had occurred in such a short time amazed her.

"It's not just that." Steph shifted in her seat and stared at her hands.

"I'm totally puzzled." Jessica put her hand on her friend's shoulder. "We've shared fantasies, told our innermost secrets. What is making you uncomfortable?"

"Brian."

"I'm still confused."

Steph sat up straight and looked Jessica in the eye. "If you and he want to fool around while I'm away, I want you to know it's really okay with me." She let out a deep breath. "This is silly, you know." She took Jessica's hand. "I know that you turn Brian on. I also know that you are attracted to him but that you wouldn't do anything, even knowing our odd lifestyle. I want you to under-stand, deep down, that it is really all right with me. The thought of you two together, knowing you both as I do, is very delicious. I think you'd have a great time."

"You're right. This is weird. My best friend is giving me permission to go to bed with her husband."

Steph laughed. "Only in America."

"Have you discussed this with Brian?"

"I wanted to tell you first. If the situation arises, say yes or say no. But do it because it's what you and Brian want. Not for any reason that has anything to do with me. That's all I'm trying to say."

"And you know what I'm going to say? Let's go buy some new lingerie, for your weekend and for my whatever."

Later that afternoon, the two women arrived back at the Carlton house with their purchases. They carried their shopping bags up to Jessica's room and dumped the contents of the bags on the bed. "I love that little green thing you bought," Steph said, stretching out on the bed.

Jessica rummaged through the boxes, then held up a deep green lace bodysuit with a triangular cutout just above the breasts. "I got matching thigh-high stockings too, you know. And I have just the shoes."

"Try it all on, Steph said. "Let's see how it all goes together."

Jessica pulled the shoes out of her closet then, boxes in hand, went into the bathroom. She changed into the outfit, pulled on the stockings and slipped into a pair of four-inch-heeled black opera pumps. Then she looked at herself in the mirror over the sink. She grabbed a comb and teased her titian hair into a wild tangle around her face, then added dark green eye shadow, liner, and heavy black mascara. She applied a thick coat of deep coral lipstick, then opened the bathroom door.

"Holy shit," Steph said. "Brian would love you in that."

"You're serious, aren't you."

"I love Brian with all my heart and I love knowing he's having fun. That's all there is to it."

"You have no doubts about him."

"I set him free and he always comes back. He's his own person and I'm mine."

"Thanks, Steph," Jessica said, hugging her friend.

* * *

When Brian arrived home from work Friday evening, Jessica had prepared dinner. "I haven't cooked in so long that I wasn't sure I still could. I thought this would be nice." She had grilled a thick steak, made hash-brown potatoes, biscuits, and apple, celery and walnut salad and, while they ate, the two friends talked. As they pigged out on rum raisin ice cream, Brian asked about her plans.

"I'm leaving the day after Labor Day."

"I'll miss you like crazy, JJ. I've really enjoyed having you here."

"Me too," Jessica said, licking her spoon.

Brian took her hand. "You know Steph's away."

"Yes."

Brian kissed her fingers. "I want you."

"I know you do, Brian," Jessica said, gently disentangling her fingers from his. "And in some ways I want you too. But you're my friend. I'm very afraid that if we do end up in bed together part of our friendship will never be the same."

Brian looked crestfallen.

"And I understand what Steph said, and I know about your adventures at the party and all, but it just doesn't feel right to me. Not right, as in right and wrong, but right as in comfortable."

Brian sighed. "I'm disappointed."

"I'm sorry you are and in a way I am too." She picked up the ice cream bowls and put them into the dishwasher. "Let's go to the video store, rent a couple of old westerns, and make a bowl of popcorn."

As the credits rolled on the second John Wayne film, Brian looked at Jessica. "This has been a wonderful evening, JJ."

"For me too," Jessica said with a sigh.

"Steph never did get into old westerns."

"If your next remark is going to be 'My wife just doesn't understand me,' it won't float."

Brian's amusement was obvious. "You know, I must confess something. Part of me still wants to make long, leisurely love to you, but part of me has been making passes at you for so long it sort of got to be a habit."

"Well, don't break that habit," Jessica said, kissing him firmly on the lips. "One of these days I may just change my mind." They went to bed that night in their own rooms.

Jessica's remaining time in New York raced by. She spent evenings with Eric and Cam, and had a fantastic overnight with Gary in the special room. She especially enjoyed Steph and Brian's company, doing everything from crossing New York Harbor on the Staten Island Ferry to nude swimming in the Carltons' pool.

On the day after Labor Day, Steph and Brian drove Jessica to Newark Airport. The three friends hugged and finalized plans for Jessica to fly out for Gary's party in October. As her row number was called to board, Jessica kissed Steph. "We'll see you October sixth, right here. I'll miss you till then."

"Me too," Jessica said, turning to hug Brian.

"Maybe that weekend, JJ," Brian whispered, then nipped her earlobe.

"Maybe," Jessica said, grabbing her suitcase and almost running to the gate. She walked the length of the runway, boarded the 707, found her seat and stowed her small suitcase, glad she had packed several boxes and mailed them to herself at her office so she wouldn't have to check baggage. She was sad to leave Steph and Brian, but exhilarated to be returning to Ottawa.

She had called Viv and in response to Jessica's request, Viv had lined up several condos for her to visit, any one of which, according to Viv, would be perfect for her in her new life. She had appointments to see three of them the following morning. And she had a date with Steve over the weekend.

She realized she'd miss Eric and Cam. It wouldn't be as easy to see them and she had no real idea where she would find an outlet for her creative sexual energy, but if she had to, she'd suppress her libido until her next trip to New York. She snapped her seat belt, opened the new suspense novel she had bought the preceding day, and began to read.

"Terrible book," a deep voice said.

"Excuse me?"

"That's a terrible book. I read the first fifty pages and realized that if the hero just called the newspapers and told a bunch of reporters everything he knew, the whole plot would fall apart."

"Really?"

"Sorry, but I hate to see people waste their time."

Jessica closed the book. The man sitting next to her was pleasant looking, with toast-brown hair and deep blue eyes. "Well, that's that. I guess we'll have to talk. My name's Jessica. Jessica Hanley."

The man extended a large hand and engulfed hers in his warm grasp. "My name's David Scharff. And I was hoping you'd say that. You see, I hate flying."

Jessica noticed that his palms were damp. "I'm sorry. That must make this difficult for you."

"More than you know. I have to fly at least once a month on business."

Over the next hour, she found out that David lived in Joliet, a city between Chicago and Ottawa, was recently divorced, and worked as a salesman for a computer software company. When she mentioned Gary's name, the man's face lit up. "You actually met the elusive Mr. Powell? I'm impressed. He's a legend in the business. When he sold his company for all that money he dropped out of sight. Where is he now?"

"He lives north of New York City. He's a nice man with interesting hobbies and the money to enjoy them," Jessica said, smiling to herself.

As they fastened their seat belts for landing, David said, "Landing is the worst part for me. May I hold your hand? It helps."

"Sure," Jessica said. As she grasped David's hand and squeezed it tightly, she thought she felt a slight tremble that went beyond his nervousness about the flight. She slid her hand up and placed her palm over his wrist where it lay on the armrest. She pressed it down firmly and held it there, her fingers on his racing pulse.

David turned, gazed intently at her, then looked down at her hand. "Why are you doing that?" he asked, his voice a bit ragged.

"I thought it might help." She smiled as he adjusted his position to loosen his slacks. Amazing, she thought.

"It does."

Jessica leaned over and pressed her breast against his arm. Close to his ear, she said softly, "I'm sure it does. Tell me the truth. Are your pants getting a little tight?" When he remained silent, she said, softly, but strongly, "I asked you a question."

"Yes," he whispered, his voice now really trembling.

"Do you have to be home at any specific time?"

"No," he said.

Jessica looked at her watch, not releasing David's wrist. "It's almost five. Would you like to buy me dinner?"

David looked at her and smiled. "Very much." More softly but clearly audibly, he added, "Ma'am."

Jessica grinned as the wheels of the plane touched down. "You can call me JessicaLynn."

Velvet Whispers

Chapter

1

"Hi, Sugar." Liza's voice was soft and husky, not its usual speaking tone. "How's my man tonight?" She had also added just a hint of a southern accent, which softened and lengthened each word.

"I'm just great now that I can hear your voice, Liza."

Liza shifted the phone to her other shoulder and settled back into her overstuffed lounge chair in the small room that was her private space. "I'm so thrilled that you called."

"You knew I would. It's Tuesday, you know."

"I do know, but sometimes you are really naughty and disappoint me." She had already double-checked to be sure that the door was closed and locked and now she reached up and turned off the light. The room was now lit only by mid-evening moonlight shining through the window. She could close the blinds, but Liza liked the softening effect the moonlight had on her psyche. "I just hate it when you're naughty."

"I like being naughty with you, Liza," the man purred.

"Mmm," she purred back. "Maybe we should be naughty together. What should we do?"

After a slight pause, he said, "Let's take a walk in the woods."

"Good idea." Liza created her picture of him, walking beside her between tall trees, the air filled with the smell of pine. He was tall, with broad shoulders, long fingers, a broad chest, and narrow hips. Mentally she created his face, all planes and angles, with a firm jaw and soft lips. His eyes were deep blue with raven lashes that matched the long wavy black hair he wore gathered at the nape of his neck with a leather thong. "Yes, let's," she said. "Will you hold my hand?"

"Oh yes," the man said, his voice soft yet clear despite the miles between them.

"It's so cool here in the shade of the trees, but your hand is warm, and I can feel the heat travel up my arm warming all of me. Are you warm too?" She felt in the near darkness for the glass of wine she had placed on the table beside her chair and took a silent sip. As she always did, she felt a delicious tingle all over.

"You know I am," he said.

"It's so quiet here," she continued. She lifted her long hair from the back of her neck and draped it over the back of the chair. "Our footsteps are almost completely silent on the deep carpet of pine needles. I can hear a bird far away, its song faint and almost melancholy. The sky is so blue that it almost hurts my eyes. The breeze is cool, but the pockets of bright sun are warm and each time we walk from shadow to brightness, I turn my face up to the heat and feel it through my body."

"What are you wearing? Tell me how you look."

She already knew his preferences. "Well, you know that you're tall enough to tower over me. I like having to look up to see your handsome face. I'm wearing my hair in a single braid down my back, and there's only a slender black ribbon at the bottom holding it together. It will be easy to remove."

"And the rest of you?"

Liza could hear his breathing, now a bit heavy. "I'm wearing a peasant blouse of soft white cotton. It's been washed so many times that the fabric is almost transparent. And I have on that full, dark green skirt that I know you like so much and soft leather sandals. I'm afraid that I had so little time to dress this morning that I didn't put on anything underneath my clothes. It's a bit embarrassing."

"Oh, baby," the man said, "you know me too well."

"I'm afraid that from your height, you can see right down the front of my blouse. I can't help it if the cool wind makes my nipples hard. I hope you won't look."

There was a soft chuckle. "Of course I won't look," he said.

In her chair, Liza unbuttoned her blouse and slid her palm over her satin-covered breasts. In the dark she almost became the girl in the woods. "I'm so glad I can trust you that way. Let's walk for a ways. I know there's a small stream just over that little hill. If we're feeling brave, we can wade through the cold water to the big flat rock in the middle. It will be a nice place for us to sit and talk." She was silent for a moment, then continued. "Do you like it here? Of course you do. I knew you'd like this place. The sun is shining through the branches of the huge trees that line the stream and, as the wind blows softly, the sunlight sparkles on the smoothly flowing water. Shall we cross to that rock?"

"Oh yes. We really should."

"Good. But you wouldn't want to ruin your beautiful leather boots, would you? Sit down here on the bank and take them off. Shall I help you? Of course I should. I'll just unlace them. You know it's hard for me to keep my hands off your muscular thighs, but I'm a bit embarrassed and I really shouldn't touch you."

"It's all right. You can touch me." His voice was hoarse with excitement.

"Are you sure?"

His "Yes" was no more than a long-drawn-out sigh.

"Oh, your legs are so hard and tight and sexy," she said. "I love to slide just the tips of my fingers over your knees and then up your beautiful thighs. I want to touch that large bulge at the front of your pants, but I don't dare, so I'll stop my hands and just pull off your boots. Why don't you take your shirt off, too, so you can enjoy the warm sunshine?"

"Will you take your blouse off too?"

"Sugar, I knew you were a naughty boy." She paused. "You are so beautiful without your shirt. Your chest is hairless and so smooth. Your abdomen is rippled with muscles so hard, I just love to touch it." She laughed. "No, I shouldn't do that. Instead, I'm going to kick off my sandals and run through the water to the big flat rock out in the middle of the stream. Can you see it?"

"Yes."

"Ooh, it's hard to climb out of the water onto this rock. The stones in the stream are mossy and quite slippery. Okay, I've got a hold now. Good. I can sit on top. Mmm. The rock is almost hot from the sun. I've left wet footprints on the stone. Are you coming? I can see you standing there on the stream bank, so handsome and sexy. I'll pull my blouse off over my head if you want so you can see my large breasts. I'll just put it over here. Do you like the way I look?"

"Yes. I'm going to wade to your rock."

"I'm going to remove the ribbon from my hair. I run my fingers through it and pull my brown curls over my chest, but they don't quite keep my nipples from poking through. They're so hard and tight. I guess it's from thinking about you and your gorgeous body." She sighed deeply. "I'm going to lie down on the warm stone. Oh yes. I can feel the heat against the bare skin of my back. Do you need any help climbing onto the rock?"

"Not at all. I like being here with you."

"It's good to have you here beside me now." She paused. "Oh, look. You've gotten the bottoms of your pants legs wet. Why don't you take your pants off and lay them out on the rock so they can dry? Come on, take them off. No one can see." She paused for a heartbeat. "There. Isn't that better? Oh, my," she said. "You're not wearing anything under those pants, you naughty boy. Lie down on your back and let the rock warm your tight buttocks. Shall I warm you too?"

"Mmm," his voice purred.

"Maybe I'll just cuddle against you with my breasts pressed against your chest. Can you feel my hard nipples against your smooth skin? The contrast between the cool breeze and the warm sun is so exciting. And we're here in the open. If any people come by, they'll know what we're doing. Do we care?"

"Of course not. We just care about each other."

"That's so wonderful. I love the feel of you. May I kiss you?"

"Oh yes."

"Your mouth is so soft, yet strong. Part your lips so I can taste you. You taste so good." She waited just a moment. "You don't know what I'm doing. I've got my fingers in the cold water and now I'm going to drip icy water on your swollen shaft. Oooh, that's cold. Shall I warm it with my mouth?"

"Oh, God."

"Your cock is so hard it's standing straight up, urging me to take it between my lips. When I open my mouth wide, I can barely take all of you. I'm doing my best to surround your cock with my hot, wet mouth and I can suck most of you inside. You taste so good. I pull you deep into my mouth, then draw back, over and over until that cock is so hard it's almost painful. Now I'm sitting up, watching you stare at my body. I know how much you want me. You want to grab me, but I know you won't. You're so patient and you let me set the pace."

"But I'm so hungry."

"I know and I'll bet that the cool air on your wet cock feels *sooo* sexy. Would you like to suck my nipples?" Liza sighed and pulled her bra cups down and pinched her own erect nipples. The picture in her head was making her really hot.

"I love sucking you," he said.

"Yes. Suck me. I'm going to climb over you so my big breasts hang over your mouth. Don't raise your head. Let me do it. I slowly lower my breast until the nipple brushes your lips. Now open your mouth. Yes, like that." She pinched again and felt the shards of pleasure rocket through her. "I love it when you suck me, but that's not enough for me now. I need you inside me. Your large cock will fill me so completely. I'm going to move lower and touch your rigid staff with my wet pussy. Then I'll spread my skirt so that it covers us both. No one can see the secrets we hide beneath the dark green cotton. I've got the tip of you against my wetness. Do you want to be inside?"

"Oh, God. Oh, God."

"Not too fast. I like it really slow. Millimeter by millimeter I lower myself onto you. My body's so hot and wet. Do you want to thrust into me? I know you do, but be patient. Let me go *sooo* slowly until you fill me completely. Yes, like that," she purred. Without changing her voice pattern, she unzipped her jeans and wiggled them down over her hips. Then she inserted her fingers between her thighs and rubbed her bottom against the soft leather of the chair. "Like that." She found her clit and rubbed. "Just like that. If we keep doing that, I'm going to come. Are you?"

"Yes," he said, his breathing now rapid and raspy.

"I'm raising up on my knees and then dropping suddenly onto your stiff cock. Over and over I raise and lower." She rubbed. "Just a few more times. Do it for me. Drive that big cock of yours into my hungry body." With the help of her experienced fingers, Liza came.

"Yes," the man said. "Just another moment." He paused, then groaned. "Yes," he whispered.

Liza panted, the telephone lying against her shoulder. "That was wonderful, as always, sugar."

"Yes, it was. Maybe I can call you again next Tuesday."

"I'll look forward to hearing from you."

A hundred miles away, the man hung up the phone then took a tissue and wiped the semen from his liver-spotted hand and his now-flaccid cock. As he stretched back on his bed he thought about his wife of forty-three years, now gone for more than two. *I used to be like that man in Liza's story,* he thought, *and Myra was like the woman, so hot and receptive. Oh, baby, I miss you so much,* he thought, *but Liza fills some of the emptiness and I know you wouldn't mind.*

Bless Liza.
Bless Velvet Whispers.

Alice Waterman rubbed the back of her neck, trying to loosen what had become a semipermanent kink. Had it always been there? she wondered. No, she suspected, only for the past few months, since her mother had taken ill. She glanced up and peered through the square opening above her desk as the office's outer door opened and closed. A man of about fifty crossed the waiting room and casually leaned on the sill of Alice's window. "Good morning, Mr. McGillis," Alice said, making sure both her voice and her face were cheerful. Dental patients were always a bit tense and she knew that her cheery attitude tended to relax them just a bit.

"Good morning, Alice. How are you this morning?"

"I'm fine. How about you?"

"I'm okay."

"How's your son? Did you hear about medical school?"

Mr. McGillis's face lit up. "It's so nice of you to remember. Yes, we're very excited. He was accepted to Johns Hopkins, of all places. We're going to miss him terribly, but it's his first choice and he's thrilled. We never expected him to get in, even with his terrific grades."

Alice made it a point to remember details about the patients' lives, further putting them at ease. "That's great news. Congratulate him for all of us." She winked. "And be sure he comes in for his checkup before he leaves."

"I will."

"Dr. Tannenbaum will be with you in just a moment. He's just finishing up with his previous patient." The woman whose painful molar was being filled had been almost fifteen minutes late and now Dr. Tannenbaum would be a bit behind all morning.

"No problem," Mr. McGillis said. "I'll wait as long as necessary. Years even."

Alice chuckled. "I'm sure it won't be that long." She flipped the switch that would turn on the doctor's "The Next Patient Is Waiting" light in the rear operatory. As she watched, Mr. McGillis took a well-thumbed magazine from the rack and settled into a soft upholstered chair. As Alice returned to her computer, her best friend, Betsy, one of Dr. Tannenbaum's dental assistants, settled into a chair beside her. "He's almost done." Betsy shook her head slowly. "That woman's going to be the death of me," she said, sotto voce referring to Mrs. Sutter, the woman with the painful molar. "First she's late and then she's irritated that we won't sit and chat. 'Let me tell you about my granddaughter,' she says. 'She's just started walking. . . .' Then she drags out about fifty pictures." When Alice failed to react, Betsy said, "Earth to Alice. Where are you?"

Alice refocused her deep brown eyes. "Sorry. I guess I'm really preoccupied this morning."

"I gathered that when you almost charged Mr. Cardova for a root canal when all he had was a cleaning. You never do that. Anything I can help you with?"

Alice and Betsy had been friends off and on since high school. Seated alphabetically, Alice Waterman and Betsy York had been relegated to the far back of the room, free to whisper and giggle, mostly about boys and the constant bulge beneath their social studies teacher Mr. Hollingsworth's trousers. "I'm afraid not," Alice said softly. Then she sighed, knowing that Betsy really cared. "It looks like my sister and I are going to have to put Mom in a nursing home." Alice's sister, Susan, was six years older, married with a teenaged daughter. Although their mother's illness had brought them a bit closer, she and her sister had little in common.

Betsy reached out and took Alice's small hand in her large one. "Oh, hon, I'm so sorry. Your mom's really that bad?"

"She keeps having more small strokes and she's really out of it. Sue called me last night and said that the doctor's recommending twenty-four-hour care. Sue can be home with her for a few days and she's got a friend who can baby-sit for a few weeks. We can pay her about twenty-five dollars a day and she'll be happy to earn it. But she can only do it until the first of May when she moves, so in about six weeks, we'll have no choice but to find a nursing home for Mom."

Alice thought about her mother, always a robust woman until four months earlier when she had her first "episode" as the doctor put it. She had collapsed in the kitchen of her New York City apartment. Sue, Alice's sister, had phoned and gotten no answer so, after several hours, Sue had called the police. Their "check on the welfare" visit had ultimately resulted in the superintendent opening the apartment door and the ambulance screaming Mrs. Waterman away.

After three more mini strokes the woman who had raised and cared for her two daughters was now in need of permanent care herself. Alice had visited her at her sister's house in Queens just last weekend, making the long drive south to spend time with the woman who was now only a shadow of the person she used to be. As Alice had walked into her niece's bedroom, now taken over by the seriously ill older woman, her mother had smiled just a bit and her eyes had softened. Alice had sat, holding her hand and talking to her for more than an hour, until her mother fell asleep.

Betsy's indigo eyes expressed her deep concern more than any words could. "Do you have a place in mind? I hear the Rutlandt Nursing Home down-county is really pretty good."

"We've been asking around since Mom's first stroke and Sue and I would love to have her there. It's halfway between us and would be so convenient for visiting. It's supposed to be first-rate, but it costs the earth." She sighed. She'd been over it and over it and there was just no way. "We'll just have to find something more within our price range. We're going out to look again this weekend." She pictured her mother sharing a gray-painted room with some other incapacitated woman, being patted on the head, fed and cleaned, but otherwise ignored. *No*, she thought, *I can't dwell on that*. Alice grinned ruefully. "I could always win the lottery."

Rutlandt had bright colors on the walls and nurses who cared, really cared. When she and Sue had visited, an elderly man was being wheeled to a waiting ambulance on a stretcher. One nurse kissed him good-bye. Kissed him like she cared. If they could only swing it. With a child of their own, Sue and her husband were only going to be able to add a small amount to her mother's Social Security and her late-father's pension and insurance payments. Alice could manage only a few dollars as well and neither family had any savings to speak of. With just a hundred dollars a week more, they could manage it. Sure, she thought. A hundred extra dollars a week. It might as well be a million.

"You don't ever play the lottery," Betsy said.

Alice returned to her friend. "Yeah. Makes it harder, doesn't it."

Despite Alice's sad news, Betsy grinned. "You never lose your sense of humor, do you?"

"I try to keep it light, but this really has me down." Alice glanced up and assured herself that Mr. McGillis was still reading his magazine. Then she combed her stubby fingers through deep-brown hair that she wore cut short so she needed to do nothing after her morning shower but rub it dry with a towel. The extra fifteen pounds she carried was evenly distributed over her five-foot-three-inch frame and, although she wore a size sixteen, her uniform, a loose, brightly patterned scrub top and white pants, covered most of the extra weight. "So many of those places are so awful; ugly places where people go who are already dead but their bodies haven't gotten the final message yet. It's just so depressing." She tapped her forehead. "Although she can't speak, Mom's brain's still alive and I hate to see her relegated to nothingness."

A "Green" light lit on the panel on the wall, indicating that Betsy could bring Mr. McGillis back into the operatory. "You know," Betsy said rising, "I might have a solution to your problem. Can you stop by my house right after work? It's time I filled you in on a little secret."

Alice had little time to wonder what Betsy was talking about, as Mrs. Sutter bustled out of the back room. "Wait till you see. I've got new pictures of Christine."

"That's wonderful, Mrs. Sutter. I can't wait to see them."

At five-fifteen, Dr. Tannenbaum closed his office and Alice and Betsy walked down the staircase and across the parking lot. "Don't forget," Betsy said, "you're going to stop by at the house."

"Okay," Alice said, rubbing the back of her neck. "I'll see you there." She climbed behind the wheel of her seven-year-old Toyota and started the engine. It was late March and the willow trees in Putnam County, New York, had just started to get that wonderful green glow that signaled the beginning of spring. It had been a particularly cold winter, and the season had yet to loosen its hold. The forsythia were still trying to bloom with just a few errant blossoms coloring the slender, leafless branches. Twosythia her mother used to call them. Alice sighed and tried not to think about the older woman.

The weather forecaster on Channel 2 had said that the weekend should bring a dramatic rise in temperature. As she shifted into drive, Alice wondered whether she could drive down to Sue's and take her mother out, if only in a wheelchair. But where would they get one? Could they afford one? They must cost a fortune. Maybe through Medicare or maybe they could rent one.

"Stop it," Alice said out loud. "You're making yourself crazy." She turned up the volume on the radio and sang along with the Five Satins. "Show dote 'n showbee-doe. Show dote 'n showbee-doe. In the still . . ." By the time she pulled into Betsy's driveway behind her friend's new Buick, her spirits had lightened considerably.

The two women got out of their cars and walked up the well-tended front walk. "I can't wait for the azaleas," Betsy said. "It's like everything's holding its breath waiting for the temperature to go up."

"I know. The weatherman says this weekend."

"God, it's a hell-of-about time." She opened the front door and yelled, "I'm home."

Shouts of "Hi, Mom" were followed by three pair of feet pounding down the stairs. "Mom, Justin says that Mr. Marks is going to let him play third base this year. That's mine. Mr. Marks promised last spring he'd let me play third."

"Mom," another voice yelled, "can I go to the mall tonight? Everyone's going to be there."

"Mom," a third boy called, "can you quiz me on my spelling words?"

"Hold it!" Betsy yelled. "Alice and I need fifteen minutes of peace and quiet, then all things will work out."

"Oh, hi Alice," Betsy's three look-alike boys said almost in unison.

"Hi, guys. If you all need an extra chauffeur later, I can help."

"Thanks, Alice," Josh, Betsy's twelve-year-old, said.

"Okay, guys," Betsy said in her best motherly voice. "Is there anything that can't wait fifteen minutes? If not, shoo." She made pushing motions toward the staircase.

After several long-suffering sighs and a small amount of grumbling, the three boys disappeared back upstairs. "Now," Betsy said, making her way into the kitchen, "how about a soda?"

"Love it. I'm really dry." Alice dropped into a kitchen chair. "I've only been here five minutes and already your boys have me exhausted. How do you do it?"

"I haven't got a clue. They say that if a cowboy starts lifting a calf at birth and picks him up each day, eventually he'll be able to lift an entire cow. I think I'm lifting a cow now—or maybe three."

Betsy put two glasses of Diet Coke on the table and settled into the chair opposite Alice. "Now, let me tell you something about me you don't know. I hope you're not going to be mad that I've been keeping secrets but at first it didn't seem that important. Then it got bigger and I didn't know how to tell you."

"You don't have to tell me anything you don't want to, you know," Alice said. "But I must admit that you've got me curious. Do you rob banks in your spare time? Do you rent the boys out for white slavery?"

The corners of Betsy's mouth tried to curve upward, but didn't quite make it. She started to speak, then turned it into a deep sigh.

Alice reached over and took her friend's hand. "Hey. Whatever it is, it's not tragic. It will work out. Really."

Betsy clasped Alice's hand. "It's not like that at all. It's wonderful, the most fun I've ever had, but it's weird. I'm just not sure how you'll take it."

Alice took a swallow of her soda. "I'm really intrigued. Why don't you just spit it out?"

"I have another job one evening a week."

"Really, I never knew." Seeing Betsy's face, she knew there was more. "And . . ."

"I do phone sex."

"What?"

"I do phone sex. My name's Liza, or whatever the customer wants it to be, and I talk to them. You know, hot, erotic stuff."

"You're joking. What do you really do?"

Betsy withdrew her hand and sipped her Coke. "That's what I really do. I work one night a week for three hours and I average between two hundred and two hundred and fifty dollars."

"You're serious." Alice's mind was boggled. Betsy had always seemed so straight. So white-picket-fence. Three handsome boys and a great-looking husband. "What does Larry think about this? Does he know?"

"Of course he knows. Every Tuesday evening I disappear into the den, stretch out in the lounge chair, and take my calls. It works out well because the office is closed on Wednesdays, so if I run late, I can catch a nap the next day while the boys are at school."

"I have only a million questions. Do the boys know?"

"No. Of course not. They know I'm in phone sales, and that's enough. They know that on Tuesday evenings I work in the den and I'm not to be disturbed."

"How long have you been doing this? How did you start? How

does it work? Do you have regular customers?" Alice leaned forward. "I mean, it just doesn't seem like you. I mean, phone sex. Shit. I'm babbling."

Betsy smiled softly. "How about this? Larry won't be home until late tonight. If you've got no plans for dinner, let's take the boys out for pizza at the mall and we can talk then. It will also give you some time to digest what I just told you. We can then send Phillip and Bran to the arcade for a while and Josh can spend time with his friends. While they're gone, I'll answer any questions you've got. Yes?"

"Sure." Alice shook her head as if trying to get puzzle pieces to fit. They wouldn't. Not a chance.

Ten minutes later, the five of them stood in Betsy's driveway. "Alice," Brandon, Betsy's nine-year-old said, "can I ride with you? You could test me on my spelling. And I've got to be able to use the words in sentences. You could come up with a story."

Alice had always believed that learning could be fun and she had developed a game with the boys. They would give her a group of words and she would come up with a story that used them all. They would hand the tale off, one to the other, each adding a paragraph wilder than the previous to try to stump the next storyteller.

"Sure, if that's okay with everyone else."

"I love your stories," Josh said. "Can I come too?"

"That sounds great," Betsy said. "Phillip, you can ride with me and we'll talk about third base."

Chapter

2

When they reached the mall, the two women parked next to each other and the boys piled out. "That was a great one, Alice," Josh said. "Phillip, you should have heard the story we did." He insinuated himself between his brother and his mother. "It was fantastic, Mom, with monsters and people on another planet." With Phillip in the lead, the three boys ran ahead toward Festival of Italy.

"Thanks for taking Josh and Bran. It gave me a chance to have a heart-to-heart with Phillip about the Little League team."

"You're welcome. I really enjoy your kids, and the stories we get into tax my creativity sometimes. Bran had the word *gravity* on his vocabulary list so we got into life on Mars. Each time one of the boys took a turn, the story got more fantastic."

"It's that imagination of yours that intrigues me. They walked through the mall entrance. "We'll talk about it later." They sat down at a large table in the pizza parlor and, after considerable argument, agreed on a small pie with pepperoni and a small with half mushrooms, half extra cheese. "Don't let them get any mushrooms on my side," Brandon said. "Yuck."

"There will be none of that," Betsy said.

"Can we continue the story, Alice?" Brandon asked. "Maybe Josh can have a turn."

"Not me," Josh said, eyeing a table filled with other kids about his age. "Storytelling's too babyish for me."

"But, Josh," Bran said.

"It's all right, Bran," Alice said. "I understand completely. He doesn't have to join in unless he wants to. We can do a great story without him. Maybe we'll even let your mother take a turn."

"I'm getting to be a pretty good storyteller and Phil's terrific," Betsy said, rubbing Phil's hair. "Fill the kid and me in."

For the next half an hour the group tossed the tale back and forth, taxing their collective imaginations. After wolfing down three slices, Josh had moved to the table with his friends, but the other four were more than able to complete the fantastic story.

"So finally Morg got the ray gun and blasted everyone," Phil said. "Then he climbed back into his spaceship and headed for Earth."

"The end," Alice said.

"No," Bran whined, "don't make it end."

Betsy reached into her wallet and handed each boy a five-dollar bill. "How about you two go over to the arcade while Alice and I visit? We'll meet you at the main entrance in . . ."

"An hour?" the two boys chorused.

"Let's make it half an hour. In the meantime in case you need us, Alice and I will be sitting on the benches right outside the arcade. I want you two to stay together. If I see either of you alone, that will be the end."

"Make it forty-five minutes," Phillip said.

"Okay. Forty-five minutes it is." The two boys dashed off and Betsy walked over to Josh, bent down, and whispered in his ear. Then she stood, raised an eyebrow and her son nodded.

"Okay," Betsy said as she rejoined her friend. "We're clear until seven-thirty. How about we get cappuccinos and sit and talk?"

Hot, frothy coffee in hand, the two women found an unoccupied bench near the arcade and made themselves comfortable. "You've been mysterious long enough," Alice said, sipping her hot coffee. "Tell me everything."

"Do you remember when I was so depressed a few years after Brandon was born? I felt lousy about myself. I couldn't work with three boys and I felt like a slug."

"Yeah. That was a really bad time for you but you pulled yourself out of it, as I remember."

"I started working with Velvet."

"Velvet?"

"Velvet Polaski. Velvet Whispers. That's the agency through which I get the customers." Betsy hesitated. "This is really awkward. It's tough to tell your best friend that you've had a secret for six years. I'm not sure I know how you'll react to this whole thing even now."

Alice stared at her friend, wondering how you could be best friends with someone for almost fifteen years and not know something that seemed so important. Velvet Whispers. "Hey, I love you," Alice said. "You're my oldest and dearest friend. There's nothing you could tell me that would change that."

"I hope so. It all goes back to the night Brandon was born. I went into labor at about midnight but I didn't call you until the next morning. You had had the flu and were still a bit rocky, and maybe contagious. Remember? And of course Larry had to stay home with the two older boys."

"I do remember and I still feel guilty about it all. I should have baby-sat so that Larry could have been with you."

"Actually it was a blessing in disguise. I didn't mind being at the hospital by myself. After all, Brandon was my third and I hadn't had bad labors with the other two. I had a book so, for a while, between contractions, I read and watched the clock. At about 2:00 A.M., another woman came in and they put us together in one labor room, I guess to keep each other company. I think the labor-and-delivery area was really crowded and all the birthing suites were full. Nurses kept running in, checking on us and dashing out again."

Betsy sipped her coffee, then continued. "Anyway. This woman and I got to talking as we tried not to concentrate on the pains. What else was there to do, after all? Her name was Victoria, but everyone called her Velvet. The baby was her first and she was very nervous. Her husband was away on a business trip and, with no real family, I became the calm expert, the voice of reason. I helped her along, sort of told her what to expect. We got quite chummy, quite quickly. Between pains, there was a strange sense of intimacy. We talked about our husbands, my kids, like that."

Betsy's mind drifted back to parts of that strange conversation.

"Do you work?" Velvet had asked.

"With a two-and-a-half-year-old and a sixteen-month-old, I sure do."

"Sorry," Velvet said. "Dumb question."

"Actually, I did work before the boys were born. I'm a dental assistant." Betsy sighed. "I guess I miss it. When your world is populated by gremlins two feet tall who speak only single words, it gets a bit boring."

"I'll bet. I'm going to keep my job after the baby. I just can't give it up."

"What do you do?" Betsy asked.

"I'm in phone sales."

"What do you sell?"

Just then a contraction interrupted Velvet's conversation. When the pain subsided, she said, "I sell sex."

Betsy sat bolt upright. "Come again?"

"I have a phone-sex business. Men call and I talk to them. I'm really busy and I make quite a good living."

"You're kidding." Betsy looked at her new friend, and saw that Velvet was totally serious. "Okay. You're not kidding."

"No. I'm not. It started as a joke several years ago with some buddies of my husband's. They wanted to play a prank on one of their friends so they set me up to talk dirty to him. They thought it would be a lark, but, as they listened in, they realized that I was very good at it. Actually, I felt bad about it, playing such a joke, but he was a great guy and let me off the hook."

The two women stopped talking as Velvet had another contraction, making conversation impossible. When things calmed, Velvet continued, "I was so good at it that, secretly, one of Bob's friends kept calling, asking me to talk dirty to him. I did, and he paid me."

"He actually paid you?"

"Fifty bucks for half an hour. He said that's what he paid for other phone-sex lines and that I deserved every penny of it. He told someone, and they told others. Now I have men calling every night and I make a nice living. It's too bad I'll have to cut back now, with the baby and all."

Betsy turned to Alice. "So Velvet and I had our babies and crossed paths a few times that first year at the pediatrician's office. She loved motherhood and our babies both thrived. It was a couple of years later, when I was so depressed, that I ran into her again at the pediatrician's office." Betsy sipped her cappuccino. "We got to talking. Dr. Brewster was running late, as usual, so we had almost an hour to visit. It was quite a while before I asked her about the business."

When Betsy drifted off, Alice prodded. "And?"

"Business was booming and Velvet had hired another woman to answer calls but she was still having to turn away customers. When she heard that I was so down, she suggested that I give her business a try. I was horrified, of course, but, well, as time passed, the idea began to appeal to me somehow. I discussed it with Larry and he was all for it. Things between us have always been great and he thought I'd be good at talking dirty to men. He was also glad that I seemed to be perking up. A phone-based job wouldn't entail having to travel to work and he promised to take care of the kids one evening a week. Both the money and something to do were welcome."

People walked past their bench, but the two women were oblivious. "How did this Velvet know you'd be good at phone sex? Wasn't she taking a risk?"

"Actually she had a friend call me and be my first customer just to be sure, but after so many years on the phone, she's a pretty good judge of character."

"I couldn't have done it," Alice said, putting her coffee on the bench beside her.

"Needless to say, I was terrified, but after a few moments I guess I just got into it."

"Tell me about it," Alice urged.

"His name was Austin. Velvet had given me some reading to do, some ideas for how to talk to men. She'd also let me listen to her end of a few conversations. That made me feel better but I quickly learned that every call and every client is different."

"So Austin called you. Weren't you scared with him having your phone number?"

"She had given me his number and I called him at a pre-arranged time. Velvet pays me and covers my phone bill too."

"What about the real customers?"

"They call and give credit-card information to a router, who finds out what the client wants, then relays the call. Velvet doesn't take many calls anymore so she usually does that herself. Sometimes, if she's busy, one of us goes to her place and does it."

"One of us?"

"There are almost a dozen women working for her now. She pays us fifty dollars an hour for routing, and on the phone we get half of whatever Velvet charges."

"Wow. I never imagined."

"Neither did I that first time."

"Do you remember that first call?"

At that moment, Phillip dashed out of the arcade. "Mom, Bran's hogging the Duel of Death. It's my turn."

"You know the rules," Betsy said. "If you can't work out your problems, we're out of here."

"But Mom . . ."

Betsy raised an eyebrow and Phillip slunk back into the arcade. The two women clearly heard him yell, "Bran, Mom says . . ."

Chuckling, the two women returned to their conversation. "That first call," Betsy said. "How could I ever forget? I had told Larry all about it and he was incredulous, but willing to go along, especially since I was going to get paid. He said he'd put the boys to bed, then watch a ball game in the living room and that I should come down when I was done. I was supposed to call the guy at about eight so I locked myself in the bedroom at about seven-thirty and shook for half an hour."

Betsy sat in her small bedroom, alternately exhilarated and terrified. *What's the worst that can happen?* she asked herself. *So I make an idiot of myself. So I'm so tongue-tied that I can't speak at all. So what?* At exactly eight, she looked down at the small sheet of paper on which Velvet had written the number and reread it, although she had already memorized it. Velvet had said that she might want to extend the call as long as possible since she was being paid by the hour, but Betsy had rejected that idea. The call would last as long as it lasted and she'd make what she made. She wouldn't con anyone. When she had apologized to Velvet, the woman had laughed. That was her theory too.

Hands trembling, Betsy picked up the phone and dialed. "Hello?"

Betsy had a naturally soft, slightly husky voice and Velvet had told her that she needn't change anything. "Hello. I'm glad I could call you tonight." She tried to sit on the edge of the bed, but found that she needed to pace while she talked.

"I'm glad you could too," he said. "My name's Austin. What's yours?"

"What would you like my name to be?" So far, so good. She was following the pattern she had set up for herself. The standard, as Velvet had told her, was to let the man lead the way as much as possible.

"I don't know. How about Mona?"

"Okay. Mona it is. What are you wearing, Austin?"

"Just jeans and a polo shirt."

"What color shirt? I want to be able to picture you."

"It's yellow."

"Is it tight, so I can see your chest and arms as the shirt hugs you?"

"Yes," he said with a sigh. "What are you wearing?"

Betsy was actually wearing a comfortable sweat suit, but she answered, "I'm wearing a tank top that's slightly too small for me, and a pair of shorts."

"Are you wearing underwear?"

"Oh yes, but we can take them off together." Betsy listened carefully to the sound of Austin's breathing as Velvet had suggested, to gauge how excited he was. So far, he was pretty calm. She settled on the edge of the bed.

"Do you have shoes on?" he asked.

Betsy toed at her sneakers. "I do, but I can kick them off so my bare toes can wiggle. Would you like me to do that?"

"Oh yes," Austin said. "I want to hear you kick them off."

Betsy used the toe of one foot to ease her sneaker off her heel then bent over and held the phone near the floor as she pushed it off and it dropped on the rug. "I'm afraid you didn't hear much," she said, "since there's a nice thick rug. Let me kick off the other one." Again she moved the phone so Austin could hear the thud. "Now I can wiggle my bare toes in the carpet. It's so soft." Betsy could hear Austin's sigh. Although Velvet hadn't told her so, Austin might like feet, she thought, filing the knowledge away. She'd done a lot of reading, hoping that nothing could surprise her.

"I like that. I'm going to kick my shoes off too. Hear that?" She heard the slap of shoe sole on hard floor.

"It sounds like you don't have a carpet there," she said. "That's too bad. If you did you could walk barefoot on the soft rug as we talk."

"I wish I could do that too."

"Here's an idea. Why don't you get a thick towel from the bathroom and spread it on the cold floor? Then we can both walk around as we talk."

Betsy could hear Austin's excitement. "What a great idea. Hold on." The line went silent. Betsy took a deep breath. So far, so good.

*　*　*

"He actually got a towel?" Alice asked. "How did you think to do that?"

"I haven't a clue. It just came to me. Most of my calls now are spontaneous. I have no idea from one moment to the next what direction they will take."

"I'm still flabbergasted."

"You know, me too. I still can't believe I do this, but it's so much fun now."

"Back then it must have been really scary."

"Believe me, it was."

Austin returned to the phone. "I'm back, and I have a towel on the floor. I can curl my toes, and it's so soft."

"Good. Let's walk as we talk." Betsy was momentarily tongue-tied and the silence started to drag. *What can I say now?* she screamed at herself. *I have to get to sexy stuff.* "You know," she said inspired, "it's really hot in my room here."

"It is?"

"Yes. I'd like to take my sweater off."

"You mean your tank top."

"Right." Dumb. Dumb. She took the piece of paper with the phone number on it and wrote *tank top and shorts. Barefoot.* "It's a knit top and it's red. Bright red. I love red. Do you? Can you picture my bright red tank top?"

"Yes, Mona, I can," he said, "but take it off. Tell me about your bra."

Betsy jotted the word *Mona* on her pad. It wouldn't do for her to forget the name Austin had given her. "Well," she said, trying to sound as if she was removing her clothing, "it's red too. And it's lace, with thin straps."

"Are your breasts big?"

She remembered that Velvet had suggested that she always have large breasts. "Do you like big breasts?"

"Yes. I love tits that fill my hands."

"How would you like them to look?"

"Oh, they'd be white, with big, really dark nipples, and the nipples would be sticking out."

"How strange?" Betsy said. "You've just described me really well. I have a bit of a tan, but my tits are really white. I never sunbathe topless since someone might see my boobs." *Yes,* she thought, *use those hot words.*

"Can I see them?" There was a long pause. "Please."

"I guess. Let me unhook my bra. I'm cradling the phone against my ear now so I can reach around and get at the hooks."

"It doesn't hook at the front? I like bras that hook at the front."

"Not this one, but if we talk again, I'll be sure to have one that hooks in the front. Maybe a black one next time."

Again Austin sighed. "Yes. A black satiny one that hooks in the front. Have you got your bra off yet?"

Betsy made a decision. "I can't quite manage it so I have to put the phone down to take it off. Will you wait for me?"

"Of course."

Betsy put the phone on the bed and pulled her sweatshirt over her head and removed her beige cotton bra. Being clothed felt like a cheat now. Her breasts were small and tight, but at least she was naked from the waist up. She picked up the receiver. "That's so much better. My tits felt like I was being strangled in that tight bra. Now these large white globes are free. Would you like to touch them?"

"Oh God, yes," Austin said, the pitch of his voice rising.

"Close your eyes and reach out your two hands, palms up. I'll lean over and fill your hands with my boobs." She paused, then continued, "Can you feel them in your hands?"

"Oh yes," he said, his voice tight.

"What else would you like to touch? Or would you like me to touch you?" *Can I pull this off?* Betsy wondered. *Touching yet not touching is really weird, but he seems to be enjoying it.*

"I'd like to take my shirt off. Would you rub your boobs on my chest?"

"Of course. Let me help you with your shirt. I'm holding the front of your shirt and pulling it over your head. Is it all the way off now?"

"Yes."

"Good. Are you naked from the waist up now?"

"Yes."

She wanted to describe touching his chest, but she had no idea whether he was hairy or smooth. Her mind thrashed, trying to think how she could find out. "I want to rub my hands over your chest. How would that feel? Touch your chest and tell me."

"I don't know. Smooth, I guess."

"Yes, so smooth and warm. You feel almost hot. I love the way my hands slide over your skin. Would you touch me while I stroke you?" She stopped, then said, "My breasts are so heavy and feel so . . ." She fumbled for a word. "Satiny. Look at your dark hands on my white skin. That's so sexy it makes me hot. You've got great hands, you know."

"Yeah," he said.

"Now kiss me, lover. Press my hot lips against yours. I'll slide my tongue into your mouth and press my tits against your naked chest. Mmm. I'm moving my body so my nippies rub against you while we kiss. They're getting really hard. You're so sexy."

Betsy turned out the light and stretched out on the bed. She slipped her free hand over her ribs, touching her skin and trying to describe what she was feeling. "I can feel your hard ribs beneath your skin, steel beneath smooth silk." She touched her lips. "Your lips are so soft and warm. Let me touch your tongue with mine."

She heard a long-drawn-out moan and knew she was doing fine so far. "I'm getting hot for you, Austin. Maybe I'll just step back and slide my shorts off." She wiggled out of her sweatpants and bikinis. "I'm naked now. Will you get naked for me?"

"Well, sure." She heard rustling and she assumed Austin was taking off his jeans.

"Are you naked now, baby? I want to see your gorgeous body."

"I'm not so gorgeous, you know," Austin said in a small voice.

"You're gorgeous to me because you're mine right now. Is your cock all hard?"

"Oh yes."

"Touch it and pretend that it's my hand. I'm touching your cock with one hand, wrapping my fingers around the hard shaft. Goodness," she said, "it's so big I can barely close my fingers around you, and it's so hard."

"Yes, it is. I wish I were touching you."

"If you were, here's what you'd feel. My pussy's covered with dark, crispy hair and if you weave your fingers through it, you can find out that I'm wet and hot for you. My cunt is steaming, waiting for your fingers. Rub me, baby. Rub my clit. Like that." Betsy rubbed her now-swollen clit with her finger, amazed at how hot the entire scene was making her. "You make me so hungry. I'm touching my pussy, dreaming that these are your fingertips. I'm sliding my hand farther back so I can slide my index finger into my cunt. Are you holding your cock? Rubbing it?"

"Oh God, yes."

"Get some baby oil so you can rub it faster while I push my finger into my pussy." She waited a beat, then said, "Now two fingers." She actually inserted two fingers into herself, loving the way it felt to be filled.

"God, Mona, you're making me so hot, I can't stand it."

"Oh, love, hold your cock in one hand and stroke it with the other. Pretend they are my hands, with long fingernails that I can use to scratch your skin." All the sexy women had long fingernails, didn't they? "Are you rubbing? Do more. Make it feel *sooo* good. I'm rubbing myself and making my pussy feel so wonderful."

For a few moments, the phone line was silent as the two touched themselves. "Are you close, Austin?"

"Yes," Austin said, almost breathless.

"Me too," Betsy said, realizing that it was true. She removed her hand, thinking of Larry sitting in the living room. She'd have a surprise for him in a few minutes.

"I'm gonna come, Mona. Right here. You're making me come."

"Yes, my hands are so talented. Close your eyes now, baby," Betsy said. "Picture my mouth approaching the tip of your cock. Shall I suck it?" She made a few slurping sounds. Then Betsy heard a few gasps and an, "Oh, shit."

"You made me come. Just like that, you made me come."

Betsy was dumbfounded. She had actually made Austin climax. Phone sex. This was dynamite. "Was it good, lover?"

"Oh yes. I'm going to use that towel from the floor to clean myself up. I've got to go now. Can I call again next week?"

Holy shit, she thought. He wants to call again. He wants to spend real money next week. "Sure, baby. Mona will be here waiting for you."

"Bye for now," he said, still breathless.

"Bye." She flipped on the light. It was after eight-thirty. She'd been on the phone with him for almost forty minutes. She looked at the small piece of paper with Austin's phone number and the notes she had made. She added smooth chest, hard cock, and the word *suck*, which she assumed was what drove him over the edge. She'd be better prepared next time. She put the paper into her bedtable drawer.

She fumbled in her closet and pulled out an old peignoir, one she hadn't worn since before Phillip was born. She walked down the hall and glanced into the boys' rooms. All three were sound asleep.

She crept down the stairs and found Larry in the living room. "Wow, you look great. How did it go?"

"It was a blast," Betsy said. "Great money, and it's got fringe benefits." She knelt between Larry's knees and unzipped his fly, feeling him get instantly hard.

"What's this?"

"What does it look like?" She reached into the opening and pulled out Larry's erection, already rock-hard.

"It looks like some other guy made you hot."

Betsy looked into her husband's eyes. "I made me hot, and I

want you. No one else. Just you." She rubbed the end of Larry's cock over her closed lips, feeling the slippery fluid already leaking out. "Want me?"

"You know it," Larry moaned. "I kept thinking about some guy getting his rocks off while you talked to him. It drove me crazy."

"It made me hot knowing he was coming, but he's not here. He's just a voice. On the other hand, you are here, now. And I want you." She kissed the tip of Larry's cock.

"You really got off on it."

"I did, and I want to take it out on you." She stood up, opened her robe and climbed onto the sofa on her knees, straddling Larry's lap. With little preliminary, she lowered her steaming cunt on his hard shaft. Using her thigh muscles, she raised and lowered her body, fucking his cock without his having to move.

It took no more than a few moments for him to come, spurting semen deep inside of her. Then he took his fingers and rubbed Betsy's clit until she came, the spasms rocking her entire body.

Silently, they cleaned themselves up, closed up the downstairs, and went up to the bedroom. Quickly they readied themselves for bed and, both naked, climbed between the sheets. "If anything about this bothers you, I won't do it again," Betsy said, prepared to give it all up if Larry wanted her to.

Larry thought about it for a minute, then said, "I was really jealous as I sat downstairs and thought about you on the phone with some other guy, but what followed was terrific. You're right. It doesn't matter how you get hot, as long as you work off your heat with me and no one else. I'm not ready to share your body."

"I have no intention of sharing my body with anyone but you." She slipped her arms around her husband's waist. "He wants to call me again next week, this time for real money."

"No shit. You must be good at it. What did you say?"

"You know," Betsy said, her tone serious, "somehow that's private and I don't think it feels right to tell you. But anytime you want me to talk dirty to you, I'll be delighted. You will, of course, have to pay." Betsy grabbed her husband's already hardening cock. "I know just how."

"Well," Betsy said to Alice, "Larry and I didn't get to sleep for quite a while." A wide grin split her face.

"That's amazing," Alice said. "I guess I'm not surprised, though. You were always good at everything you put your mind to."

"I don't know about everything, but I have more customers than I can handle, so to speak. I spend only one night a week on the phone, and can only take three or four calls."

"Have you ever seen any of these guys?"

"Nope. I wouldn't know them if they bumped into me in the food court. It's great that way. Anonymous. We can each imagine anything we want."

"Larry still isn't jealous?"

"Occasionally he needs reassurance, but I love him to pieces and in his heart he knows there's no danger at all."

At that moment Phillip and Brandon ran out of the arcade. "Mom," Phillip said, "can we have another dollar each? Please? You can take it out of our allowances."

"Please, Mom," Brandon chimed in. "We still have ten minutes. Please?"

"Let me," Alice said. She fished her wallet out of her pocketbook and gave the boys each a dollar.

"What do you say?" Betsy said as the boys darted off.

"Thanks, Alice," they said in unison, then headed back into the arcade.

"The boys think you're in phone sales. Don't you worry that they will find out?"

"Not really. It might happen, but we are careful. They know that Mom disappears every Tuesday evening into a room behind a locked door. It's the only time doors are locked in our house, so they know it's important. Most of the time, Larry takes them out for dinner and a movie so I have more privacy. It really works out fine since Larry and the boys get to spend quality time together each week. He helps them with homework, then puts them to bed while I'm locked in the den. I paid for that room, you know. With my earnings."

"If you do so well, why do you continue at Dr. Tannenbaum's office?"

"I like the work and with three boys to put through college, every cent is important."

"If you don't mind me asking, how much do you make?"

"Velvet charges $2.99 per minute and I get half."

Alice did some quick calculations. "That's ninety dollars an hour."

"Not many calls last an hour, but yes, that's what it adds up to."

"Wow.

"Yes, wow. You could do it too."

Alice barked a laugh. "I could not."

"Of course you could. You're a great storyteller and that has to mean you've got a great imagination. Just think about it. It would solve all your money problems. I can introduce you to Velvet and you can discuss it, no commitment."

"I don't think so."

"Why not?"

"Because."

"Good answer." Betsy glanced at her watch. "It's almost eight and Larry will think I've absconded with the boys." She took the last few gulps of her coffee. "Nah. He knows that if I ever abscond, I'll leave the boys here so I can have a little quiet." She stood up, tossed her cappuccino cup in the trash and picked up her pocketbook. "I'm going to find my two darlings, then get Josh and get out of here. Alice, think about what I told you and I'll see you at work tomorrow."

"Hmm," Alice said. "You know, I'll think about it."

Chapter
3

Alice watched Betsy stride into the arcade and emerge minutes later with her two protesting boys. The three turned and waved. Weakly, Alice waved back, shaking her head. Betsy. A phone-sex person. *I wonder what you call them,* she thought. *Phone sluts?* Betsy was not a slut. She was the nicest human being Alice had ever met. But this?

Alice stared unseeingly at the front of the arcade. *What's wrong with phone sex? She never meets the guys she talks with. She's never been unfaithful to Larry and Larry knows all about it. If he doesn't mind, why should I?* She shook her head again. *Now she wants me to do it too. Ridiculous.*

Alice sipped the cold remains of her cappuccino, then stood and dropped the cup into the trash. Phone sex. Me? Not a chance. But half of $2.99 a minute. Ninety dollars an hour. With just an hour or two, she could manage to have her mother stay at Rutlandt. Could she do it? She shook her head. Not a chance.

Slowly, Alice wandered the mall, gazing into store windows, not really seeing any of the items. Her mind was whirling, both with Betsy's revelation and with the idea that she could make some real money that way. *Even if I could,* she said to herself, *who knows whether I'd be good at it. Good enough to attract regular cus-*

tomers. Could I talk about sex? What the hell do I know about good sex. Ralph wasn't worth much in the bedroom.

She pictured her ex-husband, paunchy and dull, and over fifty now. *I still have no clue what ever possessed me.* Although Alice hadn't been pretty, Ralph Finch, a longtime family friend, had watched her change from girl to woman and had wanted her. As he told her, he found her innocence appealing, her intelligence fascinating, and her sense of humor delightful. He had little chance to meet and get to know women with his job as a long-haul truck driver so he had never married. Now it was time to have a wife and start a family and what could be better than someone he already knew well. Love? Passion? They would grow in time.

Her parents had been delighted with the idea and Alice really liked "Uncle Ralph." So, the day after Alice's high school graduation, they were married in the living room of the Waterman home.

The marriage was a bore. Alice worked as the receptionist for an obstetrician while Ralph drove his long-haul truck. They were apart for long periods of time and slowly Alice realized that she was happier when Ralph was not around. When he came home, he enjoyed watching TV, eating the massive amounts of food that Alice cooked to fill him up, sex, and not much else.

Evenings, with Alice beside him on the sofa, they watched sitcoms. As the evening progressed, Ralph would drape his arm around Alice's shoulder and fondle her breast. Then he took her hand and put it on his crotch. "It's been a long time, girl. See how ready I am?"

Usually Alice wasn't nearly ready but, feeling it was her job to satisfy her husband, she allowed Ralph to lead her into the bedroom. She undressed and, after coating his cock with K-Y jelly, he pushed it into her. "I'll never understand why you don't get wet," he said during almost every session. "Maybe you should ask that doctor you work for."

She asked and was told that everything about her physiology was normal. "You might suggest that your husband take his time," the doctor had recommended. She hadn't mentioned that to Ralph.

After almost three years of marriage, Ralph arrived home one day from two weeks on the road. He set his suitcase beside the door and walked slowly into the bedroom, with Alice following. "Honey, I'm really sorry about this, but I'm leaving. There's someone else."

"What?" Alice had been completely unaware that he had any problem with their marriage. She dropped onto the edge of the bed and grabbed a tissue from the box on the bedside table.

"In L.A.," Ralph continued. "She's my age and hot to trot. She loves to do all the things that you don't. She loves *The Cosby Show* and *Golden Girls* and she's great in the sack, if you know what I mean. You just never seem to enjoy it." Alice merely stared, unable to get a word in edgewise, even if she'd had anything to say. "Anyway," Ralph said, "we've been seeing each other each time I drive to the coast. Her grown son just moved out and she wants me to move in with her. I'm gonna do it." As Alice stared, Ralph began to throw the rest of his clothes into their only other large suitcase. "You need someone younger anyway. You need to have some fun."

"I need?" Alice choked past her thick throat.

"Sure. You need a young stud. I know you're not happy."

"What do you care about what I need? This has nothing to do with me. You've found someone better." She hovered between anger and panic.

"Listen. I'm not saying this real well, but it's for the best for both of us." He pulled something from his back pocket. "I went to the bank and took a thousand dollars from our savings account. Here's the passbook." He handed her the slim leather book. "There's almost seven hundred dollars left. Use it to get a divorce. I won't contest anything."

"I put most of that money in there," Alice shrieked. "How dare you take that money so you can move in with that, that woman."

Ralph tossed his few remaining shirts and sweaters into the suitcase. "I've got a load outside and it's going to L.A. I'm not coming back."

"What about the apartment? What about my family?"

"Your job will cover the rent and I really don't care about your family."

"My dad's your best friend. At least call him and explain."

"No time. You tell him whatever you want. Tell him I'll write from the coast."

"Don't bother."

Alice had cried for several days, then she had gotten along surprisingly well. Their first Christmas apart, Ralph had sent her a card with a picture of a decorated tree standing in the middle of a beach. He'd signed the card Ralph and Missy. Alice had dropped it into the garbage. Her parents had been supportive and as helpful as they could be and life quickly took on a new character.

She worked, dated occasionally, and spent increasing amounts of time with Betsy and her family. She felt as close to Larry and the boys as she did to her own family. They had all stood beside her at her father's funeral, celebrated at her sister's wedding, and they spent every holiday together. Now she realized that she hadn't known them. Not by a long shot.

Alice wandered aimlessly around the mall and found herself in front of Victoria's Secret. She gazed in the window at a display of bra and panty sets in vibrant jewel tones. *Sure. Me. Think like a sexpot. Right. Never happen. But the money would be so nice.*

She drove home on automatic pilot, her mind still reeling from Betsy's revelations. As the door to her apartment closed behind her, Alice leaned down to scratch Roger, her brown tabby cat, behind his ears. Always noisy, Roger *merrowed* and rubbed his sides along her legs. "And hello to you," she said. "You'll never believe what I found out today."

Merrow.

She picked up Roger and settled on the sofa with him on her lap. She told the cat everything that Betsy had confessed to her. When he *merrowed* again, Alice said, "Right. I know. You're surprised too."

The ringing of the phone startled them both. Roger dug his claws into Alice's thighs and darted into the bedroom. *No one ever calls me this late.* Worried that it might be her sister with bad news about her mother, she answered, "Hello?"

It was Betsy's voice. "I thought I'd call and make sure you're not shocked or mad at me or something. You don't hate me?"

"Betsy, you know I don't hate you and I'm not mad. Shocked, maybe a little, and maybe just a bit sad that you didn't tell me sooner."

"I didn't know how you'd take it all. You always were a bit . . ."

"A bit what?"

"Sorry. That didn't come out right. Listen. Let me say it this way. Everyone in the world except me, and maybe Larry, thinks that you're a bit of a prude. I know that beneath that straight exterior, there's someone who's willing and able to give the sexy side of life a try."

"A prude? People think I'm a prude?" She slumped back on the overstuffed tan sofa, the one on which Ralph used to watch TV.

"People who don't know you like I do might think you were, well, the old-fashioned spinster type. But you're not, and I know it."

"Spinster type?" Roger jumped onto Alice's lap and she began to scratch him behind his ears. She looked down. Cat, well-worn tan sofa, empty house. Spinster type.

"I wouldn't butt into your life for anything, and you know that. It just seems to me that you've stopped living before you ever started." When Alice gasped, Betsy continued, "Now don't get all defensive and just listen for a moment. I never meant to start this, but maybe it's time I did. After Ralph left, you closed yourself off. You shut everything that was womanly away. You work, hang out with us, and you know we love you, but you need a social life."

"You mean a man."

"Or men, yes. That's what I mean. Have you ever had good sex? I remember Ralph, and I doubt it. I know what's under all that bullshit you've built around yourself. I remember the hours we used to talk about boys. You had wants and needs back then.

You used to fantasize about Ponch and John on *CHiPs,* just like the rest of us. Remember those cruises we used to plan on *The Love Boat?* You got Gopher and I got, oh, what was the name of the cute guy who took the pictures?"

Alice chuckled and put her feet up on the coffee table. "Ace. He was only there at the end. I do remember. We used to spend long evenings talking when we were supposed to be doing social studies."

"So what happened to her?"

"Who?"

"The you who used to be so alive?"

Alice was silent. She'd never heard Betsy talk this way. "I like my life."

"Spending time with my kids? I have never pushed you and I'm not going to start now. I do want you to think about all this, though, and consider that this job, if it works out, may be a way to find your sexual self without any risk. It's just the phone."

"If I'm such a spinster type," she said, bitterly, "why the hell do you think I'd be any good at this phone stuff?"

"Because I know you better than you know yourself. There's a real woman under there, with hot erotic fantasies and dreams. This would be the perfect outlet. You're a natural storyteller. Even the boys know that. You could use that talent and create erotic fantasies for nice, frustrated men who just want someone to talk dirty with."

Alice tried to keep the pain out of her voice. "I really don't think so but I understand all this a bit better now."

"Alice, don't be hurt. You know how much I care about you. I love you like a sister. Please, think over all I've said and I'll see you in the morning."

The morning. How would she face her friend? She'd have to. If she lost Betsy, who did she have? She gazed at the blank TV screen. Wasn't that the point Betsy was trying to make? "Yeah. I'll see you in the morning. Night."

"Night, babe." The phone went silent in her hand. Slowly she replaced the receiver on the base, picked up the cat, and walked slowly into the bedroom, turning off lights as she went. She flipped on the bedroom light and looked around. The room was pretty much unchanged from the day that Ralph left, nearly ten years earlier. Actually from long before that since Alice had moved into Ralph's apartment after they were married. She looked around. Heavy wooden furniture that had been Ralph's. Faded blue bedspread and blue denim drapes that she had made from an old sheet their first winter together. Dull gray carpet with a nail-polish stain beside the bed. It was pretty dismal but she seldom really saw it.

Mindlessly Alice turned on the TV, already tuned to *Headline News*. "God, Roger," she said, dropping onto the bed still holding the cat, "maybe Betsy's right. *Headline News*. It's nine-thirty and I'm watching *Headline News*. If it were Tuesday, Betsy would be on the phone to God-knows-who talking about God-knows-what." She scratched the cat under his chin. "You're the only man in my life. Prude. Spinster type. Shit."

Throughout the night, Alice tossed and turned, unable to get her conversations with Betsy out of her mind. The following morning, feeling cranky from lack of sleep, she arrived at Dr. Tannenbaum's office. Betsy was already there dressed in a light purple scrub top and matching pants, her brown hair pulled back with two gold barrettes. "Morning," Betsy said, sounding disgustingly cheerful. "You look like shit."

"I didn't get much sleep." Alice pulled off her coat, revealing a cartoon character-print scrub top and jeans. She wore only lipstick and there were faint purple circles underneath her eyes.

"I was afraid of that." Betsy took Alice's coat, hung it up then hugged her friend. "I'm sorry. I replayed the discussions we had. My diatribe, actually, and I'm afraid lots of it didn't come out quite the way I intended."

Alice hugged Betsy then stepped back. "You know, I thought it all through, too, and I have to admit that lots of what you said made sense." She smiled. "I hate it when you're right."

"Right how?" Betsy's expression was wary.

"I do need a life. I'm not sure whether I need the one you're offering, but it's certainly worth a bit more thought and I really do need the money."

The two women walked into the reception room and sat down. "I'm really sorry for a lot of what I said," Betsy said.

"It's the way you feel."

"Yes, but I don't want to push you. You don't have to do anything you don't want to do. If you want to talk more about it, let me know, but I promise that I won't mention it again."

"You won't have to. I'll wager I won't be able to think about anything else." The door opened and the two women looked up. "Good morning, Mrs. McAllister," Alice said to the morning's first patient. "How's your lovely new grand-baby?"

Over the next few days Alice spent a great deal of time talking to her sister. Her mother's condition had stabilized and even improved a bit and Sue's friend was working out well as a daytime caregiver. They had applied to Rutlandt and two or three second-best nursing homes, hoping for admission by May first. If Rutlandt came through, they'd have to figure out how to pay for it, or turn it down in favor of the less-expensive place.

The following Tuesday evening, Alice sat in her living room, holding Roger and trying to picture Betsy on the phone with her customers. *Where would I even start? I can't talk dirty. I'm not even sure what guys like. I certainly didn't know what Ralph liked. Guys like women who know how to perform oral sex. Ralph used to joke about it. "Too bad you don't give head, girl," he used to tell her. Why didn't he ever let me try?*

Since Dr. Tannenbaum's office was closed on Wednesdays, Alice ran a few errands in the neighborhood, but continued to dwell on Betsy's phone business. Bizarre pictures whirled in her head. Betsy with shiny flame-red lipstick, her pursed lips near the receiver. Men with no faces but large ears, listening, talking, touching themselves. There were moments when she thought she might be able to do what her best friend did, but there were hours when she knew she couldn't.

Thursday morning, Alice arrived at work before Betsy and expectantly waited for her friend. "Morning," Betsy said, breezing in despite a freezing March drizzle that had soaked Alice's coat and made driving hazardous.

"How'd it go Tuesday evening?" Alice asked, watching Betsy hang up her heavy coat. "I kept thinking about you."

"It went great. It almost always does."

"Almost always?"

"Oh, occasionally it's difficult to get on the same wavelength with someone new," she said, walking into the empty reception area. "You have to use some charm and skill to find out what turns them on."

"How did you learn all that?" Alice asked, feeling more daunted than ever.

"Time, and lots of calls. And Velvet's a great help. She's been doing this for almost fifteen years and she knows all the tricks."

"Where do you start? I mean how do you know what will turn someone on?"

"I get lots of those shrink-wrapped magazines and read them from cover to cover. I particularly read the stories and the ads for phone sex. You'd be amazed what you can learn from what the publishers of those magazines think men like. I assume they're right since the magazines sell."

"I could do that, but I'd feel like a fool going into a store and buying *Penthouse* or *Playboy*."

"Why? Nice folks read them, you know. Now, of course, there's the Internet. You can find thousands of stories out there. I browse occasionally for new ideas and, along with the pictures of naked men and women, there are lots of pieces of good, erotic fiction out there." Maureen, the dental hygienist, walked in and hung up her coat. After the usual good mornings, she walked into the operatory area and the two women lowered their voices.

"That's a good idea. Maybe I'll do that and see whether I could say some of that stuff."

"You know, Velvet has a large number of guys who phone regularly. I wonder whether anyone likes the reticent, shy type who'll say the naughty words only reluctantly." Betsy's eyes glazed over momentarily. "That might be appealing actually."

"Really?"

"I don't know. Look, if you think you want to do this, I'll give Velvet a call and ask. I'd want you to meet her anyway."

That night, Alice signed on to her Internet account and went searching. She found several stories that seemed like they might be good so she printed them out. When she was done, she went into the bedroom with a beer. Roger curled up beside her as she started to read.

WITHOUT A WORD
by Silent Sal

Michelle lay somewhere between sleep and wakefulness, listening to the upstairs neighbors stomp around their bedroom getting ready for bed. She glanced at the clock. Almost 2:00 A.M. *I shouldn't get too angry since it happens so seldom,* she told herself. *They're such nice people, they probably just aren't thinking.*

She felt her husband, Bill, scramble out of his side of the bed and wander to the bathroom. The door closed, the light went on, and then later it went out again. In a few minutes he was back in the warm cocoon and, with a yawn, Michelle leisurely climbed out of her side and padded to the bathroom.

Several minutes later, slightly chilled from the cold night air, she climbed back under the thick quilt, thinking how glad she was that unlike Bill, she could go to the john in the middle of the night without having to turn on the light. As she snuggled her chest against Bill's large, warm back, she had a few fleeting erotic flashes. Well, she reasoned, if she fell back to sleep, she'd awake refreshed.

Wait a moment, she told herself. *Why should I go back to sleep? I have the desire and Bill's right here. Why not do something about it?*

She had never been particularly bold about lovemaking, leaving most of the first moves to her husband. Bill was almost always the initiator of sex, but why shouldn't she be the aggressor from time to time? She cuddled more tightly against his back and felt her nipples harden in response to her wandering thoughts. Was he still awake? She'd find out quickly enough.

She stroked Bill's arm, just enjoying the feel of the short, wiry hairs that covered his skin. She seldom took the time to enjoy touching her husband so she spent several minutes stroking his arm, hands, and fingers. Then she reached around and flattened her palms on Bill's chest and stroked the smooth surface. When her palms contacted Bill's small nipples, she rubbed them, then used a short fingernail to scratch the tiny nub into life. Amazed, she felt it harden beneath her finger. She wiggled her hips so her pubic bone rubbed against Bill's tailbone and realized that she was getting wetter. Bill hadn't said anything or reacted in any obvious way, but Michelle became aware of a slight hoarseness to his breathing. *He's awake all right. He's playing possum so I'll continue, so he must be enjoying what I'm doing.*

She slid her palm down to Bill's waist and felt his abdominal muscles contract. With her cheek against his back, she could hear and feel his breathing quicken. When he tried to turn over, she held on, enjoying her position behind him. Slowly Michelle slid her palm down his belly and suddenly his cock, hard and throbbing, bumped against the back of her hand. Seemingly content now to remain on his side with his wife in charge, Bill gasped and lay still.

He's so horny, she thought, *and I did that*. It was a revelation. She knew in her mind that he would enjoy it if she took the lead occasionally, but she had always been hesitant. *What if I do it wrong or he thinks I'm being silly or he's not in the mood?* Worried, in the past, when she had considered making the first move, she had demurred. *Well*, she thought, *he is obviously enjoying this. Maybe I can do it more often.* She quieted her thoughts and concentrated on the feel of Bill's body. As her palm caressed his belly, the back of her hand caressed his hard cock.

She kissed his back and licked a wide stripe. Then, unable to get enough of his skin into her mouth to nip him, she scraped her teeth along his spine. She knew full well that he wanted her to grasp his cock, but she resisted the urge, teasing him. She knew that he wouldn't ask, leaving her to set the pace, unwilling to disturb the mood. He was enjoying the silence, the dark, the slight mystery and anonymity of it all as much as she was.

Michelle squirmed, feeling Bill's skin against her now-heated body. Her belly against his back, her thighs against his ass cheeks, her breasts against his shoulder blades, she moved like a cat in heat. God, he felt so good.

Then she did it. She grasped Bill's cock and held it tightly. She had held his cock many times before, to guide it into her waiting body, but she'd never actually rubbed it to climax. Could she do it? She wanted him inside of her, but this was too intriguing to resist. Although it was scary, she wanted to try. She held him tightly and felt his whole body tense. Her entire body was in tune with his and she was aware of his every reaction to what she was doing. She held fast, pulling her hand upward toward the tip of his erection. The end was already wet with his pre-come and she used the tip of her index finger to rub the lubricant around the head of his penis.

As she did so, she felt his body tighten still more and his hips moved almost involuntarily. *God, this is so good,* she thought again. She squeezed again and pulled her hand downward toward the base of the hard rod, using his body's own lubricant to ease her way. Again to the tip and more fluid.

Soon his cock was slippery and she could slide her hand

up and down in a slow rhythm. Feeling braver, she stopped and decided to explore a bit. She slid one finger up and down the underside of Bill's cock, then slid farther down and touched his balls. The moan she heard and felt was all the reassurance she needed. It was a bit difficult to reach, but she ran the pad of her finger over the surface of his sac. Did she want him to turn over so she could do more? No, she realized. If he lay on his back she'd be tempted to climb on top of him and she really wanted to see whether she could bring him to climax without intercourse.

She returned her attention to his cock and stroked, first toward the tip, then downward to the base. She heard air hiss out between Bill's teeth. His cock took on a life of its own and moved beneath her hand. Bill sighed, then groaned softly.

Michelle flattened her hand on the underside of his cock, pressed it against his abdomen and rubbed. She felt him pulse, then his hips jerked and his cock twitched against her palm. He came, silently, his entire body throbbing against her. Her hand was now covered with his sticky come and some of it dripped onto the sheet. Wordlessly, Bill grabbed a corner of the top sheet and wiped the goo from her hand and his abdomen.

Still silent, he turned and pushed her onto her back. His mouth found her hard, erect nipple, and his teeth caused shards of pleasure to rocket through her already aroused body. His mouth alternated between her nipples until she was almost crying with need. Unwilling to break the silence, she pushed against Bill's shoulders, urging him to use his hands to finish her off. She heard a slight chuckle, then he slithered down beneath the covers and locked his mouth on her now-needy pussy. His tongue flicked over her clit, then lapped up the fluids that had collected between her swollen inner lips.

Now almost crazy with lust, Michelle tangled her long fingers in her husband's curly hair and held his face tightly against her need. A finger pushed inside her channel and, as he licked, he drove first one then two fingers in and out of her hot pussy. Her belly clenched and her legs trembled. It was only moments before she came, spasms echoing through her body as flaming colors flashed behind her eyes. Almost unable to catch her breath, she gently pushed Bill's face aside and he slid up and cuddled against her. In almost no time, they were both back to sleep.

In the morning, Michelle awoke to find Bill propped on his elbow, watching her. "I had the most wonderful dream," he purred.

"You did?" she said, a grin spreading across her face.

He leaned over until she could feel his warm breath on her face. "I dreamed that a sexy woman held me and stroked me in the middle of the night until I came. She didn't say anything, but I could have sworn it was you."

"I had a wonderful dream too. Some sexy man used his very talented mouth to make me come."

"Hmm. Matching dreams. I wonder whether that has some significance?"

"I think it does. I certainly think so."

Alice put the pages beside her on the bed and lifted Roger onto her lap. That woman had had her doubts too. She hadn't been sure how to touch her husband, but she had done what felt good to both of them. Why hadn't she ever done anything like that? Her sex life had been a bust and she hadn't done anything to make it better. She hadn't known anything, but how was she supposed to have learned? Ralph had never told her what to do, never even suggested. She had been a failure as a wife, but didn't Ralph bear any of the responsibility? Wasn't it his job, if only a little, to help her, teach her? She had read several sex books their first year together and had tried to talk to her husband about their love life but he had always put her off. "Oh, girl, it's all right. I'm happy with things the way they are." But she hadn't been happy and she knew now that he hadn't been happy either.

So whose fault was it? Was she a prude who would never be any good at sex? No, and it wasn't her fault, nor was it Ralph's. And what about her life since? Hadn't she just given up? After Ralph left, she had her job, her family, and Betsy. Was that normal? She hadn't really dated, and she hadn't had anything resembling sex in what seemed like forever.

She sighed and said, "Roger, where am I now? Thirty-two years old. A spinster type who's never even lived." She dumped Roger onto the bed and strode into the bathroom. She closed the door and looked at herself in the full-length mirror. "Dumpy," she said. Face? Plain. She tucked her shirt into her jeans, sucked in her stomach and pulled a large gulp of air into her lungs. Figure? Ordinary. Overweight. Boobs? Average. Quickly she stripped off her clothes and looked at her naked body. "Underneath all those clothes there's nothing good." Thighs? Heavy. Belly? Rounded and getting rounder. Tits? Sagging. She lifted her arms, looked at the slight droop beneath her upper arms and sighed. She wandered back into the bedroom and pulled on the oversized New York Jets T-shirt she slept in. "You know, Roger, it's only phone sex. They'd never see me. I could look like a hippo for all anyone would know, and I could become anyone."

She crouched beside her bookshelf and found the collection of how-to sex books she had bought while she was married. She pulled one out and stared at the dust. *I could learn a lot. I remember that these had a lot of good ideas. I could do some reading and learn.* "I really could, Roger."

She climbed into bed and picked up the second set of pages she had printed from the Internet. One more before sleep. Maybe it would lead to good dreams.

Chapter

4

In the Hot Tub

It had been a terrible week for twenty-eight-year-old Eric La Monte. First, he and his girlfriend of almost a year had split. "I want some freedom," she had said, "some time to explore who I really am." Eric had sat on his side of the bed in their Palm Springs condo and watched her pack. Then he'd spent three days explaining her absence to his entire family and all his friends. Why? everyone asked. God only knows, became his litany. Finally, on Thursday, his district manager had arrived for a three-day surprise visit to the supermarket he managed. Sure, he thought later, everything could have been a lot worse on that front. He'd received only a few "needs improvement" warnings, but, all in all, it had been an awful week.

Now it was Saturday evening, and he was exhausted and alone. He lay on the bed and tried to sleep, but it was impossible. Every time he closed his eyes he thought about Marge or Mr. Pomerantz. Neither mental picture was geared to allow him to sleep. "Shit," he muttered climbing out of bed as the red numerals on the clock read 1:07 A.M. "I gotta relax." Although it was early summer, it was still over eighty degrees. The condo's hot tub and pool closed at eleven but

he could easily climb the fence and lounge in the hot bubbling water for a while. "It'll help me unwind."

With just a towel around his loins, Eric walked to the
fence around the pool, surprised to find the gate unlocked.
Most of the lights were out, so he heard rather than saw that
the bubbles were on in the tub. Through the mist, he saw a
woman's gray head. Since much of Palm Springs's population was made up of retirees, Eric assumed that the person
in the pool was some ancient specimen boiling the arthritis
out of old bones at 1:00 A.M. "Shit," he muttered again. "Some
old bitch is where I want to be." He remembered that, since
he had assumed he'd be alone, he had not worn a bathing suit.
"Fuck her," he hissed, striding to the edge of the tub, dropping the towel and climbing into the bubbling cauldron.

As he settled into the hot water, Eric looked through the
dimly lighted mist at the woman sitting across the pool. She
was not bad-looking, maybe only fifty or so, with flushed
cheeks and wet, shoulder-length hair. Eric ignored her, cradled his head on the concrete rim, draped his arms over the
edge, and closed his eyes.

"I thought I'd be the only one here at this hour," her soft
voice said over the bubble noise. "I'm Carol."

"Eric," he grunted.

"Well," Carol said, "It's going to get a bit embarrassing in
here in a minute or so. The timer on the pump has only a
short while to go and I'm afraid I'm not wearing anything
either. I usually reset the dial for a second go-around."

"No sweat," Eric said. "I promise I won't look if you
want to extend the time."

"Thanks." Eric could hear the smile in her voice. Then
he heard her leave the water and quietly pad over to the
controls. He heard the creak of the dials. He couldn't resist,
so he opened his eyes and looked. Not bad, he thought. Not
bad at all. She was slender and firm, with a slight droop to her
bosom but in general not bad. Not Marge, of course but . . .

She padded back to the steps and slowly walked down

into the heated water. "You're looking," she said, seeming unperturbed.

Eric slammed his eyes shut. "Sorry," he mumbled.

"I'm not," she said. "I like it when men look at me."

Eric opened his eyes again and saw that she was still standing, thigh-deep in the warm water. "You're not bad to look at," he said.

He watched as she slowly took a handful of heated water and released it over her right breast. Then another over her left. "I love the heat," she said.

Despite the debilitating effect of the hot water, Eric felt a stirring in his groin. "How come you're here after hours?" he asked, deflecting the conversation before his cock got embarrassingly hard.

"I couldn't sleep. I often come out here after midnight so I got a key from a particularly friendly security guard."

The way she said *particularly friendly* had Eric's ears perked. How friendly, he wondered.

"How about you?" she asked, lowering herself into the water beside him. "How come you're here tonight?"

"Couldn't sleep either," Eric said. He could sense her presence beside him although he couldn't actually feel her skin.

"I couldn't help but notice that Marge moved out."

"What do you know about that?"

"There's not much real privacy here. I hope it was your idea. Breakups can be so difficult."

"Actually it was hers," Eric said, closing his eyes. "I don't really want to talk about it." Suddenly Eric felt a hand on his leg.

"I'm sure you don't, Eric," Carol said. "It's tough."

The hand was kneading his thigh. It could be just a gesture of sympathy, he told himself, but it was having an effect on his cock anyway. *I've got to change the subject before I say something dumb.* "Are you married?" Was that a change of topic?

"Used to be, but we were divorced almost five years ago."

"That's tough," Eric said.

"Not really," Carol said, her hand still kneading the flesh of Eric's thigh. "I make do."

This is getting to be a bit too much, Eric thought. *She can't be doing what I think she's doing. This sort of thing doesn't happen. Not to me.* "Oh." Eric squeezed his eyes shut, trying to ignore the hand on his thigh. "Which unit is yours?" he asked.

"I'm in B-204. It's quite comfortable for just me."

The hand crept a bit higher, the fingers almost in his groin. "I'll bet it is," he croaked.

He felt her mouth close to his cheek. "I hope I'm not upsetting you," she said into his ear. Then she giggled. "Actually I hope I am." The hand found his testicles and one finger brushed the surface. "Am I?"

Eric opened his eyes and looked at the woman sitting next to him. There could be no misinterpreting her movements. She was seducing him. His arm was still on the edge of the pool. He draped it around her shoulders and pulled her closer. "Yes," he said, his mouth against hers, "you are. Is that what you want?"

Carol's tongue reached out and licked the sweat from Eric's upper lip. "Oh yes. I want to bother you a lot."

He kissed her then, pressing his wet mouth against hers, tasting salt and chlorine and her. His mouth opened and his tongue touched hers. So hot, deep, and wet. Her mouth seemed to pull him closer.

His hands found her breasts, soft, full, and floaty in the bubbling water. He had never played with weightless breasts before. They felt loose and incredibly sexy. Then he couldn't concentrate on anything, because her hand had surrounded his cock and now squeezed tightly. "God," she breathed, "you're so big."

She probably says that to everyone, he thought in the small part of his brain still capable of thought. It's such a cliché come-on line, but he went with it all. His cock was the biggest ever, and she wanted it.

He slid his hands to her waist and started to lift her onto his ready staff.

"Not so fast, baby," she purred. "I'm not nearly ready for you yet." She stood up and climbed out of the tub, beckoning him to follow. He was incapable of resistance. She straddled a plastic-webbed lounge chair, one foot on the concrete at either side. She patted the chair between her legs. "Here, baby," she purred and he sat facing her.

She lay back and smiled. "The air is just cool enough to feel good on my hot, wet body. Yours too?"

"Yes," Eric said, his hands scrambling in her crotch. She reached down and held her labia open. "Touch nice and soft right now," she said. "Rub in the folds. I like to be touched everywhere."

Eric had calmed a bit and was now able to think coherently. He slowly explored every crease between Carol's legs. He'd always been too hungry to pay much attention to Marge's body. Now he got to know Carol's. When he rubbed back toward her anus, she moaned and moved her hips. When he brushed her clit, she gasped. It was wonderful. She was telling him so clearly exactly what she wanted, without saying a word.

She was so wet, he noticed. Slippery juice oozed backward and wet her puckered rear entry. He ran his finger around the opening and Carol trembled. Could he?

"I like what you're doing," she said, as if reading his mind. "You can do anything you like. I'll tell you to stop if I don't like it."

He had never just sat and touched a woman like this before, watching her face and body respond to his fingers. It was arousing, yet as hard as his cock was, he was also capable of waiting, enjoying the now and not rushing forward. He pressed his index finger against her puckered rear hole and marveled at how it slipped in just a bit.

"Oh, God," she hissed. "That's incredible."

Eric slipped the finger in just a bit more and watched Carol writhe. He used his other hand to stroke her clit, knowing that she was close to climax. Part of him wanted to plunge his cock into her, but another part wanted to finish her off just this way. He pulled the finger from her ass, then pushed it back in. Her juices were flowing so copiously that his hand was soaked, his finger wet enough to penetrate her rear hole. Slowly the digit slid farther and farther into her rear passage. Faster and faster he rubbed her hard nub.

When he thought she was ready, he leaned down and placed his mouth over her clit. He flicked his tongue firmly over the hard bud and felt her back arch and her hands tangle in his hair. "Yes, yes," she hissed. "Now."

He felt her come, felt the spasms in her ass, felt her cunt pulse against his mouth. He didn't move until he felt her begin to relax. "I want to fuck you," he said.

"I know," Carol said, panting, "but let's do this my way. Please."

Eric shrugged. He was beyond caring about the "how."

Slowly, Carol got up and moved Eric around so he was sitting properly on the chair, her body stretched out between his legs. "I love it this way," she whispered. Her hands cupped his balls and her mouth found his cock. She licked the tip, then blew on the wet spot. She licked the length of his shaft underneath, then each side. She kneaded his balls, then insinuated one finger beneath his sacs, reaching for his anus.

He closed his eyes. No one had ever touched him there and he wasn't sure he would like it. He did. It was electric. Shafts of pure pleasure rocketed down his cock as the familiar tightness started in his belly and balls. "I'm going to shoot," he said, his voice hoarse.

Carol lifted her head. "Oh yes. Do it, baby. Shoot for me." She took the length of him in her mouth as she rimmed his asshole.

He couldn't hold back and the jism boiled from his loins into her mouth. He opened his eyes and looked at her cheeks as she tried unsuccessfully to swallow his come. Small dribbles escaped from the corners of her mouth and wet his balls.

A few minutes later Carol took her towel, dipped it in the

hot tub and tenderly washed Eric's groin. "I have to go in now," she said.

Limp, drained, and unable to move, Eric said, "I wish you'd stay."

"No you don't," she said, smiling. "You need to recover alone. But I'm here almost every night about one o'clock. Come back whenever you get lonely."

"Good night," Eric said. "I know I'll be here again soon."

"Oh," she said, opening the gate, "I hope so."

Eric watched her back and remembered thinking of her as an old bitch. *Gray hair indeed*, he thought. *The fire's still on in that sexy furnace. I'll never underestimate older women again.*

Alice put the pages on the bed-table beside her and flipped off the light. *I'm only thirty-two*, she thought. *I could learn. I really could. Then I'd be like Carol. I just need a little practice.* She yawned and was asleep almost instantly.

In her dream she was in a hot tub, naked. The water bubbled all around her, teasing and tickling. She looked around and all she could see were palm trees, thick and completely surrounding the tub, obliterating any houses and prying eyes. There was a man in the water with her, across the tub, an old man with thick white hair and a wizened face with deep wrinkles and smile lines. "Ralph?" she asked.

"No. He's gone," the man said. "I'm here with you."

"Oh," she said, the bubbles now causing steam to rise from the tub. What was she doing in a hot tub, nude, with some strange man? She moved to cover herself but realized that with all the bubbles, nothing could be seen below the water.

"It's your turn now," he said.

"My turn for what?"

"It's your turn for yourself."

"What does that mean?"

The man shook his head sadly. "If you don't know, well . . . It's really all up to you."

"You talk in riddles," Alice said.

"No, I don't. You don't want to hear."

"Do you mean I can do this? I should do this?"

"Only you know."

She rested her head on the edge of the tub and closed her eyes. Then his hands were on her, gently pinching her nipples, his teeth nipping at her ear. She lay, her arms stretched across the edge of the tub as his hands played with her breasts and his mouth teased hers. Then his hands were between her legs. She opened her eyes and looked down but she couldn't see what he was doing through the bubbles.

It felt good. He touched and teased, yet she couldn't quite feel where his hands were at anytime. It was just a general sensation of being touched everywhere. She felt her nipples harden and her pussy swell. She wanted. Needed.

Then she was awake, staring into the darkened room, feeling the warmth of Roger's body pressed against her side. She was lying with her arms stretched out at the shoulder and she could almost feel the edge of the hot tub. As the dream faded, she turned on her side and went back to sleep.

The following morning, she was up before the alarm and at Dr. Tannenbaum's office before eight. The first patient was early and was already in the operatory when Betsy arrived. The two women had little time to talk throughout the busy morning. At about eleven, Alice snagged Betsy as she passed. "Lunch?" she asked her friend. "We haven't had lunch together in a few weeks. How about it?"

"You sound like a woman with a purpose," Betsy said. "Have you come to a decision?"

"I think so but I need to talk to you."

"Okay. How about the diner?"

"Done."

By one-fifteen Betsy and Alice were seated in a booth and had ordered club sandwiches and Diet Cokes. "I did some reading last evening and that led to a lot of thinking. I'd like to give it a try but I'll need lots of help."

"Don't worry about that. I hope you won't mind but I already talked to Velvet and broached the idea about you taking a few calls. She'll need to meet you and chat, but I think it will work out. Her business is growing every month and she was already thinking about hiring another girl or two. You'd fit right in."

"How does it work, logistically, I mean?"

"Velvet has a pretty advanced computer system. Someone calls. If it's a prearranged appointment, the call goes directly to the right phone. If it's not, the person talks to the router and the caller can ask for the woman he wants to talk to. If she's available, then the call goes through. If she's not, then the caller can wait, in which case they pay while they are on hold. If he doesn't want to wait for a specific woman or if the caller is new to Velvet Whispers, there's a queuing system so it's the next available person. Some girls need a place to be, so they work at Velvet's house. Others, like me, work at our own homes but between the computer and the phone company, everyone gets paid."

"How many girls does Velvet have?"

"It varies. It's usually around a dozen."

"I never realized that there would be so many people doing this stuff."

"And Velvet's only one of thousands of phone services all around the country."

"Does she really charge three dollars a minute?"

"It seems like a lot, but many services charge more."

"I can't get over it. My cut would be almost a hundred bucks an hour." That number had been bouncing around in her brain since Betsy first told her about Velvet Whispers.

"I know. It still amazes me. I get to keep half, the router gets paid, and Velvet gets the rest."

"That seems fair. Is this legal?"

"Sure. It's not prostitution. Just a phone call."

The two women stopped talking as the waiter brought their sandwiches and drinks. When he turned toward another table Alice leaned forward and, sotto voce, asked, "What if a guy refuses to pay?" What if she tried it and was a flop?

"Velvet and the girl involved take the hit, of course, and he never gets to call again. Most men really enjoy the service and wouldn't jeopardize it by not paying the bill. Actually for some men who worry about the money, I have a timer that dings every fifteen minutes to keep them aware of the time. I don't want anyone to be surprised."

"Don't they want to call you directly? You know, cut out the middleman and pay you less."

"A few have suggested it, but I wouldn't dream of cutting Velvet out. Anyway, I don't want to give out my home number."

"Yeah, I understand. How many regular customers do you have?" Alice took a large bite of her sandwich.

"I take three hours of calls a night, that's usually between four and six callers. Some are prearranged, some just random. The first-time clients take a bit longer since I have to take my time and find out what they want." Betsy poured a lake of ketchup beside the french fries on her plate.

"That sounds really scary. What if they aren't satisfied?"

"There's no guarantee, of course, and they take that risk. Most men want pretty much the same things and they make their needs quite clear from the beginning."

"Lots of four letter words and adjectives?"

Betsy chuckled and chewed her fry. "Some. Others just want someone to talk to. Some want to tell *their* exploits, some want to talk about doing things their wives don't want to do, some just want to masturbate while you *watch.*"

"Wives? Are they married? That never occurred to me. I thought most of them would he horny single guys with no one to play with."

"That's what I thought when I started. Lots of them, however, are men with wives they think wouldn't understand their desires. Some want to talk about bondage, spanking, or anal sex, things they think *nice girls* like their wives wouldn't be interested in."

"I see."

Betsy raised an inquiring eyebrow. "Want to meet Velvet?"

"I think I would."

"I'll set something up and let you know."

They continued to eat, and talked about other matters. Alice felt both light and terrified, and the feelings hadn't changed by the following Saturday afternoon when she pulled into the drive-way of a small house in Putnam Valley. She had considered how to dress and had changed clothes after Dr. Tannenbaum's office closed. She had finally decided on a pair of tan slacks, a brown turtleneck sweater, and an oatmeal-colored wool jacket. As she walked up the driveway, she tried not to prejudge, but she knew that she had already created a mental image of Velvet that was surprisingly like the bosomy madam of old western movies. Over made up, slightly overdressed, with eyes that knew everything about men that there was to know.

The woman who answered the door couldn't have resembled her image less. "Hello. You must be Alice." She was dressed in jeans and a pale blue sweatshirt. "Obviously, I'm Velvet. Come on in." Alice followed in a daze. Velvet was in her mid-thirties, with carefully blow-dried hair and just a hint of makeup. She was about five foot six, and weighed only about a hundred and ten pounds. She was not particularly pretty, but she had large eyes that were so deep blue as to be almost black, with long lashes. And she was al-most completely flat-chested. Why had Alice expected big breasts?

"I thought we could talk in the den," Velvet said, taking Alice's jacket and leading the way through a neat, tastefully fur-nished, split-level house. They walked through the living room to the back of the house and stopped at the doorway of a wood-paneled room furnished with two comfortable leather lounge chairs. The den was occupied by a boy of about Brandon's age, and a girl who looked to be about five. They were stretched out on the floor, the boy working on a half-built model car and the girl carefully coloring a picture of the Little Mermaid. "Matthew and Caitlin, say hello to Ms. Waterman."

"Hello, Ms. Waterman," the two said in unison.

"I need to use this room for a little while." She opened a closet above the TV and fished out a video. "How about *Milo and Otis*? You two can watch in my room while I talk with Ms. Waterman."

"That movie's dumb. Can I work on my car?"

"Put down lots of newspaper and be careful with the glue. Okay?"

"Okay." The boy gathered the pieces of his model and the rest of the paraphernalia and started toward the door.

"Can we have ice cream?" Caltlin asked.

"It's too close to dinnertime."

"Please. Pretty please with sugar on it." Alice could tell from Matthew's expression that he usually let Caitlin do the wheedling.

"No ice cream. Daddy's in the basement. Ask him to cut up an apple for each of you and you can take that and a can of soda upstairs. But don't spill."

"Thanks, Mommy," Caltlin said.

"And after the movie, can I play Nintendo?" Matthew added.

Velvet turned to Alice. "They both have great futures as negotiators." She turned back to her children. "Okay, if there's time. Now scoot."

The two bounced from the room, yelling, "Daddy, we get sodas."

Velvet grinned at the backs of her children. "They're a handful but I love them."

Alice's mind was boggled. She had just gotten used to her best friend, mother of her godchildren, being a phone-sex operator. Now this. Velvet wasn't at all what Alice had expected. "They are wonderful. I understand that Matthew is the same age as Brandon."

"They were born on the same day. Betsy and I treat ourselves to dinner the following week, just to prove we lived through the annual birthday parties the way we lived through childbirth." Alice and Velvet settled into the matched lounge chairs. "You look slightly like the deer caught in the headlights," Velvet said.

"I'm sorry. I've only known about you and everything for about a week. It's still hard to wrap my mind around it all. You seem so . . .

"Normal?"

"I guess. I'm sorry. I don't mean to be insulting."

"You're not, and I appreciate the honesty. Can I get you something to drink?"

"No, thanks."

"Why don't you tell me about yourself?"

For several minutes, Alice told Velvet about her life and about

Ralph. She freely admitted that her marriage hadn't been a sexual revelation and that she was still somewhat naive. "I've been doing a lot of reading and my eyes are opening rather quickly."

"I'll bet. Betsy tells me you're something of a storyteller. She says you're very good at it."

"Yes. I guess so."

"I've been toying with an idea for several months and when Betsy called and told me about you, I thought you might just be the right person." Curious, Alice remained silent. "I've had several men ask me to tell them erotic stories. I've suggested that they read tales from books or from the Internet, but they said they wanted to hear really hot fantasies from the lips of a woman with a sexy voice."

"But you . . ."

"Not my thing. I'm good at different things." Velvet winked. "I can talk a man to orgasm really well." Velvet took a deep breath, dropped her shoulders and her chin and said, "Sometimes I have just the sexy voice they are looking for." Her voice had changed completely. It was soft, breathy, and lower pitched. Alice knew that if she were a man, that voice would go right through her.

"How do you do that?"

"It's really not difficult. I'll show you. Do you think you could make up really hot stories? You could write them beforehand, but your client might ask for something special. You'd have to be able to think on your feet."

"I don't know. I hadn't thought about it."

"It would make things a bit easier for you until you get the hang of this."

"I guess it would be easier." Alice had thought about having to personally interact with the men on the phone, verbally being part of the sex, and that had felt like the most difficult part. Now Velvet had thought of another way. Prewritten stories.

"It would mean that you wouldn't get too many men 'off the street.' Most would be prearranged because of your specialty and it might lower your financial expectations. I gather you need the money to help your mom."

"I need about four hundred a month to get her into the best nursing home in Westchester."

Alice could see Velvet quickly calculate. "That shouldn't be a problem. Here's what I would suggest. How about writing a few stories and letting me read them? That will give me an idea of how well you express the things that men want to hear."

"That sounds like a good way to begin," Alice said, "and it takes some of the pressure off me." That way she wouldn't have to get on the phone until she was sure she could please the client. The thought of failure terrified her.

"Then we can see where we'll go from there. How about coming over next Saturday afternoon, same time and I'll read what you've written? Or, if you write something sooner you could mail it to me. I don't want to rush you, but I gather you're under some time pressure."

Alice and her sister had found an upcoming spot in a second-tier nursing home, but were still waiting to hear from Rutlandt. The current arrangement would work for another three weeks, then they would have to make a decision. "I guess Betsy told you the whole story."

"She did, and I'm really sorry. Both of my parents and both of Wayne's are still alive and, as they age, their future concerns me."

"I'll write what I can this week, and then be back same time next Saturday and we can talk more."

"Wonderful. Betsy's one of my favorite people and I'm glad to help."

"Don't do it just for her."

"I wouldn't dream of it. This is my business and the source of all our savings. I wouldn't jeopardize it for anyone. If I don't think you'll work out, I'll tell you."

"Thanks. I just need for you to be honest."

The two women stood and Velvet handed Alice her jacket. They walked to the front door and, as she stepped into the clear late-afternoon sunshine, Velvet quickly kissed her on the cheek. "Write up a storm."

"I will, and thanks for the chance."

Chapter
5

As she drove home, Alice thought about everything Velvet had said, and realized that, as naive as she might be in her personal life, she was creative enough to give this a real try. It wasn't going to be easy, but they didn't pay big bucks because what she was trying to do was easy. It was late in the afternoon and the sun was low in the sky. Although it was late March, there was no real hint of spring yet, so as she drove, Alice turned the heater up a notch.

Heat. That was what she needed to create in any story she wrote. She'd always been good in English composition and had gotten lots of A's on her writing in high school, but this wasn't high school. Not by a long shot. Oh well. She had nothing to lose.

When she arrived home, she turned on her computer and browsed the Net. She was becoming familiar with a few of the picture sites and she gazed with a clinical eye at the photos. Most of them didn't excite her, but she found that a few, involving people being tied up, made her uneasy in a not unpleasant way. She tried to think like a researcher and assumed that most of the sites were aimed at males. She gleaned lots of pointers from what the webmasters thought would appeal to men and read lots of text that was supposed to be arousing.

How could she be sure what would turn a guy on? She hadn't a clue but, she reasoned, if it made her feel sexy, then it just might work. After several hours on the Net, she finally logged off.

What to write about? *Can I do a story about straight sex? Would anyone be interested in just a man and a woman making love? There has to be lots of hands and oral sex at least,* she thought. *Lots of sucking and stroking. Can I write about oral sex even though I've never done it?* Well, she reasoned, many people write about things they've never done.

She booted up the word processor she used for occasional letters and stared at the blank screen. She typed a few sentences, then deleted them. She got as far as the first paragraph, then stared, shook her head, and again blanked her screen. After half an hour of fruitless staring, she called Betsy and filled her in on her visit with Velvet. "She's such a nice person it's hard to believe she does what she does," Alice said.

"I know. It's sometimes hard for me to believe I do what I do."

"I didn't mean to sound insulting."

"You didn't. Are you going to write tonight?"

She turned so her back was to the computer. "I'm going to try. I've been trying."

"I know you can do it, so I won't hold you up. Get cracking. See you Monday morning."

Alice hung up and her eyes returned to the blank word-processing screen in front of her. She thought for several minutes, then got up, went into the kitchen, and made herself a bite of dinner. With a cup of soup, an American-cheese sandwich and a Coke on a tray, she returned to the desk in her bedroom. She ate and stared at the screen. When she was finished eating, she took the tray back into the kitchen and washed her plate and cup and the dirty dishes left over from the day before. Then she sponged off every surface and scoured the sink.

Roger jumped onto the counter and chirruped at her. "Okay. I know, Roger," she said, carrying the cat back into the bedroom. "I'm stalling." When he again chirruped, she continued, "Don't yell at me. I just don't know whether I can do this. It's so embarrassing." Why was it embarrassing? She was alone in the apartment. No one would read anything she wrote unless she chose to show it to them. Whatever she created was hers. Private.

Alice began to write, using several stories from the Internet as models and adding her own reactions and feelings. She wrote for more than two hours, reread, and edited what she had written, then turned to Roger, now curled in a ball on the bed. "This is really weird. It embarrasses me just to read what I wrote but I think it's not too bad. Not great, but maybe not too bad." She ran her spell-checking program, then printed out the six pages. The next step was to find out whether she could actually say the words out loud. She sat on the bed beside the cat. "Okay. Here goes."

THE BEIGE TRENCH COAT

Jenny loved to read and whenever she had a moment to pick up a book, she did. One evening she had a few minutes while her husband and her three children tried to fix their broken dishwasher, so she sat in the lounge chair in the living room and read several pages of a novel. The part she read involved the heroine showing up at a guy's office wearing only her mink coat. There followed a delightfully graphic description of the interlude during which the heroine and her latest conquest made love on the desk, his secretary just a few feet and one closed door away.

"Man, oh man," Jenny whispered as she read the scene for a second time. "I wish I could be like that, aggressive and sexy."

"Hey, Mom," her daughter yelled, "I think we found the problem. Remember those toothpick critters we made? Well, it looks like Robbie dumped a few in the dishwasher. They jammed this hoodingy here. Come check this out." Reluctantly, Jenny put her book down and "checked out" the dishwasher.

A few hours later Jenny was in bed, watching the eleven o'clock news when her husband, Len, came upstairs. "Hon," he said, "you left this in the living room." He entered the bedroom holding the novel open to the page Jenny had been reading. "This is really hot stuff."

"Damn. I forgot it. I'm glad you found it and not one of the kids."

"Me too. This is really explicit."

"That is quite a scene, isn't it."

"Sure is. That's some lucky guy."

"He is?"

"Sure. Sexy broad comes to his office hot to trot. What do you think?"

Jenny arched her back and looked down at her moderate-size bosom, filling out the top of her lacy nightgown. "It would have to be someone really sexy for a guy to take chances like that. I mean with his secretary right there in the next room."

"Nah. Just the idea of something like that," he paused and looked down at the bulge in the front of his sweatpants, "you know, dangerous, would make any guy hot." Len came around to Jenny's side of the bed, pulled off his clothes, and made quick, hungry love to his wife.

Later, as she lay listening to her husband's breathing return to normal, Jenny thought again about the scene that had made Len so excited. I *wonder*, she thought.

By the end of the following week, Jenny had made all her plans. She had taken the afternoon off and selected her wardrobe. Around 3:00 P.M., she arrived at her husband's office, dressed in a beige trench coat. "Paula," she said to Len's secretary who was busily typing into a word processor, "I've got to talk to Len about something in private. Will you hold all his calls until we let you know otherwise? And don't let anyone interrupt."

"Sure thing, Jenny," Paula said. "Nothing wrong, I hope."

"Nothing at all, Paula," Jenny said. "We just need a little time for some private business."

"Will do," Paula said.

Jenny entered Len's small private office, quietly closed

the door behind her and turned the lock. Len was fiddling with some files in his credenza so his back was to her. For a moment, Jenny almost changed her mind. Would he really find this exciting? Would she make a fool of herself? She rubbed her sweaty palms on her coat and crossed to the desk.

"Hi, Len," she said, making her voice low and throaty.

"Hi, hon," Len said, turning in his swivel chair, a folder in his hand. "What are you doing here?"

"Well, I, ah . . ."

"I am glad to see you but I'm really busy. And why aren't you at work? Is something wrong?"

"No, nothing's wrong. It's just . . ." Again Jenny ran her shaking hands down her coat.

"Honey, what's wrong?"

Slowly, before what little courage she had deserted her completely, she unbuttoned her coat and pulled the sides open. Beneath she wore only a black satin bra and panties, a garter belt, black stockings with lace tops and black high-heeled shoes. Silent, she stared at her husband. She watched surprise and shock flash across his face, then a slow smile spread over his mouth.

He cleared his throat. "It's that scene from that book," he said hoarsely.

"Yes," she said softly, "it is."

"Oh," he said, he breathing increasing. "Wow."

Encouraged by the look on her husband's face, Jenny slowly let the trench coat slide from her arms. "I hope you like what you see," she said, echoing the heroine's line from the book.

"Oh, baby, I certainly do. Come over here."

Mimicking the scene from the book seemed to make it easier for Jenny to climb out of herself. "Not so fast, baby," she said hoarsely. "This is my party." She pranced around the office, wiggling her hips and humming "The Stripper." "Do you like?"

Len sat and stared. "I like this very much, but I'm really

waiting for a very important phone call so get over here right now." He made a grab for her but she neatly avoided his grasp. "Come on, baby," he almost whined.

"In due time."

The intercom on the phone beeped. "Baby . . .

This part hadn't been in the scene from the book so Jenny sighed and said, "Maybe you'd better get that."

"Yes," Len said as he put the receiver to his ear.

Jenny settled herself on Len's lap and could hear Paula's voice clearly. "I'm sorry, Len, but Mr. Haverstraw is on the line and he's leaving his office soon. I know that your wife didn't want you two to be disturbed, but I thought you would want to take this call."

Jenny could hear Len's deep sigh. "I guess I have to," he said, wiggling out from under Jenny's almost-bare behind. He covered the mouthpiece with his hand. "Baby, just hold that sexy thought for about five minutes. Okay?"

"Sure," Jenny said, deflated.

Len pushed the lighted button on his phone. "Mr. Haverstraw. I'm glad to finally get to talk to you."

Jenny sat in a chair on the opposite side of Len's desk and pondered. What would the woman in the book have done? Certainly not just sit here. An idea formed in Jenny's head and for several minutes she argued with herself, then decided. *The hell with it. I'm going to go for it.*

Now paying no attention to his wife, Len was furiously making notes on a yellow pad.

Slowly, Jenny made her way around the desk and, as Len distractedly made room for her, she wiggled under the desk. With trembling hands, she quickly unzipped Len's pants and pulled out his flaccid cock. She cradled it in her hand and watched it come to life.

Len pushed his chair back and stared at Jenny sitting in the kneehole. With his hand against the mouthpiece, he whispered, "Baby, please . . ." He pushed the chair back against the desk and Jenny could hear his pen scratching on the pad. She leaned forward and took Len's now semierect cock between her lips and sucked it into her warm mouth.

She heard Len gasp, then hiss, "Stop that!" Then he said, "No Mr. Haverstraw, not you. No, there's nothing wrong."

Smiling, Jenny sucked. This was extra delicious, she realized. Since Len had to continue his conversation, she would continue her ministrations as well. She fondled and sucked, then reached into his pants and squeezed his testicles.

"Mr. Haverstraw," Len said, his voice hoarse and tentative. "We're having some, er, electrical problems here. Can I call you back?" There was a pause. "Yes, I think I have enough to begin a rough estimate."

Jenny flicked her tongue over the tip of Len's cock, then pulled the thick, hard member into her mouth again.

"Yes, I'll get back to you tomorrow."

When she heard Len hang up, she slid from under the desk. Len grabbed her and spun her around, pushing her down so she was bent over his desk, papers and pens flying in all directions. With one quick movement, he ripped off her panties and plunged his hard cock into her steaming pussy. "God, I'm so hot," she moaned.

"Me too," Len said, grasping Jenny's hips and forcing her even more tightly against his groin. "God, baby."

It took only a few thrusts for Len to shoot his load into his wife's hot cunt, making strangling sounds, trying not to yell. Then he reached around and rubbed Jenny's clit until she came, almost silently.

"Len," Paula said through the locked door, "is everything all right?"

Len cleared his throat, Jenny still bent over the desk. "Everything's just great, Paula."

Len collapsed into his desk chair and pulled his wife onto his lap, then kissed her deeply. "I can't believe you did that," he said finally.

Jenny giggled. "I can't either." She got up from Len's lap and grabbed a wad of tissues from her purse. "Was I too outrageous?"

"Oh, baby. It was difficult there for a while, and I'll have to make a few excuses to Haverstraw, but it was wonderful."

Jenny picked up the coat and put it back on. "Yeah, it was, wasn't it." After a few more kisses, she unlocked the door and walked out. "We're done, for the moment, Paula."

"That's great, Jenny," Paula said. "I hope everything worked out."

"Oh yes," Jenny and Len said, almost simultaneously, "it certainly did work out."

"God. I actually got through it," Alice said, stacking the pages of her story. "What do you think, Roger? Does that make it?" She looked at the cat, who was now fast asleep, and giggled. "I hope you're not a good judge of quality." Initially she had strangled on the more graphic words, but she had eventually said them all, and the more often she said them, the easier they became. "I can say *clit* and *pussy* and *cock*. I've come a long way, baby." She giggled again, then laughed out loud. "If Ralph could only see me now."

The following day was Sunday, so after a quick visit to Queens, Alice spent the rest of the day either writing or surfing the Internet for ideas. She worked until almost midnight and, by the time she climbed into bed, she had written three more stories. The following morning she put them all in a large brown envelope and dropped them off at the post office on her way to work.

The week dragged. Alice visited her mother and sister on Wednesday and on the drive to Queens, she worked out exactly what she was going to tell her family. "I think I might have a really exciting new job one or two nights a week," she told her sister and brother-in-law.

"Doing what?" Sue asked.

"Phone sales," Alice answered, as she had rehearsed. "It's a bit complicated to explain, but it pays really well and I don't have to sell anything I don't believe in." She almost choked on the last phrase, but she hoped she would cover all the bases so there wouldn't be any awkward questions. "Any luck with Rutlandt?" she asked, changing the subject as quickly as she could.

"I got a letter from them. They have Mom at the top of the waiting list but they have no way of knowing when they will have an opening. I don't know whether we can afford it." Sue looked like she was coping as best she could, but it was difficult for both of them.

Alice patted her sister's hand. "I'll have a better idea by Saturday, when I find out about this new job. If it pans out, we'll be okay." If Velvet gave her the go-ahead, she'd empty her meager savings if she had to and replace the money as she got paid.

"Then I'll keep my fingers crossed for you."

Alice held up her hands, all fingers linked to others. "I've got everything crossed but my eyes."

She tried not to count on the job too much but the following Saturday afternoon she had her heart in her mouth as she drove to Velvet's house. As she had the previous week, Velvet, dressed as Alice was, in jeans and a man-tailored shirt, escorted her into the den, this week free of children. "They're at the movies with Wayne. You didn't meet Wayne the last time you were here, did you?"

"No." Alice was having difficulty focusing on Velvet's conversation.

Velvet picked up Alice's envelope and paced as she talked. "I'm sorry. Let's get to it. The stories are sensational."

Alice let out a long sigh of relief. "Do you really think so?"

"I do. You've got just the right amount of hot sex without the raunchy stuff that Velvet Whispers usually avoids. There are so many 'You phone, I'll pretend to suck you off' phone services that we try for something a bit more upscale and our clients have responded. I have a few guys who will love this stuff."

"That's wonderful."

"I know this must come as a relief to you. I've been giving this a lot of thought and I have one idea. It would sound more personal if the stories from a woman's point of view were in first person. Like 'I did this and that.' They could sound like they were personal revelations that you've never told anyone before. The ones from a man's might be stories someone told you. Personal tales, not something someone made up. I think that would go over better. What do you think?"

Alice considered Velvet's suggestion for only a moment. "You're right, of course. I'm annoyed that I didn't think of that."

"Great. Now here's my idea. We'll call you Sheherazade and I'll tell a few guys that you're a new erotic storyteller I've found. They might want to hear something specific, like," Velvet tapped her front teeth as she thought, "like the first time you made love or something naughty you did last week. You could write them out in advance but you'd have to roll with it from time to time. You'll have to be able to think fast and vary the story to go along with their ideas and desires." Alice could see the wheels turning as Velvet created her identity. Sheherazade's Secrets.

The more Velvet talked, the more it seemed to Alice that she might be able to make it all work. "Can you say this stuff out loud?" Velvet asked.

Alice smiled. "Well, I've read all these stories to my cat, if that counts. After listening to these tales I'll bet he's the hottest animal in town."

"Great," Velvet said with a chuckle. "This might just make us each some money. Let me make a few calls to men who I think would be interested, and I'll see what I can set up. Are you willing to get started next week?"

Next week! "I'm game." She took a deep breath. "Let's do it."

"Wonderful. I'll call you midweek and we'll nail down the specifics. What nights do you want to work, for now?"

"I thought about Mondays, Wednesdays, and Fridays. Are the weekends your busiest times? I could work Saturdays too."

"You know, it varies. Some weekends it seems the entire male population of the world calls, and others it's really silent. You get fifty percent of whatever the callers are charged, based only on actual time on the phone, of course. The usual rate is $2.99 per minute. I'd like you to get a timer that will ding every ten minutes so those who care will know how much they're paying. For the most part, however, I've found that most of these guys don't give a damn."

"How long should the calls go? I know Betsy said some of hers go more than half an hour."

"Yours will too," Velvet said. "It should take twenty minutes to half an hour to read a seven- or eight-page story, more if your tales get longer or if you talk slowly. If someone wants to limit the amount of money he spends, you can suggest that you can continue the story next week. You'll have to take notes and pick up just where you left off. Your clients will remember every detail." Velvet continued to think out loud. "To create regular customers, you might want to have some of your stories continued, like X-rated soap operas. Everyone should get off in each segment, but you can reuse the same characters. That's all up to you."

"Do you want me to start with someone who's not a paying customer to make sure that you like what I'm doing?"

"We can if you like," Velvet said, her smile warm and open, "but I'm confident that you can do this."

Suddenly unsure, Alice asked, "How can you be so sure? You don't know me at all."

"Actually, I do. I know you through these wonderful stories you wrote, and I've talked about you with Betsy several times this week. We both think it will work out wonderfully well for you. Anything else?"

"I'd like to start with only one or two people and test it all out. I don't want you to make any promises we can't keep."

"That sounds fine with me." She stood up and walked Alice to the front door. As Alice stepped out onto the porch, Velvet said, "Go get 'em, Sherry."

"Sheherazade. Sherry. I like that." With a quick motion, she kissed Velvet on the cheek. "Thanks."

"You're certainly welcome. And I'm not a charity. We're both going to make some nice bucks out of this. I'll call you."

Alice called Betsy as soon as she got home and filled her in on the meeting with Velvet. "She's a love."

"She certainly is, and, with the women she's got working for her and very little overhead, she makes a really nice living too."

"I'll bet. I've got stories to write now. I want a few of every type that men might ask for. Give me some clues. What kind of sex do men want from their encounters?"

"Most of my clients enjoy the idea of a woman performing oral sex on them. I guess it's something that their wives won't do."

"Oh. Don't women like that sort of thing?"

"I guess not. Did you and Ralph . . ."

"No. He was just a missionary position kind of guy. Do you and Larry?"

"Of course. It's wonderful. You might think about having sex in semipublic places, too, for your stories. I have a few clients who love the idea of possibly being found out. And of course, you need lots of control stories."

"I know. I've read a lot of those, where the men almost rape the women."

"Don't overlook the men who want to be dominated too. Oh, and one more thing: Men love to think about two women making love. Lesbian sex seems to turn guys on."

Alice was taken aback. She had never considered that men might want such a thing. "Phew. I don't know about that."

"You don't have to *do* it, just talk about it. I do. Several times I've told stories about my supposed adventures with another woman."

Alice gasped. "Have you ever?"

"No. But I can invent stories and before you say it, no, it's not lying. These men know who and what you are. It's the fantasy they're after, not the reality of who you really are. They understand. It's just a way for them to get off."

After Alice hung up, she booted up her computer and began to type. For the rest of the weekend, except for her visit to her sister's, she did nothing but write, edit, and rewrite. When she temporarily ran out of ideas, she prowled the Internet, not stealing stories, just getting her mind loosened up.

On Monday evening, she got a call from Velvet. "I talked to a man named Vic. He's a really sweet guy who's always asking me to tell him about my lurid past. I told him about Sheherazade and he's really psyched. He'd like to call you on Wednesday evening at about nine. Would that work for you?"

Vic. Her first client. Alice's hands trembled and she could barely get out the words, "That would be fine."

"I know you're probably nervous, but try not to be. He's just a really nice, sort of shy guy who just enjoys getting his rocks off once a week with a dirty conversation. And he's got the money to be able to do just that."

Alice barked out a rueful laugh. "He's shy and I'm terrified. What a pair we'll make."

"You'll do fine. He usually stays on the phone for about half an hour. That's forty-five dollars for you for just a short bit of work. Think of it that way if it makes it easier."

"Is there anything special he wants in my story?"

"He likes hot, aggressive women who like a bit of danger. That's about all I can think of."

Alice thought about a story she'd just finished. "Actually that will work out nicely."

"Good. I told him to call me right after he talks to you so he can let me know how he likes you and whether he wants to call again next week. Then I'll call you. If you both think it went well, he'll become as regular as he wants. We can use him as a sort of test case. If it works out, I'll see who else I can set you up with."

"Great. It's kind of like the ultimate job interview."

Velvet's laugh was warm and comforting. "I know you'll be great. A few tips. When you talk, deliberately relax your shoulders and drop both the pitch and volume of your voice. Get just a bit of breath into it, but don't get all Mae West or Marilyn Monroe either. You might want to have a few beers before he calls, just to relax you."

After a few more minutes, the two women hung up and Alice reread the story she thought Vic might like. *This might just please him*, she thought.

All week Alice was in a tizzy. She talked with Betsy almost incessantly, looking for reassurance. The women met Wednesday for lunch and Alice asked Betsy several times whether she thought that her storytelling would work. Over coffee Betsy finally said, "I think I'm going to strangle you. If you don't want to do this, then don't. If you do, then just take your chances and do it. If it all falls apart and you're terrible, you're no worse off than you would have been if it had never happened."

"I guess that's right." Alice smiled and winked at her friend. "Thanks. I needed that."

On her way home from lunch, Alice bought a six-pack of Budweiser. She didn't particularly like beer and she hated the calories that went with it, but tonight she'd need to unwind. The afternoon dragged by and she was sorry that her first call had been planned for a Wednesday, the only day during the week that she didn't work. At least at Dr. Tannenbaum's office the day would pass more quickly. As it was, the afternoon seemed about three days long.

Alice sipped a beer with dinner, one for dessert, and yet another at about eight-thirty. Like medicine, she told herself. When the phone rang at nine o'clock, she was seated on the edge of the bed, just slightly buzzed. She listened to the first ring, then picked it up on the second. "Hello?"

"Is this Sheherazade?"

"Yes," she said, her heart pounding. "You must be Vic."

"That's me. How are you tonight?"

"I'm fine. I've been waiting for your call. I have a story for you that you might enjoy."

"That's great. First, tell me what you look like."

"Tonight, I'm twenty-five, slim, with 36D breasts and long legs."

She heard a deep breath. "That's great," Vic said. "Blond hair and blue eyes?"

"Why yes," Alice said, putting a bit of surprise in her voice. "How did you know?"

"I guess I'm just lucky. That's the way I like to picture women."

Alice made a few notes on the pad beside her. "That's really lucky. I'm glad I'm just what you wanted."

"Are you ready to tell me your story, Sheherazade?"

"Oh yes. I love telling stories about all the women inside of me."

"Okay. I'm putting my feet up and I'm ready."

Alice picked up the pages she had written. She'd use them as a guideline, and improvise when she had to.

Chapter
6

"You know, Vic, I have a secret. I love tollbooths. I know that's a ridiculous statement, but after you've heard my story, I think you'll understand. It happened a while ago, but I still remember it.

"Let me back up. Throughout college, I loved to wear tight jeans, and sweaters cut just low enough to reveal my cleavage. I enjoyed the way guys in my classes looked at me. I developed a clumsy way of dropping my books so I could bend over and watch them as they watched me.

"When I graduated, I got a job as a secretary in a large, very formal accounting firm. It was all terribly gray-flannel: women in tailored suits worn with blouses buttoned up to the neck. Each morning, I put my long hair up, using dozens of pins to keep it neat. By the end of each day, all I could think about was taking my clothes off, unpinning my hair, and relaxing. But the work was interesting and the pay was great so I put up with the minor disadvantages. You know how it can be."

"Oh yes," Vic said. "I do. I used to work in a place like that myself."

"Then you do understand. Well, after almost a year, I treated myself to a tiny red convertible. Instead of taking the commuter train, I started to drive to work every morning on the parkway, my blouse primly buttoned and my hair up. Unhappily, I had to keep the top of the car closed or the wind would have ruined my appearance.

"On the way home, however, I was under no such restrictions. I could unbutton, unpin, and unwind. After a few weeks, the weather turned warm and I decided to lower the top of my car for the drive home. The spring air was soft and warm one afternoon so I removed my jacket and unbuttoned my blouse. Then I took five minutes and pulled every pin out of my hair, until it fell in soft waves down my back. I felt free."

"Was it long and blond?"

"Of course. A soft yellow like . . ." she struggled for a phrase, "new wheat."

"Wow."

"So that afternoon I shifted into first and eased my car out of the garage and into traffic. As I drove along the parkway toward my apartment I was exhilarated by the feel of the wind in my hair and down the front of my blouse. I could feel my nipples harden under the silky fabric. I pulled into the line of traffic and, quarter in hand, I slowly inched my way toward the tollbooth just before my exit. As I reached out to put the quarter in the outstretched hand, I glanced at the toll taker. What do you look like, Vic?"

"I'm about thirty-five, with brown hair and brown eyes."

"Do you have a nice body?"

"It's not much," Vic said softly.

"Oh, I'll bet it is. I'll bet you have nice shoulders, just like the toll taker. I remember him. He had great shoulders. Do you have good hands?"

"I never thought about it. I guess I do."

"Wonderful. Just like him. So each evening, I drove home the same way. About a week later, I found myself gazing at the same guy. Brown hair, brown eyes, and great shoulders and hands." She sighed. "Anyway, as he took my quarter, he looked me over and then he squeezed my hand. I smiled at him and pulled away.

"For the next few days, I made sure to be in his lane. Each day, I gave him a better view of my body. I began to deliberately hike up my skirt and pull my blouse open so he could see my low-cut bra."

"You did?"

"Oh yes. I loved it that he liked looking at me. By the end of the third week, I realized that I was wet just thinking about my drive home. I said hello to him each night and he stared down my blouse and said hello too.

"One evening I casually asked him when his shift was over. 'Midnight,' he told me. That was just what I wanted to hear.

"Well, Vic. You'll never guess what I did. The following evening, I had dinner near my office and returned to work. I had a desk full of things that needed my attention so I had no trouble finding enough work to keep me busy until almost eleven. When I could concentrate no longer, I stretched, rubbed the back of my neck, and smiled. I was going to be so bad.

"When I got to my car, the garage was almost empty and the corner I had parked in was not well lit. I glanced around and saw no one so I quickly pulled off my skirt and my half-slip. I glanced down at my sheer black stockings and black garter belt topped by tiny black bikini panties. Can you picture it, Vic?"

"Oh yes. I'll bet you looked sexy."

"I think I did. As I slid into the car I enjoyed the feel of the leather upholstery on the backs of my thighs and the slithery feeling of my soaking cunt. I had put a large silk scarf in the car that morning and now I pulled it across my lap, covering me up to the bottom of my blouse. My show was for only one man.

"It was almost 11:45 when I lowered the top of the car and drove through the warm spring air toward the toll plaza. As I drove up to the booth I could see the familiar face as he stretched to take money from a car in front of me. I unbuttoned my blouse all the way and pulled it open to reveal my black lace half-bra that barely covered my nipples. I moved the scarf over onto the passenger seat and pulled up next to him.

"Distractedly he leaned out to take my toll, but when he saw me, he just stared. It was the most beautiful look I've ever received. His eyes caressed every inch of my skin until I couldn't sit still any longer. Fortunately there were no other cars around so, as he watched, I slipped my hand between my legs and stroked my wet pussy through the thin crotch of my tiny panties. It took only a moment until I came, waves of orgasm engulfing my body. When I calmed and looked at him, I could tell that he wanted to touch me, but his fingers couldn't quite reach."

"Oh, wow. That's fantastic," Vic said.

"That's what he thought too. 'I get off at midnight,' he said. 'Why not save some of that for me?'

" 'Where?' I asked.

"Quickly he wrote an address on a piece of paper and handed it to me. I'll wait for you in front of my building at about twelve-fifteen.' "

"Did you go?" Vic asked, his voice hoarse.

"I hadn't decided yet, I guess. Without saying yes or no, I drove away, my quarter and his address in my hand. As soon as I got to an exit, I turned off of the parkway, pulled my car to a stop, and considered. I was still high and hungry. I rubbed my soaked crotch until I came again, but the orgasm was unsatisfying. I needed a cock inside of me, preferably his. I guess I had made the decision before I even left work that night.

"So I buttoned my blouse, wriggled into my skirt as best I could and drove to the address the man had written down. I didn't even know his name, Vic, but I guess I didn't care."

"You actually did it? Met him?"

"I did. He drove up at exactly twelve-fifteen and I got out of my car. 'I don't even know your name,' we said simultaneously.

"I didn't want to tell him my real name so I made one up. 'Mine's Christine,' I said.

"You know," Alice said to Vic. "I just remembered. His name was Vic too."

"Really?" Vic said.

"Oh yes. 'I'm Vic,' he said. 'Come on. I'll let us in.' "

"I know his name wasn't Vic, but I like it this way," the phone voice said. "Go on."

"The apartment was small and inexpensively furnished but I

barely got a chance to look around. We got inside and, without waiting, Vic wrapped his arms around me and his lips engulfed my mouth. He tangled his hands in my hair and held my head while his tongue invaded and explored. He pressed his body against mine and I could feel his huge dick pressing against my belly. I wrapped my arms around his neck and surrendered to his kiss.

"His hands roamed my back, pressing my full breasts harder against his chest. It was as though he wanted to pull me inside of his skin.

"I slowly pulled away and looked into Vic's eyes. 'You enjoyed watching me before so let's not change things just yet,' I said."

Alice switched the phone to her other ear. "Vic. Would you like to hear about how I stripped in the story?"

"Oh yes. Very much," he said.

"Well. I unbuttoned his shirt and pressed my toll taker into an easy chair. I ran my hands over his chest, loosened his belt, and unsnapped his jeans. Then I backed away.

"One button at a time, I unfastened my black silk blouse. I watched his eyes. They never left my fingers as I played with my buttons.

"He reached out and tried to rush me but I pushed his hands away. 'This is my show,' I told him. 'Just be patient.' "

It was obvious to Alice that Vic was getting into the tale. "Can you be patient, Vic?"

"I'll be patient," he said into the phone.

"I'm sure you will. My toll taker sat, looked into my eyes and smiled. 'Just don't take too long,' he said. 'I may be able to wait, but I'm not sure about my cock.' "

Alice could hear Vic's warm laugh. "I opened the side button on my skirt and let it fall to the ground. I hadn't put my slip back on, so I could watch him stare at my nylon-encased legs and tiny panties. I slipped my blouse off, dropped it next to my skirt, and watched his eyes as they roamed my body.

"I began to run my hands over my belly and breasts. I stroked my nipples through the satin and lace of my bra. I ran my fingers over the soaked crotch of my panties. I closed my eyes and let my fingertips drift over my skin.

"After a few moments, I pulled my long hair forward, over my shoulders and breasts, then I unhooked my bra and pulled it off. The strands of hair parted only slightly, just enough to allow my erect nipples to protrude."

Alice heard a long-drawn-out sigh and a whispered, "Yes."

"I swayed slightly, enjoying the feel of my hair as it brushed back and forth across my breasts. Suddenly, showing Vic my body wasn't enough. I needed his hands and mouth on me.

"I knelt down in front of Vic's chair, looked up at him and smiled. He reached down, pulled my hair out of the way and took my breasts in his hands.

"His fingers found my hard nipples and he squeezed, tiny pinches that sent shivers up my spine. He pulled me up so my tits were level with his mouth and he licked the hard buds with the tip of his tongue. He swirled his tongue around and flicked it back and forth, wetting and teasing me. He leaned back slightly and blew on my wet skin. The sensation almost made me climax, but I held it back. This wasn't how I wanted to come.

"When I just couldn't wait any longer," Alice said, "I pulled him to his feet and almost ripped off his jeans. He was magnificent naked, with his hard cock beckoning me. I needed him inside me.

" 'Take off those panties,' Vic said, 'but leave the rest on. I like you that way.'

"I pulled my panties off as he sat back down in the chair and grabbed my arms. I half dropped, half fell onto his lap, facing him. He lifted me slightly and then drove my body down, impaled on his huge cock."

Alice could hear the rasping sound of Vic's breathing through the phone. She trembled, feeling like the woman in the story. Brazen and able to ask for what she wanted. Able to do anything. " 'Yes, fuck me,' I screamed as he penetrated me. 'Fuck me hard.'

"He wrapped his hands around my waist and rhythmically

lifted and dropped me. My knees were buried in the deep chair cushions, my hands held his hair. He pounded inside of me until we both came, screaming."

Suddenly there was a loud gasp through the phone, then an, "Oh, shit."

"Is anything wrong, Vic?" Alice said.

"No. Not really. I just don't like to come so fast."

There was a long pause during which Alice couldn't stop grinning. She had done it. She had made a man come just from her words. *I really am hot stuff.*

"Did you ever see him again?"

"We met at his place occasionally for a night of hot sex but eventually he moved to the west coast."

"That was wonderful. Sheherazade, can I call you again next week? Please. Can you tell me more about your history?" He paused. "I know they're just stories, but I want to hear more."

"Of course. I'd love to tell you lots of tales about my past. Is there any kind of story you'd particularly like to hear?"

"Oh, no. I'll let you pick. And thanks."

"I'm glad you called and I'll look forward to hearing from you next week, at the same time."

She heard Vic hang up, and Alice dropped on the bed, pounded her fists, and kicked her heels. "Yes!" she yelled. "Yes!"

A half an hour later, the phone rang again. "Vic was delighted," Velvet said without preamble. "He said you were just the right kind of a slut for him." When Alice gasped, Velvet continued, "He meant it as a compliment. He loved hearing about your supposed lurid past." She chuckled. "I gather you took my advice and moved into first person."

"Did he really believe I had done what I told him in the story?"

"Probably not, but who knows, and who cares. He loved what you said and wants to call you again next week, and that's the only testimonial I care about. I've got a few more men I can recommend. How about Monday evening? I think I can set up two or three, starting at about eight. Would that work?"

"Would it? That would be terrific."

Velvet took a few minutes to tell Alice about the men she had in mind. "I'll call you over the weekend and make it official. Welcome to the family."

"Thanks."

After she hung up with Velvet, Alice called Sue. After a few pleasantries and the news that her mother was essentially unchanged, Alice said, "If Rutlandt calls, tell them yes."

"You got the job?" Sue shrieked. "That's great. I hope you aren't taking on too much."

"Not at all," Alice said, hating to deceive her sister. "I'm really going to enjoy what I'll be doing."

"That's fantastic. I'll call Rutlandt tomorrow and tell them that we're a go whenever they have a room. They said last Friday that they thought there'd be something this week."

The following Monday evening, a man named Scott called for a story. Velvet had told Alice that he would probably like a story about a man being educated by older women. Alice had decided that he'd want it told from the boy's point of view so over the weekend she had given a lot of thought to how to pull it off. Finally, Sunday evening she had had an idea, so after she and Scott had chatted for a few minutes, Alice said, "You know, Velvet said you might like to hear about my brother. He had an experience, well, he was very naughty. He told me in confidence but I don't think he'd mind if I told you."

"Really? Tell me."

"I have to tell you that Carter, that's my brother, wasn't very knowledgeable at all. My family was extremely protective and he had been more sheltered than most boys. He was also rather unattractive and painfully shy. He was just eighteen years old and a senior in high school when his first time happened, and it happened on a snowy winter weekend. He used to shovel driveways to earn extra money.

"He had already done two that afternoon so he was really exhausted. His last driveway was owned by a female customer who was unmarried and quite well to do. Let's call her Mrs. Jones.

This particular afternoon, she invited him in and asked him to sit down and have something to eat. 'Lord knows your parents don't seem to feed you, so someone should,' she said.

"He was wet and shivering as he sat down at the table in her kitchen. 'They feed me, but I'm always hungry,' he said.

" 'Carter, your clothes are wet and you're chilled straight through. Why don't you take off those wet things? I'll put them in the dryer and you can wrap yourself in this big towel.' She handed him a tremendous bath towel and hustled him into the bathroom."

Alice dropped her voice to a slight whisper. "We know he shouldn't have taken off all his clothes, but he was so naive."

"Maybe he wasn't," Scott said. "Maybe he knew exactly what was going to happen."

"You know, maybe he did," Alice said. "So anyway, when he returned to the kitchen wrapped in the towel, Mrs. Jones said, 'Now isn't that better? I've made you a sandwich and some hot cocoa. It will help to warm you up while I put your things in the dryer.'

"Carter told me that after a few minutes he became really sleepy so Mrs. Jones suggested that he lie down for a bit. She said she'd wake him in a little while when his clothes were dry. He agreed, knowing that he would still have enough daylight to finish shoveling the driveway." Alice paused. "At least that was what he told me."

"I think he was fibbing just a bit."

"I think so too. Mrs. Jones led him to a bedroom and tucked him in under soft blankets. She shut the door and he fell asleep quickly."

Alice grinned. "Carter told me that he really fell asleep. Maybe he was just playing possum. Is that what you would have done, Scott?"

"I might have. Don't stop now, Sheherazade."

"He told me that he had no idea how long he had been asleep when the bed moved beneath him and he woke up. He turned and saw Mrs. Jones laying beside him. He started to get up but she gently pushed him back down and giggled. 'Is this the first time you've been in bed with a woman?' she asked. When he just blushed, she continued, 'You're a virgin? I never suspected.' She smiled at him. 'That's all right,' she said. 'I'm glad that you are.' Her hands parted his towel and slid down his smooth chest."

Alice took a deep breath. "Can you picture all this, Scott?"

"Oh yes. I certainly can. Did your brother tell you more?"

"He told me that he started to breathe like he'd been running a race. 'Good,' Mrs. Jones said as she noticed the blankets sticking up below his waist. 'Very good. You won't be a stranger to sex much longer.'

"She parted the sides of her robe and said, 'Now look at me and touch me. Touch me anywhere you want.' He placed his hands on her face and started to caress her. When he tried to touch her large breasts, however, he became scared and froze. She took his hand, pressed it to one breast and said, softly, 'It's okay, Carter. It's really okay.' "

"Oh yes," Scott sighed. "I can see it all."

Alice smiled. "Her breasts were soft and smooth. Then she reached under the towel and gently held his dick in her hand as she started to slowly stroke it. My brother told me that he almost came right then, but he was afraid to.

"Mrs. Jones uncovered herself and removed her robe, all the while stroking his dick first with one hand, then the other. Carter stared at her and felt the heat rise in his face. 'You've never seen a naked woman or a pussy before, have you?'

" 'No,' he said, 'I haven't.'

" 'Well, just like my breasts, my pussy is soft and warm, but it can also get wet, Carter. All you have to do is touch and stroke it. Touch my pussy. It's okay, really it is.'

"So he touched it. Isn't that what you would have done, Scott?"

"I would have touched her all over."

"I'll bet you would have," Alice said. "My brother touched her pussy and it was soft just like she'd said it would be. 'Now,' Mrs.

Jones said, 'take your finger and follow mine.' He watched as she put her finger inside her. Then she removed hers and nudged him, so he slid his finger into her. 'Now, Carter, move your finger back and forth.' He did and then she said, 'Yes. That's right. Keep it going until your finger and my cunt are sopping wet. Then comes the fun part.'

" 'Fun part?' he whispered.

" 'Yes, Carter. You're going to put your dick into my soft, warm pussy and gently move it back and forth.'

"Carter didn't think a woman like Mrs. Jones would actually let him but when he pulled his wet finger from her pussy, she was so wet. 'Why me?' he asked, puzzled and so excited.

" 'I chose you because you're not like the other boys. You're sensitive and quiet. You keep to yourself.' She held his hot, hard dick then touched her pussy with the tip of it. He leaned toward her, dick throbbing so much it almost hurt. He closed his eyes so he could better feel what was happening. 'That's okay, Carter,' she said. 'Just feel.'

"Carter told me that Mrs. Jones's pussy was so warm and wet."

"I'll bet it was," Scott said.

"Mrs. Jones said, 'Your dick feels so good, all firm and warm and young.' She rubbed it over her wet pussy, then said, 'Now, Carter, push it all the way in.' He pushed gently but she said, 'Push harder. *Yesss*.'

"She pulled him so he was lying on top of her, his dick pushed into her cunt. My brother told me that he wanted to move but he didn't know whether he should. Should he, Scott?"

"Oh God, yes. Fuck her senseless, kid."

"Mrs. Jones said, 'Yes, Carter, move. Rock back and forth.'

" 'Can I go faster?' he asked."

Scott's voice was hoarse as he said, "Go faster, kid. Fuck her hard."

" 'You can,' she said, 'but since this is your first time, try to go slowly. See how nice it feels when you go slowly. We've got a long time.'

" 'But your driveway . . .' "

"To hell with the driveway, Carter," Scott said, panting. "Do it."

" 'It doesn't matter,' Mrs. Jones said. 'We can stay here as long as you like. Now move gently, slowly in and out.'

" 'I gotta . . .' He didn't know what.

" 'I know,' Mrs. Jones said. 'That's good, Carter. It means you're going to shoot. You'll lose your cherry and be a real man.' "

" 'I'm gonna . . .' He did, didn't he, Scott?"

Alice heard rhythmic rustling noises through the phone. "Is he still fucking her," Scott gasped. "Young studs can come over and over. Tell me he's still fucking her."

"Oh, he is," Alice said. "His ass is pushing, driving his dick into her. He spurted, but he was hard again almost immediately. He just kept fucking her until he spurted again.

" 'That was wonderful, Carter,' Mrs. Jones said, 'but now you've got to help me. I can come like that if you lick me.' "

"Oh God, do it, kid. Lick her pussy," Scott said.

" 'I don't know how,' he said. He was so tired, but he wanted to do all the things that Mrs. Jones would let him do.

" 'Of course you don't,' she said. 'I'll teach you. Now kneel between my legs.' He looked at her pussy, the hair all wet from his come. She smelled sweet and salty. He didn't know what to do but she put her fingers on her pussy. 'Lick here like I'm a piece of candy. Lick everywhere. You'll get the hang of it quickly. I just know you will.'

"He licked until he thought his dick would burst again. 'Can I put it in again?' he asked her.

" 'In a minute,' she said, showing him where to lick more. 'And rub right here,' she said, putting her finger on the hard, swollen place. 'Yes,' she said. 'Like that.' And she was breathing hard. 'Yes,' she said again and he felt her body move and wet juice ran from her pussy. 'Now put it in again,' she said and he did. Didn't he, Scott?"

All Alice could hear was harsh breathing, then a shout. She just kept talking, waiting for Scott to tell her to stop.

" 'Now, Carter, make me feel it,' Mrs. Jones said. This time Carter wasn't as scared so he could move and rub her at the same time. He thrust in and out, pulling it out and ramming himself in as far as he could. He came quickly but she didn't let him pull out. She held him tightly, rocking against him."

"Wow," Scott said, his breathing slower now. "That was quite a story. Did he go back another day?"

"My brother told me that it was just about dark when he left her house. 'Come back again tomorrow and you can finish all kinds of things,' she called after him. My brother went back lots of times that winter. He got quite an education,"

"I'll bet he did. Thanks for the story, Sheherazade," Scott said. "Can I call again next week?"

"Of course."

It was going to take a lot of writing time, but this was going to work out just fine. Just fine indeed.

Chapter
7

A s the weeks passed Alice's business grew. She now had four steady clients and a few times Velvet had called and asked whether she could take a new customer. She was beginning to think of her income as real. A week earlier the Rutlandt Nursing Home had finally had a vacancy and her mother had been moved there. The older woman seemed happy, spending much of her day in a wheelchair in the sunny solarium with several other older residents.

One Thursday morning, both Alice and Betsy arrived at Dr. Tannenbaum's office early to catch up on some paperwork. As they updated files, Alice said, "Betsy, I have a strange problem that I need to talk to you about. I take these phone calls and that's great. The guys enjoy it and I can usually hear them climax, but it all leaves me a bit frustrated. With Larry away this week, weren't you . . . well, what do you do?"

"For someone who can talk a man to orgasm, you sure have a way with words. Don't you masturbate?"

Alice couldn't get the word out. She talked on the phone about all manner of sexual topics in graphic detail, but she couldn't bring herself to say the word *masturbate* when talking about herself. "No," she said softly.

"Ever?" Betsy said, her eyes wide.

"Not really," Alice whispered.

"Well, you should. The only way to learn about how a woman gets pleasure is to get pleasure yourself." Betsy smiled. "Let me ask you a very blunt question. Have you ever had an orgasm?"

Alice snapped out an answer. "Of course."

"That's what you tell all your other friends. This is me you're talking to. Now, think again. Have you ever had an orgasm?"

Alice sighed. "Okay, okay. You're right. I'm not really sure. Ralph wasn't the best lover that ever was. He was pretty much the stick-it-in-and-wiggle-it-around type."

Betsy guffawed. "You're impossible."

"I know," Alice said, smiling ruefully. "Seriously, all I've ever had was Ralph. I've never been with anyone else."

"Then it's time you found out. Think of it as research. It will make you so much better at entertaining your clients if you know what you're talking about."

"I guess you're right. I've been making up a lot of what I say, using stories and other people's experiences."

"So go home tonight, read a sexy story or make one up in your head and just do it. Touch where it feels good. You certainly know how, in graphic detail."

Alice blushed. "I guess I do."

That evening, Alice had a regular client named Marcus at eight and Vic called at nine. By quarter of ten, she had told two sexy stories, had two men climax on the phone with her, and she was very excited herself. Masturbate. There would never be a better time. *How can I do this?* she wondered. *It feels so awkward and so wrong. It's my body,* she told herself, *and I'm allowed to touch it if I want to. And I want to.*

She stripped out of her clothes, pulled on her jets T-shirt and climbed between her cool sheets. Her nipples were erect and as she wiggled around in bed, they rubbed erotically against the front of the shirt. As she lay on her back, she placed one palm against her nipple, rubbing the nub against her hand. She pulled her hand back. "Stop being such a sissy," she said aloud. "You can make men quiver but you're embarrassed to touch your own body. It's yours after all." Hesitantly, Alice raised her hand again and rubbed her nipple. Small spikes of pleasure knifed through her body. She rubbed the other, feeling the rockets slice from her breasts to her belly.

She slid her hand beneath the shirt and touched her naked breasts. She played with the nipples, feeling the heady pleasure for the first time. Hands shaking, she reached lower and touched her pubic mound, sliding her fingers through the springy hair.

"Why am I so reluctant to do this?" she asked. She moved her fingers deeper and found the soft flesh that was now so wet. Slowly she explored, her fingers gliding through the thick lubricant. When she touched her swollen clit she felt a jolt of pleasure and, surprised by how strong it was, she touched again. She rubbed and pressed, finding places where the pleasure was greatest, but, although it felt wonderful, she found that no matter how much she stroked, she was unable to get over the precipice to what she knew would be her first real orgasm. She needed something inside of her. She looked furtively at her bedside table, then at the top of her dresser.

"What am I feeling so guilty about?" she asked, climbing out of bed. She opened her top dresser drawer and found an old lipstick. The tube was plastic and, she reasoned, should be the right shape. She grabbed a tissue and rubbed it all over the plastic, removing any dirt then, lipstick tube in hand, she returned to the bed. She rubbed her clit for a moment, then took the tube and stroked it around her wetness. Trembling, she pressed the tube against the opening of her vagina and felt the end slip inside. She held the tube tightly with one hand, and rubbed her clit with the other.

Suddenly she felt a tightening low in her belly and a sort of tickling and twitching in her pussy. It took only a moment for her inner spring to wind tighter, then explode. She gasped, colors whirling behind her closed eyes. Her entire body shook.

She gradually eased her rubbing and then she removed the

tube from her cunt. "Holy shit," she said. "So that's what it's all about." Still panting, she wiped off the lipstick tube, then went into the bathroom and dried her pussy. "Holy shit."

For several more nights, after fevered storytelling, Alice touched her body, experimenting and quickly discovering what felt the best.

About a week after her first orgasm, when Betsy arrived, she put a brown envelope in the drawer where Alice kept her purse. "What's that?" Alice asked.

"It's something you need to look at. Call it research."

Alice pulled out the envelope and glanced at the catalog inside. "Shop till you drop," Betsy said as Alice stared at the catalog in her hand. "You need toys to play with to add to your stories."

As Alice turned to the first page of the publication, the outer door opened. She quickly replaced the catalog in the envelope and dropped it back into the drawer. She'd definitely look at it later. She'd seen a dildo that would certainly work better than a lipstick tube. Then turning, she said, "Good morning, Mrs. Grumbacher." She focused on the six-year-old trailing behind the woman. "And Tracey. How are you this morning? Are you ready to have your picture taken with Barney?"

"Only if I have no cavities," the little girl said, her chin pointed at the floor.

"Have you been brushing?"

"Oh yes," she said. "Mommy and Dr. Tannenbaum showed me how."

"Then I'm sure that your teeth will be in great shape."

The little girl smiled. "I think this one's a little loose," she said, pointing to her top tooth.

"Wow. That means you're getting older. We'll just let Dr. Tannenbaum look at it."

Mrs. Grumbacher finished hanging up her coat. "You're so good with her," she said to Alice. "She's always so nervous coming here, despite how nice the doctor is. But she cheers right up for you."

"I'm glad I can help," Alice said.

"You're such a people person."

Right. Oh, the people I deal with. Alice winked at Betsy.

That evening, Velvet called. "Alice," she said, "I have a new client and no one to give him to. You know what Fridays are like. He just wants the standard, not stories or anything. Would you like to give it a try?"

Alice thought about it. She'd been doing very well with her stories. Somehow, telling a story was different from straight phone sex. Less personal, somehow. However Velvet had been so good to her and she really wanted to help, and yet, she didn't want to disappoint anyone either. She took a deep breath. "Sure. I guess."

"Listen. Just roll with it. I've heard a lot about you from a few of your clients and I've gotten several calls from friends of theirs. You'll do fine."

Alice took a deep breath. "I certainly will. Put him through." She hung up and perched on the edge of the bed. It was like flying without a net or without a script. Of course, she often changed her prewritten stories to fit the needs of the man she was talking to and the stories seldom ended where her written material had, but she always had the safety of those pages to fall back on. Now she would be completely on her own.

Moments later the phone rang. She dropped her shoulders and lifted the receiver. "Hello?" she said, softly.

"Hi, Sherry," the voice at the other end of the phone said. "I'm Tim."

"Well, good evening, Tim. Are you feeling horny tonight?"

"That's why I called. I need you."

"Oh, baby," Alice said, "it's nice to be needed. Tell me what you need."

"I need to poke my hard cock into your sweet pussy."

"Ohhh," Alice sighed. "That sounds really good. Are you in a real hurry? I usually like it slow. Would you like to touch me first?"

"Yes. I really would. Do you have big tits?"

Always big tits, Alice thought, considering her medium-size breasts. "Oh yes. I have real trouble finding bras large enough."

"What kind of bra are you wearing right now?" Tim asked.

"What would you like it to be?"

"I like the lacy ones so I can peek at your nipples. Are they big?"

"Yes, of course. Just listening to you has made them really hard. My bra is red, you know. Red satin, with small slits at the point of each cup so my hard nipples can just stick through. Can you see them? Close your eyes and see them reaching for you."

There was a long breath. "Yes. I can see them."

"I'm wearing red panties, too, small ones that barely cover my bush. I'm a redhead," she said, "so my pussy hair's deep auburn."

"Pinch your nipples for me," Tim said. "Make them really hard."

Alice was wearing a beige nylon bra, but she opened her robe and pinched her nipples, already hardening with erotic stimulation. *"Ohhh,"* she squealed. "That's nice." And it was. "Can I touch your cock too? Take off your pants so I can touch your prick."

There was a rustling and the squeak of bedsprings. "Okay. You can touch me."

"I'll touch it, but I'll have to use your hand. Wrap your fingers around it so I can feel how very hard it is."

There was another long sigh. "Are you wearing just your red bra and panties?"

"Well, I have red stockings with lacy tops that come up almost to my pussy, and red high-heeled shoes too."

"Rub the stockings and tell me how it feels."

Alice rubbed the inside of her thigh. "It feels smooth and cool to the touch. I can feel the heat pouring from my pussy too. Are we touching your cock?"

"Yes. I'm going to get some baby oil."

"Oh yes. Do that."

"Will you rub your pussy for me, through those red panties?"

"Will you be peeking? I don't know whether I can touch my pussy with anyone looking."

Tim laughed. "I won't peek, I promise. But I want you to really touch your pussy. Will you really do it for me?"

Alice reached down and touched the crotch of her beige nylon panties, lightly brushing the tip of her clit through the fabric. "Yes, I'm doing it."

"I love the feel of wet pussy," Tim said, "and the smell and the taste."

"How does your cock feel? Is it very hard?"

"It is, but I don't want to spurt until you do. Are you rubbing your pussy?"

"Yes," Alice said, finding to her surprise that she was very aroused. The muffled sensation of her fingers on her flesh, through the nylon, was delicious. "It feels really good and I'm getting really horny."

"Tell me exactly what you're doing and how it feels."

"I'm rubbing my clit through my bright-red panties. It feels hot and really good."

"Slide your fingers under the panties and feel your naked pussy. I want to see you doing that while I rub my cock."

Alice slipped her fingers beneath the waistband of her panties, down through her pubic hair to her sopping cunt. She was so wet. From her few sessions, she knew where to touch so it felt best. "You know, this makes me so hungry for a cock inside of me. What should I do?"

"Get something and fill your snatch. Stuff it full and pretend that it's my big cock."

"I've got a big dildo and I'm putting it into my pussy." Alice propped the phone against her ear, reached for the lipstick tube and pressed it into her pussy. It wasn't enough. She wanted something bigger, something that would really fill her up. Something she could fuck herself with without being afraid of it slipping all the way inside. She flashed on the catalog Betsy had given her, then Tim said, "Is your snatch full?"

"Oh, I wish it were your cock that was filling me up. I'd wrap my legs around your waist and jam that cock deep into my pussy."

"Oh, Sherry," Tim groaned. "I'd drive into you so hard that you'd scream. I'd pound harder and harder."

Alice rubbed her clit through her panties while the lipstick tube rubbed the walls of her pussy. She felt her orgasm building. "You're going to make me come, Tim," she said. "Does your big cock feel good inside of me?"

"I'm fucking you so hard." She heard his rasping breaths and his moans.

"Yes, baby," she said as the orgasm flowed from her pussy to her thighs and her belly. She curled her toes and her breath caught in her throat. "I'm coming. Yes," she gasped.

"Oh, Sherry. I came all over the bed."

"I came too," she said, surprise obvious in her voice.

"That makes it so much better somehow. Thanks, Sherry."

"You're welcome, I'm sure. I hope you'll call again."

"Maybe. My wife's away and I just needed something."

"I hope to hear from you the next time your wife's away."

"Yeah," Tim said, and she heard the click as he hung up the phone. Alice grinned and slowly stood up, pulled off her clothes and climbed between the sheets, naked tonight. As Roger curled up against her side, Alice looked at the blue denim drapes she had made for the bedroom when she and Ralph had first moved into the apartment. "You know, Roger, I think I'll get some new drapes. And maybe a matching bedspread." She reached over, turned off the light and was asleep instantly.

One Thursday morning a few weeks later, Betsy arrived at work. It was the second week in May and everyone was in a great mood. "I've got a plan," she said to Alice. "I called Velvet last night and she's free this evening. Larry's taking the boys to see *Friday the Thirteenth, Part Seventy-six, Jason Runs for Congress,* or something like that, so I'm off the hook too. I thought we'd all have a girls' night out, just the three of us, maybe at Patches. Silly drinks with lots of orange juice, rum, and those little umbrellas. How about it? Got any calls tonight?"

"No. I've settled on Mondays, Wednesdays, and Fridays."

"Great. We're meeting at Patches at seven."

"I really should get down to Rutlandt and see Mom. I haven't been there since the weekend."

"Come on, babe. You need some time for just you. You work here five days a week, you take calls three nights, you visit your mom each weekend and at least once during the week. Take some time off."

Alice leaned back in her chair. "Maybe it would be all right. God it sounds nice."

"Great. I'm counting on you. Seven at Patches."

At just past seven, Alice arrived at Patches, a restaurant and watering hole at one end of a long enclosed mall. The place was crowded with couples with small children enjoying overstuffed sandwiches and fries, teens sharing secrets and stuffed potato skins, and businessmen in suits and ties downing a few drinks before going home. Servers of both sexes wandered between the tables, dressed in outrageous outfits, tight white T-shirts and black jeans, both covered with squares of brightly patterned fabric.

Alice looked around and found Betsy and Velvet sitting at a small table off to one side. As Alice approached the table, Velvet stood up and embraced her lightly, kissing her on each cheek. "I'm so glad this worked out. I've been meaning to get together with you."

"Yes," Betsy said. "I was afraid you'd changed your mind and gone to visit your mom after all."

"I decided I needed some time out," Alice said as she dropped into a chair. She looked at the tall glasses filled with orange liquid that stood in front of each woman. "What are those?"

"Those," Velvet said, "are Bahama Mamas: rum, pineapple juice, coconut liqueur, and heaven knows what else. They are delicious." She lifted her glass and took a long drink through the straw.

Their waitress arrived and Alice considered ordering a diet soda, then changed her mind. "I'll have one of those," she said, pointing to the tall golden drinks.

"One Bahama Mama," the waitress said, scribbling on her order pad. "Any munchies for you ladies? The buffalo wings are terrific tonight and so are the skins."

Betsy tipped her head to one side, then said, "Why not? One of each. We only live once and to hell with the calories."

"I'll bring them right over."

Velvet leaned toward Alice. "You are really quite something," she said. "You've taken to this so quickly. The men I talk to when I route the calls rave about you. They feel they know you personally, particularly about all your daring exploits."

Alice grinned. "Thanks. It's really gotten to be fun."

"Betsy's an old hand at this, so I don't have to tell her how terrific she is now," Velvet said, patting Betsy on the hand, "but she took several months to get into the swing of it all. You've developed quite a following in the few weeks you've been doing it."

"I like my guys," Alice said. "They are really nice people. There are a few losers, of course, but most of them are just lonely men who want a warm voice with a lurid story to tell. I fit the bill."

"The men really surprised me when I first started working the phone," Betsy said. "I expected maniacs, kinky guys who wanted bizarre stuff with lots of sweaty sex but most of them are just ordinary men who want bizarre stuff and lots of sweaty sex."

The three women laughed, all sharing the same feelings. "How did you get time off this evening?" Alice asked Velvet.

"I've got another woman working the routing tonight. She's been doing it a few nights a week and it's great for me to get some time off."

The three women talked for an hour, sipping several rounds of drinks and munching on wings and skins. "Has he got the greatest buns or what?" Betsy said, gazing at one of the waiters who walked past them in his almost obscenely tight jeans.

Alice looked at the young man and sighed. "He's got a really great body. Remember that bulge in the front of Mr. Hollingsworth's pants?"

"Who could forget?" Betsy told Velvet about their high school social studies teacher.

"Maybe I'll use him in one of my stories," Alice said. "High school teacher and unruly student."

"How about him?" Velvet said, indicating a man sitting in the corner, watching the people and sipping a glass of red wine. "That's my style."

Alice turned and looked at the man Velvet had indicated. He was in his mid-thirties, with long black hair caught in a thin, black leather thong at the base of his neck. He wore a tight black turtleneck shirt and black trousers. "There's something both attractively compelling and dangerous about him," Velvet said. "That's the stuff of my fantasies."

"Umm. I love a little danger," Betsy said.

"I'd love a little anything," Alice said, then slammed her mouth shut.

Betsy turned to her. "What does that mean?"

"Sorry. Just my big mouth and one too many Bahama Mamas. It's nothing."

"No, it's not nothing. Don't tell me you've finally decided that it's time to get out into the world." Betsy leaned toward Velvet. "She hasn't really dated since her husband split on her."

"I have too. You've set me up with lots of guys."

"Yeah. Right. You meet them at my house, have maybe one date, then nothing."

"You're kidding," Velvet said. "I would have thought you had a rich and varied dating life, from what your fans tell me."

"My fans. Guys who have no clue who I am. They all think I'm some kind of swinger with an exotic past and a spectacular future." Alice realized that she was just a bit tipsy and willing to talk about her lack of a social life. "I'm starting to think I've missed the boat. You two are married, you've got kids. Me? I play on the phone three nights a week and otherwise, nothing."

"So why don't you do something about it?"

"Like what?" Alice sipped her drink to keep the slight buzz that was allowing her to talk about herself so freely.

"Like date," Velvet said.

"Excuse me. I don't seem to see the line of nice guys queuing up to take me out. I don't know a soul except you two and the guys on the phone, and I couldn't consider them as date material."

"Why not?" Betsy chimed in. "You just finished saying that most of them are really just nice, lonely guys. Haven't any of them asked to meet you in person?"

Alice thought about Vic, her first and steadiest client. "Sure. Remember Vic, Velvet? The first guy you put me on with? He's a decent guy, lonely and alone. At least that's what he tells me. He asks me out almost every time we talk."

"So?" the two other women said in unison. "Does he live around here?"

"He lives in the city, but get real. He thinks I'm a sexual sophisticate, with blond hair and big . . ." She looked down at the front of her green blouse. "Anyway. He has no clue what Alice is like. He likes Sheherazade." She lowered to her phone voice. "Woman of the world."

"So meet some businessman who doesn't know you from Eve," Betsy said. "Go out. Have a blast."

"Where would you suggest I meet this Mr. Business? I'm not the type to sit at a bar and wait for some guy to ask me what my sign is."

Velvet sipped her drink. "I've got several single male friends, one in particular I think you'd like. If you wouldn't object, I could introduce you. I'd give him your phone number."

Alice giggled. "You're pretty good at occupying my phone."

"So," Betsy added, "why don't you let one of your phone friends take you out. What have you got to lose?"

"A client," Alice said.

"Bullshit," Velvet said. "You could have more clients than you know what to do with. Pick one who sounds nice and go for it."

"These guys will expect Sheherazade, not Alice."

"Next time someone asks you out, take some time and tell him who you are." Velvet continued, "Call him off-line and just talk."

"I couldn't do that. He'd never believe me again."

"I'm sure that only a few of the men believe you now," Velvet said. "You don't think that these guys think you've actually done all the things you tell them about, do you? They're into the fantasy. They close their eyes and live those experiences with you. They know you're making it all up but it just doesn't matter."

"Like this Vic," Betsy said. "Let him learn who the real you is and he won't be nearly as surprised as you think."

Alice giggled. "Are you two ganging up on me?"

"Yes, we are," Betsy said. "I've been trying to get you out of your shell for years. Now that I've got the chance, I'm using all the help I can get." She reached across the table and, with an exaggerated movement, shook Velvet's hand. "This is a campaign to get Alice out into the big, wide world. Right, general?"

"Right, admiral," Velvet said. "And you, private, are taking orders. Do it. Soon."

"Private," Alice said, laughing. "I'm about the most public private that ever was."

Later that night, Alice crawled into bed beside Roger. "What do you think, cat?" she said. "Are Betsy and Velvet right? Am I still the spinster type despite Sheherazade?"

Roger rolled over and allowed Alice to scratch his belly. "Right. You agree with them. Well, if the opportunity presents itself, maybe . . . I'll think about it."

Merrow.

Chapter

8

The following Monday evening, Vic called. "Hi, Sherry," he said. "Got a story for me tonight?"

"Sure thing, sweet cheeks," Alice said in her Sheherazade voice. "It's about a night when I was very naughty."

"Tell me."

"Well, you know I was married a long time ago."

"Yes. I remember."

"Well it happened back then." She thought about the story she had written about a game of strip poker. She couldn't think of Ralph ever playing like this so she decided to rename her husband. "Ted and I had met this other couple, Barb and Andy, the day after they moved in next door to us. Nice folks and we hit it off right away. It hadn't hurt that Andy was quite a hunk. He wasn't actually gorgeous, but he had great eyes and the best pair of buns I had ever seen."

"Women always like buns, don't they?"

"Actually, what appeals to me now is a nice personality and a good sense of humor, but back then I was really into looks."

"I think I've got good buns, but only a woman would know for sure."

"I'll bet you have great buns, Vic." Alice was amazed. She was actually flirting with Vic. Back to work.

"The four of us had found ourselves meeting often beside the pool in the center of the condo complex. Friday evenings we were all tired from work and sat in the water, talking about everything from our jobs to television to sports to religion, politics and, of course, sex. As the summer wore on, we started to bring potluck suppers out to the pool area. As fall approached and we had to give up the pool, we started to alternate Friday dinners at each other's houses, and eventually Ted and I succumbed to Barb and Andy's shared love of poker.

"It started with matchsticks, then chips, and eventually we began to play for small change. We won and lost a few dollars and we put the winnings into a kitty to take us all out to an expensive restaurant."

"I like an occasional game of poker but I'm not very good," Vic said. "I can't bluff worth a damn. You can tell exactly what I'm thinking by just looking at my face."

"Me too. I'm hopeless."

"That's good. Go on with the story."

"Well, one night Barb had lost five dollars, the maximum amount allowed by our house rules. 'Okay,' she said, as Ted raked in the pile of coins from the center of the table, 'I'm tapped.' She wiggled her eyebrows. 'What shall I wager now?'

"I just stared. Her suggestion was obvious but I thought that she must be teasing. 'I'll ante for you,' I said, pushing a nickel into the center of the table."

"You were really embarrassed?" Vic asked.

"Yeah, I was." Alice smiled. "I wasn't always the sexually sophisticated woman I am now."

Softly, Vic asked, "Are you really so sophisticated or just a good storyteller?"

Alice gasped. Did he know her that well? Without answering, she continued her story. "Barb thanked me but looked a bit disappointed.

" 'Rats,' my husband said. 'I was hoping for something better.' I playfully slapped him on the back of the hand. 'Not a chance, buster.'

"He laughed. 'Rats, I say again.'

"Andy, Barb's husband, dealt seven-card stud. In deference to Barb, the betting was small and we allowed her to stay in despite her continued losses. Soon she had a small pile of coins in front of her to keep track of her indebtedness. 'I'll bet a nickel. I'll win this one for sure,' she said, grinning at her cards. 'Whatever would I do if I lost?'

" 'Call,' Ted said.

" 'I'll call too,' I said, hoping that Barb would win and the game could continue without the double meanings that seemed to pepper the conversation now. I was really embarrassed.

"Andy called and said, 'Time to show what you've got—cards, that is.'

" 'Full boat, tens over threes,' Ted said. I was sure my husband had won and confused as to what would happen then. Andy and I turned our cards face down, signaling that we couldn't beat Ted's hand. 'And you, my indebted friend?' Ted said.

" 'Shit,' Barb hissed, 'I really thought I had you. I have a flush, queen high.'

" 'Phew,' Andy said. 'I haven't had a hand as good as either of those all night. Ted, since you're the winner, you get to decide Barb's payment.' "

"What did he ask for?" Vic asked.

"He asked her to take off her blouse. I was shocked at my husband, but I said nothing. I was sure that Barb would be insulted and I was afraid that our wonderful Friday evenings were suddenly gone. I'll have to admit, Vic, that I was also aroused."

"I'll bet," Vic said.

" 'You've got it,' Barb said, and with little hesitation, she unbuttoned her shirt and pulled it off. I kept my gaze on the coins in front of me, then slowly raised my eyes. Barb was an average-looking woman with a nice figure, shoulder-length brown hair, and green eyes covered with glasses. As I looked up, I saw her medium-size breasts, now covered only by a wispy bit of white lace. I swallowed hard, then glanced at Ted. He was looking at Barb's body, but I felt his fingers link with mine. He glanced at me and squeezed my hand.

" 'I love those sexy things my wife wears,' Andy said, 'don't you?'

" 'I guess,' I said. Actually Barb wasn't wearing much less than she often wore at the pool but this was so much more intimate. I could see the outline of her nipples through the sheer fabric and I was sure that the men could too.

"Andy reached over and rubbed his palm over the tips of Barb's breasts. 'God, she has great tits.' I watched Andy's hand, unable to look away.

" 'Okay, that's enough,' Barb quipped. 'Let's deal.'

"It was my turn to deal and, with shaking hands, I picked up the cards and shuffled, staring at the table. 'Hey, Sherry,' Barb said, placing her hand over mine, 'I didn't mean to embarrass you. I'm really sorry. I wouldn't hurt you for the world.' She reached for her shirt and stuffed one arm into a sleeve.

" 'Of course not,' the men said.

"I sighed. 'I guess I'm just a bit more of a prude than you all are.'

" 'Not in bed you're not,' my husband said. 'This woman's a wildcat under the right circumstances.'

"I could feel the heat rise in my face. I loved good hot sex, but up till then I had been very private about it. Yet here my husband was, telling everyone. He was such a beast. Or was he? Was there any reason to be so afraid to let anyone know that I enjoyed good lovemaking?"

"No reason at all," Vic purred. "Do you enjoy good lovemaking now, Sherry?"

Suddenly breathless, Alice said, "Yes. I guess so."

"Do you get enough?"

"Let's get back to the story. Okay?"

"Sure," Vic said, but Alice thought she heard reluctance in his voice. "Tell me more."

"Well, I was chagrined. I wasn't a prude and I knew I had to lighten up. These were my best friends. 'Listen,' I said, 'leave the shirt off. You lost fair and square. But you'll win this hand for sure.'

"Barb did win that hand and a few more and by the end of the evening, everything was the same as it had been. After Barb and Andy were gone, I found that the thought of Barb without her shirt had me terribly turned on. Ted and I cavorted on the bed for almost an hour. Finally we lay side by side, hands clasped, our breathing slowing. 'You found that bit with Barb's blouse a turn-on, didn't you?' Ted asked.

"I thought about the answer for a minute, then said, 'I didn't think so at the time, but I guess I did. The sight of her in that bra and watching Andy's hand rubbing her made me hot.'

" 'Yeah, me too,' Ted said. 'Not the sight of her tits, but watching Andy touch her. God, it made me hard as stone. It's not personal, you understand,' he continued. 'It doesn't mean I love you any less.'

" 'I know that,' I said, and I did know that. I knew he loved me, but the sight of a half-naked body was a turn-on. Nothing more was said, but I lay awake for quite a while that evening.

"The following week we were at Andy and Barb's house and after dinner we moved to the card table. As the play began, Ted cleared his throat and broached the topic we were all a bit afraid of. 'I say that we cut the maximum loss to a dollar. I liked what happened last week when Barb got tapped out.'

" 'I have to say that sex was great that night,' Andy said. 'Watching my wife revealed for all to see made me really hot.'

" 'Dollar losses?' Ted said. He looked at me. 'Okay, babe?'

"I found my head nodding. Soon I was down my limit and then some. 'Shirt please,' Andy said."

"Could you do it?" Vic asked. "I mean just like that?"

"I didn't think about it, I just did it."

"I'll bet you have a great body."

Alice sighed. "I guess every woman wishes she had a better one."

"Every man too. Go on with your story."

"I had worn my sexiest black lace bra under my sweatshirt. I guess I had known what would happen and the whole idea really turned me on. 'God,' Andy said, 'you've got a great body.' I never thought of myself as having a good shape, but, as my face got hotter I looked at Andy. He had the most wonderful look in his eyes.

"Over the next half hour, Barb was clearly the big winner and had almost all the coins in front of her. I had almost become used to sitting at the table in only my bra. When Andy was tapped, Barb said, 'Listen, losing shirts isn't as revealing for you guys as it is for us. I demand your jeans.' I remember thinking, *God, she is a daring one.*

"I swallowed, wondering whether I would get to see those gorgeous buns covered only by a pair of shorts. Andy agreed and quickly removed his jeans. He was wearing the smallest pair of briefs I had ever seen and they barely covered the bulge caused by his obvious erection. As he sat down, he said, 'As you can obviously tell, this has gone a bit further than before. Let me be honest with you two. Barb and I have been talking. Before we moved here, we had a pair of friends and we all used to play together on occasion. No one actually did it with anyone else's husband or wife, but there was a lot of fooling around and a few times we each made love with the other couple watching. It was a great turn-on.'

"I remember how shocked I was. 'You didn't,' I said, horrified yet also soaking wet.

" 'Yes, we did,' Barb said. 'We never actually swapped, but it was so hot to play and to watch. We touched one another with hands and mouth and it was incredibly exciting. We wouldn't jeopardize our friendship by asking anything you two weren't willing to do but that bra you're wearing, Sherry, says a lot.'

" 'It does?' I said, trying not to sound anxious. My mouth was dry and my hands trembled.

" 'I think you wore it on purpose, hoping this would happen,' Barb said.

"Ted grinned at me. 'That's what I thought when I saw you dressing, and that's why I suggested what I did.' "

"Did you 'fess up, Sherry?" Vic asked. "Had you done it on purpose?"

Alice chuckled as she looked at the story she had written. "I admitted it."

" 'Have you ever played with another couple before?' Barb asked.

" 'Never,' Ted said. 'We'd never even considered it until last Friday night. After you guys left we had some of the hottest sex I can remember, and I must admit that I was thinking about the sight of your body and of Andy touching you.'

" 'Me too,' I whispered.

"Andy stood up and quickly slipped Barb's sweater over her head, revealing another tiny bra and her gorgeous breasts. 'Let's all get more comfortable,' he suggested, removing his sweatshirt, shoes, and socks. Barb stood, slipped out of her shoes and pulled off her jeans. She was wearing a pair of bikini panties that barely covered her mound. Ted took a deep breath, and said to me, 'Babe? Is this all right with you? If it's not we can stop now.' "

"Was it okay with you?" Vic asked, clearly excited by the picture Alice was painting.

"In answer, I stood up and pulled off my jeans. Like Barb I had worn a pair of tiny bikini panties.

" 'You really are gorgeous,' Andy said. I knew better. I had a not-bad body with a little extra flesh here and there, but the look on Andy's face said that he thought I was wonderful and that made my knees turn to jelly.

"My husband was the last to strip. When he was finally down to a pair of tight briefs, I stared, then giggled. 'Those are new. I'll bet you bought those special, thinking something like this might happen.'

" 'Busted,' he said. 'Last Friday made me so hot, I was just hoping.' Suddenly everyone was laughing, and moving into the living room. Standing in the middle of the room, Ted placed his lips against mine and kissed me long and deeply. His hands roamed over my back, cupped my ass, and caressed my calves. Calves? My eyes sprung open. Andy sat at my feet, his hands stroking my legs. At first I stiffened, but then I relaxed and enjoyed the feeling of someone else's hands on my body. Slowly his hands slid to the fronts of my thighs, then quieted. 'I can feel you tremble,' he said softly. 'Are you afraid? Has this gone too far?'

" 'No,' I whispered. 'It all feels good.' "

"I wish I had been there," Vic said. "I'd love to touch you."

"I wish you had been too," Alice said, realizing that as she told the story, she thought about Vic. "So Barb moved behind Ted, her palms flat on his upper back. Then she turned my husband so he was facing her and she gazed into my eyes. 'If this bothers you,' she said to me, 'I'll stop.' When I didn't say anything, she slipped her arms around Ted's neck and pressed her lips against his.

"I should make them stop, I remember saying to myself. Another woman's kissing my husband. But it was so sexy. As I watched, Barb rubbed her lace-covered breasts over Ted's chest. *Funny, I said to myself, I'm not really jealous. It's really erotic watching my husband enjoy what's happening.* And he was. His arms were around Barb and he was kissing her with the same mouth that had just been against my lips and it was all right. I knew that this wasn't going to go too far, and I could call it off at any time. But I didn't want to.

"Suddenly Andy's hands were on my naked belly, stroking, caressing, kneading. He stood up and his hands slid to my ribs. 'May I? I want so much to touch you.' "

Alice could hear Vic groan.

"I looked into his deep brown eyes, smiled, and touched his face. 'Yes,' I whispered. 'It really is all right.'

"His hands were on my breasts, cupping me, feeling the weight of my tits in his palms. His fingers found my nipples through the silky fabric and he pinched. 'Oh God,' I said as my eyes closed and my knees buckled."

"Oh God," Vic moaned.

"Quickly Andy guided me to the sofa. As I lay back on the soft material, I knew that nothing else mattered but hands and mouths and satisfying the rising tide of heat. Andy crouched between my spread thighs and his mouth found my nipples. Then his teeth. That had always been my downfall. The slight pain on my nipples drove me crazy. I held his head as he nipped and nibbled, moisture flowing between my legs, soaking the crotch of my panties. I ran my fingers through his curly hair, so unlike Ted's straight soft hair. This wasn't my husband, but it was so good.

"Suddenly there was a mouth on my other breast. My eyes flew open and I saw Ted's head bent over me. I had a mouth on each breast and Barb stood behind, stroking each man's back.

"Ted unsnapped the front hook of my bra and now mouths engulfed naked nipples. Sharp teeth. Pinching fingers. A hand stroked me between my thighs. Ted's? Andy's? I found I didn't want to know so I closed my eyes.

"Fingers rubbed through the silk of my panties. My clit swelled to press against those hands. Fingers slipped under the edge of my panties and found my wetness. Fingers slowly found my center and one penetrated just a tiny bit. Not enough, my body cried as I thrust my hips upward. Fill me.

"Hands removed my panties and still my eyes remained closed. I wanted to imagine that they were Andy's fingers, not my husband's. Then the fingers filled me, first one, then two, then three, filling my emptiness. I drove my hips upward, forcing the fingers to fill me more deeply. I had to know.

"I opened my eyes. Ted was on his hands and knees, his head bent over my breast. Barb had one hand on the small of his back, the other obviously rubbing him between his thighs. Andy was between my legs, one hand buried in my pussy, the other stroking his now-naked cock."

"I'm going to come, Sherry," Vic cried.

Alice knew that the best way for him to get off was for her to continue the story. "Then Andy's mouth found my clit, his tongue ceaseless in its exploration, his fingers still filling me. It was too much and I came. Waves and waves of molten heat washed over me and I heard myself screaming. As I climaxed, Andy straightened and I watched a stream of come arch from his cock onto my belly. As I calmed, Ted and Barb pulled off their remaining clothing and Barb lay on the carpet. Ted bent between her legs and pressed his mouth over her clit.

"I was now almost unconscious on the couch so Andy slid to the floor and sat beside me. He reached out, laid a hand on his wife's arm and spoke softly to me. 'You've never felt anything like touching your husband while he makes love like this. Touch him.'

"Hesitantly I reached out and placed my hand on my husband's back. I could feel the movements of his body as he licked Barb's pussy. 'If you're up to it,' Andy whispered, 'come here and touch him right.' He pulled my hand and, although I was exhausted from my own climax, I moved onto the floor until I could reach between his thighs and place my hand on Ted's cock. He was hard and hot and so smooth. I squeezed and felt his entire body tighten.

"I smiled and stroked him the way I knew he liked as I watched his head bob between Barb's thighs. I rubbed and squeezed until I knew he was getting close. I kept him there, on the edge of climax until I heard Barb scream, then I took one finger and scratched the special spot between his ass and his balls. He came, his come spurting onto Barb's thigh."

"Oh God, yes," Vic cried, his voice relaxing.

"Except for the sound of heavy breathing, the room was silent for a while. Then Ted said, 'I need a shower. Do you think there's room for four?' "

"Oh, Sherry," Vic said, his breathing slowing, "that was wonderful."

"I'm glad you enjoyed my story. It happened a long time ago."

"Did it really happen?"

"Of course."

Vic's voice got serious. "Really? Sherry, tell me about you. Are you really the woman you seem to be?"

Alice hesitated. She really liked Vic. Although she hardly knew him, she sensed that he was really lonely. "Some parts of me are, some aren't."

"We've been teasing for weeks. I ask you out and you change

the subject. Let me ask again. I already know that we only live about fifty miles apart. So how about meeting me for dinner some evening? I could come up from the city and we could meet somewhere in Westchester."

"I'm not the woman you think I am, you know."

"I don't know what I think you are but I'll bet you don't look at all like the picture I have of you."

"Not at all."

"Long blond hair? Blue eyes?"

"Brown curly hair, brown eyes. About five-three."

"Are you married? Living with someone?"

"No. I'm alone." Why had she said it quite that way?

"Listen. I've been calling sex lines for a long time and somehow you and I have some things in common. You sound like a nice person and maybe a bit lonely like me. I know a nice informal restaurant in northern Westchester." He mentioned a place called Donovan's in Mount Kisco, a twenty-minute drive from her house.

"I know the place."

"What nights do you work?"

"Mondays, Wednesdays, and Fridays."

"Okay. Saturday sounds too much like a date and this isn't. Just two friends meeting for dinner. Let's make it next Tuesday. I'll be at Donovan's at seven. I'll get a table and sit with a copy of Shakespeare's sonnets. It's hokey, but who else would have such a book. I'm thirty-eight and not much to look at so you might see me and decide to run for the hills." His laugh was self-deprecating, but warm. "I'll wait until seven-thirty, then order dinner and eat slowly. Please come."

He was so sweet and thoughtful. "I don't know."

"I don't either. I'll just hope. Okay?"

"Okay, but don't expect anything. I might not be there."

"I know. Good night, Sherry. Oh. Is that your real name?"

Alice sighed. "It's Alice. Alice Waterman. And I'm thirty-two and not much to look at either."

"Nice to meet you, Alice. I'm Vic Sanderson."

The following Thursday evening the three women met again at Patches for girls' night out. Besides Betsy, Alice had never had a good female friend and the more time she spent with Velvet, the more comfortable and the closer she felt. The three women had arrived at six-thirty and had decided to try Caribbean Romances: pineapple juice, orange juice, rum, and amaretto. After one drink and lots of small talk, Alice broached the topic that had been troubling her since her conversation with Vic.

"I've got a problem," she said without preamble. "Vic asked me out again."

"And?"

"And I don't know what to do."

"What do you want to do?" Velvet asked.

Alice chuckled. "It depends on what time of day you ask. Sometimes I tell myself that he's a lonely, sensitive man who seems to like me. The rest of the time I think he's a man who has no clue who I am and who likes to call phone-sex lines."

"Did you make a date?"

Alice filled them in on Vic's arrangement. "Sounds sensible," Velvet said, understanding that Alice didn't want a flip answer. "Each of you has a car so you have a way out if it all goes wrong. No one knows enough about the other to be troublesome. It sounds like a good plan to me."

"I guess he must have given it quite a bit of thought," Alice admitted.

"He's obviously been planning this for quite a while," Velvet added.

"Okay," Betsy said, "let's look at this seriously. What's the downside?"

Alice considered. "He's expecting Sherry, girl sexpot. Someone who's been with everyone and done everything. And what will he get? Me."

"Do you think he wants sex with you? Right there in Donovan's?"

"No, of course not."

"Right. You'll just talk, have a nice dinner, and get to know each other. I repeat, what's the downside?"

Alice smiled ruefully. "I don't know. It just so embarrassing to have to admit that I'm not what he thinks I am."

Velvet leaned forward. "You know he doesn't believe all that sexy stuff you tell him over the phone. He knows you're not Sheherazade. Maybe he wouldn't be interested if he thought you were."

"What do you mean?"

"He's a small, lonely man who's probably never actually made love to a woman like Sherry. Maybe the idea of dating her would scare him to death. It would be like making love to some porn star, a constant judge of his technique."

"She's right, you know," Betsy said. "Most of the men I talk to aren't the worldly type who would enjoy being with the woman I pretend to be. They'd probably enjoy fucking my brains out as long as they didn't have to watch my eyes or talk to me afterward." She paused. "I'm probably pretty threatening. Maybe if they could say, 'Down on your knees, bitch,' then make me disappear."

"I never thought of it that way," Alice said.

"I don't know," Velvet said. "I've never dated any of my clients, but then I've been married the entire time and I wouldn't have even considered it."

"So we're back to the question of what's the downside," Betsy said.

Alice grinned. "I don't know. Maybe there isn't one." With two Caribbean Romances making her feel a bit mellow, Alice had to admit that if she showed up at Donovan's the following Tuesday, she had very little to lose.

Chapter
9

Alice was almost useless at Dr. Tannenbaum's office on Tuesday. At unexpected moments she'd drift off into a fantasy about her dinner date with Vic. In one, she walked into the restaurant and was greeted by a hunky guy dressed in a tuxedo, and in another he was dressed in a gorilla suit. In another dream, they sat, had dinner, and then Vic asked her to climb under that table and suck his cock. None of the dreams left her feeling comfortable.

"So what are you going to wear?" Betsy said, dropping into a chair in the reception area.

"Huh?" Alice said, returning from a vision of the two of them in a heart-shaped, vibrating bed.

"Tonight. What are you wearing?"

"I've decided not to go."

"You're crazy. At least go to Donovan's and see what he looks like. If he scares the daylights out of you, turn around, and walk out. Give it a chance."

"Why? He'll just be disappointed and I'll feel terrible."

"Both Velvet and I tried to convince you that he won't be disappointed. I think he's very perceptive to be able to see the wonderful woman you are. I'm sure it comes through in your stories.

You're always considerate and thoughtful and you're such a caring person."

"Thanks for that. This whole thing's making me crazy."

"Okay. Here's what you do. Go home after work, put on those new gray linen slacks and your soft mauve silk blouse, the one you bought a few weeks ago at Macy's.

"I don't know."

"I do. Wear a pair of chunky silver earrings and that silver chain with the disk at the end." Betsy stopped to think. "Let's see. I've got the rest. Your deep burgundy wool vest in case it's chilly, and your trench coat. See? Nothing more to think about."

"But . . ."

"Enough of the buts. Just do it because Betsy says so. End of thought."

"Yes, Betsy," Alice said in a little-girl voice.

"That's a good girl," Betsy said, smiling. "You only have to walk into Donovan's and look. Then I give you permission to turn around and walk out. Okay?"

"Okay. I'll do it."

"We'll meet for lunch tomorrow so I can hear everything, good or bad."

After she and Betsy arranged their lunch, Alice hurried home from work, both exhilarated and terrified. She showered and dressed as Betsy had suggested and at seven-ten she was parked in the lot at Donovan's. She got out of her car and approached the green and white striped awning. The restaurant was American-style, the entire place decorated to resemble someone's patio, with white walls, white slatted wood tables, green and white striped chairs, table cloths, and napkins. At first look, it was blinding and it felt like being inside of a lime candy cane but it was all softened by the dozens of green plants that filled white pots throughout the dining room. The restaurant was extremely popular with well-priced dishes and a list of specials that took up half of one wall.

As she wandered toward the host, a woman offered to take her coat. "No thanks. I might not be staying." She stood at the entrance to the huge dining room and looked around. She saw a few single men, but finally her eyes rested upon a middle-aged man with a copy of Shakespeare on the table in front of him. He had shaggy brown hair, deep brown eyes, and deep laugh lines around his mouth. Alice saw that his ears were oversized, which was probably why he wore his hair long. She smiled. *He looks like a basset hound*, she thought, *comfortable somehow*. She squared her shoulders and walked into the room. The host approached and asked whether she needed a table. "No thanks, I'm meeting someone."

Vic caught her eye and when she nodded, his face lit up. He stood as she neared his table and quickly the host pulled out a chair for her. Vic was several inches taller than she was, maybe five foot eight or nine. "I'm so glad you could come," Vic said. He extended his hand and she took it briefly. His palm was warm and a bit damp, his hands soft.

"I almost didn't," Alice said, releasing his hand and settling in her chair.

"If you want the truth, I almost didn't show up either."

"How come?" Alice asked, handing her coat to the host. "Could you put this in the checkroom for me?" she asked him. She'd stay for a while at least.

"Of course," the host said, bustling away.

"All day I had these visions of you," Vic admitted, "looking like one of those Baywatch women with long legs and a big bosom. You'd take one look at me and run for the hills."

Alice laughed. "I had the same thoughts. Funny. You don't look like Hulk Hogan in a suit."

The two laughed together. "My ex-wife used to say that I looked like a basset hound with big friendly eyes."

"No," Alice said, trying to hide her chuckle. "I think you look just fine. It was so nice of you to drive all the way up here."

"Actually I love driving and I do a lot of it, usually by myself to get away and think."

They ordered a house-special chicken dish with baked potatoes and broccoli and throughout dinner the two talked like they were old friends. It turned out that they were both New York Jets fans and they talked at length about the team's prospects for the coming season. They also liked folk music. Vic raved about a small fifty-seat auditorium in Greenwich Village where they had unusual groups perform each weekend. "A few weeks ago they had a really wonderful group of Andean musicians. They played some fantastic stuff on the charango, guitar, and bombo."

"I have an album of Andean music that I particularly enjoy. Isn't one of the instruments a drum sort of thing made out of the hide of an armadillo?"

"I don't believe it," Vic said, obviously nonplussed. "No one I've ever met knows anything about Andean music. Alice, I think I love you." Alice gasped. "Don't take that seriously," Vic said quickly. "I was just kidding."

"No problem," Alice said, her heartbeat returning to normal. "I know almost nothing about you. What do you do for a living?"

"I create computer games. I'm working on one now, but eventually I'd like to write an X-rated one. I haven't worked out any of the details yet, but it will probably have a superstudly hero who has to kill the bad guys who have taken over a whorehouse. Along the way he stumbles into several rooms and takes part in the fun and games or something like that."

"You're kidding."

"Actually, I'm not. If I ever get the time, I'd love to use a few of your stories as the basis for some of the adventures."

"My stories?" Alice blushed.

"You're a very talented storyteller and the fantasies we've shared live on in my mind."

To change the subject, Alice said, "You talked about an ex-wife so I gather you're divorced. Any kids?"

"I have two teenaged daughters who live with my ex. We've been divorced for almost six years. They live on Long Island and I see them every other weekend, although it's getting harder and harder."

"How come?"

"The girls are growing up and they have their own lives. Both are in high school, and dating and hate to have their social lives messed up with a father." When Alice looked saddened, Vic added quickly, "It's okay, really. They're almost grown and will be in college soon. It's just Dad who has a bit of trouble letting go. It's great that we are really close and talk on the phone often." He paused. "Although they talk to everyone on the phone often."

"Where would any of us be without the phone?" Alice said, grinning.

"Right. How about you? I know you're not married now. Let's forget about that story you told me last week. I assume that was just fiction. Have you ever been married for real?"

Alice told Vic an abbreviated story about Ralph. "He was a nice man whom I never should have married. We got together for all the wrong reasons."

"At least there were no kids to get caught in the middle."

"Amen to that," Alice said.

When the waiter arrived to take dessert orders, Alice hesitated. "Maybe I'll just have coffee."

"Come on, Alice, be brave. Have something completely frivolous. You're entitled for putting up with me all evening."

"I didn't put up with you. I'm having a delightful evening. You're right about dessert, however. I'll have the cheesecake."

Vic grinned. "Make that two."

Alice considered. "Make that one cheesecake with two forks, if that's okay with you, Vic."

"Nice compromise. And two coffees."

As the waiter disappeared, Vic asked, "How did you get connected with Velvet Whispers? Where did you work before that?"

"I work as a receptionist in a dentist's office. You know how long I've been with Velvet Whispers. You were my first call." She told Vic a short version of her connection with Betsy and the discussion that convinced Alice to give it a try.

"You're kidding," Vic said. "I knew I was your first caller at Whispers but I assumed that you had been working somewhere else before. You were so professional and so good at it."

"Thanks for the compliment." Alice beamed.

"You mentioned your mother earlier. Is she better now?"

"No, and she won't be. She's well into her seventies and in really frail health. She's happy, however, at the Rutlandt Nursing Home and my jobs make ends meet." And more, Alice thought. She was actually putting some money in the bank.

"Fortunately my parents are still going strong," Vic said. "My dad works for American Airlines. He was a pilot and my mom was a stewardess when they met."

"How great! Does that mean you get to fly free? I've always wanted to travel."

"I can fly standby, but I seldom do. I used to when my wife and I were still together. We took the kids to Europe every summer, but now it just doesn't happen anymore. I guess I'm too caught up in my work."

"That's really too bad. I always dreamed of going to Europe."

"So come with me. We can tour for a few weeks, see London, Rome, Paris."

"Sure. We can go next week. Don't I wish I could!"

"Why can't you?"

"For starters, my jobs—both of them."

"You could work it out if you wanted to, but we can let that pass for now. By the way, I think we have a little problem regarding your job."

"Oh?" Alice said.

"Well, I'd feel a little silly calling you up on business now."

Alice blushed. "You're right. I would be mortified talking like I do to someone when I've seen his face."

"You mean you couldn't talk dirty to me over the phone."

Alice's color deepened. "Only on a very personal basis, not for money."

Vic took her hand. "Thanks. That's nice." He kept hold of her hand. "Have you ever met any of the other men you talk to?"

"Nope, and if I had, I don't think I could look them in the imaginary eye while I was talking to them. When I don't know them, they're just voices."

"I feel a bit guilty not calling you anymore. Will that louse up your income? I could call and pay, but we could just talk about anything we like."

"Don't be silly. You can call me if you like, but not for money. I have all the callers I can deal with as it is."

"Will you give me your home number?"

Alice considered. In the business she was in, giving out her home phone number was a large step, but she felt completely at home with Vic. As Velvet had said, he was a thoroughly nice and very lonely man. "Sure." They exchanged home addresses and phone numbers.

The waiter arrived with their cheesecake and the conversation wandered into other areas. When they had finished their desserts and their coffee cups had run dry, the check arrived. Vic reached for it. "I'd prefer if we split that," Alice said.

"I come from the old school. The man pays for his dates."

"You said yourself that this isn't a date. Please. I'd feel better."

"Okay. You're right. It's a not-date. Your wish is my command," Vic said. When they had worked out the details and paid the check, he stood to leave. "This has been a wonderful evening," Vic said, helping pull out her chair. "I don't want to rush you, so would you meet me again next week? Same place?"

"Another not-date?

"I would like to make it a date this time." He placed his hand against the small of Alice's back and guided her through the maze of tables.

"That would be nice. I'd like that."

As they hit the cool, late spring air, Vic leaned over and kissed Alice softly on the lips. "I've enjoyed the evening tremendously. You're nothing like what I expected, and more wonderful."

"Thanks. I've had a great time myself."

They parted without any awkward moments.

The following day, Alice met Betsy in the Italian restaurant in the mall. "Well?" Betsy said as they settled into a booth. "No, don't tell me anything. Velvet's meeting us and you can tell us both."

At that moment, Velvet walked into the darkened room and spotted them immediately. She quickly made herself comfortable in the booth beside Betsy. "Now tell," Velvet said. "Everything."

"He's very nice," Alice said. She told the two women about the evening in great detail. "We have another date next Tuesday."

"Fan-flippin'-tastic," Betsy said.

"Great," Velvet said. "I have something to tell you, however. I know more about Mr. Sanderson than you might think."

"Yes?" Alice said, terrified that she had dated a mass murderer or a spy.

"When he first called several years ago he said something that triggered something in my brain," Velvet said. "I let it go, but when you said you were going out with him, I looked him up in *Who's Who*. He said he works on computer games." She mentioned a very popular adventure game.

"I know that one," Betsy said. "My boys have it."

"I remember playing it one evening with Phil. He beat me seven ways from Sunday." Alice made the connection. "You mean he worked on that one?"

"He didn't just work on it," Velvet said, conspiratorially. "He invented it. Or wrote it. Or whatever you do to computer games." She mentioned several more very popular games. "Those too. He sold his company last year and made buckets of money. That's how he can afford your phone calls, among other things."

Alice was taken aback. He was rich. That cast a different light on everything. *Oh, shit,* she thought, *I argued about splitting the check. I told him about my problems needing money to support my mother. I probably sounded like a jerk.*

"You said he seemed like a regular guy," Betsy said. "I'll bet he didn't want you to know about all that money. Women don't like to think that they are being courted for their money and maybe he's the same way. He just wanted to be a nice guy you were dating."

"I know," Alice said, "but we're not in the same league."

"Hey wait a minute," Velvet said. "I didn't tell you all that to intimidate you. He's asked you out and that's that."

"I know, but he's not the man he pretended to be."

"Listen," Betsy said. "You aren't Sherry either, but does that change who you really are?"

"You are who you are," Velvet said, "and that's that. So if you had fun, just enjoy and let the chips fall where they may."

Alice sighed. "I guess you're right. Gee. All that money."

"Listen," Velvet said, bringing Alice back from her reverie, "since we're talking about dating, Wayne's got a business friend in from out of town. Interested in dinner? My place, tomorrow evening?"

Alice raised an eyebrow. "A blind date?"

"I guess you could call it that. He's not rich, and since he's from the west coast he's not geographically desirable either, but he's a really nice guy, single again, sort of hunky and cute."

"Single again?"

"Yeah. He's twice divorced, but you're not marrying him, just having dinner with him at my house."

"I don't think so," Alice said.

"Please? I really like him and he seems like a lost ship right now. Just pay a little attention to him and let him feel like a man again. Think of it as a charitable contribution."

Betsy chimed in. "Once again, what have you got to lose?"

"You two are trying to convert me into a social butterfly."

"Hardly," Velvet said. "We had nothing to do with Vic asking you out and this is just a one-night stand." She giggled. "So to speak."

"Come on, Alice. Make the big plunge."

Alice sighed. "Okay you two. How can I argue with both of you?"

"The kids are staying with Wayne's folks overnight so we'll be able to have a grown-up evening for a change. Wayne's dad will drop them at school Friday morning so I can sleep in and Karen's routing for me so I'm off duty. This is such a pleasure. Can you be at my house about six?"

"As long as the doctor's schedule accommodates. One question. Does he know about your business, about what I do?"

"No. I don't tell too many people, especially Wayne's business associates."

Instead of the jitters she had had before her date with Vic, Thursday passed quickly and easily. Alice had already decided to wear the same gray linen slacks with a white blouse with a thin gray stripe so she dashed home from work and changed quickly. It was a warm late spring evening so instead of a coat, she put on a deep green blazer. After feeding Roger, she made the short drive to Putnam Valley in record time and arrived in Velvet's driveway with two minutes to spare.

"I didn't expect you so promptly," Velvet said as she ushered Alice into the living room. She had met Velvet's husband, Wayne, briefly before and took his outstretched hand warmly. A very ordinary-looking man, he doted on his wife and family and Velvet seemed completely in love with him.

"It's good to see you again," Alice told Wayne and shifted her gaze to the other man in the room. To say he was hunky was an understatement. He looked to be in his mid-thirties, gorgeous in a Kevin Sorbo kind of way. Soft, sandy hair that he wore curling at his shoulders, straight nose, and piercing blue eyes. The tan sports jacket and brown slacks he wore only served to accent his deliciously wide shoulders and narrow hips. Alice found herself wondering what he would look like in Sorbo's Hercules outfit: leather pants and a cloth vest revealing most of his upper body.

"You're Alice," the man said, his voice sounding like hot fudge. "It's nice to meet you. I'm Todd." He extended his hand and Alice took it. His grip was strong and he held her hand for just a fraction longer than she had expected.

Over drinks before dinner, she learned that Todd was a salesman for a California-based manufacturing firm that did business with Wayne's electronics company. "My business is really deadly dull. Tell me about you."

Alice explained about her job in Dr. Tannenbaum's office. "Do you enjoy what you do?" Todd asked.

"It's a job, and I really like the people I deal with."

"I'm sure they like you too. I know I do."

He really comes on like gangbusters. Slow down, she said, hoping he'd read her. "Thanks. Tell me more about you."

He told her briefly that he was recently out of a messy divorce. "We'd only been married for two years, but it's amazing what you can accumulate in such a short time."

"I'll bet," Alice said.

"You know what we fought about most? Cleopatra." When Alice looked puzzled, he said, "Our brown tabby Persian cat. We each wanted to keep her and it became like a custody battle. Fortunately, about a month into the arguing, we discovered that Cleo was going to have kittens, so my wife got the cat and I got two kittens."

"How wonderful," Alice said. "I don't know how I'd manage without Roger. He's a domestic short hair and my best friend."

"I know what you mean. Cocoa and Cognac are mine."

"Great names."

"Cocoa is a little girl and Cognac is a male. They're all tan and brown so the names seemed to fit.'

"What do you do with them when you travel?"

"I have a neighbor who takes care of them for me. You know, cleans the litter pan and puts down new food. They are totally indoor cats so they don't require much."

Somehow, with cats in common, Alice and Todd began to relax with each other. Over dinner, the group talked about anything and everything, the conversation never lagging, each fighting for an opening to express another opinion. After coffee, they adjourned to the living room with glasses of brandy, where the lively conversation continued until Alice glanced at her watch. "Holy cow," she said. "It's after eleven. I'm going to be useless at work unless I get some sleep." Between her date with Vic, her work Wednesday evening, and the dinner tonight she was going to have to sleep all weekend to make up for it. And she hadn't visited her mother since the previous weekend. She stood, retrieved her jacket, and thanked Velvet and Wayne.

"And Todd, this has been a wonderful evening. I really enjoyed your company."

"I'm going to take off, too, back to my motel. Let me walk you out to your car." He grabbed his jacket, which he had taken off earlier, and slipped it on.

Alice hugged Velvet and planted a quick kiss on Wayne's cheek. "Thanks for dinner. Velvet, I'll talk to you over the weekend."

"Good night," the couple said.

Todd walked Alice to her car. "I'm going to take a risk here," Todd said, and he wrapped his arms around her lightly and leaned forward. Their lips met softly and the tender kiss totally overwhelmed Alice's senses. She pulled back slightly and looked at Todd in the moonlight. It had been years since she'd been kissed and she discovered that she liked it. She leaned forward again, touched her lips to his and sighed.

Todd made a soft sound deep in his throat and gently pressed her back against her car door. The feeling of being trapped against the cool metal made Alice tremble. Todd jumped back. "I'm sorry. I got carried away."

Alice cupped his face in her hands. "Don't be sorry. It was really nice."

Todd grinned. Then he tangled his fingers in her short curls and brought her face to his. Again they kissed, this one no longer tender. Now his mouth was hungry, heating her body and moistening her. When he pulled back, he gazed into her eyes. "My God, woman. No one should be allowed to kiss like that."

Alice was puzzled. "Like what?"

"Like you're a great vortex and I'm yearning to fall in. I want to devour you and your mouth tells me that you want it too."

Was that what her mouth was saying? It had been so long. Maybe the combination of her long time away from men and her conversations over the phone had changed her from the woman Ralph divorced to something more. Todd kissed her again, and this time she melted into it, letting her tongue roam at will, testing things she had talked about but never done. She slid her hands up his back beneath his jacket, questing the warmth of his body through his shirt. He pressed his obvious erection against her lower body and she allowed her body to press back.

They broke the kiss and, panting, she let her head fall back as Todd kissed his way down her throat. His hands slid up the sides of her shirt until his palms held her ribs and his thumbs brushed the tips of her breasts. She felt her nipples harden and her thighs shake. Without the support of her car against her back, she would have fallen from the sheer eroticism of it all.

"What's going on here?" Todd asked, his voice breathy and hoarse. "This is crazy."

Obviously he felt the burst of passion too. "I know. I have to tell you that I haven't kissed anyone in a very long time."

"I'd like to do a lot more than kiss you. I'm aching for you and this isn't the way I would have this happen."

"Why?" she whispered.

"My home's three thousand miles away and I don't get here more than once or twice a year. I'm leaving on Tuesday to other places, other people."

"Other women?"

"Yes, and I want to make that clear up front. I have other female friends and I don't deny it. But I've never had anything hit me so hard and so suddenly and after such a short time. I want to bury myself in you until we're too exhausted to move. I want to feel you beneath me. I want to make you scream and beg and cry for it, then make you climax over and over."

Alice hadn't said it any better to any of her clients. Was it a line? Maybe. He certainly knew what buttons to push and how to push them. But was that bad? Didn't she feel the same things? "So what should we do about it?"

"Ordinarily I'd ask you out a few more times, then try to convince you to join me in bed. We don't have a few more times. Can I see you tomorrow night?"

It was Friday and she had a regular caller. "I'm afraid I have something else I have to do."

He sighed and backed away. "I understand."

She shouldn't do this. Not for any reason. Except one. She wanted to. "No, you don't. I can't tomorrow, but I'm free Saturday." She didn't confuse love and lust. This was sexual, pure and simple, and from all of her phone relationships she had learned that there was nothing wrong with sexuality just for fun. And this was going to be fun, pure and hopefully simple.

In the dim light, she could see his eyes light up. "That's great. I'll call you during the day on Saturday and we'll make plans. Pick someplace nice and we can talk. Get to know each other better. That's the place to start."

Alice didn't have to ask what they were starting. It was obvious. Something really short term and really explosive.

"Yes, it is." They exchanged phone numbers and Alice got into her car. Before she closed the door, Todd kissed her again. The kiss was just as incendiary as the last, leaving Alice's hands shaking and her mind numb. Nothing even vaguely resembling this had ever happened to her before or would probably happen to her again. She didn't care.

"Until Saturday," she said.

"Until Saturday."

Chapter
10

"So tell me about Todd," Betsy said to Alice the following morning.

"He's sexy as hell and we have a date Saturday night."

"Wonderful. Tell me everything."

"Listen. I know that this is a short-time thing. No hearts and flowers, no," she made quoting marks in the air, "*relationship*, and I really want to keep it to myself for a little while."

"Are you okay?" Betsy asked, obviously a bit put out at Alice for not sharing.

"I'm great." She gave her friend a quick hug. "I just want this to be all my decision. If I talk about it, I might change my mind and I don't want to. For once in my life I don't want to be logical."

"Hey, I wouldn't ask you to change anything. Does what you're doing feel right?"

"I'm not sure, but it feels like another 'What have I got to lose' so I'm going to wing it."

Betsy hugged her friend back. "Good for you. Have a blast."

She was going to do just that. She was going to invite Todd to her apartment for dinner and let things happen whatever way they happened. She wanted it and it was about time she took something just because she wanted it. She talked to her sister Friday evening and made plans to visit her mother on Sunday.

Then, after work on Saturday, she dashed to the market and bought a thick sirloin steak, a rice mix that cooked in fifteen minutes, salad makings, and a package of frozen vegetables. Then she stopped at the liquor store and picked up a bottle of nice red wine and a bottle of rather expensive brandy, the drink that Todd had had after dinner on Thursday. Then she decided on one more stop, at a local convenience store for a three-pack of condoms. If what she expected to happen happened, she would be ready.

At home she quickly made a salad and put it into the refrigerator. It was not yet five so Alice decided that she had enough time for a bath. She turned on the hot water in the tub and poured a capful of bubble liquid beneath the tap. As the bath ran, she stripped off her clothes and stared into her closet. She quickly decided on a soft cotton sweater in a becoming shade of light blue, her softest jeans, and a pair of loafers. Easy on, easy off, she thought. Then she stashed the condoms in the table beside the bed and looked around the bedroom.

The previous evening, between phone calls she had tidied up and this morning she had changed the sheets. Three weeks before she had bought new drapes and a matching quilt in a pink and green floral pattern, and had coordinated several pillows. *Well,* she thought, *that's the best I can do.*

Back in the bathroom, she turned off the water and climbed into the tub. With a chirrup, Roger jumped onto the toilet seat. Tail swishing, he reached out a paw and batted at the mound of bubbles just within his reach. "I know," Alice said. "You're not used to this, are you."

Merrow.

"Well, I'm not either, but I'm not too old to learn, so I'm going to do just that. It's a hell of about time, don't you think?"

Roger batted at the bubbles, his paw now covered with foam. When he started to lick it off, he sneezed. "See? Something new for all of us."

Fascinated, Roger spent the next fifteen minutes trying to understand bubbles while Alice relaxed in the tub, surprised that she wasn't more nervous. "You know, Roger," she said, finally standing up and grabbing a bath towel, "I should be really upset about this. If everything goes all right I'm about to get into what several of my callers refer to as sport fucking." She wrinkled her nose and stepped out of the tub. "Ugh. That sounds terrible, but I guess that's what it is. It's not lovemaking since there's no love involved, but it's not going to be just fucking either. It's going to be two people doing things that feel wonderful."

Merrow.

"Right. He's really cute too. Wait till you see. He likes cats but you stay out of the way. Hear?"

In her bedroom, she opened her underwear drawer. She had nothing particularly sexy, nothing like the lingerie she described in such detail three nights a week, so she did the best she could. She pulled out a stretchy, beige nylon bra and matching bikini panties. "I wish I had something lacy," she said to Roger, now washing his front paws in the middle of her new quilt. "I'll have to take some time next week and shop, in case this happens again."

Roger rolled over and Alice sat on the bed and scratched his belly. Roger's purr filled the room as Alice dressed. At ten minutes to six, Alice faced herself in the mirror. She smoothed on eyeliner, redoing it twice before it looked the way she wanted it to, then added soft pink blush and lipstick. She considered mascara, but rejected the idea. Who knew when it might smear, and under what conditions? She fluffed her short curls, unable to do anything to her hair that it didn't want. She added small pearl earrings and a strand of pearls that rested between her breasts.

She started out of the bathroom, then quickly took a small bottle of Opium that Betsy had given her last Christmas, and dabbed just a touch behind each ear and in her cleavage. "Ready as ever," she said to Roger, now fast asleep on the bed. "You'd better stay out from underfoot."

As she closed the bedroom door behind her, the doorbell rang. Her heart lurched but she calmly walked to the front door. Todd stood in front of her apartment dressed in a navy-blue blazer, gray slacks, and a yellow knit shirt. His eyes were even bluer than she remembered and gazed at her in appreciation, and puzzlement. "Hi. Am I overdressed for wherever we're going?"

"Not at all," Alice said ushering him inside. "Actually I thought we could eat here. I'm not a great cook but I broil a mean steak." Todd grinned. "Great idea. Come here." He reached for her and drew her into his arms. "I've been thinking about this for two very long days." His lips met hers and the electricity she had felt when they first kissed surged through her again. His hands alternately massaged her back and grabbed her hair. "You know," he said when they paused to catch their breath, "I've been thinking about you and about this evening." He released her and walked into the living room. "I don't want to pressure you or anything. We're both grown-ups. I want you. I want to make love to you, with you. I don't want you to think I jump on every woman I meet but this isn't true love either. I don't want any confusion." When she didn't respond, he continued, "I don't want anything going on under false pretenses."

Alice walked up to him and smiled. "I understand everything and I don't jump every man I meet either. Can I take your jacket?"

His grin made him look about ten years younger. He slipped his jacket off his shoulders and dropped it on the sofa. "Come here." He tangled his fingers in her hair and gently pulled her head back, then buried his mouth in the hollow at the base of her throat.

This is exactly what I wanted, Alice thought in the small part of her mind that could still think. Then that section shut down beneath the onslaught of her senses. His mouth was hot, his tongue rough as he licked the tender spot where her shoulder met her neck. His hands roamed up her sides until his thumbs brushed the lower curves of her breasts. She thought about foreplay and the slow building from embers to flames, but the flames already existed and were quickly devouring both of them.

She combed her fingers through his hair, marveling at the softness. Like baby hair, she thought. His hands were beneath her sweater now, branding her bare skin everywhere he touched. One hand cupped her buttocks and pressed her lower body against the hard ridge of flesh beneath the crotch of his slacks. "God," he purred, "I can't get close enough to you."

She marveled at the core of calm and rational enjoyment that existed beneath the raging fires that consumed her conscious mind. This was what she had been talking about all these weeks. She took the lower edge of her sweater in her hands and pulled it over her head. Then she grabbed his shirt and did the same. "Better," she whispered, rubbing her hands over his chest, sliding her fingers through the light furring of blond hair.

"This too," he growled, unhooking her bra and dragging it off. "God yes." He cupped her breasts, his thumbs flicking over her already erect nipples. "Yes. So good."

Alice's knees threatened to buckle. "In here," she said, the words difficult to get past the passion in her throat. She led him to the bedroom and, as she opened the door, Roger trotted through. He stopped to sniff Todd's slacks, then rubbed briefly against his legs and headed off toward the kitchen.

"I'm not usually this impatient," Todd said as he entered Alice's bedroom, his fingers working at the fastenings of her jeans, "but I don't seem to be rushing you."

"You're not," Alice said, smiling at his assumption that she was an old hand at all of this. She pushed the door closed.

Quickly they removed their remaining clothes and, both naked, fell onto the bed. Todd's mouth found Alice's nipple and her back arched as shards of electric pleasure knifed through her. His fingers pinched the other nipple, causing pain that was both sharp and erotic.

She had talked about women's hands on men's cocks for weeks but she had never actually held a man's penis in her hands before. Now she touched him and he felt wonderful, like velvet over rigid muscle. His skin was soft and hot as she held him, squeezing gently.

"Do that any more and I'll lose it right here," he said hoarsely, moving her hand away.

Then his fingers slipped between her legs and found her hot and wet. "Yes," she whispered. "Oh yes." He touched and explored, then slid one finger into her channel. "Oh shit," she hissed, her back arching and her hips driving his hands against her.

When he withdrew she felt bereft, but then she heard the ripping of paper and understood. Only moments later his condom-covered cock pressed at her entrance and with one thrust Todd buried himself inside of her. It was fast, hot, and hard, Todd's hips pounding and Alice's legs wrapped around his waist. They clawed at each other's backs trying to drive deeper.

"Touch me," she cried and Todd's fingers slipped between them and found her clit. With a shout he came, and then, only moments later, Alice felt the familiar bubble growing low in her belly. Todd was still driving into her, his body spasming when she exploded, her orgasm bigger than any she had created for herself.

"God, baby," Todd said later as they calmed. "You're something."

"You're not bad yourself," Alice said. "That was amazing."

"You're amazing," he said, using a tissue to clean himself up. Then he rolled over and cuddled her against his side, her head on his shoulder. "I love a woman who enjoys good sex. There's nothing coy or reticent about you. It's wonderful."

Alice thought about what had happened. She had enjoyed it. More than that, it had been one of the greatest experiences of her life. Nothing that she had had with Ralph had prepared her for the unbridled passion of what she and Todd had done. It seemed so simple.

They had dinner and, over coffee and brandy, Todd kissed her again, more slowly this time as hands and mouths discovered erotic places. For the first time Alice touched a man's cock and was delighted when she obviously excited him. She knew what she had read and talked about, and whatever she did seemed to please Todd. When Todd touched his tongue to her clit, Alice thought she would fly into space and, with his mouth lightly sucking on her flesh and his fingers inside her pussy, she came. "God, woman, you're so responsive." Then he was inside of her and she came again as he did. They pulled the quilt over them later and, with Roger on the bed beside them, they slept until the following morning.

Todd was still asleep when Alice awoke the next day. She lay quietly and thought about the previous night. It had been wonderful, fulfilling, and electric. She had no regrets about anything and that surprised her. For weeks she had been talking a good game, and now she was playing. It was sensational. She stretched, slipped from the bed, and padded to the bathroom.

Minutes later she stood in the shower under the warm spray. She lathered her body and wondered at the slick, slipperiness of her skin. She felt her hands on her flesh and tried to feel what Todd had felt. She wasn't pretty, she didn't have a sexy body, but he had seemed to really like touching her and making love to her. In her stories she was always the ideal-looking person she had always dreamed about, but now it didn't seem to matter. Todd was gorgeous and that was what had attracted her in the first place, but after the first few minutes, it was his love of cats and his sense of humor that had kept her interest.

Suddenly the shower curtain moved and Todd climbed into the tub behind her. "Good morning."

She thought she'd feel awkward after all that they had done the previous evening, but she didn't. "Good morning. I have to visit my mom today so I thought I'd get started early so maybe we could get together again later."

"A woman with a plan. I like that. But must we waste this wonderful opportunity?" He took the shower scrubby that she used with her body wash, squeezed a large amount of aromatic gel onto it, and began to lather her body. Slowly he soaped her skin, taking time to cover her breasts and mound with bubbles. She parted her legs as he slipped the plastic sponge between her thighs and caressed her pussy with it. As he rinsed her off, she took the sponge from him and moved him beneath the spray so his back was turned toward her.

With more lather on the pink sponge, she slowly stroked it over his back, taking time to appreciate his tight buttocks. She remembered a story she had told several times about a couple who made love in a shower and she realized that she had a perfect opportunity to get to know Todd's body better. She crouched and washed down the backs of his thighs and felt him tremble as she parted his cheeks and rubbed that hidden valley between.

Water cascaded over her head as she turned him and washed his feet and the fronts of his legs. Then she stood and lathered his softly furred chest and shoulders, his arms and hands. Now she could move to the part of his body she was most interested in. She put more gel on the sponge and knelt, stroking the slightly rough surface over his semierect penis. She allowed herself to look at his body and watch his penis react to her ministrations. She lifted his cock and gently scrubbed his testicles, then rubbed the tender area behind. As she touched, she watched his cock react and twitch, making his enjoyment obvious. She slid her fingers between his thighs and touched the slippery skin behind his balls, then slipped further backward and touched his anus. His knees almost gave out.

She had touched his erection the previous evening but now she wondered whether she could take it into her mouth as the women had in her stories. Still touching his balls and asshole, she licked the falling water from the tip of his cock with the flat of her tongue. Todd grabbed her shoulders. "Don't do that, baby," he groaned. "If you do, I'll shoot right here and now."

"Is there a problem with that?"

"Oh, God."

She was going to do it. She didn't think she could deep-throat it as her characters often did in her stories, but she drew the end of Todd's cock into her mouth. She created a vacuum and pulled her head back, creating suction. Todd tangled his fingers in her hair and held her tightly, more for his own balance than to restrain her. She felt his muscles tighten and knew that he was ready to climax. "Baby," he shouted. She wrapped one hand around his erection, feeling it swell and jerk.

She wanted to taste his come, but she didn't think she could swallow it so she opened her mouth and, as jets of thick, white jism shot from Todd's cock, she allowed most of it to flow from between her lips. The fluid was thick and viscous and tasted slightly tangy. She avidly watched his cock and her hand and she instinctively pumped the last of his climax.

"Shit, baby," Todd said. "That's not fair."

"What's not fair?" Alice said, a grin splitting her face.

"You did that to me and I didn't satisfy you."

"I am satisfied. That was amazing."

Together they lathered and rinsed and, wrapped in thick towels, wandered back into the bedroom. As Alice rubbed her curls dry, she felt herself grabbed from behind. "Get over here," Todd said. He pulled her toward the bed and then pushed her down. "We're going to play a little game," he growled. "You're going to lie there and I'm going to do to you what you just did to me."

Alice giggled and tried to get up. "That's not necessary. This isn't a tit-for-tat kind of thing. I enjoyed what happened and that's that."

"Tit for tat, eh? Well I want those tits, do you understand? Now lie down," he snapped and pushed her back onto the bed.

Alice suddenly stopped laughing. "Yes, sir," she said softly. She settled back onto the bed. There was suddenly nothing soft about Todd. There was a hard edge to his voice, ordering her to follow his instructions. She felt herself tremble with excitement.

"That's more like it. Now, spread your legs and make it quick." He stood at the foot of the bed, arms crossed over his naked chest. He was beautiful, powerful.

She did as he commanded and felt herself immediately wet. "Wider," he snapped.

Alice spread her legs as wide as they would go while Todd looked down at her. "You like that, don't you?" he said, his question not requiring an answer. "I suspected that you would. I love giving orders and seeing a beautiful woman obey."

Obey. The word made her body jolt. She did like it. Very much.

Todd parted her towel and stared at her. "I want to suck your tits. Offer one to me."

What was it that made her cup her flattened breast and hold it for him? The mastery? His aura of command? The domination? It was all of those and more, she realized.

He knelt beside the bed and placed his mouth on her fully erect nipple. She felt his teeth bite down, just enough to cause her pain. When she grunted, he said, "I wanted to do that and you wanted me to. You want this and both of us know it. Is this new for you?"

"Yes," she whispered. It was all new to her and now she wanted it all.

He grabbed her hair and held her head against the mattress. Then he ravished her mouth. There was no gentleness, but rather power and hunger. When he leaned back, he said, "Since I climaxed before, I'm not feeling impatient to have you. You're mine and I can do whatever I like to you. And I'm in no hurry." He settled onto the edge of the bed. "I've played a lot of games with women," he said as Alice stared at him. "I love sex in all forms. Now it seems I've discovered something that makes you crazy." He rubbed his finger through her sopping pussy. "Oh yes," he said. "So wet. This obviously makes you hungry."

He pulled off his towel and stretched out on top of her, his feet holding hers down and his hands grasping her wrists. She could feel the length of his body against hers and her heart pounded. His mouth devoured hers while he held her so she couldn't move. Briefly Alice wondered whether she should be reacting this way, then she stopped caring. Over the weeks she had been telling stories, she realized that everyone had their pleasures and she was entitled to feel whatever she felt and enjoy whatever gave her pleasure. And this did.

Todd stood up. "You are not to move. Just lie there with your legs wide apart and let me do whatever I want."

She choked out the word, "Yes."

Todd spent long minutes playing with her breasts. He kissed, licked, sucked, and bit until it was all Alice could do not to grab him and make him satisfy the gnawing hunger he was creating. Yet she didn't move. It had become a challenge. He had told her not to move and she wouldn't.

Finally he moved between her spread legs and gazed at her pussy. "I'll bet you've never seen a pussy," he said, "but they are so beautiful. Yours is so wet I can see the moisture." He touched her inner lips with one finger. "God, you're so hot, baby." He touched the end of her clit lightly and her hips jumped. "I told you not to move," he growled.

She concentrated on keeping her body still. "That's better," he said. He looked around the bedroom and she could see him stare at the candle she had in a holder on her dresser. She had intended to light it the previous evening but things had proceeded so quickly that she had not had the chance. He stood up and grabbed the candle, a taper about eight inches long and over an inch in diameter. He hurried into the bathroom and Alice could hear the water running. Knowing what he must have in mind, Alice felt her muscles tighten.

He returned with the candle in his hand. "See this? You've figured out what I'm going to do with it, haven't you."

She nodded.

He settled back between her legs and rubbed the wax through the folds of her pussy then over her clit. "Here's what I'm going to do. I'm going to fuck you with this dildo. I'm going to slowly force it into your beautiful pussy. It might be a bit bigger than a cock but your body will take it, and you won't move while I do it. Then I'm going to suck your clit and I'm going to feel you come. Being fucked with a candle and having me in control of your body will make you so hot that you won't be able to help it. You won't be in control of it, I will."

He placed the candle against the opening of her pussy and, ever so slowly, pushed it into her body. It was larger than any cock she had felt and it seemed to force its way into her. Alice had never had anything but fingers and cocks inside of her and she noticed with the rational part of her brain that the candle felt cool and filled her in a way that no cock had. Deeper and deeper it penetrated until it seemed to fill not only her body but her mind. She was overwhelmed with sensations and Todd now pulled, now pushed, fucking her with the candle.

She was so close, she realized. So close that when his mouth found her clit she came, screaming. Her hips bucked so hard it was difficult for him to keep his mouth on her, but he did, pulling on her clit and drawing the climax out longer and longer. She couldn't control her body as wave after wave crashed over her. For long minutes she came and came. She finally placed her hand against his forehead and gently pushed him away.

Totally limp, she lay still as Todd climbed up the bed and settled against her side. He cradled her head against him and kissed her curls. "My god, woman. I've never seen anyone come like that. You're incredible."

"That was incredible," she whispered, unable to make any louder sound. They dozed for another hour, then dressed quickly. "I don't have anything in the house for breakfast," Alice admitted.

"Then how about the diner?" he asked.

"Sure. I've got to be at my mom's nursing home at noon so we've got some time."

"Can we get together again tonight?" Todd asked.

"I was hoping to. I'll be back here about five." She had planned to do some writing for her clients, but that would have to wait. After this morning she had so much to say and there was no possibility that she would forget any of it.

Alice and Todd talked almost nonstop while they ate and Todd kissed her deeply as they parted, to meet at her place at five-thirty. As she drove south she smiled. It had been so fantastic and she had learned a lot about herself.

Her mom seemed to be doing a bit better and Sue arrived at the nursing home at about one. Together the three women sat in the sunny garden and although she said nothing, her mother seemed to be enjoying the conversation. "Are you okay with the money?" Sue asked at one point.

"Yes. My new job is fun and pays well. I can afford this without any problem. Don't worry about a thing."

"Well, I don't think I've ever seen you look better. You've got a glow. Whatever you're doing must agree with you."

If you only knew, Alice thought.

Chapter

11

Todd arrived at Alice's apartment at five-thirty that evening with a pizza in hand. They both knew that going out to dinner wasn't going to happen so they made quick work of the pie and ended up in bed again. They made love twice that evening and again at 3:00 A.M. When the alarm rang at seven, Todd reached for her again. "Sorry," she said, "but I have to be at work at eight and a shower and a bowl of cereal are a necessity."

"Oh, baby," Todd groaned. "You're such a spoilsport."

Alice kissed him thoroughly, then said, "You can stay in bed if you like, but I'm out of here." When she returned from the bathroom, Todd was already dressed.

"I have a nine o'clock meeting that I have to dress for anyway so I thought I'd go back to my motel and shower and change there." He dragged her close. "Tonight?"

"I'm sorry, I can't."

Todd's eyes widened. "I had hoped . . ."

"I wish I could, but I can't. I have a commitment I can't change." She had three regular callers who were in for a surprise that night. She had several stories whirling in her head, all based on what she had experienced all weekend.

"I'm flying out at noon on Tuesday," Todd pouted.

Alice put her arms around him. "I know and I wish there were something I could do, but there isn't. I just can't."

"I'll see whether I can arrange a trip to New York in the fall. "

Alice beamed. "Wonderful. I'll look forward to that. In the meantime, we'll e-mail and call each other."

"It won't be the same. We've only known each other for a few days but . . ."

"Don't. You said you've got other female friends and I've got men I date too. Let's just leave it that it's been great and we'll do it again when we can."

"You sound like me. I'm usually the one who makes that speech."

"Well then, you're usually the wise one."

Alice could feel Todd's chuckle deep in his chest. "It feels really strange to be on the receiving end." He pulled away and slapped her lightly on the bottom. "All right, woman, let's get going."

Alice arrived at Dr. Tannenbaum's office at exactly eight o'clock to find Betsy on the phone and the doctor's first patient sitting in the waiting room reading a magazine. Betsy put her hand over the mouthpiece of the receiver. "He's going to be about fifteen minutes late."

"Oh, Mr. Fucito," Alice said to the waiting patient as she hung up her coat. "I'm sorry. I'm sure it was unavoidable."

"No problem, Alice," the man said. "I'm not due at work until ten-thirty. "

As she arrived in the reception area, Alice tried unsuccessfully to wipe off the grin that had been on her face all morning. "You look like a cat who's just eaten several very fat canaries," Betsy said. "What gives?"

"I had a weekend to write stories about."

"Tell all, and quickly."

The phone rang and Alice adjusted an appointment for the following morning. As she hung up, she said, "About this weekend . . ."

The door opened and Dr. Tannenbaum arrived with a flurry of

questions and instructions. "Listen," Betsy said. "We're never going to get a chance to talk here. I know you usually have errands to run at lunch but I'm meeting Velvet. Come along and you can regale us with your weekend adventures."

Alice couldn't suppress her grin. She wanted to keep it all to herself, but she also wanted to crow a bit. "Done." Betsy disappeared into the operatory and Alice returned to her computer.

At ten after one, the three women were seated in a booth at a diner and had already ordered sandwiches and drinks. "All right," Betsy said. "Enough stalling. Tell us everything."

"You had a date with Todd," Velvet said.

"You might say that." Alice burst out laughing, then filled the two women in on her adventures of the weekend.

"Wow. A one-weekend stand," Velvet said. "God, I envy you."

"Why?" Alice said, genuinely puzzled. "Isn't Wayne good? You know what I mean."

"He's great, but there's no thrill like a new man and the adventure of new and great sex."

"As good as Larry is," Betsy added, "and we're very in tune and totally compatible, first times are something totally different, the stuff fantasies are made of."

"Well this was certainly the stuff of fantasies," Alice said, sipping her soda. "It's like I've discovered a new toy. I knew creative sex existed and I've made up dozens of stories about it, but that was from the outside looking in. Now I've opened Pandora's box and I want to sample everything inside." She thought about the catalog Betsy had given her that she had never gotten around to exploring. "I want it all."

"And you should have it," Betsy said. "Good sex is the best stuff. I know from experience."

"Are you going to see Todd again before he leaves?" Velvet asked.

"Unfortunately, no. He's leaving tomorrow and I have callers tonight."

"That's really sad."

"No, it's really not," Alice said. "This was a slice out of a fantasy. It's not real and in some ways I wouldn't want it to become too real."

"Like how?" Betsy asked.

"I don't want to know what he's like when he's cranky, or sick. I don't know whether we have much in common and this way it doesn't matter. It was neat, and now it's done. Maybe we'll do it again, and maybe not but it's all okay."

"Aren't you sad that it was so short?" Betsy continued. "I mean, that might have become something more permanent. Don't you want that?"

"In some ways I do, but this wasn't it. If he were a local, we would have dated and gotten to know each other before we ended up in bed together and that's the basis of something more. Like Vic and I are doing. Since this weekend I have a bit more of an open mind about men and dating now that I've found out more about the real me."

"Who's the real you?"

"Someone who enjoys sex for the sake of sex."

"Indulging in one-night stands isn't life. It's not real," Betsy said.

"Exactly and I know that, but it's not wrong either. Obviously if someone comes along and we hit it off, that's wonderful. For the moment, however, I want to experiment, to explore, to experience firsthand all the things I've talked about with my callers. I want to play."

"What about Vic?" Velvet asked.

"We're meeting tomorrow night for dinner."

"Which category does he fit into?" Betsy asked.

"I haven't the faintest idea." She raised her glass. "Here's to not knowing and not caring." The three women touched glasses and toasted.

That evening Sheherazade's stories took on a new dimension. They were a bit more adventurous and there was a special music in her voice. Two of her regular callers noticed and told her that they enjoyed her tales even more than usual.

The following evening, Alice met Vic for dinner. The evening passed delightfully quickly, with good conversation and lots of laughter. There were moments when Alice thought about her split personality. Although she and Vic had become acquainted through their phone calls, so far their two "dates" had been chaste with no conversation about sex in any form.

As they sipped coffee, Vic asked, "Can I see you next Saturday? Like a real Saturday night date?"

"I'd like that." Alice stared at Vic's hands that now surrounded his coffee cup. Short, blunt fingers, wide palms. Nice, functional hands. How would they feel touching her? she wondered. *Stop that*, she told herself. *Every man isn't Todd. Every evening isn't a prelude to a romp in bed.*

"I'd love to find someplace a bit more subdued. All this green and white has me wondering whether I'm growing roots."

Alice's smile widened. "I'm not too familiar with this area. How far north do you want to drive?"

Vic winked. "Your place?" Over the sound of her breath catching in her throat, Vic continued, "I'm so sorry. I promised myself that I wouldn't mention anything like that. I don't want you to think that I'm here because of the way we met. I mean I'm not after sex. I mean . . ." Obviously frustrated, Vic ran his fingers through his shaggy hair.

"Whoa," Alice said. "Sex doesn't have to be a taboo topic between us. We met under really bizarre circumstances so maybe it's a bit awkward but we can't trip over our tongues either."

"I know, but I don't want you to get the wrong idea."

"I won't. When two people get to know each other, like we are, it's natural that the conversation will eventually turn to sexual topics. We both understand that I'm not Sheherazade. I'm just plain Alice Waterman but I'm not a prude either." *Certainly not a prude anymore*, she thought.

"You're a delightfully creative person and I think you're terrific." Alice could see Vic begin to blush. It was strange how different he was in person from the sexy man she had known over the phone. "Let's change the subject. Is next Saturday evening okay with you?"

"I'd like that. There's a great little place in Brewster that has good food and a small dance floor. Do you like to dance?"

"I love it," Vic said.

She'd been to a few dances in high school but had gotten discouraged when the only boys who asked her to dance had had octopus hands and were interested in where they could touch. She liked music and had tried to talk Ralph into going out a few times, to no avail.

"Great. Let me check on the name of the place and I'll get directions for you and call you later in the week."

As they approached her car in the parking lot, Vic became silent. "Alice, this is really bothering me."

"What is?"

"I want to kiss you good night but I'm in that same bind I was in before. I don't want you to get the wrong idea."

Alice turned and cupped Vic's face with her palms. "This is really silly." She touched his lips, softly tasting his mouth. As they kissed, she felt his hands lightly stroke her back. She couldn't help contrast this kiss with the toe-curling ones she had shared with Todd. This was entirely different, soft, shy, questioning, hopeful.

"Phew," Vic said as they separated. "Maybe there's more of Sheherazade in you than you know." He kissed her this time and she enjoyed the undemanding feel of his mouth on hers.

"Nice," she purred. "Very nice." Unwilling to go any further yet, she turned and unlocked her car. "I'll call you."

As she settled behind the wheel, Vic leaned over and kissed her again. "I'll look forward to that."

Nice man, she thought as she started her car. Nice, uncomplicated man.

When she got home, she found that she wasn't tired. Betsy's catalog lay on her dresser waiting for her to have some time to look through it, so she picked it up and stretched out on the bed. With his usual chirrup, Roger leaped up beside her and stretched out on his back. Idly scratching the cat's stomach, Alice propped the catalog on her raised knees and looked at the model on the front cover. "I guess that's what my guys think Sheherazade looks like," she said. "What do you think, Roger? Nothing that ten years, a face-lift, twenty-five pounds, and the right makeup wouldn't fix. Right?"

Merrow.

She flipped to an inside page. "Oh my," she said, gazing at a page full of dildos, in all colors, shapes, and textures. "I never imagined that anyone would want one of those in hot pink." Actually, she'd never imagined anyone owning one until she began telling her stories. She turned the page and found vibrators in almost as many varieties. As she thumbed through the thick catalog, she found lubes, anal plugs, cock rings, and several devices she didn't quite understand. She also found that her body responded to the pictures and the ideas they fostered. "I guess it's all research," she told the cat.

For a second time, she went through the catalog and decided to order several items. She noticed that the company had a Web site so, thinking it would be easier and less personal to purchase that way, she logged on and placed an order for a three-dildo collection and a battery-operated vibrator. Now anxious to receive the objects, she clicked on the overnight delivery icon, gave her credit-card number, and logged off. "Well, Roger, I've now ordered my first sex toys. Am I a sophisticate or what?"

Friday, when she arrived home from work, the package was waiting on her doorstep. She had almost two hours before her first client, so she made herself a peanut-butter and jelly sandwich and poured herself a diet soda. Dinner and package in hand, she adjourned to the bedroom. Still chewing her first bite, she grabbed a pair of scissors and stabbed at the tape. Finally the box opened. "Well, Pandora, I know just how you must have felt."

On top of the packaging material she found lots of literature from the company with this month's specials, movies for sale, and three paper folders from affiliated companies. As she placed them on the bed beside her, she noticed that one was for an erotic book sales business, one from a company that specialized in leather items, and one from a phone-sex line. She looked more carefully at the slick paper phone-sex ad. HOT WOMEN WITH SOPPING PUSSIES ANXIOUS FOR YOUR PRICK, one headline read. "Makes what I do sound so dirty," she said. "Amazing."

Beneath the literature, she found two boxes, one with her dildos and one with the vibrator. She opened the dildo box first. Each of the objects inside resembled an erect penis, one in soft pink plastic, about one inch in diameter with thick ridges at half-inch intervals down the shaft; one blue, shorter than the first and very thick around; and a third in soft green plastic curved to, as the box indicated, "stimulate her G-spot." She placed the three on their wide bases on the bed-table and giggled. "Three blind mice," she sang. "Oh Roger, this is so silly." Roger sniffed at the now-empty box, then put his front paws on the bedside table and sniffed at the three dildos. Then he sneezed from the plastic smell and settled on the bed. "Right attitude," Alice said.

She opened the box with the vibrator and looked at each of the tips that came with it. One was flat, with little cuplike structures all over it, one a soft nob, one a long slender rod that was for insertion and one with a long shaft with a ball at the end covered with soft, inchlong flexible fingers of latex. "Looks like the Spanish inquisition to me, but I won't dismiss any of it. Some women must like it."

She munched on her sandwich and let her mind wander. Toys. They hadn't played much of a part in her stories up to now, but with this inspiration, she might just create something new for one of her callers tonight. She also understood that as strange as these items might appear when she was calm and cool, when she was aroused, they would look entirely different. She thought about the lipstick she had used many times as a dildo. Now she had the real thing and ideas flooded her mind.

Her first caller was new and she used a story she'd told several times in the past. When she was done, she was pleased, especially when he asked whether he could call again. Her second was a regular and she continued the story she had begun several weeks earlier.

Her third caller was a man named Jacques whom Alice had

spoken to a few times. Many men used assumed names and tried to change the tone of their voice when they called her so it didn't faze her that Jacques put on a thick French accent when they spoke. He also had a delightfully creative mind. Once he had even helped with a story, making suggestions about what the characters should do. Alice gazed at the three dildos still lined up on the table beside her bed. Jacques was the perfect man for a story that had been smouldering in her mind all night.

"Jacques, you sweet thing," she said when the router put him through. "I've been waiting for you."

"I've been waiting for you too, *cherie*," Jacques said. His accent was particularly thick that evening. She had no idea what he looked like, but even though the accent was phony, he sounded sexy as hell.

"I thought I'd tell you about a date I had a few years ago."

"Ohh," Jacques said. "I wish you would date me."

"Well, if you keep sounding so sexy, I just might."

"If I'm ever where you are, maybe we can be together."

"Well, you keep asking and maybe I'll break down one of these days." She knew this was all talk since neither of them had any idea where the other was. "What if I call the man Jacques? Then we can pretend that we were there together."

"Marvelous," he said. "I don't want to think of you with other men. Me, I would please you so much you wouldn't need anyone else."

"Oh, I know you would. Anyway," Alice began, "it was summer. Jacques and I had dated about a dozen times and, since we stayed up late making love one Saturday night, we had decided that he would stay over. Now it was morning and, when I woke up I found that his side of the bed was empty. Puzzled I got up and headed for the bathroom. On the counter beside the sink I found a large box with a note that said,

Do not open until exactly 9:00 a.m. Then unwrap this and follow the instructions inside to the letter! I'll pick you up at 10:00.

"It was only seven-thirty but I couldn't wait to see what was inside the large box. As I started to untie the bright red ribbon my eyes found the note again . . . exactly 9:00 A.M. . . . *What the hell*, I thought, *I'll play along*. Thinking about what might be in the box was making my nerve endings tingle."

"That sounds like quite a date you had. Tell me about the man. Was he tall like me, with big biceps and big shoulders? I'm big all over, you know."

"I'll bet you are," Alice said, grinning. "Actually he wasn't much to look at, but he had a gleam in his eye and a very sexy mind." In many of her stories, the men were ordinary-looking, unless her caller wanted it otherwise. No need to further the myth that sexy men were gorgeous. "Anyway, I showered, carefully washing all my special places, reveling in the feel of my bath sponge rubbing my skin. I slipped on a robe and went to the kitchen to find some breakfast. On the table, beside the morning paper was another note.

I HOPE YOU'VE FOLLOWED MY INSTRUCTIONS AND HAVEN'T OPENED THE BOX YET. THE ANTICIPATION IS MAKING YOU HOT. IS IT?

It sure is, I thought. The note continued:

GOOD. BREAKFAST IS READY FOR YOU. I'LL SEE YOU AT 10:00. AND REMEMBER, NO TOUCHING YOURSELF.

"I found a carefully cut grapefruit half and a bowl of cereal on the counter, with hot coffee on the warmer. He was so considerate. I ate my breakfast, unable to concentrate on anything. What was in the box?

"At 8:55 I walked back into the bedroom, fetched the box from the bathroom and put it on the bed. As the digital clock clicked from 8:59 to 9:00 A.M., I opened the red ribbon and tore through the white wrapping paper. I pulled the top off the box and folded back gobs of tissue paper. Then I found a note.

Darling, in here you'll find a new toy I bought for us. Insert it, then put on the clothing, and nothing else. Wait for me in the living room. I'll be there at ten. And no playing with yourself!

"I'm quite the devil, am I not, *cherie?*"

Jacques had gotten into the story as he always did and Alice grinned. She picked up one of the dildos, thought about an item she had seen on the Internet the previous evening, then continued the tale. "I rummaged in the box and found a sizable dildo with a narrow bulge about halfway up and another at the blunt end, and a door with some batteries inside. I tried to find a switch to turn the thing on so I could find out what it did, but there was nothing. Although it was pretty thick around, I knew it would fit inside of my pussy with little coaxing, especially since I was so excited at the sight of that new toy. As I put it aside, I wondered again what the electronic gizmo was for. I reached back into the box and pulled out the clothing, a pair of jeans, a bustier, a sheer blouse, and a pair of soft black slippers. 'There're no underwear,' I said aloud. Then I smiled. 'Fine with me.' "

"Umm. Fine with me too," Jacques said. "Tell me what you looked like. What did you do?"

"I removed my robe and stared at the dildo. Then I slowly inserted it into my hungry pussy. At that moment I wanted nothing more than to stroke my clit and get myself off, but the note specifically said that I was not to masturbate so I reluctantly removed my fingers from my crotch. As I moved around, I discovered that the dildo stayed in place, tightly inside my cunt, held securely by the bulge in the center. Very little of it stuck out, just enough of the second bulge to keep it from sliding all the way in. I wondered where Jacques found it.

"Slowly, I stood up and put on the bustier. It was a size too small so once it was hooked up the center of the front it squeezed my ribs tightly, lifting my breasts until I almost spilled out the top. I saw that if I positioned my breasts properly my nipples poked through tiny holes. The fullness in my pussy and the tight almost corset-like fit of the bustier combined to keep my heat turned up high."

Jacques sighed. "I know you have beautiful breasts, *cherie.*"

"Oh yes, I do," Alice purred. "I pulled on the jeans and found that they, too, were a size too small. I knew that Jacques knew my sizes well, so this must all be calculated to make me hot. It was certainly working. As I wiggled into the jeans I suddenly became aware that the crotch of the pants wasn't sewn closed, just laced with a red ribbon. The jeans were so tight that I had to lie on my back and loosen the ribbon to get the zipper closed. Now, if I spread my thighs, I could see the ends of the ribbon and feel air on my crotch. The dildo was held firmly in place, yet my lips were exposed to the air. Oh, Jacques, you devil."

Jacques's chuckle through the phone was warm and liquid.

Alice stood and pulled down her sweatpants. She stretched out on the bed, aroused and already wet. "I looked at the clock and discovered that it was only nine-thirty. I had thirty minutes to wait and think about Jacques's arrival home. I hoped that he would pull these clothes off and fuck me senseless, but I knew Jacques well enough to know that this was just the beginning.

"I slipped the sheer blouse on and felt the fabric brush against my fully erect nipples. It was quite an outfit but despite all of the erotic details, it was almost decent. Since my nipples were dark and the blouse was navy blue, no one could really see that I wasn't decently clothed, and, although the ribbon showed, it could have been a decoration, not a covering for my naked crotch. And, of course, no one could know about the dildo.

"I walked into the living room and realized that, as I walked, the dildo shifted slightly inside me. God, I was hot. I wanted to wiggle my hips and touch myself, rub my clit until I came, but still I hesitated. Jacques didn't want me to. So I sat on the sofa and waited.

"At exactly ten, I heard the key in the lock. The door opened and Jacques walked in. He wore jeans, a white cotton sweater, and sneakers. He looked so ordinary. 'Stand up,' he said and I stood. 'God, you're sexy,' he growled, 'and you make me hard.'

He unzipped his jeans and his fully erect cock sprang forth. 'Fix this for me,' he said.

"I love sucking him, so I quickly got down on my knees and drew his hard cock into my mouth. I did all the things I know he loves, fondled his balls, tickled his anus, flicked my tongue over the tip of his cock, and it was only moments until he filled my mouth with his come."

"Would you do that for me, *cherie*, if we were together?"

"Of course, Jacques. What would you do for me?"

"I would untie that red ribbon and kiss and suck and lick you until you begged for me. I am very talented, you know."

"I'll bet you are. And the other Jacques was a very clever lover too. Just like you. When I finished with his cock, he said, 'That's better,' and zipped up his pants.

" 'Not for me,' I whispered, wanting his hands, his mouth, his cock to relieve my incredible need.

" 'I know but you've got a long day in front of you.'

"I frowned, then slipped my fingers into my crotch. Jacques slapped my hand. Hard. I had known he would and I smiled, enjoying the erotic teasing. 'Bad girl,' he snapped. 'You have to wait.' He started toward the door. 'Come with me.'

"I followed. In the driveway was a small red convertible with the top down. I smiled as I realized that he had rented it for us. He opened the door on my side and I saw that the passenger seat was covered with a furry pad. As I went to slide into the car, he grabbed my wrist. 'Just a minute.' He loosened the ribbon that held the crotch of my jeans together until the sides were widely separated. 'Now sit.'

"The furry pad rubbed against my wet lips and pressed the dildo tightly into my channel. Softly, Jacques said, 'The dildo doesn't hurt, does it?'

" 'Well, yes and no,' I answered. 'It makes me really hot and so hungry I would love to jump you, but hurt? Not really.'

"Jacques grinned. 'Good.' He slammed the door and leaned into the open car. 'I don't want you to touch your pussy,' he said, 'so these are for you.' First he fastened a wide leather collar

around my neck, then he pulled a pair of connected leather man-
acles from his back pocket and cuffed my wrists together. Then
he took a small padlock and locked the short chain between the
cuffs to a large ring on the collar. My hands were now at breast
level and I was unable to touch my cunt. He reached in and carefully fastened my seat belt, then walked around and got into the
car."

"Oh, *cherie*," Jacques said into the phone. "I can just see you
like that. Tell me where you are and I'll run to your house and we
can play together for the rest of our lives."

"I'm so sorry, Jacques, but you know that giving out my address or phone number is against the rules."

He sighed long and loud. "I know and I'm so sad."

"I am too," Alice said with a small sigh. "Anyway, we drove
into the country, the wind in my hair, the fullness in my pussy. I
was in plain sight and people in other cars must have wondered
at my unusual position, but for the most part the drive was uneventful and slowly, my body calmed. At about eleven-thirty,
Jacques pulled the car to the side of a tree-lined lane and
stopped. 'We have a bit farther to go, but I think it's time for you
to find out the secret of the dildo,' he said. 'Did you notice the
battery opening? Curious? Well, here's the control.' He showed
me a small box with several dials. 'Let's see how it feels if I turn
this.'

"Suddenly there was a whirring and the dildo began to hum,
moving inside of me like something alive. Shards of pleasure
shot through me, stabbing from my pussy to my nipples. I moved
my hips trying to drive the dildo deeper into my cunt." Alice
pulled the crotch of her panties aside and slipped the ridged pink
dildo into her pussy. As she pressed, the rings of thicker plastic
pushed into her like the vibrating dildo she was creating in her
story. " 'And this one,' Jacques said, turning another dial. The
sensation was like having my pussy channel massaged from the
inside. I guessed that the bulge around the girth of the dildo was
moving deeper inside of me, then further toward the base of the
shaft of the artificial penis. The feeling drove me higher.

" 'And this,' he said, finding another dial. The bulge around the base of the dildo moved, rubbing my clit. 'Oh, God,' I cried. 'Don't stop.' My eyes closed and my back arched. I squirmed, confined in my seat belt, unable to get my hands to my crotch. 'You can reach your tits,' he purred, 'so pinch them. And move your hips to make it better.'"

Phone propped against her ear, Alice pulled the dildo out, then pushed it in again. She allowed some of her breathlessness and excitement to flow into the story. "Jacques, can you imagine how it felt? I'm playing with a real dildo now."

"You are? Wonderful. My cock is so big and hard. I wish you were playing with it instead of my hand."

"I wish it, too, Jacques. Tell me, did you make it slippery?"

"Oh, *cherie*. It feels so good. I can picture you with that machine fucking you, so hot waiting for orgasm, just like I am right now."

"Yes, I was. I wanted it, needed it. I sat in the car, parked in the open and rolled my hardened nipples between my fingers, squeezing hard as I tried to drive the dildo more tightly into my pussy. I was higher than I had ever been, hot, swirling colors filling my vision. 'Come for me. Now!' Jacques said, and he reached between my legs and touched my clit. I came, deep, hard spasms of pleasure ricocheting throughout my body, reaching my breasts, my mouth, my cunt. It was as if every muscle in my entire body joined in the pleasure. It went on and on, lasting for long minutes."

"Oh, baby," Jacques said, his accent disappearing as it always did when he came, "damn you're good. Are you fucking yourself with the dildo? Are you close?"

"Yes," Alice whispered.

"Good. Now come for me. I want to hear it."

Alice plunged the dildo into her pussy then, leaving it in place, she rubbed her clit. "Yes," she purred as she rubbed. "Yes."

"Oh, *cherie,*" he said, his accent as thick as it had been, "rub your sweet pussy. Touch it and stroke it and think of my big hard cock. Think how it would be if my fingers were stroking you and my cock was filling you."

"Yes," Alice said, feeling the now-familiar pleasures swirling through her. Soon. Just another moment.

"Now I will bite your nipple and you will come, just like you did in that car. I rub, I bite, I fuck you so hard. Come for me, *cherie.*"

"Yes!" she shouted as the waves of orgasm pounded through her body. "Yes!"

There were a few moments of silence, then Alice said, "You always do that for me, Jacques."

"And you always do it for me. When I call next time will you tell me about the rest of the day you spent with the dildo in your sweet cunt?"

"Of course. The day had just begun."

"I'll call again soon."

"I hope so."

"You know so."

Chapter

12

At six o'clock Saturday evening Vic picked Alice up at her apartment. "This is lovely," he commented. "So like you, organized and conservative."

Alice wasn't sure she liked that characterization. "You make me sound almost dull."

"Not at all but so unlike Sheherazade. I like you just the way you are, Alice." He looked at her outfit, black linen slacks and a white open-collar shirt with a small tan geometric design. "Yes, I definitely like you just the way you are."

Alice thought about the way Vic saw her. *That's the way I was until I started working at Velvet Whispers. Now I'm so much more. I don't want to be conservative Alice Waterman anymore.* "Let me get my jacket," she said, leaving Vic in the living room. In the bedroom she peered into her closet. A classic tan linen jacket lay on the bed but suddenly she didn't want to wear it. She flipped through hanger after hanger of basic slacks, blouses, jackets, and vests. How ordinary, she thought. Then, from the very back of her closet she grabbed a bright red blazer with gold buttons. *I must go to the mall and update my wardrobe.* She found several pins and scattered them on her lapels. Finally, she took a small ladybug pin and attached it to the top of one shoulder. Better. Then she added a bit of mascara and put a coat of red lipstick over the soft coral she had been wearing. Finally she removed the combs that had been controlling her hair and fluffed out her curls. *Conservative indeed. Maybe I want to be a little more like Sheherazade.*

When she arrived back in the living room, Vic had his back to her, gazing at her music collection. "Very eclectic," he said. "Andean, Balkan, country and western, even some Chopin and Mozart. Very nice assortment."

"Thanks," Alice said. "Shall we have dinner?"

He turned and looked at her flame-colored jacket. "Well. Not so conservative after all. You look great."

As it had the previous two dinners, the meal sped by. Conversation roamed from the situation in the Middle East to several new sitcoms on TV. They talked about the unusually warm weather and the possibility of Alice's coming into the city to see Vic's latest video game. When the music began, they danced, Vic holding her at a proper distance. Slowly she moved closer, wanting to feel his body against hers but each time he realized that they were pressed against each other, he backed up. Finally, at about eleven o'clock, they left the restaurant, with Alice aroused and frustrated. She really wanted to crack Vic's uptight facade. They had taken Vic's Buick and, when they arrived back at Alice's apartment, she invited him inside for a nightcap.

"You don't usually drink," Vic said, following Alice into her living room.

"I feel like something silly tonight. Friends and I go out once a week or so and I've gotten quite fond of a concoction made with orange juice, melon liqueur, and vodka. I got the makings recently. Can I interest you in one?"

"Okay. Sure."

Vic followed Alice into the kitchen and watched as she prepared the drinks. "They're called Melon Balls. What do you think?"

Vic sipped. "Delicious," he said downing half the drink as they walked into the living room.

As nice as Vic was being, Alice was becoming impatient with his reluctance to venture into anything even remotely resembling sexuality. She knew he wasn't gay from the stories she had told him. So what was with him?

Vic settled onto the sofa and Alice sat beside him. She touched the rim of her glass to his. "Here's to good sex." *That ought to shake him up a bit*, she thought.

"You mean now?" Vic said, staring.

Alice put her drink down. "Why not?"

"But . . . well . . . I'm not really in your league. I mean. . .

"Vic, I think there are a few things we should get out into the open. We both know how we met and that's making this really strange. I find you attractive and sexy. This is our third date and I just thought that, since we're here, together, that we might experiment a bit."

"Experiment?"

"See whether we're compatible. Of course, if you don't find me tempting, I will certainly understand."

"Oh, Alice, I find you most tempting. It's just that, well, I'm a bit intimidated."

"I frighten you?"

"No." He paused and stared into his glass. "Sheherazade does."

"I thought we had agreed that she's not real. She's just a character I put on and take off at will."

"I know that, but somehow she's always there, in the back of my mind. I'm sorry."

Alice was somehow amused. "Sheherazade scares the daylights out of you, doesn't she?"

"I'm afraid so." He turned toward her. "Oh, Alice, I've dreamed about making love to you, but in all the dreams, just when we're about to do it, you know, there's Sherry, watching, judging how creative I am. And I always fail. Although I enjoy your stories and have my fantasies, I'm not really very adventurous."

Alice stroked Vic's check. "This is all silly. I am who I am and you are who you are. If we're good together, that's great. If not, well nothing's lost."

"A lot is lost. That's what you don't understand. I like you very much. I don't want to sacrifice our friendship. If we go to bed and it's terrible, then what?"

Alice touched her lips to Vic's. "Why should it be terrible?"

"My wife always said that I wasn't much in the bedroom department."

Alice sat back. "There are good and bad lovers, of course. But the bad lovers are the ones with no imagination, no ability to play, to enjoy, and to communicate. We've been communicating and imagining and playing for months on the phone so that shouldn't be a problem."

"On the phone," Vic said. "Not in real life. Face to face. I don't know whether I'm good enough for you. I might disappoint you."

"I really believe, and not from a lot of personal experience, mind you, that couples are good or bad, not individuals. I find you attractive and I'm excited by the possibility of making love with you."

"You want to make love to a basset hound?"

"That's the second time you've used that term. That really bothers you, doesn't it?"

"I guess it does. My wife used that as a term of endearment early in our marriage. Then later, it became her little joke, but eventually I didn't find it funny."

"I can imagine you didn't." Alice put her hand on Vic's thigh. "Are you going to let her get between us too? There are too many of us here already: you, me, Sheherazade, and now your ex-wife. Let's just be you and me and see what happens."

Vic gazed into Alice's eyes, then his expression softened. "You're right, of course." He put his arms around her and kissed her, putting all the longing he was feeling into the meeting of mouths. Suddenly hunger seemed to sweep over them, ending all of Vic's hesitation. Hands unbuttoned, unbuckled, and unzipped. Mouths quested and found erotic spots, hard flesh, and wetness. "Oh God, baby," he murmured as he paused to unroll a condom over his erection. Then, still on the sofa, he was inside of

her. Alice's nails dug into his back while he drove into her. She
wrapped her legs around his waist and pulled him closer, bucking
her hips to take him more deeply inside her.

Their climaxes were fast and hard. And loud.

"Still think you're a basset hound? I don't know any basset
hounds that make love like that."

"It was all right?" Vic asked.

"It was fantastic."

Later they lay on Alice's bed, naked, side by side, sipping
drinks. "Do you remember the first story you ever told me?" Vic
asked, mellower than she had seen him since they'd first met
face to face.

Alice thought. "It was about the toll taker, wasn't it?"

"Yes, and they made love hard and fast like we did. I lived that
story a thousand times in my mind, seeing me and you. Remember? Long blond hair and blue eyes?"

Alice grinned. "Not like the real me at all."

"Nor the real me either. But in my fantasies, I was young and
virile and you were blond and blue-eyed. You know what? This
was much better."

"This was great," Alice said.

"Can I ask you for something really strange? Would you tell
me a story, like Sheherazade used to do? I've always fantasized
about being able to touch you while you were telling me one of
your wonderful tales."

Alice considered it. Sheherazade was an illusion, a voice on the
phone, a figment of her imagination just as surely as her stories
were. The real Alice was solid and down to earth. But were they
really so separate? Hadn't the gap between her two selves nar-
rowed over the past weeks? She had always believed that she
couldn't talk as freely about lovemaking when she could look
someone in the eye, but now that Vic had asked, she wanted to
tell him a great story. And maybe she could find out what kinds of
lovemaking he liked at the same time.

She stood up and padded around the apartment, turning out
all the lights. Then, before turning out the small bedside light in

the bedroom, she lit several candles, the ones still left from Todd's visit.

She stretched out on the bed and pulled a quilt over the two of them, then cuddled against Vic in the flickering light. "You have to help me," she said. "Close your eyes. Set the scene. Tell me where you are, what you're seeing. Think about the most perfect encounter you can imagine. How would it begin?"

"Boy, you're really asking me to reveal my deepest secrets, aren't you?"

"No. You can create anything you like, so go wherever you want. Let's create people for our story who are gorgeous, perfect creatures who are so sexy that no one can resist us. That's what I imagine when I tell a story."

"You have those fantasies too?"

"Sure. I have long flowing hair. Sometimes it's black, sometimes blond, sometimes red but it's always long and it blows in the wind like a shampoo commercial." She'd shared so many fantasies, but had never been this personal and honest before. She wanted Vic to know that they both had the same insecurities. "I'd have blue eyes with long black lashes, a perfect small nose, and those wonderful full lips that sort of pout, the ones that men find so kissable."

Vic propped himself on one elbow and kissed her softly, nipping at her lower lip. "I think you've got a great, sexy mouth." He lay back down.

"What do you look like in your dreams?"

"I'm tall. I'm always about six foot four, with broad shoulders and lots of muscles. I have black wavy hair and black eyes. I guess you'd say I was a stud, with women panting to get dates with me."

"So you've got all the women you want in your dreams?"

"In my dreams, the one I want most doesn't want me, except on her terms."

"Oh." Alice vaguely remembered that Velvet had told her that Vic liked aggressive women. "She's forceful?"

"Very."

"How do you two meet?" She wanted to hear, and possibly play out Vic's fantasy. "How about at a party? The wine and booze are flowing freely and everyone is feeling quite mellow. Is she there?"

She heard Vic's long-drawn-out, *"Yessss."*

"Does she excite you?"

"Oh yes. I can't take my eyes off of her. She's tall, almost five feet ten and has long red hair that hangs almost to her waist. Her body is firm and trim with small breasts. She isn't wearing the usual party uniform: the slinky dress that advertises her availability. Instead, she's wearing a black blouse buttoned up to her throat and knotted at the waist and tight, black stretch pants. She has accentuated her waist with a silver concho belt, which matches her large silver squash-blossom earrings. She has completed her outfit with knee-high black leather boots that lace up the front with silver rings at the top.

"I start toward her. As I get closer, I admire her green eyes and smooth skin. I gaze at her red lips and feel a further tightening in my pants."

Alice felt Vic take her hand beneath the quilt. As long as Vic was willing to continue the story, Alice was anxious to listen.

" 'Hi, gorgeous,' I say, using my most charming voice. 'How about I get you a fresh drink and then we can get to know each other?'

"The girl looks at me. Her eyes roam my body, making me a bit self-conscious. Then she looks away.

"I want to get to know her, then take her to bed even." Vic chuckled. "Actually I don't care if I ever get to know her, I merely want to fuck her senseless, lose myself in her body."

"I'll bet it's not going to be as easy as you think," Alice said.

"No, it's not," Vic said, squeezing her hand. "You know, this storytelling isn't as easy as I thought. It's a bit scary, like I'm telling you all about me."

"I know. If anyone listens to my stories they will find out all the things that turn me on. I can't invent a really good erotic fantasy about activities that don't get me excited." She paused. "You really don't have to make it so personal if you don't want to," Alice said. "We can certainly tell this story other, less scary ways."

"I know, but it's a sort of delicious-scary. I'd like to continue as long as I can." He took a deep breath. "So I say to the woman, 'I'm sorry. Are you with someone?'

" 'No,' she says with her back to me.

" 'Then why not me?' I ask.

" 'You're not my type,' she says.

"Well, I am surprised. 'And what is your type?' I ask.

"She turns and looks at me. 'My type always waits for me to make the first move. As a matter of fact, my type always waits for me to make every move.' "

Alice felt his grip tighten and knew he was telling her something he wanted her to hear, something he'd probably never told anyone. In his fantasy the woman is the aggressor and he is the follower. "I'll bet that gets to you, makes you hard."

"Oh yes, it does," Vic said. "My whole body shudders and I can hardly control my excitement. My pulse is hammering and I'm panting. I can hardly get the words out. 'W-w-what would your type do right now?' I stammer."

Alice leaned close to his ear and whispered, "What does she say?"

"She smiles and says, 'My type would light a cigarette and hand it to me,' so I take out a cigarette, light it, and hand it to her with shaking fingers.

" 'Hmm,' she says. 'Very good,' then she just wanders off through the crowd."

Alice held his hand tightly. "I'll bet she comes back. I would, if I were her. I like men who know how to behave and you knew exactly what to do." She heard the hiss of Vic's indrawn breath. She wanted to make him hotter, make it easier for him to talk, she realized, and she'd read enough stories to understand what he would like. "You were such a good boy."

"I was? Oh yes. Well eventually she does come back, almost an hour later. I stare at her, but she says, sternly, 'Never look me in the eye. You may only look at me from the shoulders down unless I give you permission. Understand?'

"I looked at her shiny boots, staring at the sharply pointed toes, the heavy silver rings through the zippers, and the high spike heels. 'Yes, I understand.' I can hardly speak."

"What's her name?" Alice whispered. "We can call her anything you want."

"Valerie," Vic said. "She says that her name is Valerie. 'You must learn to say, *Yes, Valerie,* or *Yes, ma'am.* Now practice that.'

" 'Yes, Valerie,' I say. 'Yes, ma'am.'

" 'Not bad for a beginner,' she says. As she speaks, I watch her hands with those long red fingernails that are sliding up and down the hips of her tight pants. 'Now go into the bathroom,' she says. Her voice is soft but firm and seems to brook no objections. 'Take off your shorts and bring them to me. Quickly, with no dawdling.'

"God, I'm so hot." Vic hesitated, so Alice said, "I'll bet you're a good boy and do as you're told?"

"Oh yes, I do. I almost run into the bathroom, pull off my slacks and shorts and allow my huge erection to poke from the front of my crotch. I want to touch it, rub it, but I know she's waiting, so I pull my slacks back on, ball my shorts in my hand and hurry back through the crowd. I find her where I left her, standing beside the bar. I remember and gaze down at her boots, as I surreptitiously hand her my shorts. Valerie props her elbow on the bar as she dangles my shorts from her index finger for all to see. There are several snickers from other people at the party but I'm willing to risk anything. I start to reach for the shorts but Valerie glares at me. I drop my hand and blush for the first time in years, lowering my eyes to her leather boots."

"You were being such an obedient boy," Alice says, still holding his hand, using his grip as an indication of his excitement. "I like obedient boys."

"What would you say now?" Vic asked, his voice hoarse, his need evident.

Picking up the story, Alice continued, "I would be very glad that you did as you were told. I find you quite attractive and you would be a good addition to my collection. 'I see we understand each other,' I would say. 'Go and find my coat. It's long, black leather. Bring it to me and we'll get out of here.' Will you do that, Vic?"

"Yes. Of course. I go into the bedroom and root through the coats. I find hers, then I stop for a moment and wonder why I'm doing this. Has this girl cast some kind of spell over me? She has and I know it. And I don't care. I have to have her. I will do anything she wants just to get a chance to make love to her."

Alice shifted her grip to his wrist and held it tightly. She recalled Todd's commanding tone and trembled. She knew just how Vic was feeling, wanting to be controlled by an erotic fantasy woman. She wanted Vic to continue so she said, "Tell me what happens then."

"Well, later, in the cab on the way to her apartment, she says, 'Give me your wrists.' She pulls a length of soft black rope from her purse and stares at me. I know what she wants, so I offer her my wrists and she ties them together, then reaches down and lifts the heavy silver ring that's attached to one of her boots. She takes the free end of the rope and ties it to the ring.

"When we reach our destination, the rope forces me to get out of the taxi carefully and walk bent over with my head level with her breasts. Twice, I almost stumble when Valerie takes a particularly long step." Vic hesitated.

"Tell me," Alice urged.

"This is really kinky but when I regain my balance, she laughs and I'm so aroused by her laughter that I think I'll come right there. Am I perverted, Alice?"

"Not at all. I think it's really hot," Alice said. "Does she take you to her apartment?"

"Yes. We enter her apartment and she turns on the lights. All the furniture is chrome, glass, or black lacquer. The rug is dark red with deep pile and it silences our footsteps.

"Without a word she unties the end of the rope attached to her boot and reties it to a ring embedded in the wall. Then she turns and disappears into the next room. It's very warm in her apartment so, since I'm still wearing my winter jacket, I begin to sweat and feel a trickle of perspiration run down my side. I wiggle as much as I can, trying to brush my shirt against the tiny river.

" 'Don't squirm!' she snaps as she reenters the room. She has changed into a black corset that reveals her full breasts and pussy and she has put on long black gloves without fingers. She has also pulled her hair back tightly and wound it into a tight knot at the back of her neck. She's still wearing her boots and is banging a short riding crop against the top of one. God, this is really hard to talk about."

"Your story is really getting me hot." Alice took Vic's hand and placed it on her mound. His fingers slipped naturally between her lips and she knew he could feel her wetness. She didn't know whether she could actually become the character in Vic's story and play the scene out with him, but the tale was making her hungry. Now she understood exactly what her callers felt when she spun one of her fantasies. "Tell me what happens then," Alice said, an air of command in her voice.

"Valerie flicks the crop against the back of my thigh," Vic continued. "The effect is muffled by my jeans but the crop still stings. 'You were looking at me,' she snaps. I immediately drop my gaze.

"Valerie reaches up, unties my hands, and unfastens the rope from the wall. As she stretches, her naked breasts brush against me. I wonder how much of this I can take before I come in my pants."

Alice placed her hand gently over Vic's extremely hard cock. "Go on," she said, squeezing. She can hear Vic's hoarse, quick breathing and feel his body shake.

"Valerie walks over to the sofa and sits down, the rope still in her hands. 'Strip,' she orders. I obey as quickly as I can with my hands shaking as hard as they are.

"I stand before her, naked. Her eyes roam over my body, my erection poking straight in front of me, aching for relief.

" 'I demand stamina from my men,' she says. 'You may not come unless I give you permission. The first time is always the most difficult so I will give you some help. Crawl over here.'

"I do it, on my hands and knees. I'll do anything she wants. 'Stand up straight,' she says, 'and touch yourself.' I have never masturbated with anyone watching so I hesitate. The crop swishes through the air again and lands on my right ass cheek. It stings but it also heightens my awareness of my body and its needs. I reach out and wrap my hand around my huge cock."

Alice took Vic's hand and placed it on his cock. "Ohh," he groaned, trying to pull his hand away, but Alice placed her hand on top of his and urged him to keep it there. "Keep it there," she said, "just like in the story."

"Yes, ma'am." He kept his hand around his cock as he was doing in the fantasy.

" 'Stroke it until you come,' Valerie says. 'Then you can serve me properly.' "

"Yes," Alice whispered, "do that for me. I want to feel your hand move."

As he continued the story, Vic's hand slowly moved over his erection. "Valerie settles back and stares at my hand.

"I am very embarrassed but also very excited. I squeeze my cock and run my fingers up and down it." With Alice's hand on top of his, Vic's hand moved faster as he lost himself in his fantasy. "Oh God, Alice, oh God." It was only a moment until he spurted all over her legs. "I'm so sorry," Vic said. "I don't know what came over me."

"I do, and it pleases me very much. The power of the images you created was erotic as hell and drove you over the edge." She handed Vic several tissues and he cleaned himself up quickly.

"I've never done that with a woman," Vic said.

"Why not? It was wonderful."

"What about you? You haven't come."

Alice placed his hand on her pussy. "Fix it! Touch me!" She felt his body react to the command in her voice. His fingers worked, rubbing her clit. She grabbed the back of his neck and pushed his face against her breast. "Suck!" Quickly, his mouth and teeth drove her upward as his fingers played her pussy like a fine instrument. He seemed to know when to stroke softly and when to press hard. "Good boy, don't stop." He slipped two fingers inside of her and found a spot that made her body jerk with erotic pleasure when he pressed. "Very good. You serve me well."

He continued to fuck her with his fingers, then slid down and took her clit between his lips and sucked. She tried to hold back, wanting the wonderful sensations he was creating to last, but she was unable to prevent the waves of erotic pleasure from engulfing her. Suddenly the orgasm burst through her clenched muscles, and lasted several minutes.

Later, Vic said, "I asked you to tell me a story and I ended up telling you my deepest secrets. You must be a witch."

They dozed and, after making love once more, Vic said, "I think I'd better go home."

"You can stay if you want," Alice said, barely able to stay awake.

"I know, but I'd prefer to head home. It's almost morning and I have a lot of thinking to do. I want to take some time alone to consider what we did tonight."

"I could order you to stay," Alice said, unsure of where Vic's head was.

"Yes, you could, and that's what I have to think about. It's really unnerving to find out that you're not the basset hound you always thought you were."

"You're no basset hound. That's for sure." Alice yawned.

"I'll call you tomorrow. Actually today. Okay?"

Still a bit insecure, she thought, even after all that they had shared. "I'll look forward to hearing from you." As she heard him close the front door behind him, she burrowed beneath her covers and slept soundly.

Chapter

13

After their first sexual encounter, Alice and Vic dated almost every weekend. There were a few repeats of the dominant games they had played, but for the most part, the sex was good, hot, and traditional. In addition, through the summer Alice continued both of her jobs working at Dr. Tannenbaum's office and taking calls three evenings. She also visited her mother at least once a week and tried to join Betsy and Velvet for girls' night out. The three women became, if possible, even closer. When the doctor's office closed for two weeks in August, Alice and Vic spent a week driving around the south, enjoying sightseeing by day and playing in motel bedrooms by night. She also dated several other men, two of whom she met through Velvet Whispers and three who were introduced to her by her two best friends. Some of these dates resulted in more dates, a few ended after one evening.

In early September, Mrs. Waterman went to sleep one evening and died quietly before morning. Although it was sad, both Alice and her sister agreed that their mother's death was peaceful and she was now beyond the pain that had begun to debilitate her. Without the drain of nursing-home payments, Alice had a new-found financial freedom, and had some serious decisions to make. She knew that she was exhausted, burning the candle at more than two ends. She needed to simplify her life but she wasn't sure how. Should she give up Velvet Whispers? That seemed the most logical thing to do.

Maybe she should tell her callers that she was taking a vacation and that Velvet would be in touch when she was ready to take calls again. Yes, she should do that.

The following evening, a regular client named Hector was her first caller. "Hi, Sherry," he said. "Got a story for me tonight? Tell me a really hot one. It's been a long, tough week." She knew the kind of stories he liked and tonight she was going to tell him a doozie. One last present for him before she retired.

"Sure thing, sweetness," Alice said in her Sheherazade voice. "It's about a night when I was very naughty."

"Tell me."

"Well, several years ago I took a job waiting tables at a place called La Contessa. I was good at my job and I liked the work, not as much as I like talking to you, but that was before. Anyway, I got as many huge tippers as I got nasty customers so it was okay." Alice laughed, remembering her short stint as a waitress just after Ralph split. "I remember the man who slipped me a thirty-dollar tip for a sixty-dollar dinner check and one who yelled at me for fifteen minutes for delivering his steak too rare."

"Yeah, I'll bet," Hector said. "I always try to be nice to waitresses. My ex-wife used to wait tables and I remember the stories she used to tell."

"I don't think your ex-wife had any experiences like this one and she probably never had a customer like this guy. I know I never had. The man was not really good-looking, but he had a sensuality that was almost palpable. He wore his ebony hair long so you just wanted to run your fingers through it. His eyes were the blue of glacial ice, yet they also seemed warm and inviting. He wore a tight black turtleneck that fit his body like a second skin with long tight cuffs that almost caressed his wrists. His black jeans were, if possible, tighter than his shirt, his boots were black with silver studs and toe tips. His only jewelry was a silver hoop in one ear."

"Sounds like quite a stud."

"He was. I spotted him as he stood waiting to be seated. Although I tried not to stare, I found myself unable to move. I wondered whether he was meeting someone." Alice's breathing quickened just thinking about the man in black she was creating and she knew her excitement would add to Hector's enjoyment. "Well, the host sat him in my section. In the corner at table thirty-five. 'Good evening,' I said in my best waitress voice. 'My name is Sherry and I'll be serving you this evening. May I get you a drink?'

"His eyes met mine and our gazes locked. He stared at me, then his eyes caressed my body from my neck to my toes. You see the outfits we wore were quite revealing. Very low-cut peasant blouses and full, red-print skirts.

"He stared, then said, 'Yes, of course. I'll have a glass of sangria, Sherry.'

"I saw that the host had put only one menu on the table so I asked, 'Will you be dining alone?'

" 'Alas, yes,' he said, still staring into my eyes. 'I have set my last lover free and I'm looking for another. Are you available?'

"Whoa," Hector said. "He was really something. Set his last lover free. What did that mean?"

"I wondered about that myself, but he kept staring at me and I found that my knees began to tremble and my brain locked up tight. I couldn't concentrate. Was he asking me out? Several customers had done that over the months, and, although there was no strict rule against dating patrons, I had always said no. 'I'm sorry,' I answered, 'but no.' "

"I'll bet he was sorry too. I know just how he must have felt," Hector said. "How often have I gotten that same answer from you?"

Alice laughed. "Lots. But don't stop trying. It's good for my ego and sometime I might just say yes." Alice knew Hector lived in the New York area and maybe, with more time on her hands, she would agree to meet him. What did she have to lose? She dragged her thoughts back to her story. "So the man in black said, 'That's a shame.'

"I cleared my throat," Alice continued, "then said, 'I'll get your sangria while you decide what to order.' As I walked toward the bar's service area, I could feel his eyes on me. My knees shook and I could feel the wetness between my legs. He was the sexiest man I'd ever seen and there was something more. Something deeply, darkly erotic.

"When I returned with the man's drink, my hands shook so much that, as I placed the glass on the table, several drops of the blood-red liquid fell on his pants. 'I'm t-t-terribly s-s-sorry,' I stammered. I grabbed a napkin from a nearby table and dabbed at the almost-invisible stain.

"The hand that snapped around my wrist was like a vise. 'That was very careless,' the man said softly. Then he smiled. 'You really should be punished for your clumsiness.' "

"He really said that?" Hector asked, his breathing a bit faster.

Alice caught Hector's reaction. He was as excited at the way the story was unfolding as she was. Interesting. "Yes, he said *punished*. I wondered why he had said that? Would he punish me? How? Oh God. I swallowed hard.

" 'That excites you, doesn't it?' the man purred. 'I can feel your pulse race.' "

"Does that idea excite you, Sherry?" Hector asked, his voice filled with longing. "God, I'd love to do bad things to you."

"Let's finish the story, sweetness, then we can talk." She heard Hector's breath catch. She was definitely tempted. "So there I was, with him holding my wrist, telling me how excited I was getting. Well I couldn't speak. All my life I had had fantasies of someone controlling me, spanking me, loving me." *Did I really have such fantasies?* Alice wondered. "Although I had had a few lovers, I had never shared my dark desires with any of them. They were too kinky. Too black. Yet here he was, a man who seemed to know my deepest wishes. Or was it just an accident. 'I'm sorry, sir,' I said, taking a deep breath. 'Can I take your dinner order?' *That's good*, I thought. *Fall back on the familiar routine.* But he was still holding my wrist."

"I know these are just stories," Hector said, "but they make me so hot. Do you really have those fantasies, Sherry? Do you really want someone to take over like that? Control you?"

What could she say? She had never thought about this kind of sex play happening to her until that weekend with Todd. It had always been just a story. Now it was becoming much more. She returned to her tale. " 'Your pulse is still pounding,' the man in black whispered. 'We'll continue this later.' I wondered what he meant, but I concentrated on my job.

"I took his dinner order and tried to involve myself in caring for the other diners. When his order was up, I put the plates on my tray and served him calmly and efficiently. Or at least I tried to be calm. Tried to sound calm. His expression told me he wasn't fooled.

"As I waited on other tables, I frequently looked at him, and each time I glanced in his direction, I found his eyes on me. It wasn't just a coincidence. It felt like he was seducing me with his gaze. It was almost half an hour later when I returned to his table to retrieve his empty plates.

" 'That was delicious,' he said, his voice little more than a purr, 'but not totally satisfying. I need something hot for dessert. Any suggestions?'

"Me, I wanted to say. Instead I murmured, 'We have a wonderful hot apple cobbler.'

"The man looked at his watch, hidden beneath the long sleeve of his black shirt. 'It's almost nine-thirty. What time do you finish here?'

"I cleared my throat. 'I do recommend the apple cobbler.'

" 'You want this. I know you understand that you deserve what I have for you, and I also know you crave it. You are telling me that with every fiber of your being. I can read you like a book and I know exactly what you want.' "

Alice could hear Hector's heavy breathing and knew her story was having the desired effect. She also knew that her body was responding too. Fortunately she had changed into an old sweat suit after work so she rubbed her aching nipples as she continued.

"Again I swallowed and tried not to let my voice squeak. 'And what, exactly, do you think I want?'

" 'You want to be punished for spilling my drink. You want me to restrain you, then spank you like the naughty girl you are. You want the feeling of surrendering to me.' The idea of spanking appealed to Alice when she had read a story the previous week. Now it just became part of the fantasy she was creating. Did she want something like this to happen?

"I wish I could be like that guy," Hector said wistfully. "I'd love to dominate a woman like that, but I'm too much of a chicken to ever do it for real."

"Are you really?" Alice asked, then didn't wait for an answer. "Well, you'll never guess what happened next. I was standing close to the man's chair and my skirt covered his movements. Suddenly his hand was between my thighs, his fingers touching my panties. 'You want this like you've never wanted anything else. You're hot and wet and you can barely keep your thighs together.'

"He knew me too well. Much too well. Then the hand was gone. 'I get off at eleven.' I had said it, committed myself to him and to whatever he wanted from me.

" 'I drive a black BMW,' he said. 'It will be parked by the back door at eleven and I will wait for fifteen minutes. Be there or regret it all your life.' "

"Did you go?" Hector asked.

"Well, silently I took his credit card and returned with the charge slip. I knew I was blushing and I could barely keep my hands from shaking. He signed and as he stood to leave, he leaned close and whispered, 'For you, my love, I might wait until eleven-thirty. Please don't disappoint us both.'

"Then he was gone. I spent the remainder of my shift in a daze. I took orders, served food and alcohol, but my mind was on the man with the BMW. Could I trust him? Could he fulfill my fantasies? Yes, I admitted to myself, to both questions."

"Wow," Hector whispered.

"It's been more than fifteen minutes, Hector," Alice said glancing at the clock. "Shall I continue?"

"Hell yes," Hector said. "Tell me the rest."

"At eleven-fifteen I walked out of La Contessa, my nipples tight and aching, my pussy soaked, my body craving what was to come. I spotted the BMW immediately, opened the passenger door, and slipped inside.

" 'I'm glad you came,' the man said. 'I would have been quite sad had you not appeared.'

" 'I think I would have been too,' I whispered."

"Me too," Hector said with a laugh.

" 'Good girl,' he said, sounding genuinely pleased. He reached around my waist, grabbed the seat belt and pulled it across my body. Since it was a warm midsummer evening, I hadn't worn anything over my blouse. 'Now we have some rules to agree to. Can you snap your fingers?'

"Strange request, I thought, but I snapped. 'Good,' he said. 'If you snap your fingers or say the word *marshmallow*, I will stop whatever I'm doing. Do you understand and agree?'

" 'Yes.'

" 'You will call me Sir. Nothing more, and nothing less. Do you understand?'

" 'Yes, Sir.'

" 'Excellent.' With deft fingers, the man untied the string that held the top of my blouse. The tie loosened and he pulled the top down so my bra-covered breasts were exposed. He withdrew a small pair of scissors from a compartment in his door and quickly cut the straps of my bra. It took only a moment before the bra was gone, my breasts free, the strap of the shoulder harness cold against the skin between them. My nipples were already swollen, but he pinched the turgid tips until they were aching. Then he took two small suction devices and fastened them to my tits, causing almost painful pressure. Almost painful, but not quite. It was like two mouths sucking on my breasts as hard as they could."

Alice moved her hand down her belly and slid her fingers beneath the waist of her sweatpants. She found her pussy already wet from the images imprinted on her brain.

" 'Put your hands on your hips,' he said, softly but firmly, 'and don't move them. Close your eyes and think about your tits. Think about the pressure, the almost-pain and the cool wind against your skin. Think that anyone who looks carefully will know what your breasts are feeling and think about how hot this makes you. I want your tits and your mind at their most sensitive when we get to our destination. It won't take long.'

" 'Yes, Sir,' I said, placing my palms against my hipbones and closing my eyes.

"We drove for only about five minutes, then I felt the car slow, turn, and stop. I heard a garage door open and the car move forward and the door close again. 'We're here,' he said.

"I opened my eyes to what had obviously been a two-car garage once. Now half of the structure was walled off. I got out of the car, the sucking devices making every move pleasure and torture. My large breasts swayed as I walked propelled by his hand in the small of my back.

"We walked through a doorway into the other half of the garage and I gasped. The room was paneled in dark wood, with a thick cream-colored carpet cushioning my steps. There were mirrors on one entire wall and the ceiling. In the center of the room there was a large X-shaped wooden frame that stood about six feet tall and was about three feet wide at the ends of the arms. In the corner was an armless desk chair. 'First,' he said, 'snap your fingers.'

"I did, remembering that I was to snap if I got into trouble. 'I understand, Sir,' I said.

"He led me over to the chair, sat in it and quickly removed all of my clothes, leaving the suction devices on my breasts. Then he pulled at one wrist and I tumbled across his lap. 'You were very clumsy earlier,' he said, his voice soft and oily. 'You deserve more than this, but I will go easy for our first time.' "

"He was going to spank you?" Hector asked. "Man, oh man."

I wondered how the story had gotten to this, but it was obviously where Hector and I wanted it to go. "Oh yes," I said. "He was going to punish me for my clumsiness."

"And you let him?"

"I not only let him, I wanted it."

"Man," Hector said, "I can see it and feel it."

"I had no time to wonder as his palm slapped my ass cheek. I felt the sting in my tender nether parts, but it was just a sting. The second slap merely stung a bit more, but by the fifth, the sting had become pain and my entire backside was tender. Then he stopped."

"Did it hurt?" Hector asked. "My cock's all hard just thinking about it."

"Oh yes. But I was surprised that the pain was also pleasure. I was so wet and hot." Alice's fingers were rubbing her clit and she knew she was close to coming.

"Tell me more," Hector said.

" 'You enjoyed that. You have discovered the pleasure in a little pain.' The man caressed my ass cheeks tenderly. Then his fingers slipped into my slit. It was sopping. 'Oh yes,' he said, laughing. 'You liked this a lot.' His fingers penetrated deep into my cunt and his thumb rubbed my clit. I climaxed, my entire body quaking as the spasms took me. 'Oh my God. Good. So good,' I cried.

" 'My dear, you're perfect,' he said, still gently rubbing my pussy lips as I came down from the strongest orgasm I remembered. I knew from the moment I saw you that you could be a most wonderful playmate. I would like to do so many things with you, teach you so much about your own sensuality. Would you like that?'

"I could barely get the words out. 'Oh yes, Sir.'

"The man unzipped the fly of his jeans and pulled out his swollen cock. See how excited you make me?' "

"Oh, Sherry, you make me crazy too," Hector said. "I'm going to come soon."

"That's wonderful," Alice said. "Remembering that night is

making me hot too." She rubbed her pussy, almost over the edge.
"So I gazed at the man's cock, then into his eyes. He nodded and
I knelt between his spread knees. I took the nob into my mouth,
licked and sucked at the tip, then my mouth engulfed the entire
staff. Deep in my throat I worked the base of my tongue and my
cheeks, trying to give him as much pleasure as he had given me.
When I cupped his balls through his jeans, he climaxed and I
swallowed every drop." Alice came then, but managed to keep
telling the story. "When his cock was flaccid again, I sat back on
my haunches and gazed at his face. He wore an expression of
pure joy, an expression I had helped put there.

" 'That was beautiful,' he said softly.

"I couldn't speak.

" 'Do you see that frame over there?' he asked as he removed
the suckers on my tits.

" 'Yes, Sir,' I said.

" 'If you come here after work tomorrow night, I will tie you to
that, arms spread wide over your head, legs tied far apart so I can
play with your pussy at my leisure.' "

Hector gasped and I knew he was coming, but I finished my
tale anyway.

"I looked, first at the frame, then at the man who had awakened so much in me.

" 'And we can make love in so many ways.' He lifted my face
and kissed me gently on the lips. 'Please,' he said, passion and
desire in his eyes. 'I want you so much. Climb into my car each
night and I will show you so much, and share pleasure you have
only dreamed of.'

" 'I'll be there,' I said. 'Yes, I'll be there.'

Alice heard Hector's long sigh. "That was a wonderful story.
Did you meet him the next night?"

"Yes," Alice said softly, removing her hand from between her
legs.

"Will you tell me about that night next time I call?" Wasn't she
going to tell him that she was retiring? One more call. What
would it hurt?

"Of course, Hector."

"Next week? Monday? Same time?"

"Sure. It's a date, sweetness."

"Great, then I'll talk to you then. Will you also think about going out with me sometime? We could meet and, well, explore."

"I'll think about it."

Still unsure what she was going to do, she hung up.

Chapter

14

That Saturday night, Alice and Vic spent the evening in the city at a small club in Greenwich Village, listening to jazz. Afterward, they went back to Vic's apartment and made love. She stayed over and the following morning, they went to brunch at a trendy local restaurant. "I'm thinking about leaving Velvet Whispers," she said, sipping orange juice and champagne.

"You really should. You don't need that stuff anymore. I've been telling you that you've been doing too much and I've given it a lot of thought. I think you should marry me. Then you can give up the phone business, quit your dentist job, and move in with me." As Alice watched, Vic began to talk faster and faster. "I'm very well-off, so we could travel. See the world. I've been doing more thinking about that X-rated game I talked to you about too. We could do it together. I could pay you as a consultant if you want."

When he paused for breath, Alice put her hand on his. "You sound like you've got it all planned."

"I have. It will work. We're good together, in and out of bed."

"Vic, you know I care for you, but have you listened to yourself? You're talking like a pitchman. Who are you trying to sell, me or you? You talk about all the reasons we should get married except the most important one. You haven't mentioned love once."

"Of course I love you. That goes without saying."

"No, it doesn't and you didn't say it because it's not the most important element of your thinking. Maybe it's there between us, I don't know." Alice was sorting things out as she spoke, and she found she was seeing things more clearly. "I do know that I'm not ready to settle down yet."

"Oh, Alice, I just want to make you happy."

"I love spending time with you and I don't want that to stop but I have a few other men I date and I don't want that to stop either." When Vic looked dejected, she continued, "I can't be exclusive with you. Not yet, maybe not ever, but does that really change the good times we have?"

"I guess not, but I hate the thought of sharing you."

"I know and I'm sorry that it makes you unhappy, but I've got to have time to decide what I want. I've never had that luxury before. First I had my parents making my decisions, then Ralph. I spent a lot of years after Ralph left in limbo, drifting, then I had my mother's illness. Now I'm free to do whatever I want, and I need time to figure out what that is. I hope you can accept that."

Vic took Alice's hand across the table. "As long as I can spend time with you and you're happy, it's great. You're really going to leave Velvet Whispers?"

"I think so. It's the logical thing to eliminate. It takes up my evenings and keeps me up much later than I really want. One night last week I was up until almost one."

"Good. I hate to think of you on those sleazy phone calls."

"You didn't think they were sleazy when you were calling me."

"That's different."

Alice raised an eyebrow. "Is it?"

"I don't know, but I'm happy you're leaving."

The idea of leaving Velvet Whispers is logical, Alice thought. *Why then does it make me so sad?* Changing the subject, Alice asked, "Did you mean what you said about the video game?"

"You mean about you helping me? Absolutely. I've got dozens of ideas for it and you'd be just the person to write the scripts."

"I think that would be a gas. Between my stories and your computer skills, we'd make one hell of an adventure game." And if she left Velvet Whispers she would have her evenings, all day on Wednesdays, and the weekends to go into the city and work with Vic. It was entirely logical.

Vic squeezed her hand. "Just tell me that you'll occasionally think about marrying me. Maybe you'll change your mind."

That afternoon, after she arrived home, Alice phoned Velvet and told her of her decision to leave Velvet Whispers. "Are you sure that's what you want to do?" Velvet asked. "I know how much you enjoy your calls and we will all miss you if you leave. You have quite a group of regulars and they will be really upset."

"I know, but it's the logical thing to do. I'll stay with Dr. Tannenbaum and keep the medical coverage and all, and Vic has asked me to work with him on his computer game."

"Oh, honey, I know that you have to make your own decisions but I just don't want to lose you, as an employee or as a friend."

"Oh, Velvet. We won't lose each other. The three of us can still have girls' night out. That will be just like it always has been."

"Shall I take you out of the computer? I won't tell any of your regulars yet. Maybe you'll change your mind."

"I don't think so. Hector is calling tomorrow night and he'll be my last caller."

"I can see I'm in for lots of disappointed men."

After she hung up with Velvet, Alice called Betsy and told her the same thing and, as she had expected, she got the identical reaction. Betsy, however, was more forceful in her suggestion that leaving wasn't necessarily the best idea. "I know it's the logical thing to do," Betsy said, "but I think you're nuts."

Through the day on Monday, Alice thought about her twin conversations. Was this really the right thing? Talking with Vic the day before, it had seemed so simple. Was it really?

That evening, Hector called precisely at eight. "You're right on time, Hector," she said.

"I'm really anxious to hear what happened to you and that guy the next night."

Alice settled onto her bed, Roger beside her. Was this going to be her last call? She could take some time, of course, and taper off, but cold turkey was the best. Well, she'd go out in a blaze of glory. "His name was Daniel. I had learned that as he drove me home after our wonderful night together. Daniel. I couldn't imagine anyone calling him Dan or Danny. I couldn't imagine myself calling him Daniel. He was just Sir.

"I arrived at La Contessa at the regular time the following evening and went through the motions of setting up for the dinner crowd. Would he be here? Would he eat at the restaurant? Would he be waiting at the back door in his BMW?

"The evening crawled by. I looked at my watch and it was six o'clock. An hour later it was only six-fifteen. It took weeks for it to become eight o'clock and decades until ten-thirty. And always my eyes scanned the incoming diners. He wasn't among them. I poured coffee for a customer, brought a check to another, all in a daze. Several times the maitre d' had to remind me to give a customer the dessert menu or refill a water glass. But I was barely functioning. He would be waiting for me outside. He had to be.

"He had given me an instruction. 'Wear no underpants,' he had told me, 'so that every time your thighs brush together and rub against your pussy, you'll think of me.' As if I could think about anything else. Would he be there? Please, be there.

"When my shift was over I grabbed my purse and ran out the rear door. I looked around the back parking lot. His car wasn't there. *Oh God*, I thought. *He isn't coming.* I looked at my watch. Five minutes to eleven. It was still early. My breathing was rapid and my hands shook. I fumbled in my purse, found my car keys and opened my car door. I'd sit in my car and wait for him. He would come."

"He did come, didn't he?" Hector asked.

"Oh yes. 'Leave your purse in the car,' a voice said from behind my shoulder. 'You won't need it.'

"I closed my eyes and took a deep breath. He had come for me after all. 'Yes, Sir,' I whispered. I put my purse under the front seat and locked the car door. Still behind me, he took the keys from my trembling hand. Then he pressed his body against mine, trapping my chest against my car's closed door. He reached around my hips and his hand quickly burrowed beneath my full flowered skirt, his fingers dipping into my sopping cunt. 'Good girl,' he said. 'You did as I asked.'

"Asked, told, demanded, it was all the same. And I couldn't do anything else. I nodded.

" 'Remember last night and those suckers on your tits? Well tonight I want all your concentration between your legs.' He maneuvered a harness of some kind around my hips beneath my skirt and hooked it in place. It was soft leather, held together with cold steel rings and bits of chain. 'Spread your legs wide,' he said, still pressing me against the car with his chest.

"When my legs were spread, he bit my earlobe, just hard enough to cause me pain. 'I said wide,' he growled. I widened my stance.

" 'Now hold very still and don't move.' He released the pressure against my back. For a moment I considered how this would look to someone coming out of the back door of the restaurant. I was leaning against the side of my car, with a man laying his hands all over me. What would someone think? I didn't care.

"He lifted the back of my skirt and I felt cool air against the backs of my thighs. I jumped when I felt something cold against my hot pussy lips. 'I said stand still,' he hissed.

" 'I'm sorry, Sir. You just surprised me.'

" 'Nothing I do, nothing we do, should surprise you,' he said, chuckling."

Alice thought about the candle Todd had used to fuck her, then continued. " 'True,' I whispered, as much to myself as to him. Suddenly I was filled. My pussy lips were stretched and my passage was as full as it had ever been. A huge dildo was being pushed deep inside me. Relentlessly filling, stretching, demanding. I felt him push the rod in deeper and deeper until I knew I could take no more, yet he kept filling me. Then he stopped and

I felt a strip of something pulled down my belly, between my legs, and up between my cheeks to fasten to the harness in the back. As he pulled the strap tighter, the dildo pressed even more tightly inside me.

"He quickly pulled my blouse down in the front and, with a deft flip, my breasts were out of the cups of my bra. He leaned against me, forcing my engorged nipples against the cold metal of the car. 'You're so hot you'll come with almost nothing more from me, won't you?'

" 'Yes, Sir,' I said, barely able to stand, barely able to breathe.

" 'We can't have you this high all evening, so I'll let you come now.' His small laugh warmed my ear. 'Let's see whether you're so high that you can come without me even touching you. Feel that artificial cock fill your cunt. Feel your hot, hard nipples against the cold window. Are you close?'

" 'Yes,' I groaned.

" 'How close? How close to grasping that dildo with your pussy and squeezing it, coming against it.'

" 'Very.'

" 'Let's measure,' he said into my ear. 'If ten is climax, where are you?'

" 'Nine point nine,' I said without thinking."

Hector laughed. "Sherry, I'm at about nine point five right now."

"Don't come too fast, Hector," Alice said. "This story has a long way to go, if you want it to."

"Oh, I do."

"Then the man I called Sir licked the back of my neck, then bit the nape. 'Tell me.'

" 'Nine point nine nine,' I said, barely able to speak.

"He pressed his hips against my buttocks and moved so the strap shifted the dildo inside of me. Then he pressed the tip of his tongue into my ear and fucked my ear with it. 'Tell me.'

" 'Oh God,' I groaned. 'Oh God.'

"He bit my earlobe hard and I climaxed. I couldn't help it. He hadn't touched me with his hands but I was coming anyway.

Hard, hot, fast, my pussy spasming against the huge dildo in my cunt. 'Yessss,' I hissed.

" 'God, you're wonderful,' he said, slowly releasing the pressure of his body that forced me against the cold car, turning me around so I saw him for the first time. Tears filled my eyes as I looked at his face, warm and inviting, his eyes, dark and all-seeing, brooking no resistance from me.

"He was again wearing black, this time a soft black shirt, with full sleeves and tight cuffs. His long black hair was tied back with a leather thong. He kissed my mouth, his lips soft against mine as I descended from the dizzying pinnacle of my orgasm. 'Come,' he said, 'let's go home.'

"Could I walk with this giant cock inside of me? I found that I could, and soon I was seated in his car, seat belt tightly fastened between my bared breasts. 'Close your eyes and think about your pussy,' he said as he started the engine. 'Feel how full it is and climb to the heights again.'

"I closed my eyes. My orgasm had been so hard and so complete that I wondered whether I could get excited again, but the dildo in my cunt gave me no peace. It aroused me as I pictured my swollen lips almost kissing the blunt end of it. By the time we pulled into the familiar garage, I was hungry again.

"He guided me from the car and into his special room. 'Remember last evening I showed you that frame,' he said, pointing to the X-shaped device that he was now moving to the center of the room. It was about six feet tall and each of the four arms was upholstered in black leather. There was a flat section at the center, against which my torso would be supported, I thought. As I looked more closely I saw that the frame had flat metal hinges and small metal rings at various points. He was going to fasten me to that, I knew, and control me totally. *Marshmallow*, I remembered was the magic word that would stop everything.

" 'Strip,' he said. When I didn't immediately move, he glared at me. 'I told you to do something.'

" 'Yes, Sir,' I said, quickly removing my clothing, my eyes still glued to the frame. As I pulled off my skirt, I saw the black leather harness wrapped around my body just above my hip-bones, and fastened at the center-front with a tiny padlock. A leather panel held the dildo in place. Wasn't he going to remove it now?

" 'Come here,' he said. It was a bit difficult to walk gracefully since the dildo held my legs slightly parted but I stepped forward and stood before him. 'I discovered last evening that a little pain gives you pleasure. You know it does, don't you?'

"I wanted to deny it. It was so sick. Wasn't it? But if both of us wanted it, and it gave us both pleasure . . . 'Yes, Sir.'

" 'But the pain is just a symptom of what really excites you. It's the fact that I can do anything I want to you. I control you. I can hurt you or tease you and it's all pleasure for you. I can do anything, can't I?'

" 'Yes, Sir.'

" 'And you can always stop me. Snap your fingers or say *marsh-mallow* and I'll stop. So who's really in control?'

"I'd never thought of it that way before and now I couldn't keep a small smile from crossing my lips. 'We are, Sir,' I said.

" 'And you trust me?'

" 'Completely, Sir.'

" 'Tonight there will be no pain, just a demonstration of what control means.' He enclosed me in his arms and softly kissed me. He slid his tongue into my mouth and I stroked it with mine. I wanted to feel him, hold him but I left my arms at my sides. If he wanted me to touch him, he would tell me. And he hadn't.

"He framed my face with his hands and kissed my cheeks, then walked to a chest, opened a drawer, and withdrew a handful of what looked to me like wide leather strips. He handed one to me. 'This goes around one ankle. Put it on.'

"I was going to have to do this myself. I was going to have to admit to myself that I wanted it. I took the strap and only hesitated a moment before I buckled it around my left ankle, leaving a large ring hanging from the back. I did the same with the one for my right ankle. Then my master gently buckled cuffs around my wrists. My master. Yes, that was what he was. He looked at the frame, then at me.

"Slowly I moved to the frame, pressed my back against it, raised my arms, and spread my legs. It fully supported my back but the leg sections parted at the small of my back, so there was nothing against my ass. Quickly, four small chains and padlocks fastened my arms and legs in place. 'Now,' he said, 'try to move. I want you to know how firmly you are held. I want you to know that now your body moves only when I adjust the frame.'

"I twisted and pulled, reveling in the feeling of being unable to free myself. 'Now you know how it feels. Tell me.'

" 'It feels wonderful. It frees me.'

"He smiled as his hand reached between my legs. He tapped the end of the dildo and erotic pleasure knifed through my body. He twisted the plastic cock and moved it around as much as he could with the strap in place. I closed my eyes and clutched at the feeling of pleasure.

"He released the phallus inside me and moved the frame so it was now horizontal, at exactly the level of his groin. He unzipped his pants and allowed his cock to spring free. Then he moved so his hips were near my face, his engorged member near my mouth. 'Lick the tip,' he said. 'Just lick it with the tip of your tongue.' "

"God, you're good," Hector said. "I can almost feel what you were feeling."

Alice smiled and continued, her hand again snaking into the waist of her pants. "I reached out my tongue and touched the wet tip of my master's penis. Thick, sticky fluid oozed from the opening and I caught it on my tongue. While I licked, he reached over and pinched my nipples, hard. I gasped, but he said, 'Lick softly. Control your actions as I control the pleasure you feel.'

"It was difficult to lick his cock gently while he was pinching my nipples, but I managed. My mind was in two places at once, jumping from the feel of his fingers on my tight nipples to the movements of my mouth.

"Still twisting my nipples, he lifted a small handheld device and, while I watched, turned a small knob. 'Shit,' I hissed as the dildo inside my pussy began to hum. And the strap of the harness pressed against my clit so the vibrations were transferred to my engorged nub. Now my mind was in three places, my nipples, my tongue, and my pussy.

" 'Control your actions,' he growled. 'Don't stop licking me.'

" 'Oh,' I groaned, trying to concentrate on my tongue. I began to get used to the buzzing in my cunt, then he turned the knob and the frequency changed. Each time I became accustomed to the devilish object inside of me, he changed its method of torture, from buzzing to a slow throb, to a fast pounding and back to a low hum. And intermittently he pinched my nipples. Everything in my body was driving me closer and closer to orgasm, yet I was supposed to lick his penis in the same, soft rhythm.

" 'Are you close to coming?' he asked.

" 'Oh yes,' I moaned.

" 'Don't! Just lick.'

" 'But Sir.'

" 'No buts. You will come only when I say you may. Do you understand?' He pushed his cock closer to my lips.

" 'Yes, Sir.'

" 'A lesson in control, yours and mine. Now,' he said, pushing his cock against my lips, 'take it.' "

"Are you close now, Sherry?" Hector asked. "I am."

Sherry's fingers rubbed her clit. "I am too," she said honestly.

"I like that. Continue with your story."

"I parted my lips and took the length of his engorged tool into my hot mouth. I ran my tongue over the sides, and created a vacuum to draw his penis more deeply into me. All the time my body sang with the sensations he was creating with his hands and with the machine in my pussy. If I can make him come, I reasoned, he will let me climax with him. I used every skill I possessed to drive him closer to orgasm.

" 'You're very good at that,' he said, 'but I learned that last night. You're a good little cocksucker but I don't want to come this way.' He pulled away.

"I didn't know where the condom had come from but now he opened the small package and, as I watched, he slowly unrolled it over his cock. He walked around the frame until he was between my spread legs. 'Do you want this?' he asked.

" 'Oh yes, Sir,' I said.

"He turned off the vibrating dildo, unfastened the strap that held it in place. And slowly withdrew it from my pussy. 'I control everything you feel,' he said, 'and I want you to feel everything. Have you ever taken something in your ass?'

"In my ass? He can't mean that. His cock was so big. He couldn't possibly do that. But I knew that he could. And if he wanted it that way, then he would do it. I couldn't stop him and I didn't want to. I wanted everything he could give me. 'No, Sir.'

" 'Do you want your ass filled?'

" 'No, Sir. I don't think so. It will hurt.'

" 'It might, but it will be incredibly exciting as well. And you won't refuse me, will you. You really want anything that I think will please you. You realize that I know you better than you know yourself.'

" 'Yes, Sir,' I said, and meant it.

" 'So, now we understand each other. Your body is mine and I can do with it what I want.' Suddenly I felt something cold rubbing and pressing against my rear hole. 'I could drive my cock into you,' he said as the cold rubbing continued, driving me crazy with lust. 'But for now, we'll be content with this.' Something hard was pressing against my anus, slowly slipping into the tight ring of muscle. He alternately pressed and remained still so my body could become accustomed to the unfamiliar sensation.

"For moments at a time, it hurt, and I considered saying *marshmallow* but just as the pain got too much, he stopped pushing and the discomfort subsided. Finally my ass was filled and the pain had disappeared to be replaced with heat deep in my belly. He withdrew the object and pushed it in again, fucking me with it. While my mind was centered on my ass, he inserted his cock into my pussy. He quickly established a mind-blowing rhythm, inserting his cock and withdrawing the dildo, then reversing, so one of my openings was filled while the other was empty and hungry.

" 'I'm stroking my cock with the dildo, through your body,' he said. 'And we are going to come together.' Harder and harder, faster and faster, he pumped both his cock and the rod until I knew he was ready to climax. Although we both knew I was close, how was he going to create the moment? I wondered with the small bit of my brain still capable of coherent thought. I was so close that I didn't think I could delay or speed my climax. Could he control the timing?

"I needn't have worried. Suddenly his finger was on my clit and I came. 'Yes,' I screamed and wave after wave of orgasmic pleasure overwhelmed my body. I couldn't move my arms or my legs but I bucked my hips as much as possible, taking his cock as deeply into my body as I could."

Alice smiled as she realized that when the character in the story came, she did too. She was even controlling her own orgasm.

"And he screamed as well, loudly proclaiming his pleasure. Over and over he pounded his cock into me, fucking my ass with the dildo as well.

"My climax was the strongest and longest as I could ever remember. Wave upon wave of erotic joy washed over me and just as I thought I was descending, I came again. After several minutes of almost unendurable pleasure, I began to calm.

"A long time passed before our breathing returned to almost normal. Slowly he pulled the rod from my ass and then withdrew his cock from me. Then, leaving me to compose my body, he sat in a chair, his eyes closed, his body limp and trembling. 'God, lady,' he said, 'you're amazing.'

" 'You too,' I said, unable to move even if I hadn't been still fastened to the frame.

" 'And this is only the beginning.'

" 'Yes,' I said, then added, 'Sir.'"

"Wow," Hector said.

Alice was unsure whether Hector had come. "Are you all right?"

"I'm terrific. I came about two minutes ago," he said, "but I stayed silent so I could hear you talk. You're sensational."

Alice grinned, and at that moment she knew that she couldn't do it. She couldn't leave Velvet Whispers. She enjoyed it too much. To hell with the medical coverage. To hell with security. She'd leave Dr. Tannenbaum as soon as he could find someone else and continue to do the things that she most enjoyed, and phone sex was at the top of her list. She'd stay at Velvet Whispers as long as she loved it and the men kept calling.

"I'm glad you think so. Call me next week?"

"Sure. Can you tell me what you and that guy did on a different night?"

"Of course I can. I'll talk to you next week."

She was about to call Velvet to tell her about her change of heart when the phone rang. "Alice, I'm in a jam," Velvet said quickly. Without allowing Alice to interrupt, Velvet continued, "I know Hector was your last caller but Marie just threw up. I can reroute all of her calls but I've already got a new client on the line and I promised him someone special. Everyone else is on the phone right now and I'm routing so I can't take him. Can you do me a favor, just one last time?"

"I'm not leaving. I've changed my mind."

"Thanks for taking this one last . . . You're not leaving?"

"Of course not. I was being ridiculous. I can't leave all my friends without anyone to talk to. And they are my friends even though I've never seen them. I'll give Dr. Tannenbaum my notice in the morning."

She could hear Velvet's laugh. "I knew you'd come to your senses. You love this as much as I do. Does Betsy know yet?"

"I just hung up with Hector and he made the decision for me. He said, 'Next week?' and I just said, 'Sure.' "

"Let's have lunch, the three of us, tomorrow to celebrate. I'll even buy."

"That will be great. Now, you said you had a new client?"

"His name is Zack and he's interested in telling you about his wild date last evening. He was babbling about a video camera and several mirrors. I don't know whether your storytelling talents will be needed, so just go with the flow."

"Will do." A few moments later her phone rang. "Sherry? This is Zack."

Alice lowered her voice, stretched out on the bed, and flipped off the light. "Hi, Zack. I'm glad you called."

GREAT BOOKS, GREAT SAVINGS!

When You Visit Our Website:
www.kensingtonbooks.com
You Can Save Money Off The Retail Price
Of Any Book You Purchase!

- **All Your Favorite Kensington Authors**
- **New Releases & Timeless Classics**
- **Overnight Shipping Available**
- **eBooks Available For Many Titles**
- **All Major Credit Cards Accepted**

Visit Us Today To Start Saving!
www.kensingtonbooks.com

All Orders Are Subject To Availability.
Shipping and Handling Charges Apply.
Offers and Prices Subject To Change Without Notice.